BURYING
the
HONEYSUCKLE
GIRLS

A Novel

BURYING
the
HONEYSUCKLE
GIRLS

A Novel

EMILY CARPENTER

LAKE UNION
PUBLISHING

Published by Lake Union Publishing, Seattle

www.apub.com

Amazon, the Amazon logo, and Lake Union Publishing are trademarks of Amazon.com, Inc., or its affiliates.

ISBN-13: 9781503935013
ISBN-10: 1503935019

Cover design by Danielle Christopher

Printed in the United States of America

For my family of men—all great champions of women.

Chapter One

Saturday, September 15, 2012
Mobile, Alabama

For a solid year, I felt like I was living my life underground. Suffocated first by the weight of the pills and, after that, by the people who helped me beat them. But as I turned onto my father's winding, crushed-shell driveway, I had the sensation that—after clawing my way through bones and fossils, roots and rocks—I'd finally broken free. Cracked the bright surface of earth.

And, holy shit, was it ever bright.

The Alabama sun blinded me as it glinted off a long line of cars snaking down both sides of the drive. I stomped on my worn brakes, and my ancient car shuddered to a stop. I shaded my eyes against the glare and peered toward the big house at the end. Maybe Molly Robb was hosting her garden club. Since I was gone and no longer a potential embarrassment, she'd probably started having it here rather than at the less-than-palatial brick ranch she shared with my brother, Wynn.

Or maybe they were holding a fund-raiser for Wynn's campaign. I knew he'd been planning a run for governor next year, taking advantage of my dad's political influence while he still could. But to have something like that at Dad's house? Surely he was too sick for guests by now. According to his doctor, Alzheimer's doesn't plateau this late in the game; it just continues its relentless downward trajectory until every last identifiable piece of the person is gone.

And as far as this gathering being some kind of a homecoming celebration for me? Not a chance. There wasn't going to be any party for me, not after this past year. Not to mention I was about a week and a half shy of my recommended release date, so no one was even expecting me.

I inched as far as I could up the drive and wedged my car into a half space between a Cadillac and a Range Rover. I could see the house clearly from my spot: white boards and black shutters, peeling in the afternoon haze. The low-country cottage, built in the early 1900s by my father's people, was protected by acres of marsh and woods on the east bank of the muddy, wide Dog River. I could smell the dank, salty air through the vents in my car, and, as I sat there, a cloud blotted out the sun.

I'd grown up on this handful of acres. Lived here, on and off after graduation. On, when Dad and I were on good terms and I was clean. Off, all the other times. I'd always considered it home, and, standing in the drive, I felt my gut twist. Wynn and Molly Robb were letting the place fall into disrepair. It looked spooky now in the half-light, framed in weeds and overgrown azaleas.

I hoped they were keeping a closer eye on Dad.

I climbed out of the Jetta and slammed the door. The thick, coastal Mobile heat wrapped its arms around me, welcoming me back to the land of the living, to my childhood home. I filled my lungs with the scent of river.

I could do this. I might be shaky and fragile, but I wasn't the same person who'd been trundled off to rehab almost a year ago. I blinked away the images of metal chairs circled on a coffee-stained rug in a sodium-lit room. The women filing in, broken, haggard. Numb from their inability to save themselves. I guess this time they had scared me. For some reason, I'd finally seen myself in their faces.

Walking on tiptoe so the heels of my new boots wouldn't sink into the shells, I started up the drive. I'd bought the boots with a gift card from the women at the halfway house, and they'd given me a little surge of confidence when I'd tried them on in the outlet store an hour ago. Of course, I'd forgotten about the stupid shells.

I hadn't taken twelve tiptoe steps up the drive—actual steps with my feet, not the proverbial AA kind—when I saw something that, in a split second, sent me hurtling back twenty-five years, to when I was just a little girl.

A red raven.

The huge bird perched on the newel post of the banister that flanked the wide front steps. Glossy, black tail feathers dipping low, curved beak bobbing up at the sky, the thing was twice as big as a crow. Closer to the size of a hawk. Every few seconds, it stretched out its wings, and on its feathers I thought I saw streaks of red flash in the sunlight.

I squeezed my hands into fists, shut my eyes, and took a deep breath—my head vibrating with the heat and humidity and smell of the river.

I am not my mother.
The honeysuckle girl isn't real.
I do not have gold dust on my fingertips.
There's no such thing as a red raven.

I spoke the words aloud into the hot air, just for good measure, the way I'd been doing for months back at the halfway house. Firm and clear. Like I believed them. When I opened my eyes, my breath whooshed out shakily. There was no trace of red on the raven, not anywhere that I could see. It was just a normal, everyday black bird, watching me with blank, black eyes.

I unclenched my fists, took another breath. Coming home might be stressful, but I could handle it without the old coping mechanisms.

I didn't need them anymore—the gold or the red raven or any of the other things I used to pretend to see. It hadn't been easy to let them go—they'd morphed and taken on lives of their own—but now I had the affirmations. I didn't have to play these old childhood games. I could be present and handle my life like a normal person.

The bird spread its wings again and lifted off the newel post, and I moved to the steps and touched the spot where it had been. I looked closer at the post for a trail of gold dust left under my fingers. There was nothing. No raven, no gold. Everything was going to be okay. I just needed to trust the affirmations and myself. Keep moving forward. Let the process carry me.

I climbed the steps and stopped, wondering whether I should knock on the door or just walk in. It'd been only a year since I'd been here, but still. It had been a long one. A long, grueling, hope-sucking year. Three months in a spectacular oxy-Percocet-anything-pill-shaped flameout. Three more in rehab, another six (almost) in the halfway house. A hell of a year.

It was a wonder I wasn't seeing purple, polka-dotted elephants too.

I pushed open the door and blinked in the light. The crystal chandelier and every lamp and sconce within eyesight blazed. Weird. Bright lights set Dad off, making him irritable and confused. I stopped and let the heavy oak door thunk shut behind me, then clicked off the row of light switches, dousing the room in shadow. I dropped my purse on the antique needlepoint bench.

Low voices drifted in from the back of the house. If it was a party, it was a quiet one. No music. No laughter. I felt a spike of fear. Had he died and no one told me? I stepped into the long center hallway and noticed the spray of carefully arranged roses, lilies, and hydrangea on the round, marble-topped table. Funeral flowers. I couldn't take my eyes off them.

My sister-in-law, Molly Robb, entered the far end of the hall from the living room, and I stiffened in surprise. She wore a beige, draped pantsuit—clothes a fiftysomething woman might wear, not a thirty-four-year-old. Certainly not her usual yoga pants and tank top. Her hair looked freshly cut and straightened. She moved toward me, arms outstretched.

"Althea, what are you doing here?" She clasped me to her bony frame. I nearly gagged at the smell of her unfamiliar perfume mingling with the flowers' scent.

"I left a message . . ." My voice died. I had called my father, but he'd never called me back. It hadn't surprised me at the time. Some days I knew he just couldn't face talking to me. "Is he—did he die?" I could barely get the words out. Surely Molly Robb would have called if something had happened. I knew she'd been more than a little pissed at me when I left, but at the end of everything, we were still family.

Molly Robb pulled back, her mouth forming a perfect, lipsticked *O.* "Honey, no. No." She hugged me again, tighter this time, and relief flooded me. I clung to her.

"God, you scared me," I said.

She didn't smile, just pushed me out of the hug, squinted into my eyes. The pupil check. I was used to it. Then she looked down, her gaze flicking over my faded black jeans and shapeless gray T-shirt, and frowned. "A lot has changed while you were gone, Althea."

"What's going on?"

She took my arm with both her birdlike hands. "He's not doing well, Althea, so Wynn and I moved in. We thought we'd give everyone an opportunity—" She looked back into the house. "He doesn't recognize a soul."

"You should've called me."

"We thought it was best to let you finish out—"

I didn't wait to hear any more, just pulled out of her grasp and headed down the hall. When I stepped into the living room, I stopped dead, struck by the sheer number of bodies. People were everywhere. Some I recognized from my childhood days or from high school. There were friends of my father's who hadn't come around in ages. One elderly man, mottled and yellowed, leaning on a deer-antler walking stick, I knew—that would be my father's friend Mr. Northcut.

He was older than Dad by a good twenty years, and he'd always been a kind of mentor to him. A rich mentor, who'd funded Dad's run for attorney general. Personally, I'd never liked the guy. He gave off the unmistakable scent of old-South patriarchal entitlement and never had more than two words to say to me.

He nodded at me now, but I turned away to scan the room so I wouldn't have to engage. In response, a thrum of panic vibrated through me. Names and faces that belonged to different places, different eras of my life, swirled together in a disconcerting mash-up. I wasn't ready for this.

Then I spotted, with a painful jolt, somebody entirely unexpected. A face I knew well, even though I hadn't seen him in . . . over a decade, probably. Gentle eyes, irresistibly warm smile. Perpetually sunburned nose, like most of the men around here who spent three-quarters of their lives on boats.

Jay.

He was talking to old Mrs. Kemper from next door, nodding and laughing, and I watched him, hypnotized. He looked exactly the same as he did ten—no, eleven—years ago. Maybe even better. I'd always been a sucker for his face—from the first time I saw him across Ms. Huffman's crowded second-grade classroom—but not because it was the most handsome. It was more the way everything fit together, an evolutionary one-in-a-million that just did me in. It killed me when I was seven—although it took me ten years to admit it—and it was killing me right now.

Damn it. Seeing him again gave me the sensation of having my heart mauled by a pack of wild dogs, which was less than enjoyable, to say the least. I'd successfully steered clear of him once we'd graduated from high school, then heard he moved up North somewhere. He must be visiting his parents. Or had moved back. Fantastic. I looked away quickly, tried to melt into the room.

I finally found my father seated in a wing chair by the back wall of windows that looked out over the porch and the sloping bank of grass to the river beyond. Somebody, probably Molly Robb, had dressed him in a crisp, white shirt and blue blazer. But his freshly shaven face was slack, his blue eyes unfocused, and he looked so much older than his seventy-three years. Propped up by two chintz pillows wedged on either side of him, he balanced a small dog—it looked like a Pomeranian or a Chihuahua, maybe—on his knees.

The dog brought me up short. My dad was a Lab man. Ever since I could remember, we'd had a string of chocolates, all named Folly. I could still picture him, standing on the front porch almost exactly a year ago, watching me leave. He hadn't hugged me, just kept his hand on the last Folly's head, moving it in measured circles.

This new dog set off alarm bells in my brain.

I squatted by his chair, my face a little lower than his. He looked down at me, blank blue eyes and trembling lips, and I mustered a smile. The dog stared at me with its bulging eyes that for some reason reminded me of Molly Robb.

"Dad."

His expression didn't change.

I put a hand on his knee, and the little dog growled. "I'm home," I said. He said nothing, but he didn't look away, so I kept going. "I'm so glad to see you."

I saw his pupils constrict and flash with recognition. "Althea." He said my name fast, like it had produced a bad taste in his mouth and he was trying to spit it out.

"That's right," I said, trying to sound bright. I patted his knee and managed to keep my eyes on him, instead of checking to make sure I hadn't left any gold dust behind on his pants.

"Get out," he said.

My heart contracted, and I inhaled sharply. Looked into his eyes and smiled, tried to connect with him. To remind him who I was. *I'm your daughter. I'm Althea. I'm not Trix. I'm not my mother—*

"Get out," he repeated, so low I barely heard him.

I rocked back on my heels but kept my head down, reminding myself that I'd heard those words from him before. A couple of times, in fact, before he'd sent me packing for good. He was sick. He didn't remember all our conversations—that I'd done everything I'd promised to do. That he'd said I could come back, stay here until I found a job and saved some money. I took a deep breath and reminded myself that the man before me wasn't *my father*, exactly.

"Dad, I'm back." I didn't add *from rehab*. If he didn't remember, I sure wasn't going to remind him. I smiled again. "I'm doing good. Really good."

"Is it your birthday?"

"No. This is a party for you."

"You're thirty."

I shook my head, still trying to smile. It was getting harder. I could feel the tears I hadn't let myself cry at the halfway house threatening to spill out. "In a few weeks. I'm thirty on September thirtieth. Remember? Thirty on thirty?"

As I said it, I felt a chill run down my spine. Even though every psychologist and therapist I'd ever seen had assured me my mother had been ill and had had no right to scare a five-year-old like that, I still remembered everything she'd said to me the night of her own thirtieth birthday, the last night I saw her alive. *"Wait for her. For the honeysuckle girl. She'll find you, I think, but if she doesn't, you find her."*

My father swiped my hand off his knee and shrank back into the chair.

"Get out!" he said. The dog yapped at me, two short, ear-piercing barks. Little fucker. I wanted to toss him across the room. Dad looked

past me, one hand wildly clawing out. "Get her away from me! Get this crazy bitch away from me!"

The room went silent, and I felt people move away from the wing chair. I didn't look up, but I knew that everyone—including Jay—was watching. My face burned, and the tears were coming, like it or not. My father. My own father was screaming at me to get out of his house. But I couldn't obey him. I couldn't move. All I could do was huddle there on the floor.

My brother, Wynn, dark hair slicked back and dressed in a navy blazer identical to my father's, appeared beside the chair. I looked up at him, started to shake my head and babble something about not having said anything to upset Dad. But the light in his eyes dimmed just a bit—the way it always seemed to whenever I showed up—and he held up one hand. I clamped my mouth shut.

"You're out early," he said through a frozen smile.

"Just ten days. Wynn—"

Gene Northcut materialized between us, and I stopped abruptly.

"Excuse us, everyone," Wynn announced to the room. All the faces turned toward him, like flowers to the sun, and I noticed his easy grin and the flash of white teeth. He was good at this. Very good. "My father would like to bid you all good night, so my sister and I can take him upstairs and get him comfortable. Please, carry on. We won't be long. Althea?"

Under Northcut's watchful eye, Wynn lifted Dad up by one arm and led him out of the room. I didn't follow.

From out of the crowd, Jay materialized. "Hey, Althea. You okay?"

I felt frozen. Confused. Everyone was looking at me with expressions of pity and concern. Judgment too, if I was to be honest. Word had spread about me in the past year; it was foolish to think it hadn't. And now this. This shitstorm of a homecoming. I couldn't move. I couldn't speak.

"Can I get you a drink?" he said. "Water or something?"

"Hon." It was Molly Robb beside me. She touched my elbow. "Let's go."

"It was nice to see you," Jay said. I didn't answer, just let Molly Robb lead me out of the room and into the front hall. Wynn was already at the top of the stairs with Dad. I took off after them.

"Althea!" she said behind me, but I ignored her and kept going, taking the stairs two at a time.

At the end of the hall, I saw Wynn's carefully combed head disappear inside my father's room. The door clicked neatly shut. I ran down the hall and grabbed the knob. I rattled it, but it wouldn't budge. He'd locked it—my brother had locked me out of my father's room. I knocked on the door. "Wynn." I tried to keep my voice low. "Let me in."

Molly Robb appeared beside me. "Althea, hon? You're making a scene."

"I'm not. I just want to see him."

She gave me a sympathetic look. "You really ought to leave."

"I want to see my father."

"He doesn't want to see you right now, hon. I don't know why you seem so surprised. After what you've put this family through." She lowered her voice. "You have some nerve. Some nerve."

I turned away from her, closed my eyes, and pressed my fingertips against them. *Breathe,* I told myself.

Yes, it had been a bad year. I'd stolen money from Dad and others. I'd spent ninety percent of my days in a haze from Percocet. So, naturally, he'd packed me off to rehab. And, yes, I'd fought it all the way. But after a while, after I'd been there a couple of weeks, I'd broken. I'd attended the meetings, shared in group. Worked the program. Dad and I traded phone calls, and he sent funny cards. When I moved to the halfway house, he sent me cupcakes from my favorite bakery.

Maybe it was just the strangeness of me being home again. The women in my group had told stories about how tough it could be for family to see you after a long rehab, clean and sober. Healthy, but a stranger.

"You've made things very awkward for Wynn," Molly Robb said. "For me. The questions we have to answer, you wouldn't believe it."

"Fine. I'll stay away from both of you. But I will see my father."

"He has Alzheimer's, Althea," she hissed, inches away from my face.

"I'm aware of that," I said. *Don't cry.*

"It's much worse than before you went away." She paused. "He's about to die."

Even though I'd known it from the minute I'd seen the cars lining the drive, the news hit me like a gut punch. First my mother, now my father. Fury mixed with despair tingled into my arms and legs.

"So you were gonna just leave me in that hellhole while he slipped away?" I said. The tendrils of anger morphed into vines now and were squeezing me from the inside out. "You weren't even going to tell me?"

"We didn't want to interrupt your treatment. We thought it was best. If you had told us you were coming, we could have prepared him. As you can see, your being here upsets him."

"He's not in his right mind, Molly Robb. You and Wynn should've told me, you should've let me come home." My voice broke. "I'm his daughter."

"Althea," she said. "Pull yourself together. We have a house full of people, here to honor your father. And"—she lowered her voice to an urgent whisper—"to support Wynn's campaign. Gene Northcut is almost single-handedly funding the whole thing."

"I don't give a damn about Gene Northcut or Wynn's campaign."

"Which just proves how unbelievably selfish you are. This family has sacrificed everything for Wynn's campaign. Everything. You know how much this means to your father. He's wanted this for Wynn since he was a boy."

She was right. Dad's hopes had always been pinned to his golden boy. Never to his daughter. The most anyone could hope from me was that my fuck-ups wouldn't ruin Wynn's shot at political stardom.

"I don't care about any of this. I want to see my dad," I said.

"How could you be so cruel?" She shook her head. "He's terrified of you."

Before I could wrap my mind around the impossible idea that my six-foot-three bull of a father was afraid of me, I heard his voice boom from behind the locked bedroom door. It sounded strong. Self-assured, like I remembered.

"You tell her," he shouted. "Tell that girl I said thirty's a bitch. If her mother was here, she'd say the same. Thirty's a goddamn bitch!" And then he burst into a gale of laughter.

Chapter Two

September 1937
Sybil Valley, Alabama

Women came from the holler, the mountain, even as far as the next valley over to buy Jinn Wooten's honeysuckle wine. Usually they walked. Once in a while they rode mules, which drove her husband, Howell, plumb crazy. He was a farmer, his father a farmer and his grandfather before him, and to his way of thinking, mules were for plowing and not for transporting ladies on their errands.

Howell had been planning on pulling it all out, the mass of honeysuckle vines that had taken over the lower meadow. It was that Japanese stuff the government had put in across the eastern part of the country, over a hundred years ago. It was nasty as cancer and useless besides. Howell had been considering putting in some cotton down there, for extra cash, but lately, he'd been thinking cotton might need too much fertilizer and fussing over.

When the women came around, yoo-hooing for Jinn and asking for the honeysuckle wine, Howell usually vanished. All the same, times being what they were, she gave him whatever money she made. Well, most of it. At the beginning, anyway.

The honeysuckle wine had started off like any ordinary wine. Jinn had followed her aunt's recipe for dandelion wine the first couple of times, but then she figured out some *tricks*—some extras here and there—and it became, more or less, a cross between a brandy and the white lightning her father made.

Jinn said she didn't know exactly how the recipe had evolved—she was one of those cooks who said *a little of this* and *a little of that* when she told people how she made peach pie or rabbit stew—and she always told her customers she couldn't quite remember the process of making the wine. Or what, exactly, made it so intoxicating.

But she knew if she mashed the blossoms by hand, rather than with a potato masher, it made the flavor purer. She knew just how many extra days letting the concoction ferment would give it that extra kick. She was the only one who knew about the special yeast she ordered from that fellow over in Cedartown. She knew.

While the men of Sybil Valley—all drinkers of moonshine—wouldn't be caught dead imbibing honeysuckle wine, the ladies were a different story. They had discovered, a couple of years ago, that it was just as potent, but far smoother, than corn liquor. Word spread all the way across the state line to Chattanooga: Jinn Wooten, the girl whose hands always smelled like crushed honeysuckle, made an elixir that got you nice and toasty without taking a bite out of your fanny the next morning.

One day, when Howell was working in Huntsville with the Conservation Corps boys, and Jinn was fixing dinner for the kids, a pair of ladies from Chattanooga knocked on the Wootens' door. They wore smart wool dresses with matching hats and velvety red lipstick, and drove a silver car that looked like a dragon.

They were nothing like her regular clientele, but they'd come for the same thing. They bought out her supply, and, as she watched them lay the milk bottles on the floorboards of the car and cover them with blankets like newborn babes, one of them shaded her eyes with a gloved hand.

"You ought to go to Hollywood," she said. "Get yourself a screen test. You're about the prettiest girl I've ever laid eyes on." She turned to her friend. "Madge! Don't you think she ought to go to Hollywood?"

Walter and Collirene had joined their mother on the porch. The boy stood, feet apart, arms folded, watching the proceedings. His eyes darted like a crow's, from his mother to the women, and his mouth turned down at the corners.

Madge straightened up and gave Jinn an appraising look. "She's way prettier than Myrna Loy. How old are you?"

"Almost thirty. In a month."

"Woo-wee, girl, you don't look it. You look all of about seventeen."

Jinn's daughter, Collirene, moved close and gathered a fistful of her mother's skirt.

"You want to go to Hollywood, sugar?" Madge asked her. "Like your mama?"

Collirene didn't answer.

"You want to be a star of the silver screen?"

Collie tried to bury herself in the folds of the skirt, and Jinn placed a protective hand on her curly head. Walter was her fearless child. He carried himself like one of the rangy backwoodsmen who lived up in the laurel wilds of the mountain—watchful eyes and a smart mouth, even at twelve. Not her Collie.

"She's too shy for that, I guess," Jinn said.

"Shy don't set the world on fire," Madge pronounced, then the two ladies climbed into the silver dragon. They promised her they'd be back, and, when they'd driven off in a cloud of dust, Jinn folded the wad of bills in her skirt pocket. There was over one hundred total, but she wouldn't tell Howell about it. She would ask him who Myrna Loy was, though.

During supper, Walter's crow eyes stayed fastened to his mother. "Who was they?" he asked.

"Who were they?" Jinn corrected. "Just friends. That's all." He gave her a look—and for one brief second, she thought how much he resembled her own father. Without a word, he pushed back from the table and clattered out the back door. He hadn't finished his collards, but she didn't call him back.

Later that night, after tucking in the children, Jinn crept down to the cellar where she kept her buckets and tubes, cheesecloth and corks. She slid the one hundred dollars, a couple of bills at a time, into an empty jug. She corked it, then set it up high on a shelf, next to the jugs that held the fermenting wine. Howell generally stayed out of the cellar and out of her business, other than an occasional question about whose wives and daughters and grandmothers were buying how much, just to keep track.

When Jinn had been a girl, there'd once been a madwoman in Sybil Valley. One of the Luries, who'd gotten ahold of her husband's stash, drank near about the whole thing, stripped down to nothing, and climbed the fire tower on top of Brood Mountain. People came for miles—mostly men, of course—to stare. The next day, after it was over, Jinn heard that the Lurie girl hadn't even tried to hide herself. She'd just stood there bare-assed and bare-breasted like some kind of cheap whore, hollering about her brother getting after her. She'd threatened to jump from the tower all day and then, when the sun finally went down, she did. She should've broken her neck but her luck failed, and her family packed her off to Pritchard Insane Hospital instead, with nothing but a purple ankle and a gash down her side. People said that was what her husband got for losing track of her.

Like the Lurie girl, Jinn had figured things out. She knew that when her mama was locked in her bedroom, sick or having one of her spells, her daddy went roaming the mountain like a tomcat. She knew what he got up to; she saw the way his hands brushed the backs of certain girls in town.

She knew some things about Howell too. Nothing near like what her daddy did. But, all the same, illegally poached deer steaks did show up in her kitchen once in a while. And moonshine from a still in the grove behind their house.

Unlike the Lurie girl, though, she knew how to keep her mouth shut.

Jinn had loved Howell once, although it'd been so long ago, it seemed like another life. She used to wear her hair down, the way he liked it. Used to let him shimmy off her nightgown and run his hands over her every morning, even before the sun had come up, even though she'd been up half the night with babies.

But these days he jumped out of bed right when his eyes cracked open. He got dressed, even down to his boots, and headed out with a curt nod. He sure didn't notice which way her hair was done. He didn't notice much, except when she did something wrong.

That kind of thing—that *settling*, her mother called it—happened in a marriage, and there wasn't no sense in crying over it. The secrets he kept from her, that was part of the settling, she reckoned. And now she had her own secrets. The ladies from Chattanooga. And the other, most important one, the secret she held like a love letter, close to her heart.

The conversations with Tom Stocker.

Jinn blushed and pushed the jug a bit farther into the shadows. One hundred dollars! With the money hidden away, she'd have time to figure out what to do with such a windfall. Maybe she *should* cut out and go to Hollywood. Pack up the children, hop a train, and get herself a screen test, like the ladies said.

Howell would be fit to be tied. He might even come after her. For sure he'd want Walter back. Collirene, he'd cut loose pretty easy, but he'd need the boy on the farm. Maybe she should leave Walter behind.

But Collie was five, her baby. She wasn't going nowhere without Collie. The girl still sucked her thumb and cried for her at night.

Jinn decided she needed to lay out her options side by side, like laundry hung on a line, so she could examine each of them clearly. But it would have to be just the right time. When she was out in the meadow gathering her honeysuckle, Collie by her side, as always, collecting dried locust skins for her cigar box. In the meadow she could think, work it all out in private. She couldn't do that in the house. Howell could tell what she was thinking just by looking at her. He'd suss out somehow what she was plotting, for sure. Then he'd get to stomping and swearing through the house, and there was no telling where that would lead.

Chapter Three

I ran, coward that I was, from the party. Away from my angry, confused father, from Wynn's cold face and Molly Robb's baffling new look. From Jay and his unbearable kindness.

So that was it. Eleven months of therapy, sharing and learning how to face my problems, not to mention the purchase of a pair of kick-ass boots, and I'd ruined it all. Less than an hour at home, and I'd reverted back to Old Althea.

The busybody dog followed me out the front door and clicked down the front steps behind me like it thought I might want company. I growled at it to stay, and, looking confused, it plunked its miniature bottom down in the grass.

I ran to the head of the path that led into our woods, telling myself to breathe. My father was sick. Alzheimer's was a terrible disease. He hadn't laid eyes on me in almost a year. His mind was muddled, pierced with the buckshot of old memories. He didn't know what he was saying.

Unfortunately, that bit of wisdom didn't stop me from feeling like the earth had tilted and I was sliding, sliding down a sheer rock face, with nothing at all to slow my descent. To stop me from plunging into the inexorable, yawning chasm below.

It was almost dark. The party had grown louder, and the laughter and voices and clink of glasses drifted out to me now. Wynn had probably gone downstairs, made some quip to clear the air, and now everybody felt like they'd been given permission to have fun.

I hated every last one of those brown-nosing sycophants. Despised them. Which, my therapist would probably tell me if he were here right now, was precisely why I needed to go back inside. But I couldn't. Dad's words still echoed in my head. *Thirty's a bitch. If her mother was here . . .*

"I wish she were," I muttered, then kicked off the cursed boots.

I started down the winding path, deep into the piney woods, steering myself to the one place I knew would make me feel safe, would hide me from the sympathetic eyes and judgment. From my own fear. It was the one spot I had always run to when I'd felt alone as a child. Where I always felt my mother's presence. The clearing.

When I reached the small, circular patch of spongy green moss and rotted leaves, I stood for a moment, savoring the still, humid air. The mystery of the place. I smelled magnolia blossoms and honeysuckle from somewhere deeper in the woods. That's what always got me. That very particular fragrance. The scent of my mother.

I closed my eyes and her image rose up before me—dark hair curling wild down her back, eyes that curved up like a cat's, perfect creamy skin. She was kneeling on the ground. Her gold dress shimmered in the moonlight, making her look like some kind of otherworldly, flashing goddess. She was always wearing the gold dress when I closed my eyes.

I dropped down on the moss, rested my head on my hands, and sighed, cocooned in the stillness and deepening dark. I tried to quiet my mind so I could conjure more of my mother from a different time. A random day, maybe a Christmas morning or summer weekend at the beach. But all I could picture was her on her knees in that damn gold dress in the clearing. Chanting like a loon and shaking.

"Are you okay?"

I bolted up and looked down the path. A shadow, someone tall, blocked the light from the house.

"It's Jay," the shadow said. I sat up. He took a few steps forward so I could finally make him out in detail. The thick honey hair, blue shirt open at the neck. I looked away.

He sat beside me and gave my shoulder a friendly, nonthreatening bump. I bumped him back nonchalantly, but my heart was spasming inside my chest. He handed me a bougainvillea bloom he'd picked somewhere along the path. I took it, at the same time sending him multiple telepathic messages not to speak. At least, not until I could settle my heart. If he received the messages, he chose to ignore them.

"I'm sorry about your dad." I could smell his cologne, his shampoo, his breath. My God, I felt like I could practically smell his soul. Why did he have to sit so close?

"Thanks," I managed. I was being ridiculous. A child. *You're almost thirty, Althea. Thirty.*

"It's tough, I guess."

"Yeah," I said and cleared my throat several times. "It is."

"Would you like to go . . ." He hesitated. "Get a bite?" I squished the moss between my feet, stalling, knowing he had just bitten off the words "get a drink," and sent him another mind message: *Thank you.* So he'd heard the rehab rumors too.

"I'm not really hungry," I said.

"Me neither. I just thought you might want to get out of here. And talk."

For the first time I let my gaze linger on him. It was disconcerting—looking at the kid I'd grown up with, the boy down the river who'd been my best friend, and seeing a man. He looked like him, but at the same time, not. The skin on his face was rougher, more textured somehow. I could see he had a few early strands of gray at his temples, but his body was as trim as ever. It looked like through the years he'd settled into his tall frame, filled it out. He seemed at ease in his body. Unlike me.

I thought I had heard he was married. Not that he couldn't be out here talking to an old friend if he was married. Not that I cared.

I didn't care.

He raised his eyebrows, and I felt another flutter of nerves. How would I talk to him? After all that had happened, what he'd just witnessed, what was there to say?

"I could eat," I said, hoping I would somehow be rewarded for my leap of faith. Maybe there was a reason Jay had found me. The idea seemed far-fetched, and I realized I was probably getting nice shoulders and trustworthiness confused with one another. But what the hell. I could do worse.

"The River Shack?" he asked, and I nodded. "I've got my boat. Grab your shoes."

***

We pushed off from the dock in Jay's father's old outboard. The wide river was dark, calm, lit in places by dockside lights reflecting off the water. Once we were clipping through the waves, the motor growling, I snuck a glance at Jay. He drove the boat like his father always did, standing up, slouched against the arm of the chair. A memory flashed, then— Jay and I, swimming up under the boat's bright-blue hull, scratching our initials in the wood with his pocketknife. Forgetting, of course, that Mr. Cheramie would see it when he raised the boat in the lift.

We passed a houseboat—a tin lean-to lashed together with bungee cords and faded rope. Jay slowed and waved at a guy sitting on a webbed lawn chair. The guy doffed his captain's hat in response, and Jay opened the throttle. I closed my eyes and savored the lift of my hair in the wind.

I'd have to fill Jay in on the essentials of my life: rehab, the halfway house, how Molly Robb and my brother had just thrown me out of the only real home I had. I was glad for the loud motor. It gave me time to plan my strategy.

As we approached the River Shack wharf, Jay leapt out of the boat and tied us up, then offered to help me out. When I laid my hand on his, my skin prickled deliciously. As we headed up to the plywood shack strung with white lights, I wished desperately I could plunk down at the bar like a normal person and have a beer, just to take the edge off. My nerves were shooting out painful, alarm-like jolts through my arms and legs.

H.A.L.T., I reminded myself. Hungry. Angry. Lonely. Tired. It was one of those Twelve Step clichés they'd endlessly repeated in treatment. Well, I was definitely all four of those. Which meant I needed to stop whatever it was I was doing and take care of myself. Not that that was even possible at this point. Surviving the day was probably the most I could hope for.

We sat at a picnic table in the far corner, and I glanced around. It had been a while since I'd bartended here—one of the many short-term, alcohol-themed jobs I'd held in the past, oh, too many years—but blessedly, I didn't recognize a soul either behind the bar or among the tables. The owners were the same, a crusty couple in their sixties, but they usually stayed in the back room, playing poker and barking orders through the window at the limp teenage kitchen staff.

"Two sweet teas," Jay told the waitress, then he turned to me. "You look beautiful."

I touched my chest, shocked by the compliment. The truth was I was pale, too thin, and twitchy. Recovery isn't a good look on anyone.

"You're being nice."

"Well, I am, but I mean it. You're prettier than you were when you were eighteen. Not that you weren't pretty. It's just that you're . . ." He trailed off. "Never mind."

I flushed. Eighteen was an eternity away, and I wasn't so naive to think the hard years and chemicals didn't show on my face. But the way he was looking at me, clear eyed, open faced, a slight smile on his lips, I felt a twinge of hope. Maybe he could still see something good and innocent inside me.

I watched him order for both of us. He was so easy, so unselfconscious. Stupid-handsome, if I were to be honest. I had to remind myself how it was we'd never slept together. I'd been scared, for many reasons, the primary one being my father had told me if I ever had sex he would kill me, and then he would find and kill Jay. This was no idle threat. My dad had that Clint Eastwood glint in his eye, a man you didn't want to test.

The other reason I had never slept with Jay, the secret I'd held so close inside me, for so long that the poison from it felt like it had seeped into my blood and bones and psyche, was Rowe Oliver. That human cesspool who lived in the basement of his parents' massive columned house upriver. The man whose name tasted like dirt in my mouth.

To teenage Jay's credit, he took my ongoing and inexplicable sexual rejection like a champ. He never asked any uncomfortable questions, never pushed me beyond the point where I was willing, just kept showing up on my doorstep with a smile and another invitation to go get ice cream or see a movie.

One thing about Jay: he definitely knew how to play the long game.

When we were eleven and had snuck out to shoot contraband fireworks filched from Mr. Cheramie's Fourth-of-July stash, he told me so. We were crouched in the woods behind his house. He was flicking a stolen lighter below a mildewed Roman candle when he told me that he'd been thinking it over and had decided it would be smart if we got married. Not anytime soon; later, maybe, like when we were twenty or something. We could still go to whatever college we chose, but we'd never have to bother with the hassle of dating other people.

I think I probably said, "Cool," or something similarly profound, then he hooked one hand around a sapling pine for balance and leaned over to brush my lips with his. It was the first time he'd kissed me, and it felt sacred, like we'd sealed a solemn pact. In the subsequent years, I came to believe that pact was the main reason Jay stuck with me. He couldn't have really believed I was the person I pretended to be. I embarked on my long downhill slide and began to avoid his calls. There was no way I was going to be able to keep our pact. There was no way I was going to let him see the real me.

As we ate at the River Shack, he acted like sitting there with me was the most natural thing in the world. Like events had, in fact, worked out precisely as he'd planned. Like this was meant to be.

He caught my eye and grinned. "Mind if I bring up the elephant?"

"Sure, I guess."

"I thought you did your ninety days. Why is your dad being such a hard-ass?"

"He doesn't mean to be. It's the disease. The Alzheimer's."

Jay didn't look convinced.

But my father had good reason. In his tenure as attorney general in the eighties, he'd joined the war on drugs and proceeded to clear the streets of every low-level drug dealer and street-corner jockey the police could snag. As a result, Mobile's police department had doubled in size and income, and my father got a reputation for being a tough, unyielding son of a bitch. Not to mention a huge, fatherly monkey wrench in my teenage drug-procuring efforts.

"I deserve it," I added. "I've put him through a lot."

"Screw that. You're his daughter."

I looked into Jay's eyes. How easy it would be to tell him everything, to pour out my soul. And what a relief to do it with him. He seemed like a priest, therapist, and puppy all rolled into one. He'd never betrayed me, never screwed me over, not once. He'd been a solid friend, once upon a time.

I looked away. For nearly twenty-five years, I'd resisted the lure of dozens of psychologists, counselors, well-meaning friends. I hadn't told anyone what had happened between my mother and me the last night I saw her alive. Where would I even start?

"I've got plenty of room at the house, Althea," he said. "You can stay with me if you'd rather not go back."

I laughed. Shook my head. Laughed again.

He raised his eyebrows. "You think I'm kidding?"

"No. I just think you have no idea what you're saying. You don't know anything about me."

"So tell me."

"I'm a liar and a thief," I said evenly. "An addict—pills mostly, but whatever I can find that'll get me buzzed will do. I'm bad odds."

There was silence; then he spoke.

"I don't know how much you've heard—but I've been in New York. Worked on Wall Street," he said, like he hadn't heard a word of my confession. "I got laid off one day, and my wife moved out the next month. She said I didn't want it enough." He wiped his mouth, folded his napkin, and tucked it under his plate. "Whatever *it* is. So I just moved back home too. Looking after my parents' place while they're out of the country."

I was quiet. An unemployed divorcé. A recovering addict with a dying dad. We certainly were a pair.

"So what do you say?" he asked.

"Why are you being so nice?"

"Really? You have to ask that? Our history means nothing to you?"

Our history. Half a lifetime of catching fireflies and watching scary movies and fishing off his jon boat. Another half of mad make-out sessions and school dances. We'd probably made more promises than our childhood marriage pact; it was hard to remember through the scrim of the pills and alcohol.

"You're a good person, Jay," I finally said, to break the logjam in my brain.

"Depends on who you ask," he said and motioned to the waitress. "One chocolate pie, two scoops of vanilla, and two spoons." She nodded and left, and he turned back to me.

"But with you? Yes. Nothing but good intentions here." He gazed at me. "What do you say?"

I looked into his eyes and, all at once, felt that familiar sensation of something pulling me. Something tugging away at me, gently at first, so as not to raise an alarm. The thing that pulled at me glimmered with a promise of weightlessness and lightness. It whispered profound-sounding things about fate and the futility of resistance. Jay or drugs. I had the feeling those two things were not so different.

I tried to remember the steps, all the pithy sayings we'd repeated in group about powerlessness and weakness and how screwed up we all were, but my mind was a complete blank.

I was in a shitload of trouble.

"Althea?"

"I can't," I said quickly. "But thanks."

He stared at me for a minute longer, then nodded.

I thought of Wynn and Molly Robb back at the party, bidding their guests good-bye, and my father, upstairs, locked in his bedroom. Those words he'd shouted at me—*thirty's a bitch*—they'd turned my blood cold.

My mother had died on her thirtieth birthday. An aneurysm; tragic, but not unheard-of. But there was something about what had happened to her, the way she'd died, that he had never explained. Earlier, Dad had made it sound like turning thirty was somehow to blame for my mother's death. And he seemed to be insinuating, now that I was turning thirty, that the same shadowy unknown thing was somewhere just out of sight, waiting to overtake me as well.

My mother had said something like that too. Once, a long time ago, when I was a little girl. Out in the clearing that night, the night she died. She had warned me about turning thirty, given me instructions.

After his outburst this afternoon, it was obvious my father knew more than he'd ever let on. There was more. I'd always known it, always had that low hum of anxiety in my bones. And now it was coming out.

Thirty's a goddamn bitch.

I had to see him, whether he liked it or not. I had to know more.

The waitress set the pie and ice cream between us. Jay handed me a spoon, and I watched him dig in. The image of the raven with red wings perched on the banister flashed into my head.

"I have to get something from my house," I said to him. "Will you drop me off?"

"My pleasure."

I set down the spoon, my appetite gone with the thought of confronting Wynn and Molly Robb again. Suddenly, I thought I noticed a faint trace of gold, like the finest dust, on its handle. When I blinked, it was gone.

Chapter Four

Saturday, September 15, 2012
Mobile, Alabama

Back at my father's dock, Jay helped me onto the weathered boards. When his fingers brushed against mine, I moved my hands to my hair and made a show of winding it into a bun. Touching him made me nervous, and what I didn't need at this point was another weird raven or gold-dust hallucination.

One horrific thing at a time was all I could handle.

He stepped back on his boat, and it rocked under his weight. "Can I call you?"

I gave him my number.

"Okay. See you soon. I hope," he said and pushed off.

I could see Molly Robb through the windows, collecting plates and cups from the party. She pushed an ottoman back into place with her knee, narrowly missing the tiny dog. It skittered sideways, then slunk into the kitchen. She peered out the window, set down the stack of plates and cups, and slipped out onto the porch, pushing the door shut behind her.

"It's not a good time. Wynn's called his doctor." She blinked at me with her round, pale eyes.

"Do you have something you want to say to me?" I asked.

Her eyebrows shot up, her face a study of innocence.

"You seem angry."

"I'm not angry. I'm very proud of all the hard work you've done. Very proud. I support you, Althea. You know I always have."

I folded my arms. "But the campaign . . ."

She smiled slightly.

"You have to be careful," I said.

"You grew up in state politics. You should understand this better than anybody." She stared at me.

She really expected me to leave. To disappear into the darkness and erase myself from my family's life.

"I need to get a few things," I said at last. "Since I won't be staying here."

She tilted her head, her expression still mild. "Sure. What do you want?"

"I don't know. Clothes. Things."

"I'll get whatever you want."

"This was my house before it was yours."

Her face hardened.

"Just let me get my stuff, Molly Robb."

She sighed. "Fine. But don't go into his room."

I stepped around her, pulled open the screen door, headed for the stairs. I could hear the creaky door slam and her heels clicking behind me, and an image flashed into my head of me turning and smashing my fist into her smooth, overly powdered face. I jammed my hands in my pockets.

At the top of the stairs, I headed down the hall toward my room, the last one on the left. I threw open the door, stepped in, and scanned it. The room hadn't changed a bit since I was little. That's what happens when you grow up without a mother. You keep the same brass canopy bed, the old baby rocker with the patchwork pad, and the too-small, chipped dresser all your life. Forever a five-year-old's room.

I flung open the closet door and pulled the light cord. The shelves were crammed with old board games, afghans, and stacks of T-shirts and sweaters, but I knew instantly someone had been in there. Panic shot through me. I turned, my entire body burning with anger, and grabbed Molly Robb by the arms. She grew even whiter than I'd thought possible, and I felt a surge of satisfaction.

"Where is it?" I said.

"I don't know what you're—"

"The cigar box. Where is it?"

I pushed her away, headed for the door, then, turning back, pointed my finger and jabbed it emphatically in her direction. "I'm going into my father's room. Back up." She held her hands up in a helpless gesture. I stalked past her.

Down the hall, I pushed my father's door open. The room was dim; only one small lamp burned beside the bed. My father lay propped up by a mound of pillows. His eyes were closed, and somebody had changed him into pajamas. Wynn sat in a nearby reading chair. I really looked at my brother for the first time in a long time. His hair was thick, thicker than I remembered, and shiny with gel. He looked completely relaxed sitting there in the chair, fit and tanned, everybody's image of the ideal governor.

I flashed to him as a boy. Easy, toothy smile, freckles; always, infuriatingly, a head taller than me. The two of us used to take the Sunfish out on the river, him shirtless and skinny, ragged jeans falling below the band of his Fruit of the Looms. He always handled the hard part— pushing the boat out on the water, getting us pointed in the right direction—so by the time we really caught the wind, he'd be flushed and sweaty. It never seemed to bother him. He'd hand me the ropes and sit back as I tacked and shouted, "Comin' over!"

"It's 'coming about,' you ding-dong," he'd laugh. As we glided along the shore, he'd point out the gators sunning themselves among the thick reeds, even on our property. They especially liked to eat small sailboats, he warned me, manned by curly-headed little ding-dongs.

Now, my brother, a man I barely recognized, stood before me with no sign of a smile. While I'd spent the last decade charging headfirst down a path of self-destruction, he'd done all the right things. Gone to college and law school, been elected to the state legislature. He'd married Molly Robb—a woman from a wealthy family in Birmingham. They'd both been patient with me these last few years, supportive, I'd thought. But maybe I'd been fooling myself. Maybe they'd just been watching and waiting—allowing me to do their dirty work for them by destroying myself.

"It's good to see you, kiddo," Wynn said and opened his arms to me. Against my better judgment, I went in for the hug. His chest was warm, and he smelled like cigar smoke and whiskey and shampoo, but the embrace felt misaligned and awkward. I tried to get a better glimpse of Dad, but Wynn motioned me out of the room.

We walked downstairs to the foyer, where Molly Robb waited for us. Along with another man, one I would've been happy never to see again in my life. Dr. Duncan, the psychiatrist who'd advised Dad and Wynn to send me to treatment. After our first and only session, Wynn had driven me down to the coast and checked me in to the center. I hadn't laid eyes on the doctor since.

"What's he doing here?" I asked Wynn.

"Nice to see you again, Althea," Dr. Duncan said, his watery eyes huge behind reading glasses. He lowered a dog-eared piece of paper and I recognized it immediately; it was from my cigar box. My heart thumped once, hard, against my ribs. I kept my eyes on my brother.

"Why does he have that? Where's my cigar box?"

"Dr. Duncan's actually here for Dad," my brother said. "He's been consulting with Molly Robb and me about the kind of environment we should be creating here for him."

"I don't believe you."

"See, I told you. She's paranoid," Molly Robb said.

"What's he doing here?" I asked again.

"He's here for Dad," Wynn repeated.

"Bullshit."

"That's what I'm talking about," Molly Robb piped up. "We really can't have her traipsing in here, talking that way around Elder. It's upsetting to him."

"I can promise you my father's not upset by the word *bullshit*," Wynn said. Our eyes met, and I could've sworn I saw the corner of his mouth twitch. Maybe my brother was still my brother. Maybe he could be reasoned with, after all.

"It doesn't matter why he's here. I just want you to give me back my box. And that." I nodded at the paper. "And I'll go."

"Althea," Dr. Duncan said. "Why do you want the cigar box so badly?"

"Because it's mine."

"Is there something in the box that holds some sort of significance to you?"

I felt tears burning behind my eyes. *Breathe. Be polite. Speak slowly. Act normal.* "My mother gave it to me when I was young. It means a lot to me."

He looked at the paper again. I itched to grab it, to jam it into my pocket and run, but I stood still.

"Would you like to talk about what's in the box?" Dr. Duncan asked.

I shook my head.

"How about what's on this paper?"

Veni, Creator Spiritus, mentes tuorum visita. I could remember the sound of my mother chanting the words. When I was five, she'd given me the paper and all the other things in the cigar box. They were mine. All I had of her.

"It's just a prayer," I said.

"A prayer that means a great deal to you. 'Come, Holy Ghost, Creator blessed, and in our hearts take up Thy rest.' Did I get that right, Althea?"

And then, in answer to his question, the tears came. One, two, right down either cheek. What was the point in answering him? I was like an open wound to all of them; talking would only make it worse. I turned to my brother.

"Please. Just give it back."

My voice sounded so desperate. I was starting to slip, I could feel it. I would fragment, separate, and fly apart in all directions. The panic would set in next—the palpitations, the dry mouth, the dizziness. I'd start seeing gold and ravens and God knew what other kind of shit. Only I couldn't, not now, not in front of these people.

I am not my mother.

"Look," I said, wiping the tears and forcing a smile. "We're all pretty wound up here. Why don't you let me go up and talk to Dad for a minute? Maybe if he sees me again, and I can talk to him, he'll be okay."

"Althea," Dr. Duncan said. "We understand you may be feeling wound up, as you say, about coming back home. Living and working sober can be very daunting, after the time you've spent *out there*." He nodded toward the door, like I'd done all my illicit deeds out in our front yard. "With your father so sick, it's perfectly understandable that you're feeling overwhelmed."

"I'm not overwhelmed, I just wanted to talk to my father. If I can't do that, I want to collect a few things that belong to me, and go."

"I understand you see it that way. But we—Wynn, Molly Robb, and I—see things differently and would like to offer you an alternative.

To jumping right back into things, as it were. We would like to propose a facility for you, someplace more long-term, where you can get your bearings."

"I did that already."

"The halfway house was a good step, but you need more."

"No. No facility."

He didn't even blink. "Althea, we think you might need some more intensive therapy. For the childhood issues."

"I don't know what you're talking about." My voice sounded painfully high.

"When you were away," Molly Robb said, "Dad told us some things we never knew. About your mother."

"What?"

"Would you like to sit down?" Dr. Duncan said.

"No. I'd like you to tell me what you're talking about."

"There's a lot we didn't realize about Trix," he said. "Your mother had a great many secrets."

"She didn't die the way we thought," Wynn said.

"What do you mean?" I could feel my breath getting shallow. I looked at him.

He didn't answer, just turned and walked to the breakfront and pulled out the cigar box from one of the lower cabinets. Relief flooded through me when I saw it—tattered and brown-stained, a red raven on the front. He walked back, slowly, and held it out. I took hold of it, but he held it fast, so we both were standing there, each holding a corner. I gave a little tug, and he let go, watched me as I held my other hand out to Dr. Duncan. He handed over the paper. I returned the paper to the box and held it to my chest.

I am not my mother.

There is no such thing as the honeysuckle girl . . .

"Mom was mentally ill, Althea," Wynn said gently. "She had schizophrenia. It hit her when she turned thirty."

"She had an aneurysm," I said.

Dr. Duncan spoke. "We think it was because she was taking Haldol in great quantities to prevent the schizophrenia and that's what actually contributed to her death."

I knew there had been something not quite normal about my mother and the way she'd died. But my father had never talked about it, and I didn't want to let myself think about things like that. I couldn't. And anyway, there were some not-quite-normal things about me too. A streak of gold dust on a doorknob I'd touched or a hairbrush I'd just used.

I told myself they were just games, leftover from childhood. Mirages. The way heat shimmered and made you think it was water. I didn't see visions of the Virgin Mary in a bowl of buttered grits. The things I saw didn't mean anything. They were just aftershocks. Ghost images imprinted on my brain from a moment of trauma in my childhood.

I had made it worse, I would admit that. I used to tell myself they were signs, sent by my mother from heaven to let me know she was near. The gold from her favorite dress, the red raven rising off the cigar box, swooping around me. They meant she was protecting me.

But I'd gotten older and started with the drinking and the pills, and that's when the whispers took a turn. They started to come unbidden, when I was anxious, tired, or upset. When I was especially messed up. I didn't tell any of my doctors. Maybe I didn't want to let them go, I don't know. But when I went to rehab, I told myself it was time. I had to stop. I began using the affirmations. They might've sounded hokey, but they worked.

Most of the time.

"You knew about the Haldol, correct?" Dr. Duncan asked me.

"Yes," I said. "I mean, I knew she was taking the pills, but I didn't know why."

Molly Robb let out a soft snort.

You knew. Deep down, you knew why she took them.

"She hadn't been prescribed them," Dr. Duncan said. "We actually believe an overdose killed her, not an aneurysm."

"What does this have to do with me?" I asked.

"Several months ago, your father expressed a concern the same thing might happen to you. A psychotic, schizoid break."

"It's hereditary," Wynn said. "Collie had it too, our grandmother."

"That's why you took your mother's Haldol when you were a little girl, isn't that right?" Dr. Duncan asked.

I turned cold.

"Althea?" Duncan said. "You wanted to prevent the same thing from happening to you?"

I wanted to say that I had taken the pills because they were there, in my mother's cigar box, the box she'd given to me, and I wanted to be like her. I wanted to say they made me feel good. Light and other-worldly and brave. I hadn't understood what they were for, not really. Not completely. But that wasn't the truth.

You knew.

"I inspected all the empty vials in the box," Dr. Duncan continued. "Only one of them was from the 1980s. That bottle was hers, obviously. The others are only approximately seventeen years old. So they're yours, am I right?"

I was silent.

"You were obtaining drugs as far back as when you were thirteen years old, Althea? The same drug your mother had been abusing. It's illegal, you know, to take Haldol without a prescription."

I knew that. Haldol, Clozaril, Risperdal, all of them. After a while I'd discovered Xanax, Percocet, Vicodin, and OxyContin. Way easier to find and a more reliable high. I'd probably gone through a thou-sand bottles since I was thirteen. But I'd kept those few original Haldol bottles in the cigar box. More ties to my mother.

The doctor cleared his throat. "Let us help you, Althea. This is more than just a run-of-the-mill addiction. It's a pathology, connected to the traumatic loss of your mother. There's a strong chance you're predisposed for schizophrenia, just like your mother was. Add it to your substance-abuse problems, and this . . . this unusual compulsion you have, mimicking your mother's addiction—"

"You'll have it by thirty," my father shouted from the top of the stairs. "They all get it at thirty!"

We all stared at him. Stooped in his rumpled pajamas, his hair on end, he pointed a knobby finger in my direction. His face was red and mottled, the way he used to look when he'd caught me sneaking in late in high school.

"Dad," I said and started up the stairs. I felt a hand grab the back of my shirt, pull me back. I stumbled, cried out, and flailed for the banister. I saw Wynn move past me, taking the steps two at a time.

"Every last one of them," my father said. "They go crazy. Those mountain girls all go crazy the day they turn thirty." Wynn put an arm around Dad and pivoted him toward the bedroom.

"Wynn!"

My brother stopped, looked down at me.

"It's not true, is it?" I said. "Tell me it's not true."

My father bobbed his head, answering some unheard voices, and Wynn raised his eyes to the ceiling.

"Wynn. Please."

"I'm sorry, Althea," he said. "Mom knew what was going to happen to her. That's why she was taking the Haldol. It happened to all of them. It's probably going to happen to you too."

"We'd like to keep you under observation," Dr. Duncan said behind me. "In case we're right. So you're not a harm to yourself."

I felt them pressing in on me, my family and the doctor, with concerned eyes and this outlandish story. But how could my father have been keeping this secret all this time? Why hadn't he said anything? Nobody had said anything. My grandmother, Collirene, had died when my mother was young, I knew that. Nobody had ever mentioned a cause. My great-grandmother, named Jinn, was from somewhere up in north Alabama where the Appalachian Mountains dwindled to hills. One time I'd heard one of Dad's relatives say she'd run off with some man who wasn't her husband, but that was it. Nobody had ever spoken of her death.

So why now?

"This is about the campaign, isn't it?" I said to Wynn. "You don't want me messing it up for you."

"I want you to get help. I'm doing this for you."

"I'm not going back to any facility."

"You have to," Molly Robb said.

"Fuck you," I shot at her. They all gaped at me. "I don't have to do anything I don't want to." I was sounding like a child again. I hated myself for it.

Wynn looked down at me over the banister, his arm still protectively curved around our father. "That's where you're wrong. It's in his will." He flicked a glance at Molly Robb, then back at me. "We all appreciate the work you did in rehab. That was an excellent start, but you have more work to do. We"—at this, he swept his gaze over the others—"all of us feel you need continuous, intensive care, for your own safety. You have to check yourself into a psychiatric hospital before your thirtieth birthday if you want your inheritance. It's the only way you'll ever see a penny of it."

And then, he and my father were gone.

Chapter Five

Saturday, September 15, 2012
Mobile, Alabama

I burst out of the house into the sticky darkness, cursing the spike-heeled boots and clutching the cigar box and my purse to my chest. When I got in the car and turned the key, I heard a couple of clicks, then everything fell ominously silent.

"No." I tried again, pumping the gas this time, but there was no response, not even a click. I banged on the steering wheel. "No! Don't do this to me!"

I heard the coo of a dove outside my window. The buzz of cicadas. The humidity enveloped me. I laid my head on the wheel. Closed my eyes. I didn't care what the doctor said. Some things were valuable, just because they were. Even scraps of paper with prayers written on them in faded blue ink.

"Veni, Creator Spiritus," I said. "Mentes tuorum visita, imple superna gratia, quae tu creasti pectora."

I tried the key again. No response.

"Qui diceris Paraclitus, altissimi donum Dei . . . um . . . tu septiformus munere." I was saying it fast now, the words rolling out of me unchecked, working the key forward and back desperately. The car remained stubbornly silent.

"Tu septiformus munere!" I smacked the wheel with both hands. Nothing.

I grabbed my purse and the cigar box, and clambered out, getting my foot caught in the seat belt and nearly pitching headfirst to the shells. I twisted and kicked at a tire. "Piece of 1997 shit!"

I looked back at the house. Wynn and Molly Robb had probably forgotten about me by now. They'd gone about their regular evening routine: locking the doors, drawing the curtains, settling into their nail-lined coffins. They hadn't even given me a second thought. I turned to the deserted road, seething.

I'd only gotten a few houses down when Jay pulled up beside me. "Need a ride?"

I stopped, feeling my face go hot. I was glad it was dark.

"Where you headed?" he asked.

I hugged my bundle of pathetic possessions. "Away from here." I stopped. "Where are you going?"

"To be honest, I was coming back to see you."

"Why?"

"I don't know. Just wanted to make sure things were okay. C'mon." He beckoned. "Get in the car."

I didn't move.

"Please."

I relented. Once in the car, I didn't speak. I just held the cigar box and stared out into the blackness. He drove us to his parents' house, a couple of miles downriver. He said about three words total the whole way, but I didn't mind. I sat, both hands clutching the cigar box, grateful for the silence.

In the house—which smelled achingly familiar, of his mom's lavender-scented cleaner and his dad's pipe tobacco—Jay led me back to his parents' Zen-style master bath. He turned on the six-head shower and left me in the gathering steam. Forty-five minutes later, wrapped in his mom's huge (also lavender-scented) terry robe, I padded into the dim kitchen. The cigar box sat in the center of the enormous island next to a pot of violets. He pushed a mug of coffee toward me.

"Drink." He nodded at the mug and I obeyed, trying my best not to stare at my ratty, dirt-smudged cigar box. In reality it drew my gaze like a magnet, like always—the red and gold curlicues on each corner, a red bird with a jaunty crest perching on a tree branch suspended in midair, the lettering stamped below: "Red Raven Cigars." I was dying open it, to go through each item and catalog and caress them. It'd been so long. I kept my hands wrapped around my coffee instead.

A curtain of wet hair fell into my face. Jay moved behind me, gathered the wet strands in both hands, twisted and clipped it to the back of my head. I reached a hand back; he'd stuck a clothespin in it.

"Inventive," I said.

He cleared his throat. "My parents' condo in Orange Beach is available. We could go there. Eat shrimp. Drink sweet tea. Binge-watch shitty TV." He finished wiping up around the coffeemaker and followed my gaze to the cigar box. "Or not." He pushed the box toward me. "What's in it?"

"Just some things my mother left me," I said.

"I'll leave you alone," he offered. "If you want me to."

I hesitated, then nodded.

He smiled. "Better day tomorrow, Althea. I'd put a hundred on it."

After he left, I drew the box to me and lifted the lid. Closed my eyes, then opened them again, hoping nothing else had been taken. It hadn't. Everything was the same as the first time I'd opened the box all those years ago.

I pulled each item out, one by one: the prayer Dr. Duncan had held, the pill bottles (six total, all of them empty), an old wine-bottle label ("Jinn's Juice—The Most Refreshing!") with a name and address scratched on the back in pencil: Tom Stocker, Old Cemetery Road. An old brass-and-ivory hair barrette with a tiny bird, wings outstretched, in the middle of it. A postcard-size amateur watercolor painting, the paper folded into fourths, showing two women sitting under an arbor, deep in conversation. A few odds and ends like arrowheads, papery locust skins, and bottle caps.

I arranged the items in a row on the counter, the way I used to line them up across my comforter every night before I went to sleep. I touched each one now with reverent fingers, like they were holy relics.

And now that thing was happening, the way it had always happened when I opened the box. The memories were taking over, expanding inside me, suffocating me. Blotting out everything reasonable and sane. I saw the path that wound through the woods and to the clearing beside our house. It was an oasis, the clearing, cool and mossy, even in the south-Alabama humidity. Spanish moss hanging like curtains, making you feel like you were in a secret cave.

Nighttime, and my mother kneels in the clearing. She is shaking. She pushes the box with the red raven on the lid across the grass to me. I see what's inside—the prayer, the wine label, the barrette, the painting, and the pill bottles—but I don't understand what they mean. She tells me to hide the box from my father, and I promise I will.

I had kept my promise. I kept the cigar box out of sight, hidden in my closet, even when I went away to college. I hadn't understood why I was doing it. But now, more than ever, I was convinced my mother had known what she was doing. For some reason, my father could not see what was inside this box. The same reason, no doubt, that my brother had taken it. The pill bottles, the prayer, the painting, the wine label, and the barrette—they weren't just random reminders of my mother. They actually meant something. They were clues.

In the clearing, I heard my mother's voice. Practically the last thing she'd said to me before she died, about the honeysuckle girl.

She's very wise. She knows things.

Now the items—the clues—waited on Jay's kitchen counter in their orderly row. Waited for me to make the next move. They were pulling me toward them but I held back, afraid to get too close, to let them infect me again. My mother's words had been a fairy story. A lie.

No, worse than that. Her instructions had been the product of a disturbed mind.

No one had found me. No honeysuckle girl, no all-wise friend with words to save me. And it wasn't good for me to obsess like this, that's what all the doctors had said. I owed it to myself to stay strong and focused.

I am not my mother.

The honeysuckle girl isn't real.

I do not have gold dust on my fingertips.

There is no such thing as a red raven.

I swept the neat row of items into the cigar box. I was glad Jay had left. I didn't know if I would've been able to explain to him why I cared so much about its contents, in a way that didn't make me sound completely, one hundred percent crazy.

Jay had turned down the sheets on his parents' king-size bed, and I climbed in, robe and all. He took an old undershirt of his dad's out of the drawer, tossed it to me, then reached around and took the clothespin out of my hair. He pinched it on his finger a couple of times, until the tip of his finger turned white.

"It's so weird being here," I said.

He smiled.

I smiled too. "It's weird being in your parents' bed."

"You want to sleep in the guest room? My dad has his exercise equipment in there, but the bed is good."

I shook my head, and he went quiet. He made a move to leave.

"Stay," I said.

He lifted the covers and, fully clothed, climbed in beside me. Curled around me and buried his face in my damp hair. My heart began to race. "If you want to talk about it . . ." He stopped, waiting. But I didn't say anything. I couldn't. Not yet. I heard him exhale, then I did too, and, without intending to, I fell asleep.

I woke up sometime before dawn, enveloped in the lavender smell of the bedsheets and the undershirt I was wearing. I sat up and watched the stars that hung over the river and the purple glow of the coming morning from the wall of glass opposite the bed.

I couldn't stop thinking about what my father had said. *Every last one of them*—my mother, Trix; grandmother, Collie; and great-grandmother, Jinn. Other than my suspicions about my mother, I had never heard anything about them having any kind of mental illness. Or it happening at age thirty. I'd never been told anything other than the few sentences my mother had whispered to me in the clearing that night.

The new knowledge, this thing I held inside me, was too big to comprehend. I could barely swallow. I could barely breathe. After a minute or two I turned to look down at Jay. He was lying on his back, awake, watching me. I stared back, unblinking, breaking contact only once to look down at his lips. By now, the air between us was crackling, and his face had transformed in understanding.

"I don't think this is such a good idea," he said.

"Nothing I do is a good idea."

"You're wrong." His voice was soft but hoarse. "I wish you knew how wrong you are. I wish you could see how I see you, Althea."

I felt tears flood my eyes. He had to stop saying things like this, these things that made me feel like my skin had been peeled back. But he'd been surrounded by so much care, so much love, he probably couldn't imagine living in a world that wasn't brimming over with it. I wanted to tell him to stop, but I was sick of conversation and scared where more of it would lead me.

Instead, I pulled off the shirt and then my underwear and moved to him. He held aside the covers, and I arranged my body over his. Chest to chest, arms and legs entwined, my head under his chin—we fit perfectly.

"We shouldn't," he said.

"Yeah."

His arms went up and wrapped around me. And he exhaled again, like he'd been holding his breath for a really long time. After a couple of minutes, he shifted me to the side, peeled off his shirt and pants, and pressed himself against me once more.

I kissed him once, and it couldn't have been any slower and sweeter. When I felt tears threaten—*oh please God, not that*—I rolled on my back and pulled him on top of me. I wanted to feel his weight, all of it, on me. I wrapped my legs around him, and we settled into each other.

"You feel cold," he said. "In a good way. Like the river on a hot day."

He was wrong, though. It wasn't good, the way I was cold. It was bad. It was a little bit dangerous. I hurt people with my coldness.

When he finally moved inside me, I forced myself to stay detached for as long as I could, focusing on his shoulder, the way freckles dotted his skin, his smell. But I couldn't stop myself, he felt too good. I closed my eyes, pressed up and into him. And felt myself slipping away to that place where I didn't care anymore, not about anything. Only us and this.

I made a wish. Two wishes, actually: First, that Jay wouldn't realize that I was doing this, using him, to numb my fear. And second, that in spite of our long history, our friendship and the pact we'd made, this tryst wouldn't ultimately mean anything more than just two strangers doing what strangers sometimes did.

Then I let go.

Chapter Six

October 1937
Sybil Valley, Alabama

Miss Isbell, the schoolteacher, sent home a note pinned to Walter's shirt. He wouldn't even hold still long enough for Jinn to unpin the thing but tore away from her grip, ripping off the corner as he ran outside. Collie banged on a mixing bowl at the counter while Jinn read the torn note. Then she folded it into a tiny, hard square and tucked it in the pocket of her apron.

At supper that night, she told Howell.

"Walter's been picking on the young ones," she said. "Pelting them with chestnuts while they're saying their lines for the Christmas pageant." She didn't look at Walter but she could feel him, slouching on the left side of the table, swallowing down a lump of potatoes. His eyes seemed to burn right through her.

"Practicing for a Christmas pageant in October? Lord *God*, these women." Howell forked a piece of ham onto his plate and jerked his chin. Jinn hopped up and ladled a circle of gravy for him.

She didn't know if he was referring to Miss Isbell specifically or the long string of schoolteachers Sybil Valley had hawked up and coughed out over the years. Howell had driven a few to nervous distraction himself, back when he was a boy. One up and walked out of the classroom—the whole building and all the way down Main Street to the boardinghouse where she stayed—right in the middle of the day.

"I don't have time to go down to the schoolhouse and drink tea with some dried-up, horse-faced schoolmarm. You take care of it." Howell winked at Collie, who giggled. He cracked his neck and addressed Walter. "You leave them kids alone. Or I reckon I'll jerk you outta that school, and you can go to work like me and my daddy did when we was your age."

Walter sat like a stone.

"Huh?" Howell held his knife and fork over his plate like two daggers. "You gonna throw chestnuts or study your books?"

"Study."

"That's what I thought."

The next afternoon, at five 'til three, Jinn walked through the front doors of the school. As the children trooped out, she clutched her pocketbook and pressed her back against the wall. In the classroom, Miss Isbell was sitting at her desk, waiting. Walter and Willie Stocker sat at their desks. Tom Stocker stood by the window. When she came in, he grinned at her. Something fluttered low in her belly.

Tom was a widower who lived up the mountain a ways in a big brick house with his young son. His wife, a petite, refined woman named Lucy, had died soon after Willie was born, and he'd never remarried, even though he had piles of money and was probably the most eligible bachelor in north Alabama. Folks said he couldn't get over Lucy. It was true. Jinn had seen him offer Lucy his arm every Sunday she was alive when they walked out of church. She'd seen the way they looked at each other.

Tom and Jinn had kissed once—forever ago, when they were kids, in the schoolyard, long before she ever went with Howell, before Lucy and her family moved to town. But after Lucy had been dead a couple of years, Tom began to pay Jinn extra attention whenever he ran into her at the hardware store or the feed store. He bumped into her regularly enough, when she was in town, that Jinn began to take notice.

One June day after church—another Sunday Howell had begged off—Tom had appeared beside Jinn as they descended the steps. He offered her his arm. She took it.

He never touched her, other than that one time, nor said one unseemly word. But still. Any husband who was paying the slightest bit of attention would be riled. Even Jinn had to wonder: what was Tom Stocker, with his bright eyes and ready smile, waiting around for? A bolt of lightning to cleave Howell Wooten in two?

"I suppose we should begin," Miss Isbell said.

She explained that Walter and a few of the older boys, the Wise Men, had been pelting little Willie Stocker, a sheep, with chestnuts and baaing at him during the practice for the pageant. One of the chestnuts had struck his eye, leaving a bloody gash in the white of it. Miss Isbell had made Walter write *I will not throw chestnuts* on the chalkboard, which Jinn could see he'd completed. His cramped, cursive scrawl rose in row after row on the board behind the teacher's head. In addition to the punishment, Miss Isbell wanted to settle things between the parents.

Jinn promised Miss Isbell and Tom that Howell would give the boy a good whipping, and she'd take away his supper to boot, and then they all stood, shook hands. At the front doors, Tom laid a hand on her arm.

"Jinny," he said.

She liked the way her name sounded in his voice. Nobody called her Jinny anymore, except her father, and when he did, it had an altogether different sound. In fact, her father said they'd named her after a mule for obvious reasons. But when Tom said it—*Jinny*—she got goose bumps. And now, something more. Something sharp and insistent leaping up from her belly. It made her more nervous, being here without Howell with that feeling in her gut.

"You boys run on home," Tom called out to Willie and Walter. "We'll be along." Tom turned to her. "Walk with me," he said. "We need to talk."

Jinn wasn't so sure she could walk with Tom and talk to him at the same time. They'd only ever had scraps of conversation between them. Never a whole back-and-forth, not since they were kids.

He had this thing he did. He'd wait until she asked a question or said something that invited a reply, then give her a look that said, *We'll talk later* and amble off. It left her so unsettled. Yearning for, yet dreading, the next time they met and the conversation could inch one step further.

Jinn had a feeling that one day they'd reach the end of the conversation, and then what would happen? If it came down to it, would she choose Tom Stocker over Howell? Could she really and truly make that choice? If she did, she'd be turning her back not only on her husband, but on Jesus as well. Touching Tom Stocker would make her a backslider.

She followed him down the steps of the school and around back. Her heart was hammering, belly flopping like a fish. They cut across the schoolyard, just a square of hard-packed dirt, knobbed with shiny tree roots. Even though it was barely past the edge of dusk, a raccoon was already out, worrying at a brown lump of something. An apple core or the remainder of a child's sandwich.

"You remember the time I kissed you out here?" Tom said, right off.

The wind kicked up, sending dirt clouding around their ankles. A thread of cool ran through it. A tinge of the winter ahead. She didn't answer him, not because she couldn't recall the day, but because she wasn't sure what to say.

"I guess that was a long time ago," he sighed.

"I remember."

He stopped. Turned to her. Studied her.

"It was May Day," she said after what seemed like a long time. "When Howell bid on my bouquet."

"You mean, after he snuck in the auditorium during lunch and filched it before the auction even started?"

"That's right." She smiled. "I thought you were gonna pop him one good, you were so mad."

"I considered it." His eyes were flashing now, the sly grin making her weak. "Then I remembered he was three years older and twice my size. And I decided I'd be smarter finding you, so I could get my kiss in first."

He took one step closer. Hands in his pockets. Her heart thudded.

"I thought I should give you the kiss you'd be comparing all the others to for the rest of your life."

Her eyes slid to watch the raccoon scuttle around the corner of the building.

"This is what I wonder," he asked. "Did it work?"

He spoke so quietly; she almost didn't believe he expected an answer. Maybe because he already knew what she'd say.

It had worked, but then Tom had gone away to college. Howell had stayed. He'd stayed and sworn to her that if she married him, he'd keep her safe. He'd never let her daddy darken the door of their house. He'd never let Vernon hurt her again.

She looked back at Tom and felt a tremor of fear. His face had hardened, his eyes dimmed. Something was wrong, more than just Howell or what had happened all those years ago. Something was terribly wrong.

"What is it?" she said.

"I've got to show you something, Jinny. Up on the mountain."

"What?"

He was quiet.

"Tom. You're scaring me."

"It's something . . . just something you need to see."

He offered his arm, and she took it. They left the schoolyard and headed into the woods, stepping carefully through the blackjack oaks, hickories, and pines. Climbing over beds of slick needles and acorns. It was a path, nothing but a narrow deer trail, but it went for miles up the mountain, around mossy boulders and across dozens of trickling branches.

After awhile, Jinn let go of Tom's arm and fell into step behind him. Her coat had come unbuttoned but her back was damp with sweat, so she welcomed the cold air. The smells made her heady—smoke curling up from someone's distant woodstove, the musk of bear and deer and red fox and bobcats either bedding down or rousing for their night hunt. She thought she could even smell apples too, crisping on the trees.

She wondered what it would be like to tramp with Tom through the woods every night, after supper. Then turn homeward toward their big, brick house with the white painted door. Up to their bedroom to tangle together in soft sheets and blankets.

They'd been walking a good half hour when Tom beckoned her forward. "Almost there," he said. He held out his hand, and she took it, holding it the last couple of yards. At a curve in the trail, he helped her over a fallen log, its center collapsed by rot and rain, and the scene unfolded before her.

A half-circle of black tree trunks stretched to the gray sky. In their center, between them, hung a strange form. Jinn thought at first it was some sort of sign, a banner like the ones they hung at the county fair. Only this banner had no words printed on it. And it was misshapen, somehow. Nothing was right about it at all.

She took one step forward. And then she saw.

Suspended by ropes between two longleaf pines, about six feet off the ground, was what appeared to be a large dog, its legs dangling downward. A length of rope was looped around its neck and stretched to one tree; another length was tied around its hindquarters and stretched to an opposite tree. The animal was motionless, a deformed monster, against the graying sky.

"It's a calf," Tom said. "Hereford. Only a couple days old. Whoever did this stole it from my place and brought it here. They strung it up and left it here. For days. They let it starve."

Jinn moved closer. Reached her hand up and touched one small hoof. It was wet. She drew her finger back, rubbing the pads of her fingers together. Blood. She reached up again.

"Jinny, stop."

Then her fingers found the cuts—tiny razor slices along its flank. She used both hands then and felt the sliced ears. The hacked-off tail. The empty, streaming eye sockets. She stepped back. Shook her head, slowly at first, then faster.

She stepped back again but stumbled this time, and Tom caught her. She held her bloody hands high above her head, the way Brother Daley did before he passed out communion, and coughed out a series of sobs that eventually turned into screams. Tom finally had to cover her mouth.

When she'd quieted, Tom whispered into her ear, "Willie found him up here."

She tried to tell him to stop—she didn't want to hear any more—but all that came out was a strangled whimper.

"It was Walter, Jinny," he said. "Walter was the one who did it."

At supper, Jinn thought if she put one forkful of chicken pie in her mouth, surely it would come spewing back out. So she sat very still and pushed the lumps of peas and carrots around in the gravy. Prayed that Howell wouldn't bring up the meeting at the school.

He didn't. After supper, he headed out to the porch to smoke and look through the mail. Jinn sent the children off to listen to *Amos 'n'*

Andy so she could scour the dishes. But she felt Walter's eyes on her back.

She turned, wringing the dish towel to give her trembling hands something to do. "You still hungry?"

He was staring at her. "Willie told his pap what I done up there on the mountain, didn't he? And then he told you."

She knew she should speak, but she couldn't. Her throat felt all closed up.

"You ain't gonna tell Daddy, are you?" he said.

The boy was smart to be afraid. If Howell found out he'd stolen a calf and killed it, he'd be furious. He'd pull Walter out of school, once and for all, and put him to work. Calves weren't cheap, they sold at auction for more than Howell could afford. More money than Howell wanted to hand over to the likes of Tom Stocker.

But Walter's blank, cold eyes weren't afraid. They were angry, brimming with warning. She pointed at him anyway, not caring that her finger was shaking and he could see it.

"Don't you never do anything like that again, you hear? I mean it."

She turned back to the dishes, and the boy rose from the table and went out to the front porch to join his father.

Chapter Seven

Sunday, September 16, 2012
Mobile, Alabama

I woke up late, the room bright with midmorning sun. Jay lay beside me, arms flung over his head. I rolled away from him. On a morning like this, a normal girl would've been feeling . . . what, exactly? Triumphant? Possibly. Or, at the very least, she'd be replaying every lascivious detail in her head.

But I'd never been anywhere close to normal, and right now all I felt was anxiety-riddled, my nerves buzzing under my skin, mind racing with thoughts of escape.

I checked the pads of my fingers for any trace of gold. All clear, completely normal. Jay's torso and arms looked clear too. Maybe I really was getting better. I slipped from between the sheets, picked up my pants and blouse, and crept to the bathroom. I pulled open a couple of drawers looking for some toothpaste and saw it. The bottle of painkillers. Lortab.

My mouth watered and my jaw ached as I imagined the bitter crush of powder in my mouth. I shook my head. Pressed my lips together. Hard.

I picked up the bottle and could instantly feel the warmth the pills would provide; the buoyant feeling that would overtake me, if I took them. Wynn and Molly Robb and Dr. Duncan would shrink to little dots of no consequence. My dad's words would recede into darkness. I'd be free.

For a while.

I set the bottle beside the sink and eyed it as I pulled on my clothes. On my way out, I stopped. I could take it, stash it in my purse, just in case I found myself in a bind and in need of emergency help. I wouldn't go so far as to open it. Just knowing the pills were there would be enough to make me feel better. I twisted off the cap and poured the pills into my hand. Replaced the bottle in the drawer.

In the kitchen, I dropped the pills into a zippered compartment of my purse and pulled on my boots. A calendar hung above Jay's mom's neat desk, and I put my finger on the last square of the month. September 30, my birthday. Two weeks away, to the day.

Schizophrenia might be genetic, directly inherited even, but the nonsense Dad was spouting about it manifesting on the exact day I turn thirty? That was ludicrous. Medically impossible. On the other hand, if he was telling the truth about some part of it, if something really *did* happen to Trix, Collie, and Jinn on their thirtieth birthdays, how could I ignore that?

I felt it then—the dark, spidery thing that seemed to always hover around me, that fear or madness or whatever it was I'd held back for so long with booze and pills and now AA mantras. It was back, creeping through my brain again, just like when I was a girl.

If my dad and Dr. Duncan and Wynn were right, if I was genetically predisposed for schizophrenia, then I was going to get it no matter what happened. So I could either sit around, gulping Lortab to keep the visions of gold and red ravens at bay until Wynn came to lock me up in the nuthouse. Or I could fight. I could go back out there into the real world and face the darkness. Find out what had really happened to the women in my family.

I studied the Red Raven cigar box, sitting in the center of the island, and I felt a wave of dread wash over me. I couldn't do it anymore, this white-knuckling my way through life. I had to find out the truth. If I could find out what had happened to my mother—and to my grandmother and great-grandmother—maybe I could figure out a way to stop it from happening to me. Their stories were the only chance I had.

I knew nothing about our family history on my mother's side. I had an aunt and an uncle and a handful of cousins on my dad's side, but it was as if my mother had just sprung up out of the river. No one talked about her family. And now, I had two weeks to dig them up.

Fourteen days.

I needed money. A plan. I thought of my car back at the house. Maybe it would start for me today, if the stars were aligned, if I prayed just right. It would have to. I would sneak back, get it before Wynn and Molly Robb had time to formulate a plan. Head somewhere safe. Get access to a computer. I had work to do.

I reached into the cigar box and pulled out an empty vial. It was the oldest one, the one Dr. Duncan had said was my mother's. I read the label, like I'd read it a million times before. The pills were prescribed from an address in Tuscaloosa. Pritchard.

My heart revved the slightest bit.

Pritchard. The state mental institution. The original structure was over a hundred years old, deserted now, all the patients housed in another modern building on a different part of the property. Everyone in the state of Alabama knew the name Pritchard, synonymous with the worst of mental-health-care abuses. There had been a brief move in the eighties to restore the place, a limp effort that died as soon as the state legislature saw how much it was going to cost, and then, shortly thereafter, the state finally admitted it couldn't keep up the Victorian behemoth and shut it down. As far as I knew, the place was just waiting for a bulldozer.

My mother had never been a patient there. I didn't think.

But I did know someone who'd been connected to Pritchard. Someone I had tried my damnedest to forget.

I lifted the lid of the cigar box, dropped the old empty bottle inside. I tucked the box under my arm and walked outside, turning toward my house. The air was still and thick and humid, like right before the first winds of a hurricane.

I was bathed in sweat from the sticky, two-mile trek by the time I reached Dad's drive. A tow truck, my car piggybacked on its bed, rumbled past me, and I began waving my arms like an idiot. The driver glanced at me but kept driving. Choking in the cloud of white dust he left behind, I glared up at the house. Molly Robb, in another beige old-lady dress and matching headband, watched from the porch. I stormed up the drive and stopped in the turnaround, hands on my hips.

"You can't do that!" I shouted up at her. "That's my car."

"No, it's our car," Molly Robb said imperiously from her perch. "You sold us the title a couple of years ago, remember? And I don't know what you've done to it but Wynn's going to take care of it for you, so you should be thanking him."

"I want to talk to him," I called up.

"He's busy," she said. "Talk to me."

"You're gonna make a spectacular first lady, you know that? You're like an entire Secret Service squad squished into one bony little beige package." She rolled her eyes. "But you're going to have to get over yourself, because I"—I enunciated each word in a loud, clear voice— "*want to talk to my brother.*"

She shifted. "Wynn is busy. You probably don't care, but Folly is missing, and your father is frantic with worry."

"Folly?"

"His dog."

The Pomeranian or Chihuahua or whatever. Molly Robb must've named it Folly. What a bonehead.

"Tell Wynn he'd better grab his shotgun," I said. "I've seen plenty of gators up and down our banks."

"You're a monster," she said. "Your father loves that dog."

"My father can't stand little dogs. If he was in his right mind, he would punt that dog into the river like a football. As it is, you're probably too late. The gators have probably already had him for brunch."

Without a word, she pirouetted and disappeared inside the house. Slammed the door, rattling the row of windows. I walked to the end of the drive, trembling with fury. On the long walk back to Jay's, I kept repeating the same words in a loop in my head: *Don't let him be awake, don't let him be awake.*

I could hear the shower running from the back of the house. I guessed Jay had woken and, when he'd found me gone, decided to let me have my space. This, and the fact that his keys were still sitting on the kitchen counter, were better than an answered prayer. It was a divine gift.

I headed outside and slid into the fragrant leather seat of Jay's BMW. Pressed my fingers to my temples.

Don't think, just go. Go.

I said a quick *Veni, Creator Spiritus* in penance—even though I was pretty sure it wasn't that kind of prayer—and threw the car into drive. I headed upriver about three miles, to a sprawling, stone-and-glass contemporary house that lay almost adjacent to the mouth of the bay. The sight of the place always caused my gut to twist and my pulse to speed up, but if I was going to get information about my mother, this was where I had to start.

Miraculously, there were no cars in the drive, so I parked and knocked on the double front doors. A maid answered, thank God. (A maid, not a housekeeper, mind you, a woman who had to be over seventy and who still wore one of those gray-and-white uniforms from back in the day.)

I said I was an old friend of Hilda Oliver's—well, all the Olivers really—and wanted to say hello. She told me that although Mrs. Oliver was out, she did know that Mr. Oliver was playing golf at the club with Rowe, their son.

Nervous excitement bubbled up inside me as I nosed the car toward the country club. I sang snatches of the song on the radio, trying not to think about how easy it was to slip back into my old ways. What a terrible person I must be to feel this good about lying, stealing, and speeding eighty-five miles an hour toward another bad decision.

Chapter Eight

Sunday, September 16, 2012
Mobile, Alabama

Mobile Country Club's rolling golf course shimmered in the waves of heat. I parked at the edge of the lot, under the shade of an old oak, and punched at the baffling row of buttons above the windshield until one of them closed the sunroof. I slid the cigar box under the driver's seat. Along with my phone.

The kid in the pro shop told me the Oliver foursome was close to finishing. I was thinking about getting a golf cart when I spotted the snack cart parked outside on the path. They were always hiring the biggest dingbats to run the carts: morons with mermaid hair, big tits, and skirts so short you could see a faint swell of ass under the hem. In other words, women who could sell an ungodly amount of beer and turkey clubs. I sauntered out. No surprise, the key was in the ignition. I started it up and took off down the cart path.

After whizzing past a couple of players who attempted to flag me down, I parked at the fifteenth hole, just in time to see Rowe Oliver tee off. I sat in the cart, under the stand of pines, trying to collect myself. It had been a long time. Years. But now that I was this close to him, I felt like a thirteen-year-old girl again. A trembling, panicky, thirteen-year-old girl.

Rowe was dressed in an atrocious combination of purple, kelly green, and yellow with a wide white belt holding his pants under a substantial gut. I did some mental math. He was forty-two. His face was bright red, salt-and-pepper hair sprouting above the white visor, stained with sweat.

I could handle him, I told myself. I could. And not just because I knew his weaknesses but because he was nothing to me.

Nothing.

Rowe squinted down the fairway, leaned on his driver, and swore. The rest of his group headed to their cart. I slid out of my seat. Struck a pose—legs apart, one hand on my hip, chest out.

"Thirsty?" I called out. My voice sounded strong. Saucy. And, like a puppet on a string, Rowe Oliver turned my way. I smiled.

He returned his driver to his bag and waved at his father and the other two men. "Y'all want a beer?" They declined, and Rowe walked toward me. "You're new," he said, whipping off his sunglasses, wiping his face with his arm. His eyes roamed over my body. My stomach turned.

"You want something?" I asked.

He narrowed his eyes at me, and I thought I saw a flash of recognition. He hesitated. Stepped back. "No, thanks."

I grabbed his wrist. It was hairy and slick with sweat. "Well, I do."

"I don't do that anymore." He jerked his arm away from me, but he didn't move, and I saw him look me over again. I pulled off the sunglasses and smiled at him.

"Hey, Rowe."

He was shaking his head now. Smiling at his own stupidity. He had recognized me. "Althea. Long time no see."

"Ten years," I said.

"Yeah. Wow. Where you been?"

"Oh, here and there. Around. You know." He allowed himself another quick check at the opening of my blouse. *Asshole.*

"C'mon, Rowe." I moved closer to him. "I know you've got some oxy or Percocet or something lying around. I know it."

"Rowe!" His father called out. Rowe waved at him.

"Meet me when you're done," I said in a low voice. "Just give me whatever you have. I can pay, any way you want." I winked. He swallowed. "Second row from the back. Silver BMW." I held my breath and moved my finger to the front of the horrendous green pants, hooked it into his white belt. Gave one gentle tug. His mouth parted. I could smell his breath, cigars and onions.

"See you soon," I said.

I climbed into the cart and drove back down the path to the parking lot. I was being unquestioningly, horrendously stupid. But the last twenty-four hours had made something all too clear to me: I'd spent a lifetime letting other people push me around, letting them use me and hurt me. Today, finally, the time had come to push back.

Rowe had plenty of pills—they were in one of those vinyl money bags banks use—and we settled ourselves in the hot backseat of Jay's car. Right off, I told him to remove his pants. He didn't even question me, just pulled them right off and threw them onto the floor. He was wearing black boxer briefs. And from the looks of it, really looking forward to what was about to happen next.

I studied him. He was practically trembling with anticipation. "Now your shirt. Don't worry, the windows are tinted." He peeled it off too, then went for my neck again, his hands spidering up and down my arms.

"So you're married?" I pulled away. "Kids? What do you do?"

"God, Althea. Now? Really?"

"Sue me. I want to catch up a little first."

He sighed. "I run my dad's business."

"The timber company?"

"And I'm on the city commission." He cracked one eye open, assessing my reaction.

I smiled. "The underwear." He hesitated. "I have money, Rowe, if you'd prefer." He whipped off the briefs then, and I averted my gaze to the zippered money bag on the console.

"So what do you have?" I said.

"Xanax, Vicodin . . . Whatever you want."

"Impressive," I said. "I mean, for a guy who doesn't sell anymore."

In answer to that he reached up, wrapped one hand around the back of my head, and pushed me down as hard as he could in the direction of his crotch. I tucked my head and, just missing him, hit the seat, my nose bent uncomfortably sideways. I opened my mouth and drew in a breath. I could smell the sharp new-leather scent and his odor.

"Get busy," he said above me.

"Give me a minute, okay? Jeez."

"What, you want to say the blessing before you get started? Quit stalling."

I carefully reached under the driver's seat and slid out my phone. I opened the camera app just as I felt a sharp tug on my scalp. He was pulling my hair, trying to get me back up to him. I switched the phone to my left hand. Then sat up, pointed it at him.

"Say cheese."

I snapped a couple of pictures.

"What the hell—?" he yelped.

I jabbed at the button until he slapped the phone of out my hands, and it tumbled between the console and the driver's seat. I bent back, reaching for it, but he pushed me aside and jammed his hand into the crevice. His face contorted with the effort.

"It's too late," I said mildly.

"What did you do?"

"Sent a few to the cloud. And my email."

"The fuck you did. You barely even got a shot."

"Why don't you pull it out and see?"

"I would if I could get my goddamn hand in there." But after a few more fruitless seconds, he sat back and glared at me. I smiled.

"Okay, well," he said. "This has been great. An absolute riot. What do you want?"

I reached down under the driver's seat, pulled out the cigar box, and opened it. I held out the oldest vial, no more than an inch from his nose. He just sat there, quivering, red-faced, hands over his cock.

"A long time ago, you sold these pills to my mother," I said. "Start talking. Now. I want to hear everything."

Chapter Nine

October 1937
Sybil Valley, Alabama

One late-October afternoon, Jinn's daddy sent for her.

He did this every so often when Vonnie—the girl who looked after him and Jinn's mama—got held up with her own father and brothers or couldn't make it down the mountain in the winter ice. He'd let things pile up around the house until he ran out of clean dishes or discovered the coffee grounds in the pot furred with mold. Then he'd call Jinn to come tackle the mess.

"We'll go to Grandpap's after I put the collards and sausages in the oven," Jinn told Collie. "How about we make a cobbler over there and bring home half?"

Collie nodded. "Daddy'll like that."

The mist hadn't even burned off the grass when she and Collie tramped into the apple orchard that bordered the Alfords'. Jinn watched the little girl dart into hazy puffs of moisture like they were magical clouds. Like she expected everything would feel soft and fuzzy once she was inside them. It made Jinn laugh. Collie had such an imagination.

Jinn pushed open the front door of her parents' frame house and crinkled her nose at the smell. There was a trail of chicken shit leading through the hall, a few pellets squashed on the linoleum floor. She could see the deep grooves from her daddy's work boots imprinted in the mushy blobs. Farther inside the house, Jinn could hear Binnie and the other two hens clucking and scratching their claws on the wooden floor. Somebody'd probably left the back door open. Maybe Mama had got up this morning.

Her daddy's .22 rifle hung in its spot over the fireplace. The brass stock plate, engraved with oak leaves and acorns, glinted in the morning sun. Jinn let out a relieved breath. Her mama had been known to take the gun down on bad days, when her nerves got the best of her. She'd shoulder it, say she'd had enough of Vernon's nonsense, and, by golly, she was going to shoot him if he didn't straighten up. These episodes never amounted to much—Vernon kept the gun unloaded and hid the bullets—and it hadn't happened in a while. Anyway, by now, her mama had to be too sick to heft a gun.

Jinn shooed the chickens out of the den and into the kitchen, which was also liberally sprinkled with the sharp-smelling pellets. She clapped her hands, and Binnie and the other two hens squawked indignantly, racing in crazed circles all the way out the back door. They darted across the dirt-packed yard and to the coop, where she shut the gate behind them.

Back inside, the house was quiet as a graveyard. The rays of the morning sun slanted in, splashing bright blocks on the rag rug. Jinn had forgotten how the house flashed with light in the mornings. She remembered being little, standing in one shimmering square that lit up, on and off, like an electric lamp.

She walked to the bottom of the rickety staircase and looked up. She thought about her sleeping mother, what would happen if she tiptoed upstairs and peeked in the bedroom. She could do it, just creep to her mother's bed and smooth back her fuzzy gray hair. Press her lips against the dry, crinkly skin. She only thought about those things, though. Howell had told her in no uncertain terms that her father said she wasn't to bother her mama. "Your pap says she don't feel well, and she needs her rest." He'd made Jinn promise she wouldn't go upstairs.

Her mother had been sick for a long time now. Tumor in the gut, they said, and not much to be done about it. That, on top of being touched—well, any surprise might set her off. Howell was right; going upstairs wasn't a good idea. But Jinn couldn't help thinking about it. She hadn't seen her mother in months.

The cuckoo clock on the mantel tick-tocked in the still morning air, and she surveyed the room. The chickens had left a mess, sure enough. She'd better get to work; she had to be back by one o'clock to give Howell his lunch. She handed Collie a little broom and dustpan, sent her off to the kitchen, and busied herself with her own broom.

Around eleven, when the den and kitchen sparkled, she started on the roast, another batch of collards, and the biscuits. As she kneaded the dough, the thought crossed her mind that her father might not have given her mother anything to eat. Not that he'd do it on purpose. He had a lot to keep up with, and he was getting on in years. He might've even been the one who'd left the kitchen door open.

There was a bad stretch last year, when her daddy had been laid up with emphysema and a stove-up back. He'd let things slip, long enough that Mama had gone downhill quick. He'd felt bad when Jinn and Howell had found her up on their bedroom floor, sobbing from the burning in her stomach. Vernon had even cried a bit himself, something Jinn had never witnessed. He said he hadn't meant to forget her medicine.

For a while after that, the ladies at church would stop by with casseroles and pies for them. But that was a year ago, and Jinn was pretty sure the church ladies had other people to think about. She rolled out the dough and thought about her mama. Even if she'd had breakfast, she still might like a piece of toast or a sliver of one of the plums Jinn had brought.

Even though Jinn had said she wouldn't go upstairs.

Her father's shirts and underwear and socks might need to be washed, though. And if they did, she should get to that right away, while the sun was high, before the afternoon got too cloudy and cool to dry the clothes. Of course, she'd have to go up to the bedroom to gather the pile of dirty laundry. Daddy always threw his clothes over the back of a cane chair by the window after he wore them.

She set two slices of bread, each with a pat of butter, on the stove to warm and sliced the plum. She wiped out the sink, cut the biscuits with her mother's tin cup, and lined the dough discs on her mother's pan. She slid the pan into the oven, then put the toast and plums on two plates.

She called Collie in from the backyard and set her up at the table. She told her to eat quietly, that they'd do the wash next.

"Mama's going upstairs to tidy up," she said, kissing the top of her daughter's curly head. "Don't you come up, you hear?"

Collie picked up a wedge of plum and inspected it.

"Collie?"

"Yes, ma'am."

Jinn carried the plate up the stairs so quietly she wouldn't even startle the mice that liked to nose the cracks along the hallway baseboards. At the top of the steps, the hall stretched out before her, tranquil in the late-morning sun. A beam of sunlight streamed from the high transom at the end of the corridor. Dust motes floated and collided and danced around each other in it, and a spider's thread bisected it. A whiff of something musty hit her nose. The bathroom up here probably needed a good scouring. And the bedroom. The sheets were probably soft and yellow with stains by now.

She crept toward the closed door at the end of the hall, her heart thrumming in her chest. One step, two, three, until at last her hand was on the knob. She turned it and hesitated there, straining to hear any sound that meant Collie had followed her or that her father had returned early from the mill. After a good, long stretch of silence, she pushed open the door.

The smell hit her first. Piss and shit and something else vaguely rotten. Jinn clapped her hand over her nose and told herself not to gag. The room was dark, filled with bluish shadows from the flowered wallpaper and patchwork quilt. The blinds were drawn, the curtains pulled across them. Otherwise, it was perfectly neat. No piles of soiled work clothes on the chair back, no dusty boots or grease-stained gloves resting on the bureau.

Her mother lay under the quilt, her hair spread like a fan around her. She was still—but for the barest rise and fall of skin and bones under the quilt. Her face was as blue as the room, and it took Jinn a minute to realize it was just the light. Her mother wasn't dead. Not yet. Jinn moved closer, close enough to see her mother's taut skin hollowed under cheekbones, eye sockets, and nose. The woman's eyes stared at the ceiling, unblinking; her mouth gaped open. A line of spittle had left a shining trail from the cracked corner of her lips all the way down to the sheet.

A low rattling rose up from the bed, and, at the same time, a cry erupted from Jinn's mouth. At the sound, her mama turned her head toward her daughter, and her mouth moved just the slightest bit, a sunken hole with no teeth. She greeted her daughter with a long, creaking moan.

Chapter Ten

Rowe squinted at the pill bottle for so long, I had to wave the empty vial at him. He blinked at me.

"Let's just start with a simple yes or no," I said. "Did this bottle come from you?"

He sighed. "I'd tell you if I could read the label. I need my glasses."

"It's Haldol, Rowe. And the fill date is 1987. Did you sell this to my mother?"

"You've got to be kidding me. How the hell should I remember something from 1987?"

"Your mother worked at Pritchard back then."

"Not exactly," he said. "My mother had connections at Pritchard. She was on the board."

"And that's how you got started in your career as Mobile's premier dope dealer, right? She brought home extras."

"Can I have my clothes back?"

"Not until I get answers."

"It was a long time ago, Althea, okay? Why do you even care?"

I leaned in. "Because when my mother died, when I was five years old, this bottle was almost entirely full. It took me about eight years to finish it off. I went slow—a pill here, a pill there. My special, magical SweeTarts."

He made a face.

"Pathetic, I know. What can I say? By the time I was thirteen, I'd run out. I didn't know where to go or who to talk to. I was afraid to ask my father. You know my father, the state's attorney? The only person I knew who had anything to do with Pritchard, where this stuff came from, was your mother. So I rode my bike to your house and knocked on the front door. Only she didn't answer the door, you did. Remember?"

He remembered. I could tell by the way his face flushed to purple, the way his shoulders slumped. The way, under his big gut, he'd shriveled up to nothing.

"Look, I was an idiot back then," he mumbled. "I'm sorry."

"What are you sorry for?"

"You know."

"What are you sorry for, Rowe?"

"For . . . that time . . . in my basement."

"What about all those other times?" I said, my voice trembling. "What about all those other goddamn times?"

Quaking in the freezing air-conditioning, watching my clothes form a pile on the orange shag rug . . . I'm dying of shame . . .

He looked miserable. "I'm sorry. I'm really sorry."

"Did you sell these pills to my mother?"

"Yes. I sold your mom Haldol. What's your point?"

"Why did she want it? What was wrong with her?"

"I don't know," he said. "I don't even know how she found out I could get it for her. I was only giving some stuff to my friends back then. I was just trying to help her out."

"There's more. There has to be."

"I have a family, Althea," he said, his eyes pleading, beads of sweat rolling down the side of his face. "A wife and three children. The youngest is a baby. Do you hear me—a fucking three-year-old! I have a company with over six hundred employees depending every day on me. To see that they can feed their families. Sure, I take a little something now and then to take the edge off. But that's it. I don't sell the shit. Not anymore."

"That's not what was happening here five minutes ago. And because I'm sure you don't want anything to upset your wife and three children, you're going to tell me everything, *everything*, you know about my mother."

In one instant, I saw Rowe's eyes go flat and dark. His body rose up and out of the backseat and came at me with the force of a tsunami. I scrambled backward like a crab, onto the console between the front seats. But quicker than lightning, he swung a fist and cracked me right above my eye. I fell back, the dashboard connecting with my head.

I saw him then, looming above me, massive and red with rage, reaching for me with both hands. I felt myself lifted up and over the seat and then flipped and slammed facedown on the backseat. He yanked at the waistband of my pants as I thrashed and kicked.

"You're gonna take a picture of me?" he said, one hand pressing down between my shoulder blades, pinning me to the seat. "You little brat. I will fucking kill you."

My head throbbed, and I saw pulsing purple-edged lights. Cawing sounds filled the car, and I realized it was me, my mouth against the leather, trying to scream. I stretched out my hand, groping for the key fob on the console. My fingers closed around it, fingers pressing in desperation, and in a split second, the air was filled with the earsplitting, shrieking sound of the car alarm.

I felt him release me, and I scrambled up and away, pressing my back against the opposite door.

"Jesus!" he yelled. "Shut it off!"

I didn't move, the fob clutched in my fist.

"Althea!"

I looked down at the fob. I couldn't focus.

He was pulling on his pants, scrambling for his shirt. "Hit the red button, you idiot." He held out his hand. "Just give it to me."

"Fuck you," I yelled back. I gripped the fob to my chest and looked out the window. A couple of golfers had paused near the pro shop and were staring in the direction of the car. I felt a hand swipe at me, ripping the fob out of my grip. I turned around, clawed for it, but it was too late. Rowe was holding it up triumphantly, and suddenly there was silence.

He threw the fob at me, narrowly missing my head.

"I don't want to hurt you," he said in a level voice. "But I need you to give me that phone."

"Tell me what you know about my mother. Tell me, and I'll give you the phone."

"And you delete all the pictures."

If we'd been a pair of hyenas, we'd be circling and snapping at each other. At this point, though, between the two of us, I speculated that Rowe was the one with far more to lose. After a few seconds, I saw his eyes flicker, and I realized, with a twinge of incredulity, that I was right. I'd done it. I'd beaten him.

"I know you won't believe me," he said. "But I only wanted to help her."

He was right. I didn't believe him, but I told him to get on with it anyway. Even if his story was crap, I had to hear it. It was all I had.

"She was in a bad way the last night I saw her. She was messed up, hallucinating, and talking like a crazy person. She asked me to take her a couple of places."

"And you did it?"

"Yeah. I took her to a house up in Birmingham."

"What house?" I asked.

Rowe shrugged. He'd never seen it before, had no idea who lived there. Trix had told him to stay in the car and disappeared inside. That's when he'd left.

"You think you'd recognize the house if you saw it again?" I asked.

He shook his head, looked out the window. "Maybe."

I leaned forward, threaded a couple of fingers into the crevice between the seat and console and extricated the phone. I laid it on the seat between us. "Go to Birmingham with me," I said. "Show me the house. And tell me everything, I mean everything, you remember."

"Fine."

"Really?"

He was already thumbing furiously at the phone. "You know, I knew the first time I ever laid eyes on you, I was going to regret messing with you."

I inhaled deeply and let it out, as steadily as I could. "You're going to Birmingham with me, okay, Rowe? You're going to show me the house and then go through every detail of what happened to my mother, from the beginning to the end. Right?"

He didn't lift his head, engrossed in deleting the incriminating photos.

"You know it's too late. They're already in the cloud. Believe me."

"I don't know that I do. Maybe I just deleted them all."

"Maybe you did, Rowe. And maybe you didn't. I wouldn't think you would want to risk that kind of thing."

He stopped. Sighed. Tossed the phone down. "God. Okay, whatever."

I climbed into the front seat and put the key in the ignition. The car didn't make a sound. Not even a click. It was like a horrible replay of the incident with my own car earlier that morning.

I turned the key again. Nothing.

"Well, it's been real," Rowe said behind me. "Give me a call when you get your car fixed. We'll talk." He reached for the door, but it was locked. He jabbed at the button but couldn't unlock it. "Come on, Althea, I said I'd help. Now cut it out."

I ignored him and turned the key again but there was no response.

"Althea . . ."

I twisted the key and twisted again, but the mechanism wouldn't catch. Buzzing with frustration, I ripped the key out and sent it sailing into the passenger's-side window. Simultaneously, there was a *chunk*, and a *click*, and, all on its own, the engine roared to life. My head jerked up in shock.

Jay, standing at the nose of the car, his eyes narrowed ominously, held up a duplicate key fob.

"Good God, who is that?" Rowe said behind me.

I held my breath as Jay rounded the car, opened the door, and slid into the seat beside me. He shut the door and met my eyes. He raised his eyebrows.

"Hello," he said.

"Hi," I managed.

He waited. I did too.

"Just FYI," he said finally. "This is a very nice car. It has a remote starter, a kill switch, and a tracking system. I knew where you were the minute you left my house."

"Ah." I swallowed.

He nodded gravely, like I'd delivered a sincere apology and he'd graciously decided to accept it. He glanced over his shoulder. "Who's this?"

"I was just going," Rowe said, his hand on the door.

"Rowe Oliver," I said.

"Old friend," Rowe said.

I snorted. "Human excrement."

"So. You guys just hanging out in my car, in the broiling-hot parking lot? Just shooting the breeze?"

I felt my face flush. "He has information about my mother. He was going to show me a house she visited in Birmingham, that last night."

"Okay. Birmingham. Sounds great."

I met Jay's eyes. He was studying my face, and I knew I was going to have to explain everything to him soon.

"Why don't you let me drive?" he suggested.

Or I could always make up more lies.

Rowe led us right to the house, a mossy Tudor crouched on the top of Red Mountain. We pulled the car to the bluff side and stared. Between the crisscrossed timbers, the mildewed plaster was cracked, bits of it crumbled away. The windows were dark and there was no name on the rusted iron mailbox. One lone oak tree, half of it sawn off from disease or a lightning strike, curved its branches protectively over the house. The yard was mostly dirt with a few clumps of crabgrass.

"You recognize it?" Jay asked me.

I shook my head. "Who lived here?" I asked Rowe.

"I don't know. She didn't say."

"Spare me. You know."

"Maybe I did, but I don't remember now," Rowe said. "I just dropped her off and drove back home."

"I have pictures, Rowe. Pictures I will show your wife," I snapped.

From the backseat, he started to jabber. "Look, Althea, I wish I could tell you more, but I don't know anything. I drove your mom here, and then I left. That's it. That's all I know."

Somewhere in the middle of his speech, a tidal wave of exhaustion and despair hit me, and I felt tears spill out and down my cheeks.

"Do you believe him?" Jay asked me in a low voice.

I met his eyes and sniffed away the tears. Shook my head.

"Do you think he knows more?"

I nodded.

"Do you want me to help you?"

I hesitated. Nodded again.

"Say it."

"What?"

"Say you want me to help you."

I studied my knotted fingers. "Jay, will you help me?"

He studied me for a minute, I guess sizing up whether he thought I was going to pull my next crazy stunt. Then he looked in the rearview mirror. "You better call your wife, Mr. Oliver. Tell her you're going to be late for dinner."

Chapter Eleven

Sunday, September 16, 2012
Birmingham, Alabama

I told Jay I wanted to clean up and eat before paying a visit to whoever lived in the house overlooking the bluff. I wouldn't be doing myself any favors by showing up looking like so much hot garbage.

Jay found a Target a couple of miles down the highway, and I went inside to pick up supplies—a couple of T-shirts, jeans, pajamas, and underwear. A handful of protein bars and water bottles. We found a hotel, a shabby collection of beige buildings with "Suites" in the name and a deserted parking lot. Jay gave me the credit card to check us in, and when I got back to the car, we marched Rowe into the room. Rowe called his wife and fed her a story about going to Birmingham on last-minute business, then Jay shut him in the tiny living room and locked the door between us.

"He can't leave, and he can't get at you," Jay said.

I nodded, but I didn't really believe him. I didn't think I'd ever feel safe around Rowe Oliver.

While Jay ran a bath, mounded high with hotel-provided bubbles, I told him everything, beginning with the snack cart and ending with the cell-phone pictures. He told me he'd gone online and found the house on the bluff listed to Walter and Val Wooten. The name Wooten seemed vaguely familiar to me—maybe I'd heard somebody mention it at some point in the past. Once I was in the tub, he examined my forehead like it was the most interesting thing he'd ever seen in his life, maybe to avoid looking at the rest of me. I appreciated the effort, but at that point I honestly didn't feel a shred of modesty.

"It's not as bad as I thought," he said. "But I still wouldn't mind breaking his neck. Can we just send that loser home and call it a day?"

"No," I said. "He has to go with us. He knows more than he's telling."

"Althea, it's past eight. You're exhausted. We shouldn't go back to the house until morning. Let's let him go."

I rested my head against the back of the tub. "No. I need him."

"He's trouble."

"I know." I looked at him. "But so am I. And speaking of that, I really am sorry for stealing your car."

"It's okay. But I actually expected more out of you, after that big speech you gave me about your sordid criminal past."

"Yeah, well, I'm not a car thief. I've always been more of a steal-your-wallet kind of gal."

Or your mother's pills.

He laughed. "Really? No."

I gave him a look.

"You're serious?"

"Oh, yeah."

He leaned forward. "How was I not aware of this?"

"Because I was good at hiding things from you. I was good at hiding things from everybody."

He was quiet for a moment.

"Don't feel bad. Lying is my superpower."

I'm warning you, I thought. *This is me warning you.*

He lifted an eyebrow. "You feel like getting it off your chest now?"

I laughed. "Not really."

"I make a great confessor."

"You go first," I said.

He raised his eyebrows.

"Confess. Tell me about your wife."

He scratched the back of his head. "Okay, well. She's okay. A really good person, actually. Just not for me. She just wanted . . . a lot. A bigger place. A second place. A third place."

"And you didn't?"

"It wasn't going to happen. I wasn't on that level with my career. Ending it was for the best."

"Sorry."

"It's okay. I'm starting to feel not too terrible about it. It's in the past."

I chopped a bubble mound, leveling it. "The past matters, though, doesn't it?"

"For you, it does. Yes." He had this strange expression on his face—this look full of unspoken meaning. "And for me too, I guess. You and I were the past, weren't we?"

"Yeah."

"Okay, your turn. Tell Father Jay. Whose wallet did you steal?" He was grinning now.

I thought for a minute, then ticked off my fingers. "Leonard Albrecht's, Jeff Tole's, Scott Matthews's . . ."

"Total dick," he said. "That guy deserved it."

"Clark Duncan's, Farrell Westridge's. Coach Anderson's, three times."

"Nice."

"He always left it in his desk drawer during lunch." I sighed. "I did purses too. Many, many purses."

"And you used all that money to buy . . ."

"Pills."

He examined his laced fingers.

"Forgive me, Father, for I have sinned," I said. "A lot."

"You know, you should've asked for my help back at the country club. I could've probably been of some assistance."

"Rowe's my problem, not yours." I turned my head away. The porcelain felt cool against my face.

"Still."

"He's bad news. And he's a fighter. I didn't want to get you mixed up in all that."

"You do not know me. I will fuck a brother up."

I smiled. "Right."

He was smiling now too. There was an awful lot of smiling between us, way too much of it. It made me feel drunk. Or high. I wondered when I would start blabbing—saying things that were uncomfortably real. That I would deeply regret later.

I shifted in the tub. "Tell me the truth. Why are you here?"

He sat back on his heels, studied the tile floor or his knees or something else I couldn't see. When he spoke, his voice was low.

"Because you're somebody who was important to me."

I waited.

"And I've always been a little ashamed about how I kind of faded out of the picture when you hit your rough patch."

"My rough patch," I said. "You make it sound so charming."

"I want to help, Althea."

All of a sudden, I felt exposed, sitting there in the tub. He must've felt it too, because he turned sideways, so that we were both facing the door and the neatly arranged towel rack. He draped his forearms over his knees. Tapped his thumbs together.

"You want to talk about him?" He jutted his chin at the door separating us from Rowe.

"He didn't do anything," I said. "I took care of it."

"No, I mean, when you were younger." I felt myself flush, the heat rising up through my body. "He hurt you, didn't he? Another thing you never told me."

I pictured the Lortab. Tasted it melting on my tongue. I untwisted the bath plug and watched the soapy water swirl down.

Quaking in the freezing air-conditioning, watching my clothes form a pile on the orange shag rug—first the pink crop top, then my acid-washed denim shorts, then my white Victoria's Secret bra, the only one I have. The embarrassing, little-girl cotton underwear goes down too, and it's done. I'm naked—my back hunched, arms wrapped around myself, dying of shame. Here in this dark basement room in front of a grown man, I stand trembling in the cold and humiliation and terror. I can't help thinking how pathetic my little half-developed breasts must look, how thin and pale I am.

Rowe sits a couple of feet away on a futon, hands laced behind his head, surveying me. Then he bursts out into laughter. I want to cry, but I don't. I just wonder what could possibly be so funny about a naked girl.

"It was a long time ago," I said finally.

"I'm here, Althea. I'd like to be a friend to you, if you'll let me."

I'd never told anyone the whole story. In spite of the dozens of doctors and therapists, counselors and facilitators who'd tried to get it out of me, I'd kept that information to myself. I'd shared versions of it, of course—meandering, pathetic half-truths that got me more meds, papers signed, files closed, whatever I needed at the time. But my story—the real story—was mine alone, like the cigar box, a precious possession belonging only to my mother and me.

The bathtub was empty, and I shivered. Jay jumped up and pulled a towel from the bar, handed it to me. I wrapped it around me and stood, face to face with him. I reached one arm around his neck and kissed him.

He pulled back, gently removed my arm. "Althea, don't. You've got to talk to me."

Suddenly, the bathroom wall shook. It was Rowe, pounding on the door. "Hey!" he yelled. "Hey!"

I stumbled back, my heart thumping.

"I know you guys can hear me! Listen. You guys are going to have to let me go soon or my wife's going to completely lose her mind. I'm just warning you, she will call the police in a heartbeat. She loves 9-1-1. The dispatchers all know her by name. Listen, she calls 9-1-1 when she chips her manicure. She calls 9-1-1 when we run out of toilet paper. You guys hearing me?"

Jay leapt up and ran out. I could hear the muffled yelling, back and forth from between the rooms.

I slumped down on the toilet seat. The pills were in my purse in the room, practically calling to me. I closed my eyes. Two or three, and I'd feel weightless. Four, five, or six, and I'd be gone for hours. I'd just have to be careful, but I knew how to avoid overdosing. It was one of my many worthless talents.

Or I could go back in the room and face Jay. Tell him what Rowe had done to me all those years ago. And watch for him to get that blank look in his eye that told me he saw me for the woman I really was. That he thought I was dirty and disgusting, and he'd prefer to start his life over with somebody more suitable. A woman less damaged.

After Jay had gotten Rowe calmed down, I dressed in the unlikely flowered Target pajamas and slipped into our room. Jay was sitting on one of the chairs by the window, murmuring into his phone. I sat on the far bed, pulled a pillow onto my lap, and wrapped my arms around it. He hung up, laid the phone on the dresser.

"Friend of mine. A lawyer. I just left my name and number. You don't have to talk to him if you don't want to."

I nodded.

"Are you okay?"

"I wanted to tell you what Rowe did. If you still want to hear."

His expression didn't change. "I do."

I was quiet a moment. I had the crazy thought that the words of the story, when I let them out, would cut me. But that was nonsense, wasn't it? Speaking words didn't hurt; it was keeping them in that did that. I just hoped I could get through the story without an imaginary, gold-dust-covered red raven dive-bombing my head.

"He didn't touch me at first," I began. "He just looked. Which was bad enough. Sometimes I have to remind myself that." I dropped my gaze to the ugly patterned carpet, suddenly aware of the way my heart seemed to be trembling inside my chest. Trembling instead of beating. I inhaled. "He just looked until I turned sixteen."

Chapter Twelve

October 1937
Sybil Valley, Alabama

This time Jinn's mama was discovered doing so poorly, none of the church ladies brought casseroles to the Alford house. And Jinn's daddy didn't shed a tear over what he'd let happen to his wife.

Howell went over to Vernon's house that night and made sure there was plenty of broth on the stove and biscuits and bacon in the larder. When he returned home it was late, a long time after Walter and Collie had been tucked in. He sat Jinn down and said that they had to forgive her father. It wasn't Vernon's fault. Jinn's daddy was getting old and forgetful, and these things were bound to happen. They just needed to pitch in a bit more.

Jinn wanted to bring her mama to their house but Howell said no, it was a man's job to keep track of his own wife. And he said Vernon might take it personal if his daughter started checking up on him. He said he'd drop by and check on her mama from time to time on his way home from work, to make sure everything was in order. He told Jinn her mama would be fine and dandy. Fine and dandy as a dying woman could be, and the only things Jinn needed to worry about were the children.

There was plenty to worry about on that count. Walter hadn't gotten up to anything since the calf, not that she knew of, but Jinn felt uneasy all the same. Collie was beginning to worry her as well. Jinn had found Walter's best marble and an unopened packet of licorice snaps in the cigar box the girl kept under her bed. She made Collie take the candy back to the store and apologize to Mr. Darnell, the shop owner. The marble, Jinn slipped into the top drawer of Walter's dresser the next morning while he was at school.

All through the weeks of October, Jinn watched the leaves on the trees around her cabin turn from green to golden red to brown. They fluttered to the ground, and the wind eddied them down the mountain. Soon Sybil Valley would be swept bare. Just like her soul.

The green things—her mother, her children, the wine—she felt were turning the same gold as the maple and oaks. She thought of Walter and Collie, grown and married. Herself, sitting up in her bed— touched, maybe, or sick like her mother, with only Howell to look after her.

Even thinking about Tom made her feel like one of those pines in the meadow, grown over by honeysuckle vines. Choked by her own life.

Last time she saw them, the ladies from Chattanooga had driven up in their silver car and stood on Jinn's porch, shown her a contract their lawyer had drawn up to start a business. Fifty-fifty, they promised. They'd share all the profits. And what profits. People in Chattanooga and Knoxville sure did like honeysuckle wine. "Juice," they corrected her. "We're calling it Jinn's Juice." The ladies had gone on and on about how smart she was, called her an entrepreneur. She didn't know why she hadn't been brave enough to tell Howell about them in the first place, but now it was too late. She was conducting business behind her husband's back and hiding money.

It was her pride, she told herself. It was simple as that. She didn't want Howell taking her business away. It couldn't be the roll of bills, expanding like a sapling tree in the jug in the cellar. She couldn't spend that money anyway, not without Howell knowing, so it was useless to her, wasn't it? Who had any use for money they couldn't spend?

One Sunday at the end of his sermon, when the poplars were at the height of their gold, Brother Daley told his congregation that lately he'd felt a chill among the flock. A lull in their fervor for the Lord. He'd prayed and the Holy Spirit had told him that what they needed was revival. "Seek and ye shall find," he said, and so he had. By the end of the month, the world-renowned Charles Jarrod would be pitching his tent out back of the church and bringing the people of Sybil Valley the Word of the Lord.

Jinn reckoned it was a good time for Charles Jarrod to come. Good for Howell and her father. Good for Walter and her too. They could all use a dose of the Word to clean their consciences and start brand new.

All the same, she was careful to keep her growing nest egg hidden away in the cellar. *It's green,* she reminded herself as she eyed the fluttering gold canopy of leaves. *And it will stay that way forever.*

⁓⁕⁓

In spite of Howell saying she should keep her mind on the kids, Jinn continued to worry about her mama.

One morning, just to set her mind at ease, she dropped Collie off at Aggie's and cut through the holler to the Alford house. Tucked up under her sweater were a bottle of her honeysuckle wine and another plum from the tree out back. In her parents' kitchen, she sliced the plum and poured the wine into a glass.

Upstairs, sitting beside the bed, Jinn watched her mama sip the wine. She seemed remarkably revived, the way she closed her eyes and smacked her lips. "Honeysuckle," she said, after a moment or two. "With a dash a Howell's apple brandy."

"How'd you know?"

Mama leaned back against the headboard, eyes still shut. "I may be crazy as a betsy bug, but I know my moonshine."

"I'm selling it." Jinn couldn't believe how weak she was, telling her secret right out like that, just to get her mama's approval. Sometimes she wondered if she was a grown woman at all, or still just a ninny of a girl.

"Are you now?"

"Some ladies put it in stores for me over in Chattanooga. They call it Jinn's Juice."

"Lady bootleggers. Law. What's next?" Mama drained the rest of the bottle and blotted her lips with the sleeve of her stained nightgown. "You watch it, Jinn. Watch yourself." She thunked down the glass. Sighed with pleasure. The alcohol was probably taking hold already, Jinn thought, she couldn't weigh more than eighty pounds.

"How much money you make off them bottles?" Mama asked.

Jinn shrugged. She shouldn't say any more. Her mama wasn't right in the head. She could slip and say something to her daddy. Get them all in big trouble.

Mama persisted. "I hope you've hidden it good."

"Yes, ma'am, I have."

"Attic? Smokehouse?"

Lord, sometimes her mama sounded about the farthest thing from touched you could be. Sometimes she sounded downright conniving.

"Cellar," Jinn said and looked down. She'd twisted her apron into a coiled snake slithering across her lap. She smoothed it out, flattened it over her knees. The scent of the honeysuckle nectar on her hands wafted into the air. For a moment, she imagined the nectar had special powers. That it was a magical potion from a fairy tale, dripping from her fingers. If she touched her mother with it, she'd transform. Become a normal mama who fussed over her grandkids at church and baked batches of oatmeal cookies. If she touched Howell, he'd turn to stone, a statue that could only watch her as she moved about their house. If she touched Tom . . . really touched him . . .

"You better watch it, girl," Mama said. "He'll put you in Pritchard, if you don't watch it." She had scrunched down farther under the quilt and turned her face toward a block of sun shining down from the window.

"Howell?"

"And your daddy. I hear 'em talking all the time. Talking about Pritchard. Talk, talk, talk. All the menfolk do up here on this mountain is talk about how they gonna put their women in Pritchard if we don't straighten up. You'd think we was a bunch of kids."

Jinn ignored the ice fingering its way up her spine. She forced a laugh. "Sometimes I think I wouldn't mind getting sent off. At least I'd be getting away from this place."

Mama made a face. "You'd think that, until they get you inside that place. Then you know better." She cackled. "I went to Pritchard, you know. Once't. My daddy sent me there."

Jinn had never heard this story for real. Only bits and pieces from others.

"What did he send you there for?"

"Walked around in my sleep. Mama found me in the hog pen some mornings. Daddy said I had a nervous mind, so he sent me on down there for rest. But it weren't for long. Me and your daddy was courting around then. So I wrote him and told him what all they did at that place. I want you to know, he rode down and carried me right home. Never mentioned Pritchard again."

"Was it awful?" Jinn asked.

Mama's hand flapped at her, spotted and roped with veins. "Oh, now. It's been a long time ago."

"What did they do there?"

She exhaled, long and loud. "I don't know."

"Mama."

She rolled over and rested her hand on Jinn's. The way the sun hit her mama's skin, flattening out the wrinkles and smoothing the planes, Jinn could see the beauty she had been. She had once looked a lot like Jinn—dark curls and delicate features. The eyes too, that swept upward under arched brows.

"You hide that money in the smokehouse, Jinn," Mama said. "I recollect that Howell don't much like to go in there, so it'll be safe. Hide it in the smokehouse, you hear?"

Jinn squeezed her mother's hand and collected the plate. Her mother was remembering things wrong again, getting people mixed up. Howell and Jinn had never had their own smokehouse.

She descended the steps and, out of habit, glanced at the spot over the fireplace. The two square-shank nails stuck out from between the stones, empty. The rifle that usually rested atop them was gone. Jinn froze. Where had it gone? Had Mama taken it?

She should probably march back upstairs right now, make her mother tell her where she'd hidden it, and return it to its spot before her father got home. If Jinn was a good daughter, if she was smart, she'd do that.

On the other hand, she didn't have tell anyone about the missing rifle. She could keep her own counsel and let her mama settle things for herself. Her parents' affairs were going to come to that anyway, she thought, sooner or later, no matter what she did.

Heart thumping steadily, mouth dry as a creek bed in summer, Jinn fetched her wine bottle from the kitchen and let herself out the front door. She stood for a minute, basking in the electric flash of shadow and sun, then started off toward Aggie's.

Chapter Thirteen

Monday, September 17, 2012
Birmingham, Alabama

The next morning, we returned to the house perched on the edge of the bluff. Jay and Rowe were quiet the whole way there. I recited my mother's prayer over and over in my head, psyching myself up for whatever lay ahead.

A doughy young black woman in teddy-bear scrubs, her hair scraped up and knotted in a scrunchie on top of her head, swung open the Wootens' front door. A fusty smell billowed out from behind her and cobwebs hung from the tarnished brass chandelier.

"Can I help you?" Her eyes darted between me, Jay, and Rowe. She seemed nervous, blinking in the bright morning sun. She couldn't have been more than nineteen or twenty.

"We've come to see Walter and Valerie Wooten," I said. "Are they in?"

"Walter isn't," she said. "He passed years ago."

"What about Valerie?"

"She's in, but she's sick."

"What's wrong with her?" I knew I sounded rude, but I really wasn't in the mood to tiptoe.

"She's about eighty-nine, is what's wrong with her. And she has cancer. She won't recognize you even if you go in there. Who are you again?"

"Her niece," I said. "She's my aunt."

She rested a hand against the doorframe, and her gaze traveled over my clothes, all the way down to my shoes. "I didn't know she had a niece. Or, at least, Terri didn't say. You all from Birmingham?"

"Mobile."

"Oh, Mobile. I have a cousin down there."

I nodded. "Would you mind if we popped in for a quick visit?"

The girl looked dubious.

"You could give Terri a buzz, to okay it with her." I held up my phone. "Or I could."

"No, no." Her eyes flashed with something that looked like worry, and I filed it away for later. You never knew what could come in handy. "You don't have to bother with that. I'll just take you on back."

We filed in. Inside it smelled far worse than the whiff I'd got at the front door let on. Old food, mildew, decaying flesh. Not one lamp was switched on, and beads of sweat sprang out on my forehead and chest.

"Did y'all bring chocolate?" the nurse said. "She loves her chocolate. And Tab. You know how hard it is to find Tab around here? Terri hardly ever comes and Traci less than that, but they do always bring a six-pack of Tab and some chocolate."

She led us through a foyer layered with dingy, mismatched rugs. I folded my arms, covered my nose and mouth with one hand, and gaped at Jay. Behind him, Rowe walked with his head down, hands jammed in his pockets. We passed a dining room, a formal living room, and then a den with a huge stone fireplace. Animal heads protruded from every corner—hogs, deer, buffalo, even some kind of African-gazelle-looking thing. A gun glinted above the mantel. A rifle with a decorative metal plate screwed to its stock.

The girl, who said her name was Angela, took us through a kitchen with a jungle of plants crowded under the window, a sink stacked with dirty dishes, and appliances that looked like they were from the 1950s. Out of the corner of my eye, I could see a row of pill bottles lined up under the warped-metal, paint-chipped cabinets.

We arrived at a door tucked in a cramped hallway off the butler's pantry. Probably a maid's bedroom once. Angela turned to us and grinned. "Traci makes me keep her down here because she can't do stairs. This house actually has an elevator, can you believe that? But it's busted, and no one'll pay to get it fixed."

I didn't really care about the elevator or Traci. I just wanted to get on the other side of this door and see Valerie Wooten. Find out who she was and what she knew about my mother.

"I'll stay out here," Rowe said as Angela turned the doorknob.

"I don't think so," Jay said through clenched teeth and hooked a hand under his arm. The look in his eye had me worried a bit. I don't think he'd recovered yet from my story about Rowe.

Angela opened the door, and we all walked into the bedroom. Light filtered in through the lace curtains, and I saw, sitting on every surface—dressers, night tables, bookshelves—what must've been nearly a hundred crosses. Crosses ad infinitum. They covered the walls, from the crown molding to the baseboards. They were made of every type of material imaginable—wood, silver, brass, plaster.

"No vampires getting in here," Rowe said.

"She collects them," Angela said and walked to the side of the bed. "Wake up, Miss Val, you got visitors. Your niece is here to see you."

That jolted me, and for a minute I felt bad that I was about to trick a dying old lady. I stepped closer and reminded myself I had to do this. My future, maybe my life, depended on it.

Valerie Wooten looked mean, even riddled with cancer, even resting helplessly against the stained pillowcase. It was the lines in her face. They showed years of disapproving looks, angry glares, sour silences. Her skin was yellow and sunken, and there was a smudge of crusted food on her chin. Nobody was spending much time easing her into the Great Beyond.

She opened her eyes. They were filmy and brown, and they studied Angela, then traveled uncertainly around the room. She reached out a hand and, in response, the nurse picked up a small wooden cross hidden in the folds of the chenille bedspread and handed it to her. Her papery, vein-roped fingers clenched it.

"Say hey to your niece, Miss Val," Angela said.

The old woman's head turned, and her unfocused eyes fastened on me. "Your husband know you're here?" she said in a thin voice.

I heard my heart hammering in my ears. I took one step closer, and my fingers brushed the bedspread.

"Hey, Aunt Val. How are you?" My eyes flicked up to Angela.

"Where's your husband?" She was really looking at me now, squinting a bit, trying to work it out.

"Do you mind if we have some time alone?" I asked Angela.

"No problem." She waved a hand at me. "I got my *Housewives*. Her pills will be wearing off soon. Call me if she starts talking ugly."

Jay moved to the center of the room, and Rowe hovered near the door. I turned back to the old woman, lowered myself to sit on the edge of the big bed.

She moved the cross to her breast, wrapped her other hand around it. "She moves my crosses all around the room when I'm asleep. She took the one with garnets."

"I'm sorry," I said. "I'll tell her to return it."

"Won't do any good. That's what they do. Steal. Hide things."

Ah, yes. There was that old-fashioned, old-time bigotry. As predictable as it was, it was always such a smack in the face.

She gave me the once-over. "Does your husband know you're out? He won't like it. You shouldn't have come here." I saw the lines deepen between her eyes and around her lips. "Walter won't like it either."

"I wanted to ask you a question, Aunt Val, if I could." She was silent, so I went on. "I wanted to ask you if you knew Trix."

"But you're Trix," she said. "Aren't you? Collie's girl? Walter's niece?" I sat back, and the puzzle began to assemble itself: Walter Wooten was my grandmother's brother. Val and Walter were my mother's aunt and uncle. So Val was my great-aunt. I'd said I was her niece, but I hadn't been far from the truth.

"Yes, ma'am." My skin goose-pimpled. "You're right. I am Trix."

She rolled her head to the side, away from me. "Does your husband know you're here?"

"No, but I was wondering, Aunt Val. Could you tell me what happened to me? That night I came to your house?"

When she spoke her voice was higher, like a child's. "Walter doesn't want me to talk about it. It doesn't reflect on the family."

"But I'm family. It's okay to tell me."

"No. Walter said."

"Please. Please, Val."

She rolled back to face me. Her eyes brimmed with reproach. "How's Elder going to win the election with you running around taking drugs? And carrying on with a teenage boy?"

She was talking about my father and his campaign for state attorney general. And how my mother had jeopardized his chances. Behind me, Rowe cleared his throat.

"It makes the both of you look like trash," she went on. "Walter says it's going to get worse. It always does. Goes from bad to worse." She looked toward the door.

My heart began to thrum. "What's going to get worse?"

"Walter said not to talk about it."

"You can tell me."

"When you turn thirty. They're gonna have to lock you up."

"Why? Why are they going to have to lock me up?"

"You'll go crazy. All you girls do, Walter says. It's the mountain in you. Jinn, his mama, and Collie, his sister, you know. Those mountain girls, they were funny in the head. Even though they didn't live on the mountain. Not exactly. They lived down in that valley. Sybil Valley. He ever tell you about that one . . . what took off all her clothes and climbed up on the fire tower? But, no, she wasn't a Wooten, she was a Lurie."

She was getting off track.

"What does the age of thirty have to do with it?"

"A curse. Sins of the generation. Hits at thirty." Her eyes darkened, and I saw her lips curl in disgust. "You know. The night you turned thirty, you brought that boy to my house. You brought that boy right into our house. And then you threatened to kill us. But Elder came and took care of it. And we didn't interfere. Walter says Elder's got the say-so." Her voice had turned whiney and small again.

"The say-so? About what?"

"How he handles you."

"What do you mean?"

She gave me a look like I was stupid. "It's Elder's job to decide what he wants to do about what all you got into. With that boy and the pills. Elder thought about a psychiatrist but then he thought better of it. People talk so much around here. After a while, he decided he had to lock you up. Walter said he shouldn't. Walter said . . ."

"What?"

"Walter said he should just put a stop to it altogether."

"What does that mean?" I asked.

She turned her head. "Elder's an important man. Walter understands that kind of thing."

"Aunt Val," I said. "Tell me. What do you mean by 'put a stop to it altogether'?"

She turned back to me. And smiled. Her teeth were brown and a few were missing. "It's not the first time it's happened in your family. Those Wooten women are an odd lot. They always have been."

"So what did he do?" My voice was barely a whisper. "Lock me up or . . ." I swallowed. "Stop me altogether?"

"Why, he sent you away, of course." She looked cowed. "To Pritchard. You know that. Walter and I had nothing to do with it. It was Elder's say-so."

"But then I died, right?" I said. "On the way to the hospital? Because of the aneurysm."

She starting puffing, her bottom lip pushing in and out. Tears spilled down her papery skin and her nose ran. I could see the spots they made on the pillow. Then she was sobbing, heaving. She thrust the cross in my direction over and over, like I was some kind of ghoul from hell, back to possess her.

I grabbed her hand, the one holding the cross. "I had a clot, in my brain," I said. "An aneurysm. I died that night."

Val shook her head. "No. You called me."

"From Pritchard?"

"You asked me to come get you out. You said there were ghosts. Chained to the beds. Hanging from the doorways. I didn't tell anybody," she went on. "But I went."

"What happened when you went there?"

She thrust out the cross then, held it with two hands right in front of my face so fast I couldn't believe her strength. She was trembling.

"You're not real. You look like her, but you're not real. It's all this medicine they give me." She peered up into my face, shaking.

"You're right," I said. "But if you tell me what happened, I'll leave you alone."

She curled forward, up off the pillow. This was what I'd come for, I reminded myself. I had to press on.

"I think it was the boy who did it," she whispered. "Once Elder got you into the hospital. I think it was that boy who went there and killed you."

I shot Rowe a look, and he seemed to shrink into the shadows.

She lifted her chin then and wailed in an oddly quiet way, a dying animal, and I stepped back. If only the ground under my feet would open up and swallow me. Anything, oh my God, anything to stop that sound. She stopped then and held the cross in the center of her sunken chest, looking so much like a corpse I shuddered. I turned and ran, past Jay and Rowe, out of the room, my blood beating in my ears.

I sank down on a stained settee and dropped my head in my hands. Then, from back in Val's room, I heard a rumble and a series of thumps.

"Althea!" I heard Jay yell. Then Rowe shot into the hall, lumbering past me in a blur of sweaty skin and purple Dri-FIT. He threw open the front door and vanished through it. I jumped up in time to see him sprinting across the yard and down the street like a pot-bellied Olympic athlete.

"Well, shit," Jay said behind me, and took off after him.

I turned back to get my purse and saw another bag beside it, a straw bag embroidered with sunflowers. The nurse's. Some barely formed, purely instinctual thought flitted through me, and I picked it up and slung it over my shoulder. I walked out the door and away from the house. Reached under my arm and rummaged in the bag. My fingers closed over a prescription bottle. Jackpot.

"Excuse me," a voice said behind me.

I looked over my shoulder. Angela, a linebacker in teddy-bear scrubs and a scrunchie, held out my purse. "You left your bag."

In answer, I held up the bottle. The label "Dilaudid" in plain view. She opened her mouth, but nothing came out. I took my purse from her and dropped in the bottle. Snapped it shut, then threw it over my shoulder. I handed her the sunflower bag.

"It's not what it looks like," she said.

"Good thing," I said. "Because it looks like you're stealing my aunt's pain medication. If I were you, I'd sort that out. Take it from someone who knows."

My lecture was cut short by a bloodcurdling shriek that came from down the street, followed by a series of muffled expletives. Angela took the opportunity to scurry back up to the house, clutching her purse to her chest. I walked across the street to Jay's car and leaned against it.

A moment later they showed up, Jay holding Rowe by the scruff of his golf shirt and pushing him forward. A red-hot asphalt burn shone along the length of Rowe's face. Jay shoved him into the backseat with a warning glare and slammed the door.

I lifted an eyebrow.

"Told you," he said. "I'm a fighter."

❧

We made our way back to the hotel. "Listen carefully," I said to Rowe, who was set up in a desk chair between the two beds in our hotel room. The curtains were drawn and the AC was off. Rowe was flushed with sweat.

"You are going to tell me everything that happened that night with my mother," I continued. "Everything. Or I'm going to burn down your miserable life. Do you understand?"

The side of Rowe's face was already scabbing. He looked worse than miserable already. Jay told him to call his wife again and tell her he was going to be stuck in Birmingham for just a few more hours.

"She's not going to buy it," he said. "She'll call the police if I'm not home soon."

"You're full of shit," I shot back. "You think your wife doesn't know about your special zipper bag of pills? You think she doesn't know everything you get up to? She's not going to call the police. Not unless she's finally had enough of your nonsense and is ready to pull the plug on your operation." I snuck a glance at Jay. "Or, how about this? If you really think she's worried, I'll be more than willing to call her and tell her you're safe and sound up here, just settling some differences with one of your former underage, recently rehabbed clients."

He studied the stained popcorn ceiling, his lids fluttering down over his eyes. Jay, propped against the headboard and staring daggers at him, ordered room service. I sat, barricaded by pillows, on the other bed. I couldn't imagine eating. All I could think of were those two bottles, Mrs. Cheramie's Lortab and now Val's Dilaudid, nestled together in the zippered compartment of my purse. I pinched at the bridge of my nose and tried to think about babbling brooks and sunsets and other inane bullshit.

"Can I have one of those cheeseburgers?" Rowe asked Jay.

"Talk first," I said. "Food later."

I saw a small flash of fear in his eyes. *Good.* He should be scared. I had a wheelbarrow full of dirt on him, and he knew it.

"So," I began. "You lied about leaving my mother at Walter and Val's and driving home."

He nodded.

"You went in with her." Another nod. "And you saw everything."

He chewed at his lip. Suddenly, I saw the TV remote whiz past Rowe's head. He ducked just in time and the chair teetered. His legs flailing, he finally managed to right himself.

"Hey!"

"We need to hear words, asshole," Jay said. "Words coming out of your mouth."

"I was with her that night," Rowe said. "I saw everything."

We waited.

"I gave her the Haldol. We used to meet in the parking lot at school."

I closed my eyes. "I need to know everything," I said. "Start talking."

Chapter Fourteen

Monday, September 17, 2012
Birmingham, Alabama

"My mom was on the board at Pritchard," Rowe said. "She used to bring home a lot of stuff from there. Haldol, Seconal, and Darvocet, I think. She used to hide it in the canopy over her bed. I don't know if she was planning some grand exit or what. I think she was very unhappy."

"I don't give a rat's ass about your mother's suburban malaise," I said. "Get to the point."

I was about to find out about the real Trix Bell, and I was steeling myself for it. I'd only known one side of my mother. The mom who had played with Wynn and me in the clearing. Who'd shown us how to pull the stamen through a honeysuckle blossom and catch the drop of nectar on our tongues.

That mother had cooked collards and cornbread and had hummed songs she'd learned from her mountain-bred mother. She'd recited Latin poems when she folded the laundry or weeded the garden.

Veni, Creator Spiritus,
mentes tuorum visita,
imple superna gratia
quae tu creasti pectora.

Rowe began again. "I started off by stealing a few bottles of pills here and there and slipping them to your mom."

"You mean, you sold them to her," I said.

He shrugged.

"She paid you, right?" I prodded. "In cash?"

"I guess. I don't really remember."

"Then think about it."

"Yeah. She paid me in cash."

"You're lying." I looked at Jay. "He's lying. Call his wife."

"No—" Rowe said.

I leaned forward. "My father kept a tight rein on my mom. He gave her just enough cash for groceries, dry cleaning, the post office. She had to save receipts for him. There's no way she would've had extra money for drugs."

He swallowed, his Adam's apple dipping like a bobber on the end of a fishing line.

"Stop fucking with me, Rowe."

"Okay," he said. "Okay. But you can't tell anyone about this. It's a . . . *web*, okay? There are a lot of people—" His head dropped, his scalp showing through the spikes of his hair. A buzzing started up inside me, the faintest current. Now we were getting somewhere. Finally. Rowe spoke to the carpet. "Your father—Elder—set the whole thing up with my mom. I think they had something going on."

I went cold.

"I don't know if he paid my mom or if they had some kind of an arrangement between them." He coughed. "I knew he didn't want either of them involved in the actual transactions. I mean, he was attorney general, and she was a hot-shit diva in the community. So they got me to do their dirty work. My mom gave me the pills. I'd head out to the parking lot after school, give them to Trix, and that was that."

"What about what Val Wooten said?" I asked. "About my mom running around with a teenage boy? That was you, right? You weren't just handing her a bottle of pills every couple of weeks? There was more between you two."

His face went sheepish like a boy's, and the side of his lip curled up in spite of himself. "She liked me, okay? She used to talk to me in the parking lot. She asked me if I'd go riding around with her out in the country. We drove around like that sometimes. She really liked the country."

I rolled my eyes, but I couldn't ignore the revulsion that surged through me. How could my mother have spent time with this animal? How could she have been so stupid?

"She'd tell me things," he said. "Things about her childhood. And her mother."

It felt like my neurons were crackling. "Like what, exactly?"

"She'd lost her mom at an early age. Five or six, I think. Her mom was sent away to Pritchard. It was hard on Trix."

"Why did they send her to Pritchard?" Jay asked.

"I don't remember. She was . . . she was sick or something, I think. Schizophrenia, maybe?"

There it was again—schizophrenia, the common denominator. "Did she tell you anything about Elder?" I asked. "Their relationship?"

"Just the stuff you'd expect. That he was controlling. Hard on her. Hard on you and coddled Wynn." He flicked his eyes to me. "She said they never had sex."

"Right," I said, voice dripping with sarcasm. My middle finger itched so bad, I had to tuck it under the opposite arm. I couldn't afford to alienate my only source of information now, but Rowe was tempting the hell out of me.

"Yes," Rowe said. "That's right. Your father and your mother were in a loveless marriage."

"And you're saying that she came on to you."

"Yeah." His voice was defiant. "That's what I'm saying."

There was a beat or two of silence where I considered if I actually had it in me to wrap my hands around his head and plunge my thumbs into his eye sockets. To push and push and not let up until his blood was running in rivers down my arms. I gritted my teeth, rolling the image around in my mind, then blinking it away.

"But," Jay said, "Trix never explained why Elder wanted her to take the Haldol? Y'all didn't talk about that?"

"No, we did. She said her mom had something, and there was a good chance she'd get it too. She knew Elder was worried about his position and how she reflected on him. All that political bullshit. But I mean, I kind of understood why Elder wanted her on the pills. No offense, but your mom was kind of a basket case. Like you'd just be talking to her for a few minutes, and you could tell right away something was wrong with her."

A rush of protectiveness welled up in me. *Asshole.*

"Like what?" Jay asked.

"Like she always seemed like she was in the middle of a panic attack. She twitched, you know? Trembled, sort of. She always looked nervous. Her voice shook. And sometimes she'd mumble stuff to herself in the middle—"

I broke in. "It was a prayer she liked to say. She chanted it. Lots of people do that. It doesn't make her a basket case."

"Yeah." He caught my eye. "I remember now. It was a Catholic prayer. Which was weird because I didn't think y'all went to church."

That was a mystery to me too, why my mother had latched on to that particular prayer, but there was no way in hell I was going to tell Rowe that.

"Back to the drugs," I said. "My dad wanted her to take them to make sure she didn't flip out and jeopardize his career?"

"The election was a big deal. A lot of bigwig supporters writing a lot of checks. I think he was always worried about her. Then something happened—she got this letter—and she got worse."

My nerves crackled again. It felt like a dozen tiny chain saws sawing their way through my insides. A letter. Here was something—finally. A clue in the midst of all this mess.

"Trix told me this letter rattled her, really freaked her out. Elder didn't know about it. She didn't show it to him."

"You saw this letter?" I asked, hope lifting inside me.

Rowe shook his head. "She told me about it."

"What did it say?"

"It was kind of bizarre. I don't really remember."

"Try," Jay said.

Rowe slumped back and searched the ceiling. "It was from some lady who'd known her family, up in the mountains in north Alabama. The lady wanted to meet Trix, to talk to her, on her thirtieth birthday, at Bienville Square."

"Why?" I asked. I could barely breathe.

"I don't know. She wanted to tell her stuff she needed to know? Family stuff, I think? Honest to God, I don't really know. Mostly Trix said it was just a bunch of weird shit about Trix turning thirty and how it was a strong age—all this feminist crap about women coming into their own when they turn thirty." He shrugged. "I mean, look, I was a seventeen-year-old idiot. It didn't compute."

He was a middle-aged man, and, from the looks of it, it still didn't compute.

"Trix got really worked up about that letter. God, if I could tell you . . . It sounds strange but I think she actually had the idea that this woman was like some kind of witch. An oracle or something, from the mountains. That she was coming to impart some magical gift that had belonged to her mother and grandmother. Something that could save her from going nuts. Fucking loony toons, right?" He laughed. "I mean, it was actually kind of sad. She really believed it. But she was so messed up about her mom, I guess she needed something to hang on to. I felt really sorry for her. But honestly? That was when I thought maybe Elder had the right idea, pumping her full of pills."

"Did she meet with the woman?" I asked.

"I snuck out and drove her to Bienville Square the night of her birthday. She was wearing this gold dress . . ."

His voice thinned. He seemed to momentarily waver in and out of the room. All I could see was my mother. The gold dress, sparkling in the moonlit clearing. Tears rose in my eyes.

"She told me to stay in the car, and she walked to the center of the square. It was raining, I think." Rowe twitched, lost in the memory. "When she came back, I don't know, like fifteen minutes later, she was different. Changed."

"Changed? How do you mean?"

He blinked. "She was shaking really hard, like ten times the normal amount. I mean, really amped up. Like she'd finally snapped her fucking pencil for good, if you know what I mean. She said she had to go to Birmingham, right then, to get something. She asked me to drive her."

"Get something? What?"

I felt like I was on the final hill of a roller coaster, barreling toward that last, terrifying tunnel. Where all the answers awaited me. But Rowe wasn't ready to go there. He squirmed in the chair and addressed Jay.

"Look, man. I gotta take a piss big-time."

"Then you better talk faster."

Rowe *pfft*ed and shook his head.

"Talk, Rowe," I ordered him, trying to control the tremor in my voice. "What happened at the Wootens'?"

"She wanted to sneak in like we were spies or something. We found him . . . your uncle Walter . . . sitting in the living room. He had a gun. An old rifle."

I thought of the rifle I'd seen over the Wootens' mantel, the one with the brass plate on the stock.

"Is that what my mom wanted? The gun?"

"Yeah. Yeah, it was. But her uncle was cleaning it," Rowe said. "Or maybe . . ."

I leaned forward. "Maybe what?"

"I don't know. I mean, it looked like he had the barrel to his head. His forehead, you know?" Rowe's eyebrows lifted and he looked from me to Jay. His temples gleamed with sweat.

I pictured the rifle between the old man's knees, pressed against his head. His hands reaching down to the trigger. "He was trying to shoot himself?" I asked.

"I guess, I don't know. Maybe I'm making that part up. It doesn't seem right now. I mean, why would he have been doing that?"

Everything was buzzing now. There was a full-on electrical storm raging inside me. "Go on."

"So we come in," Rowe said. "And this guy, Uncle Walter, puts the gun down. Wait. No. That's not what happened. Trix took the gun away from him. She takes the gun, and she starts yammering about it. She's talking about the gun, saying she's going to take it with her."

"What for?"

"Beats me. But I'm telling you, she's obsessed with taking the fricking gun. And then she's peppering him with all these questions about what happened to her mother, his sister."

"Collie."

"Yeah, Collie. She asks him about how Collie ended up in Pritchard when she turned thirty, and what happened to their mother, Jinn, when she turned thirty. She's talking crazy. Absolutely bonkers. Then her aunt comes in. Val. And she says Trix needs to see a doctor, and she should probably go to Pritchard too."

"And?"

"Trix loses her shit. I mean one hundred percent flips the fuck out. She starts waving the gun, pointing it at everybody. She says she has to take the gun. Take it somewhere, I can't remember. And then she fires it."

"Walter's gun? At who?" I asked.

"I don't know."

"Well, think about it. It matters."

"I don't know, Althea. All of us, I guess? She didn't hit anybody. But I mean, Jesus, she shot a gun inside their house. Walter crawled around the furniture somehow and knocked her down. He kind of tackled her, and she went down. They fought, scuffled, for a minute or two."

"He hit her?"

Rowe cut his eyes at Jay. "He, ah—she was going wild, and I think he might've hit her a couple of times. Like with the flat of his hand or something. Just to stop her."

"You let him hit my mother?" I felt my fingers start to itch again, my blood warm in my veins.

"She fucking shot at him, Althea."

He was right, I knew it, but I couldn't stop myself. I'd been pushed past some kind of line, and all I could think was how badly I wanted to wrap my fingers around his neck. Squeeze until the breath went out of him.

"You watched a man hit my mother," I said evenly. "And then you stood there and let him put her in a mental hospital."

Rowe's eyes darted nervously to Jay. "She was out of control."

I scrambled up, aimed myself at him, and launched off the bed. At the last moment, right before I landed on him, right before I was able to sink my fingernails into his fleshy jowls and rip him to shreds, Jay caught the back of my shirt and pulled me back.

He swung me onto the bed, where I landed with a whump. I crawled under the covers and pressed my face into the hotel comforter. The pungent combination of bleach and sweat and stale cigarettes filled my lungs. I wouldn't cry. I wouldn't give him the satisfaction.

"I'm sorry, Althea," Rowe said. "I'm sorry. I was a kid. I didn't know what to do. She took a shot at us. She could've killed somebody."

I didn't answer him.

After a long time, Jay spoke in a quiet voice. "What happened next? After Walter got the gun?"

"Elder showed up," Rowe said. His voice had taken on a penitent tone. "He took Trix home. I got out of there. I didn't want any more to do with the whole situation."

"What did your mother say?"

"I didn't tell her what happened. I didn't tell anybody. The next day I heard they'd taken Trix to the hospital but she'd had an aneurysm and died. I guess that was why she'd been shaking so much. And acting so crazy. I mean she probably had schizophrenia, but I guess she had the aneurysm too. Maybe because of all the pills."

It was a lie. A ridiculous lie. My father had put her in an institution and, in despair, she'd killed herself. But Dad couldn't tell that story. An aneurysm in the ambulance on the way to the hospital looked infinitely better on his resume. It put him in the role of the sympathetic widower, made people want to vote for him.

I, on the other hand, wanted to find my father and smash both my fists into his face. I clenched into a curve over the comforter. Balled my fists.

Jay spoke. "So then, after all that, Elder just showed up out of the blue at Walter and Val's to take Trix home?"

"Well," Rowe said. "Not exactly."

I sat up. Snuck a look at Rowe.

"After Bienville Square, when Trix asked me to take her to Birmingham, we stopped at a gas station." His face sagged, and he seemed to take a deep interest in the pattern of the carpet between his feet. "Trix was asleep. While I was filling up, I found a pay phone. I called Elder and told him where we were. I told him he should come get her. It was my fault."

I didn't care anymore what Rowe Oliver thought of me, whether he was afraid of me or not. I turned away, hid my face in the disgusting hotel comforter, and wept.

Chapter Fifteen

October 1937
Sybil Valley, Alabama

As the days passed, Jinn kept thinking about the dismembered calf, her wine money, and Hollywood. She'd seen in the paper that one of Myrna Loy's pictures was playing over in Chattanooga. It was called *Double Wedding*, a comedy with William Powell. She didn't know him either but thought she would definitely like seeing it. She wondered if a person could just walk into a movie house alone.

She was thinking about the movie on her walk home from church, Walter and Collie trailing behind her, when she opened the door of their cabin and saw Howell in the kitchen. He was sitting at their small table, a glass of lemonade to his right and a wad of cash to his left. She pushed the kids back onto the front porch.

"Shoo," she said. "Go play."

Her mind worked quickly—she tried to imagine how Myrna Loy might stand and look at her husband, if by chance she found herself in this situation. She took a couple of deep breaths and smoothed the wisps of her hair that had sprung from her bun. Walked to the kitchen and stood in the doorway.

Howell pointed at the pile of bills on the table, then looked at her with raised eyebrows. His silence filled the warm room until Jinn felt a bead of sweat roll from her armpit into her elbow. She finally spoke.

"It's my wine money," she said, voice trembling.

"This ain't no goddamn wine money. Try again."

"It is."

"You telling me Sadie and Jane Tifton and Aggie and them bought six hundred dollars' worth of honeysuckle wine off a you?" He said *honeysuckle wine* like someone else might say "dog shit" or "head lice."

I can go to Hollywood, Jinn thought. *I can get a screen test.*

She could also call the ladies from Chattanooga, for that matter. Ask them to drive her away in their silver dragon, show her where the buses left for California. She thought of that and, in the same instant, knew she would never do such a thing. Who would make sure her mama was looked after? Not her daddy. Not Howell. And the kids . . .

"Jinn?"

"I'm in business," she said, her voice a croak.

"That so?"

She nodded.

"So, while I'm breaking my back, digging holes and planting pine saplings to put food on the table for this family, you got this—this *wine* money—tucked away in a hidey-hole in the cellar." She swallowed, and he banged his palm on the table. "I will not have my wife hiding money from me. It ain't fitting. It ain't respectable."

She nodded again, fast.

Then he told her how he'd found her out. While he was in Chattanooga buying a tractor part, he'd happened into a store on Market Street. The proprietor, deducing Howell was a man of discernment and extra cash and might have possibly worked up a powerful thirst since the law forbade saloons in this part of town, escorted him to a special room in the basement. There in neat rows on the shelves sat a dozen slim blue bottles of honeysuckle wine. Machine-printed labels with a honeysuckle vine curling around the gilt edges proclaimed, "Jinn's Juice—The Most Refreshing!"

He came home (after buying one of the bottles and tasting it to make sure that, yes, by God, it was his wife's honeysuckle wine), gone down to the cellar and smashed all the jugs. Including the jug with the money. Only it wasn't one hundred dollars anymore. By that time, it had grown to six.

"Why were you hiding this money?" He leapt up. "What were you planning on doing with it?"

"Nothing."

"You planning on running off?"

"No."

"You got somebody on the side? Tell me, girl, were you gonna run off, leave me and the kids?"

She began to tremble and she could feel tears threaten, but she told her feet to stay planted right where they were. This wasn't nothing she hadn't heard a thousand times. And she could make it through to the end. She just had to tough it out.

Shy don't set the world on fire.

"It's Stocker, ain't it?"

"No."

"Goddamn Tom Stocker."

"No, Howell. No."

"Goddamn my-daddy-struck-gold-in-Georgia-so-all-I-do-is-sit-on-my-ass Tom Stocker. You know, I been to Georgia, little lady. And I ain't heard nobody over there talking about Tom Stocker's daddy. Mr. Gold Strike. Mr. Fancy Britches. Ain't nobody over there ever heard a Tom Stocker's daddy, which makes me think he got his money other ways."

Jinn didn't move. She didn't even blink or breathe.

He cocked his head to the side and eyed her. "Why you think that peckerwood never got married?"

"He did, to Lucy."

"I meant after she passed. He's got a boy. Why hasn't he got married again?"

"He's still in love with Lucy."

"Now Jinn, you know that's bullshit. He's in love with you."

"No."

For a minute, Howell looked tired of this line of argument, and his eyes roamed around the kitchen. He rubbed his jaw. Rubbed and rubbed and rubbed, until his blond beard bristled and his cheeks flushed a deeper red. Jinn's heart spiked, a tiny leap of hope in her breast. Maybe he was done. But she was wrong, because when he turned back to her, she could see his eyes had hardened.

"I should tell your daddy," he said in a low voice. "That's what I should do."

The hope melted away inside Jinn.

No.

He smiled at her then, a mean smile. He could probably see on her face his threat had frightened her. He straightened, puffed out his chest, and laid his hands flat on the table. He studied his nails, unusually neat for a farmer.

"If I tell your daddy, he'll sure as shooting know how to handle this."

"Howell—"

"I should drag you by the hair over to your daddy's right now, that's what I should do."

"Please—"

"You'd tell *him* the truth, wouldn't you?" She clasped her hands together underneath her apron to keep them from shaking. She would not run. She would not.

"Please, don't tell him," she whispered. "Please."

He came at her, his hands already fists, and she curled herself toward the floor. She had one fleeting thought before he reached her:

she hoped the children had, for once, disobeyed her and gone far, far past their property line.

He picked her up off the floor, squeezing her so hard she thought her ribs would snap. She gasped for air. Then, just when she thought she was going to faint, he spun her and slung her outward, sending her flying across the kitchen and into the table. Her head hit the corner and snapped back, and she fell to the floor. He walked to her, stood above her, panting. She cracked open her eyes and looked at his boots, so close to her now. They were old, caked with dried mud. There was blood on them too, from a rabbit or a squirrel. Or a deer he'd stolen from the mountain.

She forced herself to speak as steadily as she could. "I was saving the money for Walter. For college."

The boots shifted a little, then headed to the sink. She heard the water run, and next thing she knew he was holding a dripping dishrag beside her. She took it, pressing it against the back of her head. No blood, thank God, but there was a nice-size lump.

"You shoulda said something." His voice was gruff.

"I know. I'm sorry, Howell. It kinda snuck up on me." The lie, the stuff about Walter and college, had come out as slick and easy as a six-pound baby. She should be ashamed. The truth was, the idea of saving the money for her son had never even occurred to her. She'd only ever thought of herself.

She decided to chance a look at her husband. His face had softened, his eyes glazed over. He was staring past her, lost in some kind of dream. Maybe one of Walter going to college over in Georgia, graduating in a cap and gown. Setting up a law practice or going to medical school. His eyes focused then, and he shook his head.

"I don't like you keeping secrets. A woman can't carry around money like this behind her husband's back. It ain't right."

"Okay."

"It don't reflect on the husband." He looked down at her and heaved a great sigh. "I don't know what I'm gonna do with you, Jinn."

He'd shuffled to the other side of the room, like the matter was done, but a voice in her head told her it wasn't. It couldn't be over and done, just like that. The voice told her to watch out, step careful. It sounded a lot like her mama.

Howell offered her his hand, and she took it. To show him the matter was settled, that he didn't have anything to worry about, she smiled the most winsome smile she could muster. A Myrna Loy smile. After he helped her up and patted her bottom, he gathered up the scattered money, folded it neatly, and slid it in his pocket. She tiptoed out to call in the children.

Later that night, around about midnight, Jinn woke to an empty spot beside her in the bed, voices drifting up from the porch. She recognized them right away: Howell and her daddy. She couldn't hear their words exactly, but she knew what was being said, all the same. They were making plans for her.

Chapter Sixteen

Tuesday, September 18, 2012
Birmingham, Alabama

I awoke, cotton-mouthed and sweaty, and looked at the clock. A little after three in the afternoon. I was in my underwear, cocooned in the sheets. I must've shucked off my dress sometime in the night.

Jay was sitting on the other bed, in his boxers, on his phone and his iPad. He must've sensed I was awake, because he half turned, muttered into the phone, and hung up.

"The lawyer again?"

"Yep."

"I don't want to talk to him."

"You don't have to. You thirsty?"

He tossed me a bottle of water, and I guzzled it. He smiled at me, which made me think about how heinous I must look. Bed-head hair, sheet-creased skin, dragon breath. I felt like I hadn't showered or eaten in days. I extricated myself from the sheets and put my feet on the floor.

And then everything from Rowe's story came back to me—the Haldol, Bienville Square, Walter and Val, and the gun. But in the center of all of it, the question still remained: what had really happened to my mother? How had she died?

We'd been together that night, my mother and I. I remembered it in flashes, a kind of murky slide show of the past. I heard her voice, telling me to wait for the honeysuckle girl. But after that, it was so hard to pull the bits and pieces of memories together into a coherent story.

I suddenly straightened. "What's the date?"

He quit tapping. "The eighteenth."

Panic knifed through me.

"I need to figure out what the hell happened to my mother and my grandmother and stop this fucking freight train before it runs me over."

He'd let Rowe go while I slept. Put him in the elevator and told him to catch a cab home. I think he expected me to blow up over that, but I was strangely still exhausted and decided to let it pass. The truth was, we couldn't hold Rowe forever. And I had other things to do.

Jay also said he had come back to bed and held me all night. This part, I remembered—feeling him against me every hour or so when I woke up. I wasn't used to sleeping with someone. Usually it made me feel hemmed in, claustrophobic. But something told me he was the only thing keeping me from going over the edge. So I clung to his arm all night like it was the only thing between me and utter despair.

"Well?" I said when he'd finished talking.

"Well what?" Now I had his full attention, bare chest, boxers, and all. The sight was more than a little disconcerting. I tried to stay focused on my anger, but I could feel it dissipating. Ebbing away.

I threw up my hands. "Didn't you hear what Rowe said? I have to do something before it happens to me too. I have to get a handle on this before Wynn forces me into some horrible facility."

"And to do that, you need to be strong. Well rested. Right?"

I sighed and massaged my temples. This line of conversation was going nowhere. I needed to keep my eyes on the task at hand. My birthday was only twelve days away. Less than two weeks to figure out what this thing was.

"Find anything interesting?" I gestured to the iPad.

He looked at the screen. "I was returning an email to my parents. They're in France, headed over to Tuscany for a wine tour. The apartment they leased is empty for the rest of the month. I can get you an expedited passport in twenty-four hours. We could be in Paris by Friday and you could spend your birthday walking around the Louvre and stuffing your face with croissants and macarons."

"No."

"Can I ask why not?"

"Because, Jay, that's all I need—to lose my shit overseas and get locked up in some French nuthouse like Fantine or whoever."

"They put her in a hospital, I believe, because she was dying of tuberculosis."

I shook my head. "Smart-ass."

"Just tell me where we can go, Althea, where you'll feel safe. Tell me." He sounded wounded now. Maybe a little pissed that I wasn't going along with his European getaway plan.

I swung my legs around the bed. "Give me the iPad, and I'll tell you."

I did a quick search and flipped it around to him.

"The Jefferson County Department of Health," I said. "That's where I want to go. You can get information there about anyone who's died after 1908."

"Information?" He looked at the screen. "What kind of information?"

"A death certificate." My fingers hovered over the tablet. "Listing time and location and cause of death. And we find out if Val was telling the truth. If my mom was ever at Pritchard. And what she died of—an aneurysm or an overdose. Or something else."

The next questions hung in the air. If my mother had been checked into Pritchard, how could she have gotten a hold of enough pills to overdose? And why had my father been lying to everyone about it for over twenty years? Had he been involved somehow?

I had to face it. My father had been a politically ambitious man saddled with a troubled wife. She was a problem that needed solving. He could've killed her. Easily. She had no family looking out for her. No one would've blinked an eye if he put her in the state institution. Walter, who, for whatever reason, was on the verge of finishing himself off, didn't seem like he'd be the one to spill the family secrets. And Val, poor tormented Val, she wouldn't stand up to either Elder or her husband.

One thing was obvious: if my mother had indeed died under suspicious circumstances, Elder Bell, the state's attorney general, could've easily covered it up. He could have altered the death certificate too, if he'd been really careful. I still needed to see it, no matter what it said.

I tossed the iPad aside and hugged the sheets around me, hunching deeper into myself. Even if my father had done the unspeakable, even if he had killed my mother, that still wouldn't explain what had happened to my grandmother and my great-grandmother—why they disappeared when they turned thirty too.

Something inside me, a residual thread of those women still buried in my DNA, told me it was much more than a random coincidence. It was a mystery, but one that had to be solved very carefully. If I stepped wrong, Wynn would have me committed. To him, I was a liability. Nothing but an item in the loss column of his personal asset sheet. And probably a threat to his becoming governor. But why he was so determined to label me schizophrenic and have me locked up forever, I couldn't comprehend. It seemed so extreme.

I thought of what he'd said about Dad's will—I'd inherit my share as long as I was under psychiatric care. So maybe all this had to do with money. Maybe I was due to inherit a bigger amount than I realized. I wondered if Wynn had been named my legal guardian. I'd heard people did things like that. I needed to talk to somebody with expertise. A lawyer.

I dropped my head in my hands. What I needed—probably more than a lawyer—was a therapist. I had no business carrying drugs around in my purse. I should talk to someone, a professional, about taking some sort of preventative medication, in case this thing was schizophrenia. But there was the risk that, after confiding in someone, a doctor, I'd open myself up to legal action. If Wynn got to the doctor somehow, he could convince him to lock me up. How would I be able to help myself then?

I have to get out of here. I'm running out of time.

And then, another thought: *I can't let Jay see me like this.*

I clenched my jaw in frustration. Why was I even thinking that way? Why did I care? I was acting like a high-school girl, like Jay and I were conducting an actual, real relationship. Which was ridiculous. We weren't.

God. What was wrong with me? I'd quit everything else. Why couldn't I just send Jay on his way?

He'd turned back to his phone and was texting away like mad. I surveyed the way his back curved over his phone, the lean muscles, the ridges of his spine. His skin was smooth and golden. Perfect.

"You should go," I said, pulling the words out of the air. "Back to Mobile."

He looked up from the glowing screen in front of him. "What?"

"I don't know." I twisted the corner of the sheet. "Don't you need to be looking for a new job or something?"

"I'm working at my dad's construction company. Doing the books. Tax consulting."

"Shouldn't you be . . . consulting, then?"

"I have some flexibility." He straightened. "Do you want me to go?"

"It's not that. I just think you could probably find something more productive to do with your time than chasing down my drug-dealer buddies and giving me sponge baths. Or trying to lure me down to Orange Beach or Paris."

"I don't know." He grinned. "It's not such a bad gig."

"I'm being serious."

"I am too." He was gazing at me. "There's nothing that could happen here that's going to change how I feel about you, Althea."

"How you feel about me?"

His eyes dropped and his face reddened. He looked nervous, I thought. Guilty, even. Or maybe I was imagining things. Looking for something that wasn't there, some reason to doubt him and send him away.

I spoke again. "I'm not trying to be difficult. It's just I don't even know what that means."

He shook his head. "I don't know. I just want to be here. Helping you." He scratched at his scruffy jaw, then met my eyes. "Okay. Look, Althea, this is really hard for me to admit, but I kind of need this. I need to focus on something right now, something bigger than me that actually matters, instead of sitting in my parents' house feeling sorry for myself."

His face was deeply flushed now, eyes bright. He was either extremely embarrassed or lying. And I had no idea which to believe.

He was playing the knight in shining armor in this scenario, that was for damn sure. The guy with a getaway car and limitless credit card. And the fact was, I needed those things. I had to have them. So maybe I wasn't just distracting myself with the eye candy and possibility of sex, but I was using him all the same. The way I always used people.

But he was letting me. It might be for selfish motives but he was sticking around, and this was good for me.

"If you really want to stay, I'm not going to turn you out," I said. "Because, as a matter of fact, I could use a ride to the Department of Health right now. They need a next of kin to request a death certificate."

At the Department of Health I sat on a plastic orange chair under the glare of fluorescent lights and filled out the death-certificate-request form. Mom's full legal name, name of spouse, parents' names. Date: her thirtieth birthday, October 5, 1987. Mobile County.

As I moved to turn it in, Jay stopped me. "Why don't you fill out two more?" he whispered. "For your grandmother and great-grandmother."

I asked the clerk for two more forms and filled them out with what spotty information I had. I turned in all three, paid the fee, and settled down to wait. She came back with three pieces of paper and a receipt.

There was one Certificate of Failure to Find—for Jinn Wooten— and two death certificates, for Collie Crane and Trix Bell. I flipped to Collie's certificate first. The date of death marked 1962, the place Tuscaloosa, with the cause listed as "Intentional Injury."

"Suicide?" Jay asked.

"I guess. There's nothing more here. Other than her husband's name was David."

"Tuscaloosa County means Pritchard, right?" he asked.

It had to. No one had ever mentioned anyone from her mother's family actually living in Tuscaloosa County. Jay shook his head in disgust as I shuffled the paper to the back of the pile. My mother's certificate lay on top. I rested it on my knees, skimmed the basic information, then skipped farther down:

METHOD OF DISPOSITION: *Cremation* PLACE OF DISPOSITION: *Oak Park Crematory*

LOCATION: *Tuxedo, Mississippi*

DATE PRONOUNCED DEAD: *October 5, 1987* TIME PRONOUNCED DEAD: *4:11 a.m.*

City of Death and Zip Code: *Mobile, 36607*

Was Medical Examiner or Coroner Contacted: *No*

"Tuxedo, Mississippi?" Jay said.

"Her father's people were from Mississippi. The Cranes. I knew them, sort of. It was only Collie's side that nobody talked about."

"So your mother's ashes are buried hundreds of miles away," he said. "How convenient."

I skipped down to the bottom of the page, the box marked "Medical Certification," and continued reading:

PART I: Immediate Cause of Death: *Seizures*

Seizures? And no mention of aneurysm. How could that be? I scanned farther down. There was another section below, with spaces for more details on her death. Every space was blank.

"No autopsy," I said. "Manner of death, 'natural.'" I looked at Jay. "I'm pretty sure there's supposed to be a little more here. I mean, was it a preexisting condition? An injury? Drugs? There's nothing here to explain it. Nothing."

He furrowed his brow. "Bush-league death certificate. Who signed it?"

I looked at the bottom. "Woodrow Smart."

"Who's he? Her doctor?"

"I don't know. That's all it says. Woodrow Smart."

Jay whipped out his iPad and tapped in the name. He scrolled down the page of results.

I thought back through every name I could remember, all my father's friends. Anyone that would've been able to help him falsify medical documents.

"Here we go," he said, clicking on a link.

He read aloud. "'January 11, 1988. A Mobile paramedic who fell from the I-10 Bayway Bridge into the Mobile River on Sunday night has died, according to the Mobile Fire Department. Twenty-four-year-old Woodrow "Woody" Smart suffered multiple severe injuries in the fall and was discovered drowned. He was found by Mr. Donald McLean, 58, of Daphne, who was fishing under the bridge. "I saw him hit the supports a couple of times on the way down. I knew he was a goner after that," McLean said. Smart was responding to a call by a stranded motorist. He left his partner in the emergency vehicle and walked alone to the car, which was wedged against the cement barrier. It is believed he was attempting to open the door and extricate the passenger when he slipped and fell into the river below.'"

We were silent for a moment, then I spoke. "So . . . three months after Woodrow Smart signs my mother's sketchy death certificate, he falls over a bridge and dies? A little handy, don't you think?"

"What I think," Jay said, "is that you need a lawyer."

Chapter Seventeen

Wednesday, September 19, 2012
Birmingham, Alabama

The next day, we were supposed to meet an old college buddy of Jay's for lunch, a general-practice attorney who Jay swore we could trust. Jay was going to go early, catch up with his friend and explain the situation. I was going to spend the morning seeing if I could dig up any more information on Collie Crane or David, her husband, and meet Jay and the lawyer later to hear his recommendations.

The whole scenario gave me a sour stomach. And an almost uncontrollable desire to rip open one of the bottles of pills and crunch one between my teeth. But I resisted. For the moment.

I had work to do.

A search for Collirene Wooten Crane turned up nothing. I had a bit more luck with David, even though he wasn't much more than a blip on the Internet. I did find what looked like a Crane family reunion site, based in Maryland, that briefly mentioned him. He was born in 1930 in Birmingham, a graduate of Phillips High School in 1948 and a member of the Rotary Club in 1963. Married to Collirene Wooten Crane and member in good standing at Cathedral of Saint Paul Catholic church. One daughter, Trix.

The search dead-ended there. I tossed the iPad aside and went to shower.

✺

Forty-five minutes later, circling the block in the Five Points section of Birmingham, I was tempted to point Jay's car east toward 280 and floor it. Fly right out of town and across the state line to Georgia or Tennessee. Maybe even head west to Mississippi to find my mom's grave. Skip town. Disappear.

It wasn't that Jay hadn't been great. After we'd left the Department of Health, we'd gone south of town to stock up on enough clothes and toiletries to get me through the week. And we'd finally had a meal that wasn't from a drive-thru. In other words, he'd continued his Mr. Wonderful routine.

But he was intensely distracting. And with the threat of death or insanity or being locked away forever hanging over my head, I couldn't afford to be sidetracked. What I needed to focus on was solving the mystery, not Jay's spectacular shoulders. The way the skin crinkled out in two delicious fans at the corners of his eyes. I had to streamline my operation, and soon. And then I had to figure out how I was going to untangle this mess without Jay's help . . . and his shiny silver credit card.

And then there was the issue of my complete lack of leads. There was basically no record of the women in my family, on the Internet or elsewhere, and I couldn't help but feel suffocated by the gloomy cloud of that reality. It was like history had conspired to wipe out any trace of the women who came before me. Nothing was happening in Birmingham. I was banging my head against a triple-bolted door.

I found a spot on the far side of the street and wedged the sleek BMW into it. I was early, so I grabbed the cigar box from the backseat, climbed out of the car, and walked down the sidewalk. Just across the street from the restaurant, someone had left a newspaper and a half-empty Styrofoam cup of coffee at the side of a fountain. I picked up the paper, folded it under my arm, and sat by the fountain. I hoped I looked like I had a reason for being there.

I wasn't ready to go into the restaurant. Not yet. I wasn't ready to unburden myself to a lawyer, much less to say the things I had to say to Jay. Telling him I'd decided to continue on without him was going to be tough, and he was going to fight me on it. Nevertheless, I owed him this much. I would go in there, listen to his buddy's spiel, then cut the cord. But, before that, I needed to gather myself.

From behind the row of parked cars, I could see into the window of the place. It was one of those French bistros with baskets of crusty bread and an endless wine list. I'd been fantasizing about a cappuccino and crème brûlée ever since Jay had told me about the place, and, even now, my mouth watered. In the window I could see him, seated at a table. He was alone, tipping back a beer. The waitress came up and said something. Smiled. Said something more. He laughed, and then I saw her hook a finger in her ponytail and trail it down her neck and white button-down chest provocatively.

Jealousy stabbed at me, and I knew instantly I couldn't go on, keeping this man tethered to me, dragging him all over the state of Alabama, deluging him with my family secrets. I wasn't ready for all that. I dropped my head and listened to my own shaky breathing for a long time. I had to go, that was all there was to it. I couldn't do this with Jay.

When I lifted my eyes, there was still no sign of Jay's lawyer friend at the table. Meanwhile, the flirty waitress had managed to sidle a couple of inches closer to Jay's chair. She was caressing her ponytail with feverish intensity now, her lithe frame curled toward him. He said something to her, something obviously riotously funny because she threw back her head and belly-laughed. He checked his watch.

Something, a hunch maybe, or a niggling thread of doubt, made me glance down the block. I caught a flash of movement—a smudge of dark hair out the corner of my eye. My whole body tingled with shock.

It was my brother, Wynn, walking up the sidewalk in the direction of the restaurant. Sauntering, really, like he owned the world. He was dressed in a white polo shirt, collar up, sporting a pair of sunglasses attached to a neoprene strap. He looked like he was on his way to celebrate some particularly good news. Or to crush an opponent.

My gaze swiveled back to Jay, and he flicked a glance out the window at me. We locked eyes, and I felt time grind to a halt. Jay's back straightened, ever so slightly. His face had gone slack. Pale. For the second time, gooseflesh sprang out all over me.

Sonofabitch. He called Wynn.

My brain spun into overdrive. I leapt up, and, at the same moment, Wynn stopped, his head swiveling in my direction. He pivoted, a slow, measured move, the way he might move if he was stalking a deer. My breath caught in my throat, and, in the next instant, he was running toward me, crossing the street, shrinking the distance between us with a series of easy lopes.

I backed away from the fountain, stumbling over my own feet, fumbling with the cigar box and frantically digging for the keys. I edged around the car and, hands shaking, unlocked the door, slid in. I pounded at the locks just as a set of knuckles rapped the glass beside my head. A scream shot out of me like an arrow.

Wynn leaned down, head sideways in the window, his lips stretched apart in a smile. I couldn't even fathom how fast he'd made it up the sidewalk and to Jay's car. My heart thundered; my fingertips tingled. The sunglasses blocked his eyes, but if I could have seen them, I wondered if they'd be filled with false concern. And that underlying flicker of hatred.

I heard his voice, muffled through the window. "Hey, kiddo. Come on inside with me. Get something to eat."

I reached for the keys—where were they?—then remembered I'd dropped them in the console. I snatched them up. Wynn pounded on the window, rattling it in the doorframe. "Althea? Don't be like this. I just want to talk to you."

I went for the ignition, but my hands were shaking so bad, I missed the slot. On the second try I jammed the key in, and the car roared to life. The door opened, and he reached for me, grabbing at my sleeve. I flailed back at him with one hand but couldn't shake him off. I threw my elbow, smashing his hand against the metal frame. He yelped. I slammed the car into reverse.

"Althea!" He sounded enraged.

I stomped on the gas, and the car jerked back and stalled, lurching to a stop. The door swung open, and he lunged. Suddenly he was on top of me, reaching for the steering wheel and pressing me back against the seat with one surprisingly strong forearm. I let go of the wheel and at the same time hit the gas as hard as I could. The car skidded back and crashed into the one parked behind it. The door swung closed, crunching Wynn's torso. He yelped.

With all the force I could muster, I pushed him out and slammed the door, locking it as he rolled onto the asphalt. I put it in drive, cut the wheel hard, and gunned it, doing my best to maneuver around him. But it wasn't necessary. He'd already scrambled up and stumbled over to the other lane, out of the way of an oncoming cab.

I screeched into the street, spinning out, narrowly missing the cab myself. The irate driver yelled something unintelligible at me. I was halfway down the block when I finally allowed myself to look in my mirror. Wynn was doubled over in the street, his crushed sunglasses and their neoprene strap dangling around his neck. Jay stood beside him.

I cut the wheel to the right, heading downtown. Praying for a sign that would point me toward the interstate. I couldn't think straight, and I had no idea where I was. My hands were shaking on the steering wheel. In fact, my whole body was shaking.

I thought of Val's story, Collie's death certificate, and what they had in common. Pritchard. Over and over the place had come up. Maybe Mom had been there, maybe not, but for sure Collie had been. Maybe it was time I dug deeper into my grandmother's life. And her death. I had to get to Pritchard.

With trembling fingers I switched off the GPS, although it probably didn't make any difference. No doubt Jay could find me instantaneously with his stupid, space-age, car-locating app, but why make it any easier for him? And there was a chance he'd just let me go. I hoped he still cared enough about me to do that. Or didn't care enough. Either way, hoping was all I could do.

I told myself to breathe. Breathe and try to remember the way to Tuscaloosa.

***

I was headachy and limp with adrenaline loss by the time I pulled into the parking lot of a dumpy motel on the outskirts of the college town. I rested my forehead against the steering wheel and whispered into the still air.

"I am not my mother.

"The honeysuckle girl isn't real.

"I do not have gold dust on my fingertips.

"There's no such thing as a red raven."

The truths brought me comfort, but saying them felt a little pathetic. There were new developments now, facts I couldn't just chant out of existence.

My brother is out to get me.

Jay betrayed me.

I am alone.

Alone.

Reciting mantras wasn't going to cut it anymore; I had to keep moving forward. Figure out how to root out this evil seed of mental illness that might possibly be growing inside me. And now, on top of that, I had to stay one step ahead of Wynn. And Jay.

I lifted my head and surveyed the sad sight before me. I'd bypassed the shiny Courtyards and Suites and Expresses in favor of a seedy, one-story rathole aptly named the Crimson Terrace. The bottom third of the original white brick walls was stained with red clay that bordered the L-shaped structure, and there were no shrubs in sight, just a broken-up parking lot with an empty, cracked swimming pool at its center.

Sandwiched between a KFC and a Hardee's, the place felt isolated and, at the same time, like it might be the safest spot in the world. The perfect hideout. I could get a room, settle in, and formulate a plan.

I rented a room—nineteen dollars cash for a single night—and then went back to search the car for supplies. Jay had left a pair of aviator sunglasses (good), his iPad (very, very good), and a couple of unopened bottles of water (couldn't hurt). In the trunk I found a yoga mat, multiple maps of Alabama, and a bottle of hand sanitizer.

I lugged everything out—all of it being mine now, on account of Jay being a deceitful dickhead—then hit the "Lock" button on the key fob three times, for good measure. If anyone tried to steal the tank of a car, I'd be out of the door in seconds, ready to tear them to pieces. I walked to Room 11 and let myself in. Dumped everything on the round laminate table by the window and slammed the door behind me. It bounced back open, and outside, I could see a grimy old man watching me. I shut it again, bolted it tight, and slid the chain into its rusty slot.

When the single light by the bed was switched on and the curtains were drawn, the wood-paneled room glowed red. There were twin beds, a dresser, and a gargantuan TV on a wheeled metal stand. The bathroom was like something out of a postapocalyptic novel—grime-encrusted and possibly infectious. After inspecting things, I decided to make a supply run across the street, maybe pick up some food on the way back.

A couple of hours later, fueled by a greasy fried-chicken-and-mashed-potato dinner, I cleaned every surface of the place with a pasty mix of Comet and bleach while the TV blared the local news.

Toward the end of my cleaning frenzy, something yanked me back down to earth—Wynn's name coming from the TV. I stopped midscrub and sat on the edge of the bed, riveted to the screen.

A local news anchor was talking about my brother, calling him things like "the heir to the throne" and "the newest member of Alabama's Bell political dynasty."

Dynasty seemed overshooting it, I thought, since it was really just Dad and Wynn. But whatever. Those people made up whatever they needed, whenever they needed it.

They rolled some tape of Wynn, standing by the river's edge alongside old Gene Northcut, Dad's former benefactor. A bruise shadowed the underside of Wynn's cheekbone, and, as the breeze ruffled his hair, he grinned, an act that I imagined took every ounce of his willpower. I wondered if his ribs hurt from getting smashed in Jay's car door. I hoped so.

"My sister has had her struggles in the past few years," he was saying to the reporter off camera. "She's a recovering addict and suffers from schizophrenia. She is currently being treated, a fact which my opponent is trying to twist in a sad attempt at mudslinging. The truth is, my ability to effectively govern the great state of Alabama has absolutely nothing whatsoever to do with her condition."

So I was being treated, was I? I reached out, turned up the volume.

Wynn went on. "In fact, in honor of my sister's condition, I'm actively supporting the restoration of Old Pritchard Hospital. I'm having it listed on the National Register of Historic Places as one of the few remaining examples of the groundbreaking health-care reforms our state pioneered back in the nineteenth century. This gentleman"—Wynn gestured to Northcut—"Mr. Gene Northcut, a longtime member of the Alabama Historical Association, has agreed to start with a memorial that will mark Pritchard, finally and deservedly, as the hospital that changed lives."

I couldn't believe my ears. Why in the world would my brother want to open up that can of worms? With the connection between that hospital and his family, you'd think he'd avoid the place like the plague. For that matter, how had Wynn's opposing candidate gotten dirt on me? It was like freaking junior high all over. I switched off the TV in disgust.

When I'd finally exhausted myself, and the air smelled nice and chemically, I stripped the dingy linens off the bed and laid out on the bare mattress a pink-and-purple sleeping bag I'd bought at the dollar store. I climbed into the bag and placed the cigar box in front of me. Took everything out and laid the items in a neat row. I closed my eyes and the words filled my mind.

Come, Holy Spirit, Creator blessed,
And in our souls take up Thy rest;
Come with Thy grace and heavenly aid
To fill the hearts which Thou hast made.

I opened my eyes, half expecting there to have been a miracle. An answer. But there were just six pill bottles, the prayer, the wine-bottle label, and the hair clip. I stared at them until they blurred, but nothing new came to me. It was all the same. Clues that told me absolutely nothing.

Chapter Eighteen

October 1937
Sybil Valley, Alabama

Jinn had never seen the inside of Tom Stocker's house. Even when they were kids and she'd gotten an invitation to Tom's birthday party, an event that promised store-bought ice cream and a magician, she hadn't gone. She hadn't had a nice-enough dress.

When she finally did see it, she was surprised at how simple it was. The front hall was hung with green-and-gold-striped wallpaper, but the worn wooden floors were bare, and the iron chandelier was too small for the space. Also, there were chunks of mud, leading in a trail up the stairs. It looked like a mole had emerged from his muddy underground tunnel to explore the premises.

Jinn followed Tom into a shadowy room to the left of the hall. Its windows were shuttered and curtained, and the gaslight sconces flanking the marble fireplace, cold. She stood uncertainly behind a large carved and tufted sofa. She'd never seen a library in a house before.

Tom had positioned himself a respectable distance away—by a heavy bookcase with glass doors—and was regarding her with mild eyes. He hadn't acted surprised when she'd knocked on his big, white front door just after eight that morning, just greeted her and asked her if she'd like a cup of tea.

But now that she was safely inside his house, she felt his eyes roving over her face. Searching. She thought of the lump on her temple. It was hard not to reach up and touch it.

She produced a small purse from her pocket and held it out to him. "Would you keep this?" she said.

He didn't answer.

She jiggled the purse. "For Collie?"

"What did he do to you?"

She wished he would quit glowering. She smiled brightly. "I'll leave her a note. Hide it in the cigar box she keeps. My daddy used to smoke Red Ravens, way back when. He gave me the box, to put my treasures in, and I gave it to her."

She was jabbering, like Howell said she tended to do at certain times. She clamped her mouth shut.

"What's in there? Why do you need to hide it?"

Jinn cleared her throat. "Howell found most of what I'd saved. But I hid this in the flour jar. I want to save it for Collie."

"What's he done to you, Jinny?"

She opened her mouth. The words didn't come out. They'd wilted somewhere in the back of her throat, like a handful of dead meadow flowers.

His face had gone crimson, his eyes narrow. "Jinny, I swear, I will kill him—"

"No." She laid the purse on the table by the sofa. He didn't even glance at it, never took his eyes off her. "No," she said again, with finality.

She fiddled with the button on the sleeve of her dress. Everybody minded their own business up here on the mountain, did their duty before God. It was her duty to be a good wife, no matter what Howell did.

"I haven't said anything, because it wasn't my place," he said. He was watching her—so closely she felt heat creeping up her neck. "It wasn't my place, but I swear, Jinny, I'll make it my place, just say the word. We can go away," he said. "You and me, Willie, and Collirene."

Her eyes fastened on his. She couldn't think clear.

"Go away with me," he said.

She managed one word. "Where?"

"He wouldn't find you in London. I bet he can't even find London on a map. It's beautiful there. The flowers . . ." His voice trailed off. He scooped up the purse, crossed the room, and tucked it into an oblong, black-lacquered box on the mantel. He turned back to her.

Time stopped. Everything stopped but the drumming of her heart.

"California," she said.

And then, in a split second, he was in front of her, inches away, his breath hot and sweet in her face. "Yes, California. San Francisco, San Diego. Wherever you want."

"I can't . . ." She was going to bring up something about God and the Bible and the fires of hell, but she shut her mouth when she saw the way he was looking at her. His eyes were large and sad. He looked lost in the twilight of the big room.

"All you have to do is say the word," he said.

There was more than just God. She couldn't leave her mama, in that house with her father. She couldn't leave Walter, to be raised by Howell and Vernon. He was only a boy, after all. Just a little boy.

Before she could say no, Tom kissed her. His kiss was different than she expected. Of course, there was a world of difference between kissing a thirteen-year-old boy and a thirty-year-old man, but it wasn't just that. He seemed so . . . *desperate*. His lips were different from Howell's. Softer. Hungrier. His skin too. It was soft and rough all at the same time. Her head filled with a pleasant fog at the pressure of their mouths, the burn of his whiskers. She imagined that if she could press her face against his for a long-enough time, their skin would fuse. They would become one person.

He cradled the back of her head with his hand as the other grasped the back of her dress. He pressed himself against her. Now everything was leaping and twisting inside her, pulling her toward him. She put her hands on his chest, grasped at his shirt, but he pried her fingers loose. Pushed her away.

"Jinn. You've got to go on home now," he said.

"Don't send me away—"

"We'll go to California. The first night of the revival, when everybody's busy."

"I can't—"

"I'll wait for you," he said. "You and Collie slip out. Come to the house, and we'll go. Now you've got to go on home, Jinny. We've got to play this smart." His face was so grave. Scared, she thought, with a twinge of distress. She'd never seen Tom look scared of anything. And she hated it, the both of them bruised and beaten down with fear.

"Run away with me," he said again.

She pressed the tender spot on her temple. "No," she said.

Even if it wasn't what Tom wanted to hear or what she wanted to say, the word still felt cool on her tongue. Delicious, like a sip of honeysuckle wine. If she said no to Howell like that, he'd go crazy, throw her against a wall. Then again, if he found out she'd been to Tom's house, he wouldn't just send her to Pritchard, he'd kill her.

"No," she said again, louder this time, relishing the way the word slipped from her mouth and filled up the room.

Tom smiled, like she'd said something particularly endearing, then took hold of her hand. He led her to the door and told her to go home.

Chapter Nineteen

Thursday, September 20, 2012
Tuscaloosa, Alabama

When I mentioned to the lady on the phone at Pritchard I was interested in seeing a grave of a relative who'd died while a patient, her voice took on a decidedly guarded tone. She informed me that I would need to make an appointment with an official of the hospital and, furthermore, that there was no one available for tours of the old hospital or cemeteries until Tuesday. I wanted to chuck my phone across the room in frustration.

Instead, I dropped it on the bed and pulled the painting out of the cigar box. I smoothed the tiny watercolor on the bedside table under the hanging lamp and studied it, like I'd done a hundred times before. It was the only item in the box that seemed like it could be connected to Collie, my grandmother, but I had no idea what it meant.

It was a detailed, if amateurish, work that showed two women sitting under a vine-covered arbor, facing each other. One of the women could easily be Collie—probably the younger one, the one with a dark brunette flip and pink dress. She sat with crossed legs, a cigarette aloft in her fingers. She was hunched slightly, bent toward the other woman. In fact, every inch of her—eyes, arms, legs—seemed to be trained on her companion. That woman looked older, but far more elegant. She wore a white coat with a wide collar, and her red hair was swept back in a smooth twist. Her lips were scarlet against the pale face. The initials *LW* were painted into the lower-right corner.

Collie sitting with another woman—meeting with her, maybe— the two of them deep in conversation. I thought of my mother meeting the woman at Bienville Square. The oracle, Rowe had called her.

Her honeysuckle girl.

I folded the painting and looked around the room. Four days of hanging around Crimson Terrace with nothing to do but sample all the spiciness levels of KFC fried chicken? Three more nights hiding from cockroaches in my too-short sleeping bag? It was complete and utter bullshit.

I wasn't going to do it. I couldn't afford to.

I tucked the painting into my purse and left.

❧

Driving west on 215, I tried not to think about how I'd just had to use Jay's credit card to gas up his car. And how, at this very moment, the thirty-seven-dollar charge was zooming its way to his bank statement.

I'd had no choice. But running that card through the slot on the pump released a whole herd of butterflies in my stomach. If Wynn and Dr. Duncan swooped down on me in a couple of days, I'd know Jay was an enemy. If not, I'd have to admit I'd misjudged him, and maybe, when I'd caught them about to meet in Birmingham, he'd only been trying to talk Wynn into giving up his vendetta against me.

In the distance, I saw the tall red-brick pillars that marked the entrance of Old Pritchard. I turned between two pillars crosshatched with dead vines. They bore twin bronze plaques that read, "Pritchard Hospital, Est. 1851." One of the original gates, twined with the same brown vines, had been pushed back, a rock jammed under it to keep it open. I drove between majestic rows of live oaks, bouncing over the broken-up asphalt. When I came to the circular front drive of the old hospital, I slowed. There was a huge, rusted iron fountain in the center. I maneuvered around it, marveling at the detail, then parked and climbed out.

The structure was immense—a red-brick Gothic castle, with stone-capped bay windows, crowned by a magnificent center tower and belfry that pierced the hot, cloudy sky. More towers and spires dotted the wings that flanked the main building. Two enormous magnolia trees stood sentry at the end of each massive wing. The lawn, grown high with weeds, fell away from the structure. Cicadas buzzed in the mid-morning heat. A bank of gray clouds was roiling on the horizon. I could taste rain in the air.

If what Val had said was true, my mother had been here in this very building. And my grandmother, Collie. And then both of them had died in there, somewhere, hidden away in the maze of towers and spires, windows and rooms. Once there had been hundreds of patients crammed into this place, doctors and nurses, administrators. But looking at the dark windows, I knew—my mother and my grandmother had died alone.

The sadness—their sadness—seemed to expand and fill in the spaces between my skin and veins and organs, until I wondered if I would even be able to move again.

I finally forced myself to go on. Around the east wing of the building, and down the vast, sloped grounds, I followed a promising-looking weedy path. The cemetery crowned a bald, sunbaked hill, about a quarter of a mile behind the hospital. A large filigree iron sign—new, from the looks of it, and reading "Old Pritchard Cemetery"—arched over the entrance. I was pouring sweat by the time I passed under it and looked out over the rows of neat iron crosses dotting the field.

A breeze whistled through the iron sign and lifted my soaked hair. I stared in disbelief. The cemetery was enormous; stretching for acres. There were at least a thousand graves, maybe more, stretching all the way to a line of far-off trees and crisscrossed by grassy paths. The markers—a few of which were festooned with sun-worn silk flowers—were engraved with two-, three-, and four-digit numbers. No names.

I'd never find Collie in here.

∼✦∽

"Official tours are on Tuesdays." The woman behind the desk kept her eyes trained on her computer and sucked at her teeth.

I'd managed to find the operational part of Pritchard Hospital on the far side of the property. It was closer to the interstate, across from a smattering of fields and small farmhouses. The administration building itself was a squat brick structure, the shade of an acorn squash. Just beyond it sat the three-story patient hall, a formidable U-shaped structure of matching squash-brick. Its windows were dark and covered with steel-gray screens. Over all this, in the distance, loomed the Gothic towers of the old building.

Inside, the administration building was clean and well lit, if a bit on the dingy side. Pretty much like the inside of every rehab and psych ward I'd ever seen. The smell was familiar too. It reeked of an odor I knew well—the smell of hopelessness.

"Yeah, I heard about the Tuesday thing," I said. "And I'm sorry to ask for favors, but I'm going to be out of town on Tuesday. So I was wondering"—I lowered my voice—"if it wouldn't be *too horrible* if I took care of it on my own? If you could just look up my grandmother's number, I'll scoot over there superfast, snap a pic, and be out of there in, like, nothing flat. Won't tell a soul. Tick a lock."

I flashed her a bright smile. She stared at me, dead eyed.

I leaned on the counter. "So. If you could just look up her number. Collirene Wooten Crane. Date of death, 1962."

She sucked at her teeth one more time, this time picking the offending object out with two delicately pointed coral nails. She smeared whatever it was on a napkin beside her keyboard. "Official tours are Tuesdays only," she said.

I tried my best to keep smiling as she went back to her work. But what I really wanted to do was deliver a hearty, roundhouse slap to each jowly cheek.

Down the hall, I heard a door open. An African American woman in her twenties, wearing a no-nonsense button-down and a headband that held back a sheaf of wild curls, stopped at the counter beside me. She nodded a greeting. Her eyes, behind black-rimmed glasses, were kind.

"How are you today?" she asked me.

"Oh," I said, "good, thanks." Even though I wasn't, not at the moment. But flies with honey and all that bullshit. I widened my eyes, hoping to look innocuous. "I'm just trying to locate a relative."

"A resident?"

"Former. She died in 1962."

"Oh. Well. Denise should be able to help you with that." The woman cleared her throat at her colleague across the counter. "Denise, I'm running next door for a sec."

"Uh-hm." Denise was back at her dental ministrations, this time the molars. I felt vaguely nauseated.

"Would you mind picking up my line? I've been waiting on the Foley call all day, but, I don't know, they're tied up, I guess. Anyway. I just don't want them to get my voice mail."

"Uh-hm."

The woman waited a fraction of a second, I guess for Denise to make eye contact or communicate a shred of concern, but apparently she couldn't be bothered. The woman made a sound like she might say something else, then changed her mind and left. I looked down the hall and spied her office door, opened just a crack.

"Well," I said to Denise. "I guess I'll see you Tuesday."

She didn't even grunt. I headed down the hall and glanced back quickly before slipping into the young woman's office and into her mesh office chair. Her computer screen was still up and glowing. The room smelled of spearmint and something else. Something really good, like fresh-out-of-the-oven brownies. My mouth watered as I scanned the monitor, and I realized I hadn't eaten a thing in the past twelve hours. I told myself to focus and started to click around in the open database, trying to find some file that sounded like it might contain past patients' burial numbers.

It didn't take me long to figure out that every file on her desktop was password protected. Which meant I was shit out of luck, as I pretty much sucked as a hacker.

I looked around the room, my nerves twanging. I knew I should get the hell out of there while I still had the chance, but I didn't move. I wasn't ready to give up yet. I couldn't. I hadn't found what I'd come for, and I refused to go back to the Crimson Terrace and twiddle my fingers until Tuesday.

I looked out the window beside the desk. It had finally started to rain, and there was a knot of people—patients, I guessed—working along a path leading to a soccer field. I watched them rake, hedge, and spread pine bark over begonia beds. There were a couple of teenagers too, beyond them, playing a game in the drizzle. All of them looked so normal. So sane. Why didn't they just run across the field and into the woods and disappear when no one was looking?

Then, suddenly, above them, a large, black bird appeared, circling over the kids. It cruised lazily down and landed on the top bar of the soccer goal. I sat up. The bird was huge. Not a crow. A raven. I stiffened.

There's no such thing as a . . .

In a panic, I pushed back from the desk just as the door opened, and the woman—the woman whose office I had snuck into—saw me. I stood.

"Is there something I can help you with?" she asked.

Chapter Twenty

Thursday, September 20, 2012
Tuscaloosa, Alabama

"I'm sorry . . ." I clutched my purse and rose up out of her chair, as if puppet strings lifted me.

"You're trying to locate a relative," the woman said. She clicked the door shut behind her. The sound was ominous.

My heart slammed. What should I do? *Run? Cry?* Was she going to call security on me? I found my voice. "The woman at the desk said I had to come back Tuesday, but I can't. I don't have time. It's hard to explain . . ."

Her eyebrows rose.

"I'm desperate," I said.

"Okay."

"My brother doesn't want me digging into the past. He's telling everybody I have a mental illness. Schizophrenia. He's threatening to have me committed." The words were gushing out. I ignored the churning in my gut and the blaring alarm bells in my head and let them gush.

"But you don't? Have schizophrenia?"

"No," I said as emphatically, but calmly, as I could. "I don't."

"So, your brother's a liar. And an ass."

I nodded. "That about sums it up."

She made a little *harrumph* sound. "My brother's an asshole too, for whatever it's worth. But he hasn't tried to have me committed. Not yet. That's low."

I managed a weak laugh.

"Well, I'm not a doctor," she added. "But I've got to say, you don't seem like any schizophrenic I've ever seen."

"I'm not crazy, I swear." *Not yet, anyway.* "I just want to know the truth."

She stared at me for a minute, and I could see the gears turning. "What's your name?"

I hesitated.

"Just start with your name. We'll go from there. I'm Beth." She offered her hand and I took it.

"Althea. Althea Bell."

Her eyes flashed in recognition. "Bell. You mean, as in Wynn Bell? The guy running for governor?"

"Yes."

She whistled. "Wynn Bell is trying to lock you up?"

"I know it sounds crazy." I shook my head. "But yes."

"Interesting." She regarded me for a moment, her eyes narrowed, then brushed past me and scooted up to the computer. "Would you mind telling me her name? Your relative's?"

I straightened. "Collirene Crane."

She tapped at the keyboard.

"But I'm also looking for my mom. Trix Bell. She died in 1987."

"Hm. Yeah," she said after a while. "Collirene Crane, I see. No Trix Bell here, though." She regarded me through the black-framed glasses. "I'm sorry. She was your mother, right?"

"Yes."

"Are you sure she was here at Pritchard?"

"Not exactly. She was . . . There are conflicting stories."

She tilted her head, gave me a sympathetic look. "Not surprising."

"What do you mean?"

"Even as recently as the eighties, there was a stigma attached to being hospitalized. Some families wanted it kept quiet, so they'd bury the paperwork."

"The hospital would let people erase records? Just like that?"

She pressed her lips together. "You have no idea, the things that have gone on here. Pritchard was known for being a place where a lot of things were overlooked. Accurate records, for example. So . . . Collirene Crane." She tapped again. "1962. Here she is. Buried in . . ." Her voice trailed off.

"What?"

"Nothing. It's just that—" She leaned forward. Adjusted her glasses. "It says she's buried in Historic Number Four. The black cemetery."

My stomach lurched. "I don't understand. She was white. Is that normal?"

When her eyes met mine, I saw that it wasn't. That a white woman being buried in the black cemetery was, in fact, very strange. Panic rose in my throat again, and my hand pressed against my purse. I pictured the Lortab and Dilaudid buried at the bottom.

"It's . . . unexpected," the woman said, at last. "I'll say that."

"Could it be a mistake?"

"There's no other record of her being buried in any of the other cemeteries."

"But why would she have been buried there?"

She drummed her fingers on the desk distractedly. "I don't know. But I tell you this, I'd sure like to find out."

"You would?" I said. "What do you mean?"

She bit her lip.

"You can trust me, I swear."

"Your brother," she said. "He came here, to Pritchard, not too long ago."

"My brother was here?"

"When the memorial committee toured the hospital. While the historic preservation guys walked through the wards, your brother sat in the main office. Like he didn't want to catch crazy-person cooties." She folded her arms. "I introduced myself. Talked to him for a minute or two, about the memorial. He was . . . unhelpful, to say the least. I got the distinct impression he didn't appreciate my questions."

I held my breath.

"I'll admit, I was grilling him on some things. Specifically, if the committee planned to include some kind of acknowledgment of the lost patients."

"Lost patients?"

"Most of the old state mental institutions had their share of lost patients, especially during the early 1900s, before the government cracked down and enforced the new regulations. They were the patients who 'went missing,' who died as a result of abuse or neglect. A lot of them had no family. Or had the misfortune of being black. I've been researching, reading these horrific accounts. Anyway, it's something of a pet project of mine."

I felt cold. "Do you think my grandmother is one of those, the disappeared?"

"I don't know, but we're sure as hell going to find out."

❧

Beth and I rode in one of the hospital's utility vehicles through several wood-fenced fields. The paved road led through the fields, past a broken-down barn and smaller outbuildings that were in various stages of rot. We turned left onto faint dirt tracks, which led into the woods.

We wound our way through the trees and then, with no warning at all, Beth hit the brakes.

"This is it."

I climbed out. Rain pelted the spreading canopy of leaves above us, but we stayed mostly dry. She led me down the hill to a large cleared area of about an acre, ringed by a makeshift wall of piled stones. There was no sign. Nothing announcing the resting place of hundreds of souls.

A dull dread washed over me but I suppressed it and walked past Beth, stepping over the low stone wall and into the sea of graves. Some were marked with clover-shaped iron crosses, the letters *PIH* engraved on them. *Pritchard Insane Hospital.* The rest were marked with bricks sunk into the ground. There were no paths, no grass, no flowers. Just the blanket of slick, brown leaves.

"In the old days they used to mark the graves with wooden crosses," Beth said behind me. "Then they started using iron ones. They used the stones starting around 1940." She looked down at her papers. "If I'm right, your grandma's number would be in that section." She pointed to our right.

I couldn't move.

Beth tilted her head. "Althea?"

I wanted to say I was afraid, but I didn't. I couldn't say something like that, out loud, to a stranger. But I could feel myself slipping. Jay was gone. My father and my brother had turned against me. I was the only one left who could figure out what had really happened to the women in my family. The search began and ended with me.

"Will you help me find it?"

In answer, she walked past me, up the row, head down, reading. I followed her, avoiding the bricks. There was something unbearably sad about their simplicity.

She was standing just a couple of yards down the row when she pointed down. "Althea."

"You found it?"

I hurried to her, my face a question. "You see here? There's 4627, 4628, then 4630. She should be here, right in this area. But . . ." She glanced around.

"Where is she? Could they have put her somewhere else?"

"Maybe." She looked doubtful. "Possibly on the end of a row."

We scanned every row—up and down, multiple times—even the ones that were nowhere near the sequence. After we'd been at it for more than thirty minutes, I had to accept that patient 4629 wasn't going to be found.

I pressed the heels of my hands into my eyes, making spots of color flash across my field of vision. My mother was lost to me, and now my grandmother too. Maybe finding Collie here wouldn't have answered any questions, but I'd hoped that at least seeing her final resting place would have given me a sense of resolution. And maybe the glimmer of an idea of what to do next. But it appeared she wasn't here. And I had no idea where she might be. So what was I supposed to do? How was I supposed to learn anything if all these women's lives were nothing but vast blank spaces?

And there was the issue of Wynn. I had no idea where he was; he could be following me right this minute. Waiting for me to make one wrong move so he had a justifiable reason to lock me up.

Tears pooled in my eyes, and my throat burned. Then I heard Beth's voice behind me.

"There are some documents," she said softly. "I haven't read them all as thoroughly as I'd like, but . . ." I felt the tap of cardboard on my shoulder. A brown expanding file, secured with an elastic band. She must've slipped it into the utility vehicle's cargo box before we left.

She handed the file to me. "You're supposed to fill out a Disclosure Consent Form—"

"I'll do whatever," I said.

"—and then typically it has to go through channels."

I ran my fingers along the edge of the flap, as if the contents inside were radioactive.

"It's everything I could find," she said. "Her admittance information, a visitor log, and some doctor's notes. Not much, but it's the best I could do. I haven't reviewed them myself. So"—she shifted her weight and lowered her voice—"just don't tell anyone."

"Thank you."

"It's okay. I don't know why she was listed as being buried with the black patients. She might've actually been housed with them for some reason. I imagine . . ."

"What?"

"That, if she had, it might've been some form of . . . punishment. A warning, maybe."

"Or it could've been another way to hide her," I said. "To keep anyone from finding out what happened to her."

I looked out across the cemetery into the woods. Ropes of dead vines had choked the low branches of the scrub trees that ringed the clearing. They made the place look even spookier. There should've been flowers here, with these forgotten people, instead of more death.

I glanced at Beth. "She would've been fine here. It's a nice spot."

"Yes, it is." We both gazed across the peaceful, damp clearing, then she gave me a brief nod. "I'll be in the car."

I stood where Collie's grave should've been until it started to grow dark, the closed file in my hands, rain misting down over me.

⁂

On my way out, as I passed the looming old hospital, I slowed to a stop. I studied the massive door through the rain-smeared window. It didn't make any sense, I knew, putting myself in the place where my mother and grandmother had spent time and expecting it to shed light on their situations. It was loopy, new-age-style thinking. But maybe I wasn't so opposed to loopy anymore. Maybe this was worth a try.

I grabbed the file and scurried through the sheeting rain to the vestibule. The massive door gave way when I pushed it, so I slipped in and shut it behind me. It clunked with a finality that sent a shiver down my spine. I walked into the center of the hall. Gray light shone weakly through the dirty windows. The floor had once been white marble—it was spiderwebbed now with cracks and stained brown, large chunks of it missing. A giant brass chandelier festooned with cobwebs, Mardi Gras beads, and a couple of bras and grungy underpants. *College kids*, I thought, *breaking into a haunted insane asylum for kicks*.

I looked up. A soaring staircase—marble laid with a faded red runner—rose up from the center of the hallway and then split, leading the ways to the opposite wings. Strips of mildewed wallpaper hung from the graffiti-sprayed walls. I stood as still as I could, tried to ignore my thumping heart, and listened.

There was no one here. And yet, the place seemed crowded with life and sorrow and death. A million stories.

I dropped down on a marble step and opened the file. The first sheet was a copy of Collie's visitor log. There were only two names: David Crane and Lindy Wade. David, Collie's husband, my grandfather. He'd visited once, on June 12, 1962, and he'd stayed for an hour. Lindy Wade had visited exactly seven days later, June 19, 1962. She'd come in the morning and stayed all day, signing out at nine o'clock that night. Beside her name, in the spot labeled "Description," was written *Friend*.

I turned to the next page in the file. It was Collie's medical history, forms filled out by her doctor. The words *schizophrenia, depression, mania* jumped out at me. I read more. *Patient demonstrates a blunt affect, obsession with deceased mother. Ruminating thoughts manifest in the repetition of a Latin prayer. She reports experiencing auditory and visual hallucinations, delusions of a religious and racial nature, paranoia, and suicidal thoughts.*

I looked up, afraid to read further, my heart thumping so hard I thought my ribs would crack. A Latin prayer. Hallucinations and delusions.

Like red ravens or traces of gold dust on hairbrush handles?

This sounded like it could be a description of me.

I looked back down again: *Haldol, Thorazine, Clozaril.* I read further down, hitting a line that stopped me cold.

Lobotomy.

Procedure performed by staff June 22, 1962. Successful. Patient is calmer, more docile, although intermittent episodes of paranoia continue.

There was no mention of her death. No mention of "intentional injury."

"My God." I dropped the paper.

After pouring drugs into Collie, they'd performed a lobotomy on her? The horror of it washed over me, and tears welled in my eyes. I swiped at them, but I couldn't slow my breathing. I could hear it, shallow, with a hitch of desperation in it. It wasn't just sadness I was feeling. It was overwhelming fear.

What would they do to me? More pills? Electroshock therapy? I thought I'd heard they still did it, for some people. Were there other things—more horrific procedures that awaited me?

I kept sucking in air, my face tilted to the ceiling. If I kept this up, I'd hyperventilate. Pass out in this haunted house.

Stop it. You have to stop.

I picked up the papers, shuffled them together on my lap, forcing myself to hold my breath. I moved the medical file to the back of the pile and looked at the next document.

Collirene Crane's admittance record.

It was dated June 3, 1962, and stated that she had been admitted at 8:35 a.m. by her brother, Mr. Walter Wooten. There were no doctor's orders or medical files accompanying her. Reason for commitment: *dementia.* And then, at the bottom, there was a note, written in the margins of the paper in an elegant hand. *Patient is to be housed with colored population on request of Mr. Walter Wooten.*

I looked back at the visitor log. My brain started to ping, as if I could actually feel the connections falling into place. I thought of the painting of the two women with the signature *LW. LW.* Lindy Wade—the name on Collie's visitor log.

Lindy Wade—the artist who'd painted the picture of my grandmother and the other woman.

Lindy Wade—Friend.

Chapter Twenty-One

October 1937
Sybil Valley, Alabama

Before the end of the month, Howell Wooten had to go to Huntsville three more times. The CCC boys were planting pine saplings, cutting paths through Monte Sano Park, and building trail shelters, and even though Howell grumbled that he was a farmer and not a government hand, Jinn knew they were lucky he'd gotten the job. He'd had to say he was unmarried in order to get it, but he reckoned nobody was going to bother and tromp all the way up Brood Mountain to check if there was a wife and kids sitting around the table in his cabin.

When Howell went off to Huntsville, Jinn went up to Tom Stocker's house. She waited until Walter got off to school and Collie to Aggie's, then she took a stroll up Old Cemetery Road to make sure there weren't any neighbors watching from porches or fields. If things looked quiet, she walked the rest of the way up. She wasn't so awed by the big brick place anymore. Nor did she feel one bit shabby when she stepped onto the wide front porch. It was probably because Tom broke into such a wide grin the minute he put eyes on her. That grin made him look like a boy. It made her heart feel it might crash right through her ribs.

The first time she visited Tom, he led her to a nook under the staircase, out of sight of the windows. They stood, pressed together, and kissed and touched until their mouths were raw and they'd felt just about all they could of each other's bodies through their clothes. He whispered feverishly to her, about California and Hollywood and the Pacific Ocean, and, even though she didn't say she'd go, she dropped a kiss on his neck, just under his collar. The sun shone year-round out there, Tom said, trailing kisses along the rise of her jaw, up to her bruised temple. You didn't even need a fireplace, he said. There were palm trees, a thousand cars, and castles set on cliffs. After he said this, they kissed again.

They never went upstairs. He wouldn't. He wanted her as his wife and told her so.

She didn't say yes, but she didn't say no either.

He caught her hand as she was leaving. "The Sunset Limited runs from New Orleans to Los Angeles. I could buy two tickets for you and Collie. Two for me and Willie."

She thought of Howell and her duty before God. She thought of Walter and the calf strung up, black against the sky. She smiled at Tom, but shook her head.

That night, her mother's soul finally left its tortured body and flew to glory, and Jinn felt a sweep of relief. The whole valley gathered at the church a couple of days later to bury her. Howell couldn't make it back in time for the funeral, but Jinn thought it was just as well. He might have found it strange that she didn't cry at her own mother's burial.

❧

The second time Jinn went up Old Cemetery Road, Tom led her out to the back porch. As she admired the view, he pointed across the tumbled, rocky field, to each of his cows grazing along the slope.

"There's Sally, Kit, Nat and Gal and Bun."

"Bun?"

"Raisin Bun. Willie named her."

Tom didn't say what would become of the cows if they went to California. Jinn thought folks would, most likely, steal them. Not Howell. No, he'd stand right where she and Tom were standing now, lay his head over his rifle, one eye squeezed shut, and pull the trigger. Over and over, until all of Tom Stocker's cows were dropped.

"What would you do . . . if we were to go to California?" she asked Tom, to take her mind off the cows.

"Maybe timber or oil. Or maybe I'll buy us a racehorse. What do you think? You like horses?"

She nodded. She wanted to tell him about her dream too, about Myrna Loy and Hollywood and the movies, but she couldn't push the words out. Not yet. When it was time to leave, Tom mentioned the train tickets again. Again, she said no, and his face took on an intense look.

"He will kill you," he said. "He will kill you one day, if you don't go."

Jinn thought about the Lurie girl, who'd jumped off the fire tower, and her mama, wasted away in her bed. It was true; Howell could kill her, and he might. The strange thing was, the thought didn't surprise her much. It felt about the same as hearing somebody say that honeysuckle bloomed in spring. Like Howell killing her was just the natural order of things.

Her destiny.

She felt a pang of something inexpressible. Then a small vine of doubt sprouted and began to grow in a narrow crevice of her mind.

The last time Jinn went up to Tom's, he greeted her and escorted her to the library. She sat on the tufted sofa, and he on a soft leather chair. His face was gray and hard as a tombstone.

"I have a question," he said. "Are you with me?"

Her mind shot in every direction at once.

"I got to know, Jinn. Yes or no." His voice sounded strangled.

Her lips parted, and he brightened like he thought she might say something. When she didn't, he went on. "I can't sleep, Jinny. I can't eat. I got to know what you're going to decide." He clasped his hands, leaned forward. "You can't make Howell right, Jinny, you can't. Men like that tear through the world, searching out the weak, those who can't speak up for themselves. They rip through everyone they meet, not caring if they draw blood. And I can't bear it, I just can't bear it, if that happens to you."

As he talked, the vine of doubt in her head grew and spread and pushed apart her crowded brain. She felt a surge of hope rush in—it was like somebody had opened a door in her head and swept every bit of confusion and fear right out. It wasn't her destiny for Howell to knock her around, and it wasn't natural at all. Not one bit. Her mother hadn't deserved such treatment, nor had the Lurie girl. None of them did.

She stood, blood rushing through her veins, her heart pounding hard. "Get the train tickets," she said. "The first night of the revival, during the altar call, me and Collie will meet you down at the school."

Tom bounded across the room in a couple of steps and swept her into his arms. She clutched at his shirt and threaded her fingers through his hair—for the first time, holding him as tightly as she'd always wanted to.

Chapter Twenty-Two

Friday, September 21, 2012
Tuscaloosa, Alabama

Early the next morning, I settled down with Jay's iPad in my room at the Crimson Terrace. The painting was propped up on a pillow beside me. I had to move quickly; the battery was low, and I didn't have a charger.

Lindy Wade. There were the typical social-media suggestions, and the ads for "Find a Classmate," but they all linked to people too young to be Lindy. Then, toward the bottom of the page, one link caught my eye, from a 1985 issue of the *Birmingham News*. The piece centered on the unsolved disappearance of Dante Wade, one of five black Birmingham men they'd never found during the most intense years of the civil-rights movement. His house, in the Fountain Heights section of town in the neighborhood known as Dynamite Hill, had been bombed. He'd gone missing that same night. He had a mother, a father, and a sister named Lindy.

I absorbed the information: Lindy Wade, my grandmother's friend in the sixties, was black.

Once I had the name Dante Wade, the iPad practically started making that slot-machine jackpot sound. It took me only a few minutes to connect the name Lindy Wade, sister of Dante, to Dr. Linda Wade Bradley, award-winning principal of Hillyard Middle School, in a suburb of south Birmingham. Dr. Bradley was Lindy Wade, the artist of the portrait tucked inside the cigar box. She must have known my grandmother, Collie.

For the first time, I felt hesitation. Getting to Rowe and Val hadn't fazed me in the least, but this woman . . . Lindy Wade was an altogether different story. She'd probably been hounded by the press back in the day, but it didn't appear she'd been all that obliging. The only comments I'd been able to dig up were a few curt requests that the reporters leave her family in peace. As for her current Internet presence, it was practically nonexistent; I couldn't find a phone number or address, not one social-media profile. The woman was a pro.

I had the feeling my usual bluff and swagger weren't going to cut it with this woman. In fact, there was a chance nothing I could say would convince her to talk about the past. The subject matter was incendiary—Birmingham in the sixties and the unsolved, racially motivated murder of her brother—and even if Collie Crane didn't exactly figure into all that, it was clear Linda Wade Bradley was a tough nut.

Regardless, I had to try. I had to go back to Birmingham and find her; right now, it was my only lead. Lindy Wade was the only person who'd come to see Collie at the end of her life, and I had to talk to her.

Naturally, I would've rather stuck needles in my eyes than go back to Birmingham—I kept picturing a citywide manhunt for me, with Wynn and Jay spearheading the search—but I had no choice. It wasn't just about Lindy. I also needed one more conversation with my great-aunt Val—about why Walter had put his own sister in with the black patients at Pritchard. And where she was buried. Collie's story had to hold some sort of key to my own future.

I checked out of the Crimson Terrace and headed east on 20, trying to ignore the gnawing discomfort in my stomach. Nerves. It had to be. I planned to intercept Lindy at the middle school where she worked. School let out at three, and I would be there. Meanwhile, there'd be time to swing by Val Wooten's house.

I stopped at a roadside flea market on the outskirts of town and purchased a glazed pottery cross, in the hopes that, being closer to death, the old woman might be ready to purge her secrets and cleanse her soul.

My heart sank when I saw a stream of people filing into Val's house, but I went ahead, parked, and fell in line with the rest of the crowd.

It had just been four days since I'd been here, but the house was unrecognizable. Shutters and curtains had been thrown open; fresh air had blown through the cracks and corners. Cobwebs had been cleared out, curtains pulled down, trim scrubbed and oiled. The rugs were cleaned, and the dark wood floors shone. A helmet-haired woman, standing in the foyer, handed me a chunk of Day-Glo sticky notes.

"Prices are marked," she said. "No haggling. And we accept cash or check. If you want something, write your name on the paper and stick it to the item."

"Okay. Mind if I go to the back?"

"Up to you. But the best stuff's in the living room."

I walked back into the hallway and toward the kitchen, where I slid the sticky notes onto an empty shelf.

The room hadn't changed much, except they'd cleaned it and replaced the linoleum with tile. The row of pill bottles was gone, as well as the jungle of plants under the window, and it smelled like bleach. There was no trace of Val. Nor of Angela, the pill-swiping nurse. I headed back toward the bedroom at the end of the hall.

The crosses were gone, the walls bare, freshly repainted. The bed had a new spread on it, some kind of stiff, matched, floral comforter set. I stood there, trying to take it in.

Val was gone. My great-aunt. Other than my father, the only direct link to my mother and grandmother. Why hadn't I asked her more about Collie last time I was here? I wanted to kick myself for being so shortsighted. If I'd pushed harder, she would've opened up to me. Especially after having been stifled for decades by Walter and Elder.

Elder has the say-so, my ass.

I reached in my purse and pulled out the pottery cross. It was nothing special, glazed blue with a little dove stamped into the center, but I hoped she would've liked it. I walked into the room, laid it at the foot of the bed.

"I know you," a voice said beside me. I turned to see an older woman, midfifties, with a frizzy gray braid. She wore a shapeless denim dress that hung to the floor and feather earrings that brushed her shoulders. Her skin was leathery and crosshatched with lines. "Althea, right?" she said.

My mind pulsed with a million electrical charges—*Danger! Danger!*—synapses searching for a way to dodge this woman and run out of the house. But my feet wouldn't budge.

She held up her hands in the "don't shoot" stance. "I didn't mean to scare you. I'm really glad you came."

"I'm sorry. I don't recognize you," I finally managed.

"I'm Terri Wooten. Val and Walter's daughter. You and I are second cousins."

I knew I should touch her arm, hug her or something, but I didn't want to. "I'm so sorry about your mother," I said instead, my arms folded across my chest. I could feel my brain spiraling back down, the adrenaline draining from my body.

"She told me you came to see her." She gestured at the bed. "Well, she told me Trix came to see her, but I figured it was you. She got mixed up a lot there at the end. Traci and I have always wondered what happened to you."

She moved up beside me and saw the cross on the bed. She drew a finger over it.

"I wanted to talk to her again. I didn't know—"

"Yeah. She was pretty eaten up with the cancer," she said, then broke into a smile, like she hadn't just said those horrific words. "You know, I'm really glad to meet you. That sounds so weird, but I am. It seems so strange we never met each other. But I guess families can be funny that way. I guess your father didn't want you and your brother to mix with the crazy side of the family. Your mother's side."

She laughed, but dread shot through me. Did she even know what she was saying? Had she heard about Trix and Collie and Jinn? It was hard to tell. I decided to tread lightly, see what I could get from her.

"You knew my mother, right?" I asked mildly.

She nodded. "Traci and I used to play with Trix all the time when we were little—after her mama, after Aunt Collie died."

I hadn't expected this woman—this stranger, with her earthmother getup and frank eyes—to refer to my mother with such a warm tone in her voice. My eyes swam with tears, and her forehead creased. She reached out a hand. "Oh, hon. I'm sorry. This must be hard for you too."

I shook my head. "I just have so many questions."

"Like what?" She smiled.

"Like . . ." I faltered.

She watched me expectantly.

"Well," I said. "I don't know what happened to my mother. To Trix. My father told us, told everybody she died of an aneurysm in the ambulance on the way to the hospital. Her death certificate says it was seizures. Recently, though, he told us she died of an overdose. We can't be sure. He has Alzheimer's."

"I didn't know. I'm sorry."

I nodded. "When I spoke with your mother, she said Trix was admitted to Pritchard Hospital and died sometime later."

At the word Pritchard, Terri's eyes clouded. "Oh. Well. I wouldn't really know anything about that."

"Really? Your mother never said anything?"

"No."

"Well, also I found out . . . Somebody told me Trix took a shot at your parents . . . with your father's gun. Maybe that's why they sent her to Pritchard."

"I might've heard about the gun thing," she said. "But only in passing." She shook her head. "Look, my father, Walter, was an interesting man. A product of his upbringing, you might say. I know some of his problems had to do with losing his mother, Jinn, at such a young age. But he never talked about it. Men like him just didn't do that. But it took its toll. I did have my suspicions over the years . . ."

"About what?"

"That he had his finger in some bad stuff."

"What do you mean?"

"Well, for one thing, my sister and I . . ." She smoothed her dress and shifted uncomfortably. "We've come to believe he was in the KKK."

I swallowed. "Really?"

"He used to ride night patrol with the police back in the sixties. That's what they did around here back then. In the early days, when tensions were heating up, each police car would have someone from the Klan, to help keep an eye on things. To see who was doing what. Who was stirring things up or getting into trouble or . . . whatever." She stopped abruptly, shut her mouth, then covered her lips with the tips of her fingers. Her eyes had gone wide and watery. Her face, crumpled in shame.

"It's okay, Terri," I said gently. "We're family. You can tell me."

She looked back at the empty bed. "He'd go out right after supper. He'd pull his rifle down from the mantel, and he'd be gone all night."

"Was he ever . . ." My mind went to the article I'd read about Dante Wade, Lindy Wade's missing brother. "Was he involved in any particular . . . incidents?"

She shrugged. "I don't know. That's a question I've asked myself a hundred times. Nobody talked about that kind of thing back then. It just wasn't done. But I know people got killed."

"His sister was killed. Collie."

Her eyes flickered. "No, you've got that part wrong. Aunt Collie was sick. She had a nervous breakdown, and they had to have her committed."

"Your father, Walter, had her committed," I said. "Did you know he had her put in with the black patients at Pritchard?"

Her jaw slacked. "What?"

"It's in her records."

"He couldn't have."

"I went to Pritchard. I saw the records."

She shook her head. "He would never have done that. Put his own sister in with the black patients? No. Not in a million years."

"He did, though. He requested that she be housed with the black patients. And even though she died there—from suicide, supposedly— no one can show me her grave. No one knows where Collie is buried. She's missing, Terri. Your aunt, my grandmother, is missing."

I could see her eyes harden, the lines around her mouth pinch. She was going to defend her father to the death, that much was clear. Family loyalty would prevail.

I changed the subject. "So do you know what kind of breakdown Collie had? Did anyone talk about that?"

"All my mom ever said was Aunt Collie was just like her mother Jinn and her daughter Trix. She said all mountain girls were the same."

I straightened. "What's that supposed to mean?"

"That they had mountain blood. It was just another way of saying they were different from us."

"Different?"

"Tacky. Loud and ignorant. Not like girls from down here. Mama said mountain girls were all half-crazy."

"Crazy, like schizophrenic?"

She shrugged. "More like an all-purpose kind of crazy. Everyone always told stories about the women who came from north Alabama. They were a whole species unto themselves. Growing up in those hollows, all hidden and hermit-like. Steeped in that mountain religion, getting the Spirit and falling out. Snake handling and saying they see Jesus in the pine paneling. My mama said they were all of the devil. She said Aunt Collie probably did witchcraft."

She scrunched her face in an attempt at a chuckle, but I could see she didn't really think it was funny. She believed all this nonsense—that Trix and Collie were weird, probably even insane. I smiled, even as my stomach did a slow roll. I had that mountain blood too. I'd seen things, felt reality shimmer and bend right before my eyes. I wondered what Terri would think of me if I told her all that. I took a breath, looked down at the carpet.

I am not my mother.

The honeysuckle girl isn't real.

I do not have gold dust on my fingertips.

There's no such thing as a red raven.

When my gut had settled, I cleared my throat. "Your parents didn't mention anything about Collie meeting with a woman before she had her breakdown?" I didn't say it—*the honeysuckle girl*. I had a feeling if I did, Terri would probably turn tail and run.

She shook her head. "They didn't talk about it. I think they were ashamed about the whole situation, to be honest."

So Trix had had some sort of freak-out in Walter's presence and was hustled off to Pritchard because of it. Collie had ended up at Pritchard too, courtesy of Walter. And gone missing on top of that. It could've been schizophrenia that had landed both women there, but that explanation seemed too easy. Especially now that I knew about the other strange occurrences: the woman my mother had met at Bienville Square. The woman in the painting with Collie. The strange death of the paramedic who'd signed my mom's death certificate.

There were too many missing pieces.

Terri was quiet for a minute, then looked at me with solemn eyes. "Will you come with me for a minute? I want to show you something."

I followed her out of the bedroom, back into the cavernous, paneled living room, which was crowded with people. At the soaring stone fireplace, she stopped and looked up. I followed her gaze, all the way up to the rusty rifle balanced on a couple of nails over the center of the timber mantel.

"Excuse me, everyone," she said. "Can we have a minute?" The people drifted to the other side of the room by the walls of bookcases, watching us, and she turned to me. "Dad's rifle. It's an antique. Valuable, maybe. I don't know. He got it from his grandfather when he was a boy."

We both stared up at the gun. Then Terri pulled a chair over from the corner, set it on the hearth and, hiking up her dress, climbed up and took hold of the gun. She stepped down off the chair, handed it to me.

The wooden stock was heavier than I expected, the brass plate cold. I brushed my fingers over the engraving—oak leaves and acorns—and then over the action. Even though the gun was small enough for me to hold with one hand, I knew it could do real damage. My father and brother had both hunted with guns like this. Brought home limp squirrels and rabbits and raccoons that they skinned out by the shed on the old dock.

I shivered, the rifle heavy and cold in my hands. Why did I feel like I was holding generations of secrets when I held this weapon? I wondered if my mother had felt the same.

"What do you think my mother wanted with this gun that night?" I asked.

"I don't know," she said. "And I don't care to. Some things need to stay in the past."

I looked at her, my eyes wide, then down at the gun, half expecting to find streaks of gold from the pads of my fingers. All I saw was dull, brown metal.

"Can I have it?" I asked. "Not forever. Just for a while, in case there's something else I can learn."

"Take it. Keep it if you want. I certainly don't have any use for it."

The scavengers stared as I walked out, the gun at my chest. I felt like a soldier heading off to war, amped up for action, but unprepared for the dangers ahead. Whatever they were, whatever horrors were going to reveal themselves, I needed it to happen soon. I had just over a week left.

Chapter Twenty-Three

Friday, September 21, 2012
Birmingham, Alabama

At exactly three o'clock, an assembly line of shiny SUVs and sedans began their crawl past the ivy-covered brick Hillyard Middle School. The cars opened their doors, gobbled the children up, and roared off. I'd parked at an out-of-the-way corner of the lot, under the shade of a feathery mimosa tree, and reviewed my strategy.

Find Lindy Wade. Show her the painting. Beg for help.

It was a sorry-ass plan, even I could see that, but my brain didn't seem to be firing on all cylinders these days. I felt foggy and unsettled, the way I'd felt in the broken-down ruins of Old Pritchard. Like I was slowly coming apart.

I wondered if it was just anxiety over my impending birthday or if it was something more. The sickness, inching its way toward me. The spidery curse. Or maybe it was just the threat of another appearance by Wynn. I contemplated the pills stashed at the bottom of my purse. A couple—just two measly pills—would calm me, give me that extra blast of confidence I needed.

I pushed the thought out of my mind and focused on the woman I'd picked out and identified as Lindy. She had to be in her early seventies, but looked no more than fifty. She was a stunner. Willowy, with dark-brown skin and short, white hair twisted into dreadlocks. She stood in the midst of her charges, half-moon glasses perched on the end of her nose, directing the chaotic flow of adolescents around her. Throwing out a word here, a look there, all with the calm demeanor of an elder statesman. I wondered what kept her at the school, in this job, at her age. I wondered if it had anything to do with her brother, Dante. What they'd experienced.

When the last of the carpool line petered out, I locked the car and ambled toward the main doors of the school. Dr. Bradley and a young male teacher with long hair and a beard were talking. He laughed at something she said, and she looked around, catching my eye. She froze for a nanosecond, her head cocked to the side.

I started toward her, Collie's painting in my hand. Stopped in front of her just as the other teacher headed back into the school.

"Dr. Bradley?"

She raised her eyebrows, removed her glasses. "Can I help you?" She studied me, and I could've sworn I saw her swallow nervously.

"I have something that belongs to you."

I held the small watercolor out to her. She looked down at it, then up at me, then back down again. She took a step back and raised one hand, palm up as if to ward off both me and the painting.

"I think you're mistaken," she said. She spun and hurried into the building.

I took off after her, catching the door as it closed. She was moving fast, already down the hall and rounding the corner.

"Wait!" I called out. "Dr. Bradley, wait!"

I followed her to the front office, pulled open the door, and stepped in. The space was empty, save one woman behind the long counter with silver hair and a nametag that read "BARB." The woman looked at me with saucer eyes.

"Hi, Barb. Sorry to bother you," I said. "Where's Dr. Bradley's office again?"

She pointed down the hall behind her, and I skirted the end of the counter. She held up her hands and waved them at me like I was an errant airplane on the wrong runway. "Miss! She closed her door. That means she doesn't—"

I kept going, down the hall and up to the only door that was closed. I pushed it open. Dr. Bradley, seated on a leather chair behind her desk, swiveled around, looking not so much surprised as resigned.

"Dr. Bradley."

"Who are you?"

"My name is Althea Bell."

"I don't know you."

"But you know this painting."

Her eyes dropped to the pile of papers on her desk. She straightened them. Inhaled.

"Five minutes. That's all I need."

She regarded me for a minute over her glasses, then, as if she knew that was a lie, nodded at a chair across the desk. I sat and tried to ignore the discomfort that settled in my gut—residual dread left over from my school days. I'd spent more than my share of school hours on this side of a principal's desk.

"Can I ask how that painting came to be in your possession?"

"It was my mother's—Trix Crane's." I handed it to her. She pulled up her glasses and studied it, her face softening. Then the moment passed, and the light in her eyes flickered out. She handed the painting back to me.

"How is Trix?"

"She's dead," I said. "She died twenty-five years ago. I was five years old." Dr. Bradley removed her glasses and sat back against her chair. I went on. "Trix was thirty when she died, the same age her mother was when *she* died. The same age as her mother before *her*."

Dr. Bradley was silent.

I leaned forward, pushing the painting to the side, pressing my hands flat on her desk. "I turn thirty in nine days. I don't know what the hell is going on, but I don't want to die like they did. I was hoping you could help me. That you could tell me something that would keep it from happening to me."

She turned away from me, stared out the window.

"I'm very sorry for your loss," she said at last. "I looked after Trix a long time ago, when she was quite young. She was very special to me."

"Right. Just like Collie was special to you."

She didn't flinch at my words. "Miss Bell, why are you here?"

"I need your help. I need to know what you know."

"Why? What exactly do you think is going to happen to you?"

"I'm going to—" My voice caught, and I cleared my throat. "I'm going to go crazy, like they did."

"Is that what you've been told?" she asked. "Is that what you think happened? That Collie went crazy? And Trix too?"

"That or they were witches with crazy mountain blood. I've heard that one too, believe it or not." I took a breath. Tried to collect myself. "Here's the thing: everybody agrees Trix and Collie both had symptoms of something. Schizophrenia or some kind of mental illness like it. Whatever it was, they acted crazy. So they had to be dealt with."

"What exactly did Trix do, that had to be dealt with?"

"She took drugs. There were rumors about an inappropriate relationship with a teenage boy. Oh, and she fired a gun at her uncle." I swallowed. "My father was running for attorney general. She was going to jeopardize the campaign. I'm starting to think he may have killed her. Helped her overdose on Haldol pills."

"Do you believe that?"

"I don't know what to believe."

"Miss Bell," she said. "I knew your mother as a five-year-old girl. After they sent Mrs. Crane to Pritchard, Mr. Crane, David, fired me, and I never saw Trix again. I wish I could help you, but I can't."

She stood up, which, I guess, was my cue to leave. But I wasn't ready. I wasn't giving up, not yet. I stayed in my chair.

"You can help me," I said. "You can tell me about this painting. And you can tell me about the day they took Collie away."

"I don't . . ." She gazed over my head, her eyes unfocused. "I don't see how me telling you any of that will help you."

"If I know Collie's story, I can change mine. I believe that."

"It's not just Collie's story." She folded her arms over her chest. "Or yours. And if I tell you, I could put you in danger, in ways you can't even begin to understand."

"I know about your brother, Dante," I said quickly. "You don't have to go into that. I just want to hear about my grandmother."

"I can't talk about your grandmother without talking about my brother." She paused. "And other people."

"The other people are dead," I said. "Walter Wooten and his wife Val are dead."

I stood then too, and hoped she saw the sincerity in my face. I'd been hiding and lying and convincing people to believe every word I said for so long, I had no idea what my face looked like when I actually told the truth. I closed my eyes for a minute. *Trust me*, I thought. *Please.* I opened my eyes. She was watching me, her head cocked to one side.

"I know Walter is dead," she said. "I read the obituaries every day. Which is how I know his children are still alive and well. And a couple of his friends. There are still enough of those guys kicking around this city that I keep my mouth shut."

"They're not going to hurt you. They can't."

She smiled. "If it makes you feel better to believe that, go ahead."

"It's been a long time since Walter and his friends rode with the police."

"Trust me on this. People may die. Hatred doesn't. I don't think certain things will ever be forgotten. You must understand that, even after all these years, some people will do just about anything not to go to prison. Whether you believe it or not, I could still be in danger. And my family."

"I believe you, I do. But you have to believe me too. Anything you say will be between you and me. I swear that to you." I pushed the painting toward her. She picked it up, gingerly, like it might crumble in her hands. Ran her index finger down the length of the paper, then rubbed her fingers and thumb together like the paint might still be wet.

I took one step forward. "I'm not a journalist. I'm not here to do some kind of exposé on those days. I just want to know what happened to my grandmother. So I can stop it from happening to me."

She stared at the painting. Pursed her lips.

"The story doesn't go beyond these walls."

"Whatever you say."

"We weren't supposed to be friends," she said at last. "To mix black business with white. Not back in 1962. Back then our roles were clear-cut and simple, and we were supposed to stick to them. Collie Crane was my boss, and I was her maid."

Chapter Twenty-Four

Friday, September 21, 2012
Birmingham, Alabama

"Mrs. Crane was a terrible boss. She didn't need a maid, she needed a friend."

As she spoke, Dr. Bradley looked again out the window of her tiny office. The teachers were scattering to their cars and pulling out of the lot. I took the opportunity to scan the room. It was simple, neat, and it smelled like hand sanitizer. On the beige wall behind the desk, an arc of framed diplomas haloed her—University of Alabama in Birmingham, Howard, Emory.

No photographs with Oprah or Obama, though, or any other civil-rights luminaries. As the sister of a famed, still-missing activist, she had to have been invited to every awards dinner and memorial dedication in recent history. But her wall was devoid of any such evidence.

"Mrs. Crane knew I liked to draw and paint," Dr. Bradley went on. "So she bought me supplies and let me play around after I'd finished my work. She talked to me too. All the time. She told me all about her childhood up in the mountains. Her mama had gone crazy when she was little, run off with a strange man, is what she heard. She didn't know for sure, but she was always wanting to solve the mystery. She was always wanting to *do* something about it. Or just do something, in general. She was smart. And a good person."

In addition to digging up her past, Lindy told me, Collie took an interest in politics. It was in the early sixties, when the civil-rights storm had just begun to brew. She used to talk to Lindy about the various protests that were cropping up around Birmingham. Lindy avoided these conversations as best she could until Collie insisted she tell her everything.

"Somehow Collie found out my brother and I were organizing secret meetings for the young people," she explained. "Planning marches and sit-ins. We'd show up to the white folks' church services and kneel at the front steps when the services let out. I don't know how, but Collie always managed to have at least one person at the church, taking pictures, sending them to the newspaper. Sometimes, when she could, she passed messages or found us places to meet."

"I can't believe it. I had no idea."

Dr. Bradley lowered her voice. "She suspected her older brother, Walter, was KKK. One of the big guys, involved in major stuff. Cross burnings, bombings, shootings, that kind of thing. I knew she considered me a friend. But I think that's really why she wanted to help—she liked the idea of sticking it to her brother."

Whether a result of her illegal activities or her family history, Collie's anxiety skyrocketed. David, her husband, persuaded her to meet with a priest. The priest gave her a copy of a prayer, the *Veni, Creator Spiritus*, and she began to chant it on a loop, all through the day. It was her invisible, spiritual shield against the slings and arrows of the invisible enemy. Lindy couldn't help but memorize the prayer too. As did Trix, even though she was just five at the time.

In spite of Collie's fervor, nothing much had come of her underground civil-rights efforts. With her connection to Walter, Collie was a liability, and Dante put his foot down. Lindy had to stop sharing information with her. So once again, Collie turned to the real mystery that had haunted her for years—her mother's disappearance.

She showed Lindy the cigar box and the barrette her mother had given her when she was a little girl. She believed it had belonged to someone who had known her mother. Someone who could tell her what had happened.

The honeysuckle girl.

Dr. Bradley said that one day soon after, a woman had dropped by the house. Collie and the woman met outside in the backyard, under the arbor. Like she always did when she had a free moment, Lindy pulled out her art paper and brushes and painted them. But she had been inside the house, looking through a window the whole time. She hadn't heard a word of their conversation.

"So all they did was talk?" I asked.

"Yes. And then she left."

I tightened my hands around the cigar box. "Who was she?"

"I'd never seen her before. She wasn't one of the Cranes' friends and I don't think she was a member of David's family."

"What did she look like?"

"She had red hair, bright-red hair, and expensive clothes. I let her in, and she said hello. She didn't sound Southern, not exactly. I couldn't really place her accent. Anyway, Collie took her right out back, and I stayed inside."

"And afterward?"

"Collie was a mess. She stayed in the backyard, pacing, for an hour, maybe longer. Walking in circles and talking to herself. When she finally came inside, she was crying and shaking. She wouldn't even say her prayer. I asked her to lie down, but all she wanted was to go see Walter. She wouldn't say why."

"Did it seem like . . . like a psychotic break to you? Like she was hearing voices or being paranoid?"

"She was agitated, yes, maybe acting a bit paranoid. She took Trix back to her room, and they stayed there a long time."

"Could you hear what they were saying?"

"No. But when she came out, she said we had to go to Walter's house. She was insistent we had to go right then."

"Did you?"

Lindy nodded. "I drove her. We took Trix with us. Collie went inside and left us out in the car. I told Trix stories, and we sang songs. After a while, Val came out and told me to drive Trix home. She said Collie was sick, and they were going to keep her there. Look after her. When Trix and I got back to the Cranes' house, Mr. Crane fired me. He wasn't mean about it, he just said he had to let me go. I gave Trix a hug and went home, and that was the end of that."

"What about the painting?" I asked.

She touched the paper. "I gave it to Trix. As a going-away gift, I guess." Her lips curved in a slow, sad smile. "I was scared to take it with me, scared somebody would find out I'd been messing around instead of working. I knew it could get Collie in trouble, but I couldn't bring myself to destroy it. I didn't think it was important. I just . . . I thought Trix might want it, to remember me by."

I realized I was jiggling my leg like a hyper kid, ready to jump out of my skin. I told myself to stop.

"So Collie knew Walter was Klan," I said. "But do you think the woman told her something else?"

"Like what?"

"Do you think there was something . . . I don't know, mystical? Or psychic? That went on in the backyard?"

Lindy narrowed her eyes. "What in the world are you talking about?"

"I don't know." I shifted on the chair. "I've heard people believed Collie and her mother had mountain blood—like they were witches or something. Maybe this woman was a witch. Maybe she put a spell on Collie, made her lose her shit and confront Walter."

Lindy looked like she was about to burst with laughter. "You sound like my New Orleans granny, with her holy-roller, hoodoo stuff. No, there was no cauldron in the backyard. No spells or witchcraft or anything like that. All that happened was, they talked. Then Collie confronted Walter, and it didn't go well." She leveled a look at me. "He put her in Pritchard, the very same day."

I thought of Collie's file. "He put her in with the black patients."

She sighed. Sat back in her chair.

"I don't get it," I said. "Why would he do that?"

"To teach her a lesson. Scare her. Walter was a bully and a racist. If his sister said she wanted to mix with black folks, why, he was going to see to it that she got to mix with black folks."

I let this information sink in.

"You went to see her there a week later," I said. "Right?"

"Yes. She was shaking, completely out of it, nothing like her normal self."

"Drugs?"

Lindy spread her hands. "Maybe. More likely it was because she hadn't been eating or drinking. They said she wouldn't sleep. She kept talking nonsense to me about the bones. The bones and Walter's gun."

Rowe had said Mom had been obsessed with Walter's gun too. I thought of it now, hidden in the trunk of Jay's car. If it was a clue, I didn't know how to interpret it. My eyes filled with tears, and then I felt, with horror, one slip down my cheek. I pressed my fingers against the wetness, brushed it away. I was so close but, at the same time, miles away. I had a jumble of facts—these disconnected bits of information about my mother and Collie—but nothing made any sense. Nothing fit.

"I understand why you couldn't speak up or tell anybody about Walter," I said. "But why didn't you say anything to Trix? Find her later and tell her what had happened to her mother?"

"I couldn't. It was too dangerous."

I could feel the heat rising in my body. "My mother, the little girl you supposedly cared so much about, had *no* idea what had happened to her mother. She didn't know anything about the Klan. All she knew is her mother had gone off the deep end and had to be locked up. Nobody explained anything to her." I gripped the arms of the chair. "So when she opened up that box—that stupid box—you know what she found? A hair barrette, a label off a wine bottle, and a Latin prayer. Which, as you can imagine, was not a whole hell of a lot of help."

"Althea—"

I thrust out both my hands. "No! Let me tell you what Trix's solution was. Right before she turned thirty, she found a kid to sell her drugs, a wagonload of them. It ruined her, messed with her brain and her body. She was a wreck by the time my father had her locked her up. And now all I've got is that damn cigar box and a bunch of empty pill bottles that mean *nothing*. I'm no closer to really understanding what it was she had."

She leaned forward. Her eyes blazed. "The things in that box, they mean something, don't they?"

"I guess."

"Maybe Collie and Trix did find answers. From the redheaded woman. Maybe you will too."

The redheaded woman. *The honeysuckle girl.*

I pressed my fingers to my eyes. I was doing it again, getting sucked into magical thinking. The redheaded woman was just a person. A friend of Collie's. She wasn't anybody magical, some fairy godmother or superhero who was going to swoop in and save the day for me.

I could not go down this path again, believing one woman was the answer to my problems. I was sober now. I had tools, real tools, not fantasies, to help me deal with life. The honeysuckle girl wasn't real, any more than Santa Claus or the Tooth Fairy. She was just some story my mom concocted—a fairy tale to soothe a scared little girl.

Unless she wasn't.

My stomach bucked so hard I thought I was going to gag. I clapped my hand over my mouth.

Lindy reached out a hand. "Althea. Are you all right?"

I nodded, but I didn't think I was. Dizziness was washing over me, and I felt faint.

"Have they threatened to lock you up too?" she asked.

I said nothing.

"I know I'm probably the last person who should being saying this . . ." She pressed her lips together. "I hope you'll fight. I hope you'll keep searching for the woman." She leaned forward. "You may actually find the answers, to both our mysteries."

Images flashed through my mind.

Collie. Trix. Dante. The rifle.

The older woman held my gaze, and at that moment, I was sure of two things. First, that my questions kept leading me back to this mystery woman. Second, I was about to be horribly, colossally sick. Clutching my stomach, I clawed at the arm of my chair, leaned over, and vomited out the entire contents of my stomach on Dr. Linda Wade Bradley's tastefully patterned carpet.

Chapter Twenty-Five

Saturday, September 22, 2012
Birmingham, Alabama

I lay spread-eagled on top of the hotel bed and let the shards of morning sun split my head. Awful didn't begin to describe how I felt, caught somewhere between hungover and the flu. I walked through the previous day in my head: leaving the school, driving back to my hotel. A string of catnaps punctuated by bouts of violent heaving into the toilet.

I hadn't been this sick since rehab. But this wasn't like withdrawal, it was different. Deeper in my gut, something immensely unsettled. It had to have been something I ate or a virus. A parasite I'd picked up at the Crimson Terrace.

I reached for my phone and squinted at the screen. Saturday. I had two missed calls and two voice mails. The first was from Terri, my newly discovered second cousin, inviting me to brunch at her parents' house Sunday. Her sister Traci would be there.

I should go. It was possible Traci would have more information about my mom or Collie. Something more about the mysterious days between their confinement at Pritchard and their actual deaths. Or any clue about the ever-elusive woman who'd met with Collie and my mom.

But I didn't know if I'd be able to drag myself out of this room, much less focus on what they had to say. All I could feel was the horrible, endless twisting inside.

The second message was from Jay.

"Althea." His voice sounded tentative, nervous. I closed my eyes, braced myself. "I know you're mad, but you have to know, I'm concerned about you. Everyone's concerned about you."

I hit "Delete."

He was right. I was mad. I'd trusted him with my darkest secrets, only to find out he'd been communicating with Wynn. He couldn't be trusted. I didn't want to hear a word he had to say.

I bet everyone was concerned about me. *They should be.* I was mad as hell. Jay had no idea how angry I was. The last thing I needed was his and Wynn's concern. In fact, I needed it like I needed a fifth of vodka. And a handful of pills.

At the thought of alcohol, my stomach slithered and turned, and I felt saliva rise up in my mouth. In a panic, I leapt off the bed. Raced to the bathroom, sank to my knees, and vomited again.

Chapter Twenty-Six

October 1937
Sybil Valley, Alabama

Charles Jarrod's baritone, confident and slightly off-key, rang out over the rest of the voices under the tent. Jinn held Collie's hand—she could feel the little girl's fingers tighten around hers in excitement—as they filed in behind Howell and Walter.

Jinn could feel the press of the strangers—they probably numbered over a hundred—from as far away as Georgia and Tennessee, and they filled the tent with the scents of unfamiliar laundry soap and tobacco hastily spit out in the shadows. Charles Jarrod, *the* Charles Jarrod, had come to Sybil Valley. Everyone sang with the evangelist:

> *Breathe on me, breath of God,*
> *Fill me with life anew,*
> *That I may love what Thou dost love,*
> *And do what Thou wouldst do.*

Jinn laid a hand on Collie's head as Howell led them to the right side of the tent to sit on the benches the men had hammered together just that afternoon. They slipped in, first Collie and Jinn, then Walter. Howell took the end seat, planting his elbows on his knees. Jinn looked around for her father but couldn't see him.

Jarrod led the third verse of the hymn, waving his arms at the congregation like a band conductor. Jinn craned her neck, looking for Jarrod's wife, Dove, the one everybody'd been talking about. The story went that Jarrod had seen her laid out, flat on the floor, at a revival out in California and that she was so beautiful, he'd fallen right in love with her. Jinn couldn't wait to get a glimpse. Unfortunately, the tent was packed with so many people, she doubted she'd be able to spot her in the throng.

Tom was the one who'd told her about Dove. Two days ago, while Howell was still in Huntsville and the men had met to raise the tent out behind the church, Jinn and Tom had ended up standing together under the shade of the massive oak in the yard.

"They say she's outlaw Dell Davidson's half sister," Tom had said to her. By then, the other men had gathered around the tree too, gulped a few glasses of lemonade and trooped back to work. Tom was still there; he sipped a good bit slower. Jinn stood a couple of feet from him, her arms folded over her chest.

"Of course, she and Brother Jarrod don't talk publicly about that," Tom went on. "I expect they don't want to attract the wrong crowd." He shot her a quick grin but it quickly faded. This was how he looked at her now, like she held the fate of both their lives in her hands. She pretended not to notice but she flushed anyway.

"But those are his best customers," she said. "The ones who've done something they want to undo."

He didn't smile, just looked at her until she felt the flush move from her face down to other parts of her body. He stuffed the rest of the cookie in his mouth and finished off the lemonade.

"See you, Jinny." He wiped his hands on his jeans and jogged back to the half-raised tent. Her eyes followed him, and she thought of his mouth, the pressure of it on hers, as they stood together in the nook under his stairs. She watched him shoulder a mallet. Arc it around to smash a metal peg. The muscles in his arms twisted out from his rolled cuffs, moving under his skin. She thought of sliding her fingers under the cuff, up the length of his forearms, until she reached the knob of his shoulder. Moving them across the hollow and rise of his chest.

Now, in the charged night air, the crowds filled the tent and the Wooten family settled on their bench. From her seat, Jinn spotted Dove Jarrod. The woman sat in the front row, back straight as an arrow. She was wearing a fine, ivory silk dress with a pink camellia pinned to the collar. She was young—a girl, really, but her hair was redder than any hair Jinn had ever seen, bobbed, waved, and held back with a dainty gold-and-ivory barrette. Dove's eyes were fastened on her husband, her hands folded demurely in her lap. Jinn craned her neck to get a better view, but all she could see was red lips and the curve of her jaw. And that hair. It glowed like a sunset.

Jinn felt Howell's eyes on her and forced her gaze away from Mrs. Jarrod. She told herself to concentrate. To open her heart to the Lord. He would speak to her, even though she'd strayed from the path. He would give her a sign that Walter would be safe.

"God Almighty has put the state of Alabama on my wife's heart," Jarrod was thundering. "For months and months now, in the watches of the night, she's been plagued with terrible visions . . ."

The entire tent drew in their breath. Jinn saw Dove's back straighten, then Jarrod glance at her and continue.

". . . visions too terrible to describe, but such that she implored me to travel here, all the way from California, to give you the Word of the Lord."

Everybody out in California, Jarrod said, was being filled with the Holy Spirit. Just like in the Bible days when the apostles were filled on the day of Pentecost. Every day, out there, they were witnessing the fact that God was as real and scientific as electricity. It was like you were the wire, and the Spirit was the current that would go right through you and into whoever you laid hands on. Sometimes He'd send healing. Sometimes visions or prophecies. However it happened, the important thing was to be obedient and do as He led.

Jinn thought of the Holy Spirit out in California. She pictured it flying over cars, palm trees, and castles, swooping up the faces of cliffs. She imagined it gliding down to her house—maybe they'd have gotten a bungalow on the beach—curling around the cornices, misting the windows with its breath as it spied on her and Tom. Her stomach dropped.

By the end of the message, when Jarrod gave the invitation, nearly half the tent surged to the stage, all of them dropping to their knees, sobbing and carrying on. The pianist started up playing again, and Jinn slid to the edge of the bench.

Jarrod picked his way through the people, laying his hands on their heads. Sometimes he'd kneel and speak to one of them, a few quiet words no one could hear. By now, Jinn had Collie's hand and was trying to catch Howell's eye. She would tell him she needed to take Collie home, that the girl wasn't feeling well. But her husband seemed to be lost in his own world. He was hunched over his knees, hands clasped, staring at the ground. Jinn jiggled her leg nervously. Thought of Tom down at the schoolhouse, waiting.

Dove had shifted now, in the cleared-out rows ahead of Jinn. Her arm rested along the back of the bench; her gaze roved over the crowd. The girl looked right at her, and Jinn just about stopped breathing. Her eyes were large and unflinching. And when they settled on Jinn, something seemed to awaken in them.

Then Dove's gaze moved left. Past Collie, sleeping against Jinn's side, past Walter, fiddling with his pocketknife, finally landing on Howell. As she looked at him, she lifted one delicate, red eyebrow.

Faster than you could say jackrabbit, Jinn heard a yelp and watched her burly, blond husband leap straight up from his spot on the bench and clamber over the benches that lay between him and the stage. She jolted upright, jarring Collie awake. Walter sat up too.

"What's he doing?" Walter whispered.

Howell flung himself facedown on the hay and lay there—one hand reaching up as if he was the beggar sitting at the temple gates waiting for Jesus Himself to pass.

"Where'd Daddy go?" Collie asked, scrambling up to stand on the bench and rubbing her eyes. Jinn yanked her back down.

"He's gone for prayer and healing," she said.

"He's sick?" Collie said.

Down front, Howell wept. Jinn stole another glance at Dove, who was watching him with narrowed eyes. From the masses of writhing people, Charles Jarrod materialized. He squatted beside Howell and laid one hand on the weeping man's shoulder. Howell quieted, as Charles bent to whisper in his ear. After a bit, Howell turned his head and whispered back.

Charles pulled Howell to his feet. Little bits of hay and clumps of dirt clung to his shirt and pants, and his tie was flipped over his shoulder. Jarrod laid a hand on his shoulder, leaned into his ear, and spoke again. Howell pulled his handkerchief out of his pocket and wiped his face, nodding periodically. Then the evangelist addressed the crowd.

"This man has confessed his sin and bent his knee to Jesus!" he boomed across the tent. "Will all God's people say amen?"

People from all over the tent angled their faces toward Jarrod and Howell. Jinn's heart skittered.

"Amen," they said.

"Will all God's people vow to stand beside this man as he walks in the newness of God's forgiveness? As he vows to love his wife, as Christ loves the church, and from here on out?"

"Amen," the people said with gusto.

A prickle of dread ran down Jinn's back. Howell must've told the man about the times he'd given her a thrashing, knocked her to the floor or against the wall of their cabin. But now he aimed to treat her better. He pledged it before God and everyone he knew.

"God will make this man right. The Lord God Almighty! Glory to Him!" Charles Jarrod clapped Howell on the shoulder. Howell flinched ever so slightly, turned, and found Jinn's eyes.

His cheeks were flushed, creased by his shirtsleeves, and there were traces of tears and dirt on his face. She could see, even in the dim light of the tent, beneath the film of embarrassment that lay over his features, an expression she'd never seen in her husband's eyes. It was resolve.

A quiet dread crept into her heart. She didn't know why, exactly. She shouldn't be afraid; she should be glad. She should be thanking the Lord right now with a grateful heart. Hadn't she just seen the man repent? Hadn't she just witnessed him go up front and bow his knee? God had done something tonight, under the white tent. He'd made Howell right.

She couldn't go off with Tom now. Not after what God had done. Not after He'd worked a miracle and set her husband right. If she left Howell now that he'd repented, she'd be worse than backslid. She'd be damned.

Chapter Twenty-Seven

Sunday, September 23, 2012
Birmingham, Alabama

Clouds scudded across the sky, darkening the afternoon sun so much it looked near twilight. I parked on the Wootens' road. To my left, the bluff dropped away; to my right, the Wooten house loomed. A "For Sale" sign squeaked in the wind, and I noticed that, unlike during the open house two days ago, all the shades were drawn.

Terri and Traci were inside waiting for me; we were going to have dinner and talk. But the house looked unusually dark. An odd feeling struck me, some faint premonition I should turn back.

It had to be the remnants of the stomach bug. Shaking the thing had seemed next to impossible—an uneasy feeling still rumbled in my gut even after lying motionless in the hotel bed all day. I gritted my teeth, hauled myself out of the car, and started across the street.

Halfway up the front walk, from some shadowed part of the yard, Rowe Oliver materialized before me. He had a baseball cap pulled down low over his eyes, and his chin jutted at me. He didn't look like the doughy mass I remembered from the hotel room. He looked like an ox. A really pissed-off ox. I tensed to run.

Before I could spring away, he grabbed my arm, right above the elbow, and squeezed hard, pivoting me around and pushing me forward. Away from the house and my cousins and safety.

"Rowe . . ." I said. He shoved me again, hard. My mind began ticking wildly through options. Talk to him, appease him, promise him . . . anything. Scream, run, kick him in the balls. But I couldn't do any of those.

I was frozen in fear.

He prodded me, one finger stuck in the small of my back, as we crossed the street. I looked left and right—but there was no one. The neighborhood was deserted. Just past Jay's car we came to the strip of grass that bordered the crest of the bluff. The lights of the city below were starting to blink on in the late dusk. Smog hung low between the hills.

I gave him a pleading look. "Rowe, I know you're mad. You should be. What I did to you was shitty. But I swear to you, on my mother's"— *life*, I almost said, then stopped myself—"on my mother's grave, I'd never say a word to *anyone*. You've got to believe me. I'll never tell a soul what you did."

He reached for me, and I sidestepped him, but it was too late. My vision was telescoping, the edges of things feathering to black. I felt like I was going back—back to the Olivers' dank basement, back to the smell of mildew. The feel of the scratchy old sofa.

Back to knowing I should get up and walk out, but staying anyway.

I wrapped my arms around my torso because I'd started to shake. "Veni, Creator Spiritus," I said, under my breath.

He wheezed out a sigh. "Jeez, Althea, c'mon." He took a step forward.

I stepped back. "Mentes tuorum visita."

"Don't." He beckoned me to him. "Cut it out."

I took another step back. Spoke louder. "Imple superna gratia, quae tu creasti pectora!"

He darted at me and, with a lightning-fast jab, pushed me over the edge of the hill. Tumbling down, I pitched headlong down the embankment. My hands instinctively scrabbled out, and after sliding several yards, I snagged the branch of a spindly tree. My body swung around, and my shoulder socket popped, sending shock waves down my arm. I hung on and hauled myself upright, trying to plant my feet to keep from sliding further. Panting, I peered back up the hill.

Rowe wasn't far behind me, slipping down the same track I'd cut. When he reached me, he grabbed a fistful of my shirt, spun me around, and slammed me to the ground. My head burst with a sharp, hot pain. A shower of white spots dotted my vision.

I screamed. I screamed the way I should have all those years ago, loud and long and full-throated, with every bit of resistance I had in me. I screamed and screamed until he clamped one hand over my mouth, pressed my head hard into the dirt and grass. Flashes of light exploded inside my head.

I arched against his hand. *Air. I need air.*

Even though I was kicking, Rowe managed to grab me, digging his thumb into my hipbone. I cried out in pain, but the sound was barely audible.

"Stop," he hissed. "Stop it."

I looked into his face. He was pale, but his eyes shone like two bright orbs. I thought of Walter's rifle and wished I had it. I imagined pointing it between those eyes and pulling the trigger. Exploding Rowe's skull into a thousand pieces.

"Dammit, Althea," he said. "Would you just hold still for a second?"

He jerked back, releasing his grip on my face. I sucked in a lungful of air. And another.

"Don't," I gasped. "Please, don't hurt me."

"Shut up, will you? Jesus Christ!" He took a breath. "I'm here because I need to tell you something before he . . . I remembered something."

I gulped back the rest of my diatribe, stunned into silence. I felt something crawl down my neck and into my shirt—ants, probably—but I didn't move. He'd scooted a couple of feet from me and was breathing heavily.

I sat up. "Rowe—"

He held up one hand. "Just . . . don't say anything. Not yet. I—" His head jerked up, eyes scanning the top of the bluff. He looked back at me. "I remembered something from that night. Something Trix said to me about the woman at Bienville Square."

I scrambled upright. "What?"

"The woman Trix met with was from the mountains up in Alabama. She knew your great-grandmother. Trix's grandmother."

"Jinn," I breathed.

"Trix told me her name. It was like a bird or something. A bird name, like . . ." He looked skyward. "Like Wren or Robin or something. I can't remember."

I stared at him. "You can't remember."

"I know you hate me," he went on. "And you should. You should hate my fucking guts, but that doesn't mean I can't try to make it up to you." He inhaled. "I'm sorry, okay? And I can at least try to do something to make up for what I did—"

And then his gaze flipped back up to the edge of the bluff above us, and I saw him go white. I turned my head, following his gaze. Wynn stood at the edge of the drop-off, legs apart, the jacket of his gray suit blown open and his perfectly knotted light-blue tie flapping in the wind. Storm clouds swirled behind him, a debonair Titan.

"I'm sorry, Althea. I really am. I had to do this. He said if I didn't—"

"Althea!" Wynn called down. "What the hell are you doing? Did he hurt you?" I looked back at Rowe. His face was contorted in fear.

I rolled over and struggled to my feet, and Rowe pushed me up the hill toward my brother. Finally at the top, I stood before Wynn. His eyes swept over me once, a cursory look of annoyance, then past me.

Wynn stared at Rowe. "You're pathetic. I don't know what I was thinking. I said subdue her, you donkey, not push her off a cliff." His gaze flicked over me. "Are you hurt?"

I blinked at Rowe. "You work for him?" I turned to Wynn. "First Jay, now him?"

"He said he wanted to talk to you," Rowe said to me. He turned to Wynn. "That's what you're going to do, right? Talk?"

"Yes, Rowe. We're going to talk." He smiled at me. "And Rowe," he said in a deliberate voice—the same voice he'd used when he called me a ding-dong and teased me about the gators. "Pay attention. This is how you subdue someone."

There was a pause, a split-second beat where I could hear the wind rustling the branches of the trees above me, then I felt a bright-hot explosion on the underside of my jaw. My head snapped back, my legs folded underneath me, and the world went black.

❧

I woke up in a dark room that reeked of sour beer and urine. I was lying down, and Wynn had spread a blanket over me. He sat beside me, stroking my hair. My stomach heaved in revulsion. I wanted to tell him to get away from me, but I couldn't muster the energy to speak.

I looked around. The room was inky dark, lit only by a flashlight balanced on a seat, its beam aimed up at the ceiling. I could make out words, graffiti on the walls. *Tanya is a fucktard. I love Ryan. Sigmas suck balls.* Two large windows stretched from the ceiling to the floor, all their glass smashed out. Rowe was nowhere in sight.

Wynn and I were alone, inside one of the rooms at Old Pritchard.

It looked like a pack of crazed hobos had held a rave inside the place. And it reeked. I wanted to cover my nose, but I wasn't sure I could lift my arms. My foggy brain clicked through all these facts, but

I couldn't make sense of any of them. Why in the world had he brought me here? I looked up at him, barely able to lift my eyelids.

"Feel better?" he murmured. "I gave you something for the pain. The pills, in your purse. That's our Althea, always prepared."

I managed to touch my cheek. A shock wave of pain radiated through me.

"Rowe hit you," he said.

"He—"

I lost track of my protest as the fog rolled through my brain. My purse lay on top of an old metal chair behind him. I squinted up at him. The glare of the flashlight shadowed the planes of his face, but the sockets of his eyes were two dark pools. Canyons of black. I couldn't make out the expression inside them. Or maybe he had no expression.

"Was this Mom's room?" I heard myself ask.

"Mom was never here," came the answer from somewhere that seemed very far away.

"Somebody . . ." I was slurring. I felt like I was someplace else— somewhere high on a shelf. Safely out of reach. "Was it Collie?"

"Oh, kiddo." He sighed. "Who knows?"

"They killed themselves," I said vaguely. "Or somebody killed them. I don't know . . ."

I heard another sigh from out of the black void.

"But how?" I asked. "How . . ."

"Kiddo." He pushed up on my chin, so that my lips pressed together and my teeth clacked. "Listen. What's important is that you and I are together. We're family, you and me. Whatever happened to Mom and Collie doesn't matter. It's about the two of us now."

He was right. My mother was dead, my father was dying. In the end it was just Wynn and me. He'd sent Rowe to find me so we could be reunited. I knew somewhere in the back of my fragmented brain it was because he wanted to lock me up. But right now, with my jaw throbbing and the awful roiling in my stomach, I didn't care.

He was stroking my hair again, and I closed my eyes. My mother used to stroke my hair. It always made me feel so safe. I took a deep breath, let it out slowly. Wynn was my brother, he was older than me, smarter. Maybe I should just do what he said. Let him take care of me. Drift off to sleep.

"You never told me what happened." The sound of his voice surprised me. I'd forgotten the fingers in my hair were attached to a person. And then the fingers stopped. "With Mom," he said. "The night she died . . ."

I thought of my mother in her gold dress. The way the yellow moonlight lit up the clearing. "I can't—"

"Try." His voice was so measured. So calm. "I deserve to know."

❧

I am five years old, lying in my white-eyelet canopy bed. Wynn, nine, is asleep down the hall, but my eyes won't stay closed.

The next thing I know, my mother is standing beside me. She's still wearing the gold dress from the party, and as she bends over me, she shimmers. As I breathe in her Mama smell—honeysuckle and hand lotion and something else that's sharp and bitter—she whispers, "Little Bit. Thea. Wake up."

I get up, put on my blue sweater, and together we tiptoe out of the house. It's so exciting, like we're playing a midnight game of hide-and-seek. I wonder where Folly is. He wouldn't usually miss a walk in the woods. Mama must have locked him in the laundry room.

We cross the cool, spongy grass to the edge of the woods, then slip into the thicket of pines and oaks, following the straw path. We hold hands, and as we pick our way down the path, Mama does our special thing. Three squeezes—I love you.

Finally we come to the clearing. I've never been here at night. Never seen the grassy circle in the dark. It seems almost magical. I have a secret playhouse under the spreading branches of an ancient magnolia tree, a place Wynn doesn't even know about, and I wonder if my mother's found it. If she's mad and going to make me take it apart.

She tells me to kneel, so I do, then she does too. I close my eyes and press my palms together like I've seen some girls do at school. We don't go to church, even though I've begged a hundred times, but I do know what praying looks like.

She begins to chant. I've heard it before—she usually does it when she cooks or folds the laundry—but this time it sounds spookier than usual. My scalp prickles, so fiercely it feels like my hair is moving on top of my head. I open my eyes and peek at her. She is shaking all over. She opens her eyes, catches me looking. Now my whole body begins to tingle, starting with the tips of my fingers.

"I don't know what it is, baby," she says. "The pills or the sickness. Or maybe it's something else. I'm not sure. Everything is different now."

She drops down on all fours and, as she does, I hear the breath whoosh out of her mouth. It sounds like that time Wynn hit me in the stomach with the Wiffle-ball bat. I drop down too, mainly because I want to do what she does. A bizarre, midnight Simon Says game.

She is sweaty, breathing hard, and I'm afraid she might throw up. Or die. Instead, she tells me to go find a box she's hidden under the tree in my playhouse. It's an old box with a red bird on it, the lid sealed shut with layers of yellowed packing tape. When I bring it back, she tears through the tape and then lifts the lid.

There's nothing inside but an old hair barrette, a couple of pieces of paper, some arrowheads, and an orange bottle of pills. She reaches into the neckline of her dress and pulls out an orange bottle identical to the one in the box, only empty. She lays it inside and picks up the full one. She shakes the bottle in front of me.

"See these, Thea?" she says.

I nod.

"I want you to take them when you're older. When you're thirty. They'll help you."

I nod again, but I don't understand.

"Little Bit, listen to me. I have a story for you."

I square my shoulders. I'm a good listener.

"There's someone out there, someone very special. My mama called her the honeysuckle girl."

Something in the air changes, turns enchanted and even sweeter smelling. The stars rotate their faces to us. All around the clearing, the forest hushes.

"My mama told me about her when I was little, like you. She told me she was wise. That she knows things."

"What things?"

Mama's eyes soften. "Everything you need to know to grow up strong and safe."

I wait. This sounds like a fairy tale.

"Take the pills and wait for her. She'll find you. I think. But if she doesn't, you find her. You hear? You go and find her, Little Bit."

I want to ask why, make her explain everything so I understand. But I'm used to doing what I'm told without arguing, so I don't. I watch her put the pills back in the box and close the lid. Push it across the grass toward me.

"Hide this from your father," she says in a serious tone.

I swallow. My father is a bull of a man with a square jaw and Brillo Pad hair. He's a lawyer and wears black suits with starched white button-downs and maroon ties. He throws bad guys in jail. I've never hidden anything from him.

I put the cigar box back under the tree. When I return, she asks me if I want pancakes. I say yes, and we walk back. In the kitchen, she turns on the light over the stove, opens the yellow box, dumps half of it in her big mixing bowl, and sets to work. Her gold dress flashes in the light.

Daddy appears in the doorway from the darkness of the hallway. He's still in his suit from the party. I smile at him, and he smiles back. I suddenly feel hot all over, remembering the cigar box. Mama walks up behind my chair and drapes her hands on my shoulders.

From the doorway, Daddy says her name—Trix. It sounds like a warning.

"Where have you been?" he rumbles.

"With my daughter." Her answer sounds like a warning too.

His eyes go black, and, as if in response, her arms stiffen, her hands grip my head. It's like she's trying to keep from falling. I cry out, and she jerks back, pulling my chair with her, sending us both toppling to the floor. My father rushes toward us, barks at me to go to my room.

I do, holding back my tears until I'm facedown on the bed. Later, I watch out my bedroom window as an ambulance glides up to our house— no lights or sirens—and takes both my parents away. I creep into Wynn's room. He's still asleep. I crawl into bed with him, pulling the dingy blanket he still sleeps with out from his arms. I hug it close.

When I wake up in the morning, Wynn is still asleep. I go downstairs for breakfast. Dad is sitting at the table with a cup of coffee. He doesn't look at me or smile like the night before, just gazes out the window and fondles Folly's ears. He tells me to go play outside.

Under the magnolia tree, I find the cigar box with the red bird on it and open it, deliberately disobeying my mother's orders. But I don't care. Thirty is too far off. The bottle of pills has spilled . . . She must not have screwed on the lid tight enough. I put one on my tongue and let it melt in my mouth. It tastes sour, like bad candy.

I set up my kitchen and make magnolia-leaf pancakes, drizzled with drops of honeysuckle nectar. After a while, I feel a drowse begin to steal over me. I wander out into the clearing again and lie on my back. I feel so nice, like an angel. Mysterious and peaceful. I think of the honeysuckle girl Mama told me about. I pretend to be her, drifting and wise. I close my eyes.

Later, back at the house, Dad sits Wynn and me down and tells us that our mother has died. Something with her brain—a clot, he explains. A big word I can't say.

As soon as he's done talking, I run out of the house and to the clearing. I gather the pills from the cigar box and dump them in my pocket, crunching down on another one. I am going to take every pill, one at a time, so I can feel like the honeysuckle girl again. I put the cigar box back under the tree and head to the house.

When I turn and look back at the clearing one last time, with the slanting sun hitting it just so, I see something: the grass—the spot where we'd knelt the night before—seems to shimmer gold.

Chapter Twenty-Eight

Sunday, September 23, 2012
Tuscaloosa, Alabama

Now that I was finished with my story, my brain felt locked up. Swollen and thick and sludgy inside my skull. I fell silent, drifting.

I couldn't think anymore. I didn't want to.

I couldn't focus my eyes.

Sleep seemed like everything. The only thing. I just wanted to go to sleep. I closed my eyes.

Wynn's voice: "You remember you said Dad looked at you? And smiled?"

I nodded.

"That wasn't a smile, kiddo, that was a look of concern. I think he looked at you and saw the same thing I'm seeing now."

Something prickled over me. Not fear. I was too numb for that.

"A waste," he said mildly. "Like Mom and our grandmother. A train wreck of a human being. You know what he told me, the day we sent you to rehab? He said you were just like her. Like Mom. Not because of the addiction. Because of the insanity. He said he'd known since you were little that you'd go crazy like she did."

His words settled on my skin like a thousand-pound weight, pinning me to the bed. I was crazy, just like my mother. Wynn was right. And I must've known it all along, deep down. That's why I'd taken the pills that very first day, why I thought I saw gold in the clearing and ever since then on my fingers. It was why I'd let Rowe use me all those years ago. I knew I was destined to be like her.

"Tell me this, Althea," he asked. "In all your amateur sleuthing, have you found her? Mom's honeysuckle girl?"

I tried to laugh, but it came out as a drawn-out sigh. "No."

"Who is she?"

"I don't know."

She has a bird name. Wren. Robin . . .

"But you know things about her, don't you?"

I rolled my head to face him. "She has a gift."

"What do you mean? Like a psychic?"

"I don't know. Maybe. She keeps you safe."

"What did she say to Mom when they met?"

"I don't know."

"What did she tell Collie?"

"Nobody knows."

"Bullshit." A hand cuffed my neck, and the fingers constricted. I let out one choked cough and tried to suck in another breath. I couldn't. My airway was being crushed. "You know," Wynn said. "And you're going to tell me. Now."

He squeezed harder, so that I saw the spots again, then a wash of red. I was going to die. My own brother, my own flesh and blood, was going to kill me. I gave one flailing kick and twist, and, feeling a surge of adrenaline, wrenched free of him. I clattered off the bed, down onto the filthy, rubble-strewn floor. I scrambled to my hands and knees, darting looks around the room. I was on the far side of the bed, the side opposite the door. I tried to gauge my best path of escape, ignoring the shards of broken plaster and glass that jabbed into my hands.

Wynn planted his hands on his hips. "Where is the woman?"

I could go under the bed. If I was fast enough, I'd make it to the door before he caught me. Or I could try to leap over the bed. But I felt like I weighed a thousand pounds. It would be like running through molasses.

Wynn snapped his fingers. "Althea, pay attention. Where does she come from? The mountain? Sybil Valley?" He produced the bottle from his coat pocket and twisted off the lid.

I sat back and stared at him. "I told you, I don't know."

His face darkened, folded into itself, and his body expanded like it'd been pumped full of air. He threw out a finger, aimed it at me. "I'm tired of you lying to me. This woman knows things about our family, and *you* are going to tell me where she *is*!"

I leapt to the bed, hooked my fingers under the iron rail, and pulled. It flipped up, easier than I'd imagined it would, and crashed onto Wynn. He stumbled back, tripping over his feet. I scrambled for the door.

Then my head jerked back with jolt of pain. He had my hair. I ducked and twisted, but he held fast. He pulled me to him, wrapped one steely arm around my chest, and put his mouth to my ear.

"I need you to do what's right for your family," he whispered. "For Mom and Dad. This is what they'd want."

He flipped me around and shoved me to the floor. My legs collapsed under me. He poured some pills out into his open palm. They made a neat, white pyramid. He squatted.

"Open your mouth." He grabbed my hair and yanked my head back.

I didn't move. Our eyes met. I could feel tears rising.

"Althea," he whispered into my ear. "It's not enough to kill you, I promise. You have to trust me." I kept my head turned.

Wynn held up his cupped hand, and I could feel his gaze level at me. I glanced at him. His eyes, what I could see of them in the dark, glittered. "Just stop all this," he whispered. "Stop and go to sleep."

I saw my mother, on her knees, shaking in the dark, trying to explain something she didn't even understand. Trying to protect me, give me a chance at life. It hadn't worked. Whether she'd failed or I had just screwed everything up, I didn't know. But it was over. Too late to do anything about it.

I had an overwhelming rush of homesickness, wanting to be with my mother. Wanting to be safe in her arms.

And it would be so good to taste the bitter crush of the powder between my teeth, coating my mouth and burning my throat. It would be good to feel weightless again. It had been so long.

My lips parted. My mouth opened.

Wynn was stronger than me. The past was stronger. I was alone and done with all the fighting.

He poured in the pills, and I crunched down, trying to work my tongue around the dry powder. He handed me a bottle of water, and I took it with a wave of gratitude. After I swallowed, he tipped more pills into my mouth. Shut my mouth, made me chew, poured more water down my throat.

More pills, more chewing, more water, and I waited for the buzz to drift in. Blunt every edge, make everything okay. Make me feel like the honeysuckle girl. Drifting, peaceful, and wise.

When it finally did, I closed my eyes.

Chapter Twenty-Nine

Monday, September 24, 2012
Tuscaloosa, Alabama

A wide staircase curves below me and disappears into darkness. It is old but it's real, I think—made of wood and marble and carpet.

At the foot of the stairs and across the expanse of scarred, cracked marble are doors. They lead to the outside. I want to go out to the wind and the night sounds. I want to leave this dark place forever. But I don't think I can make it out on my own. I don't know how far my legs will carry me.

If I jumped, it would be easier. But I would join the broken pieces below me. I would shatter and they would find me on a day when the sun finally decided to shine. Or they wouldn't and I would soften and rot and dissolve into the floor, between the marble cracks.

Instead I float down the stairs and the doors part and give way beneath my hands. I am standing in the night air. The wind lifts my hair. The broken ground crunches beneath my feet. I turn until I see light. I run to it. I run and run and don't even feel tired.

I am in the middle of a field. I drop to my knees, and then my hands, and release everything inside me. It burns coming up, but after that I feel the wind on my face. It's a good, clean wind. Sweet and warm. It pushes the tears out of my eyes.

I will die here. But it's good. I've found a level place that's open to the stars and the moon. There are trees here, like at my clearing. They encircle me, and I smell honeysuckle.

I turn up my palms. There is no gold. No red raven. I only see those things when I'm in my right mind. When I am Althea. Right now I'm not even her.

I am a honeysuckle girl.

I awoke in a hospital bed. Parts of my body I could still feel on fire. The rest of me, my fingers and feet, arms and legs, were completely numb. An IV tube ran from my forearm to a bag on a stand beside the bed. It was almost empty. I drew a deep breath—even my throat felt scorched—and promptly vomited down the front of my flimsy gown.

I sank back, unable to even reach the nurse's call button. I must've fallen asleep because, when I next opened my eyes, a nurse was rolling me back and forth, whipping the gown and the wet sheets out from under me. She didn't say anything, but I noticed her lip curl in disgust. My eyes swept the room. Wynn was nowhere in sight. Neither was Rowe. I was alone.

The nurse rolled me back down and snapped the blanket over me.

"Where am I?" My voice came out a rasp.

"DCH Regional," she said. "Tuscaloosa. Psych ward."

"Psych ward?"

"Forty-eight-hour hold, at least."

"I don't understand."

"Mandatory fifty-one-fifty whenever there's a suicide attempt," she said, then spun, her ponytail flying behind her like a flag, and slammed out of the room.

Chapter Thirty

Wednesday, September 26, 2012
Tuscaloosa, Alabama

When I next emerged from the fog, I found I had become, at long
last, an official patient of Pritchard Hospital. It was a little strange how
unsurprised I was to be locked inside the gray walls. How natural it
felt—like destiny had finally settled over me, a familiar blanket. The
place had been home to my mother and grandmother. Now it was mine.

They said an orderly had found me wandering in the soccer field
near the new hospital around dawn, vomiting in the grass. They'd taken
me to the hospital but didn't need to pump my stomach. I hadn't taken
enough pills to kill me.

In other words, Wynn had done his job well.

After my forty-eight-hour hold at DCH Regional, they'd bundled
me into an ambulance and shuttled me across town to Pritchard.
Because it appeared as if I had attempted suicide (and because, in my
haze, I'd mentioned I'd been in one of the rooms at Old Pritchard when
I took the pills), my brother had gotten an involuntary-commitment
order from a judge. The admittance nurse informed me I was a patient
indefinitely, that I may as well settle in. I didn't have any clothes, so

one of the nurses found an old pair of sweatpants and a Crimson Tide T-shirt from the donation closet.

I wondered if Wynn had found the cigar box back at the hotel in Birmingham. It was impossible to know. That he'd somehow gotten to Terri Wooten was clear—she must've told him she and Traci were expecting me that afternoon. The thought of Wynn tracking me like a wounded deer turned my knees to jelly.

My brother was a ruthless bastard; there was no denying it now. And I hated him.

I sat on the narrow bed, knees tucked up under my chin, staring at the gray cement-block wall of my room while the nurse ran down the schedule: meds in the morning, breakfast, group, therapy (art, music, or puppies, my choice), lunch, free time, meds again, then lights out at nine thirty. If I stayed here long enough, they'd let me work in the kitchen or the laundry or with the grounds crew. Joy.

Wynn had won. My dad was two hundred miles away, dying, and I couldn't get to him. Even if I could, I wouldn't be able to make him understand what I was dealing with. I couldn't coax the truth out of him; he was probably too far gone by now.

If my father died while I was locked up, Wynn would be appointed trustee, or guardian, or whatever it was they called it, over my portion of the estate. Giving him complete control over every cent and, it followed, my future. I could be locked up for as long as he wanted while he walked around in complete freedom. Flush with cash for his campaign or a cruise to the Caribbean, or whatever the hell he and Molly Robb had on the agenda.

I could tell someone the truth. I could tell them he'd forced me to overdose, but who was going to believe me—a known addict—over Wynn, son of Attorney General Elder Bell, state legislator and highly respected candidate for governor? Look at Trix and Collie. They hadn't had a fair trial. They'd been thrown in here like trash. Left to rot and die.

The nurse was staring at me. She must've reached the end of her spiel.

"Okay. Thank you," I said.

She pursed her lips. "I said, do you have any questions?"

"No," I said. She started for the door. "I mean, yes. I left my car in Birmingham. What do you think happened to it?"

"It was probably towed." She left.

Great. Jay's car was in an impound lot somewhere, and Wynn had my purse and probably the rifle. God knows what had become of the cigar box, back at the hotel. Wynn had done one hell of a job on me. I was fucked six ways to Sunday.

❧

New Pritchard was nothing more than an uglier, more up-to-date version of Old Pritchard. Three depressing stories of bricks and mortar—a soul-killer of a building.

I decided if there was anything that could suck the hope right out of you, it was trying to watch the *Today* show in the buzzy, mercury-vapor glow of fluorescent lighting on a TV that was imprisoned in a metal cage and suspended nine feet off the floor.

Everything was gray. The cement-block walls, the epoxied floor. The doors, the windows, the wire mesh on the doors and windows. Even the patients were gray. Most of them seemed pretty docile, and for that, I was grateful. They whiled away the day playing cards or Scrabble. Others wrote in journals, watched TV, or stared out the windows. The disturbed ones shuffled ruts down the hallway, sat motionless in wheelchairs, or jabbered incoherently at invisible companions. At least two regularly shit and pissed themselves, overflowing their adult diapers on a regular basis. The smell could practically peel the skin off your face, and someone would always have to go find an orderly to clean the mess up.

The first afternoon, I met with my appointed psychologist—a young girl with a tousled, asymmetrical haircut and pink-crystal nose ring, who looked to be just hours out of her master's program. We sat on a (gray) sofa in the (gray) hallway and talked while people passed back and forth, which I guess was a tactic to make the session seem less threatening. One patient, a gaunt teenage girl, leaned against the wall and glowered at us.

"So tell me about what happened, Althea," Dr. Hipster said.

"My brother forced me to take pills so it would look like I tried to kill myself." I smiled at her.

Her expression remained placid. "Your brother?"

She knew who Wynn was. Everybody did.

Her eyes swept over the clipboard in her hands. "Why do you believe he forced you to take pills?"

"I don't believe. I know. And I . . ." I touched my jaw, and it throbbed in response. All of a sudden, I felt exhausted. "I think there's something he doesn't want me to know. Something about my family, something terrible that keeps happening to the women in our family . . ."

I trailed off. She was looking at me like she already knew everything I'd just said. Like she'd heard this before because Wynn had briefed her. Warned her I would lie about him. I shut my mouth.

"You have a lengthy history of addiction." Dr. Hipster returned to her clipboard. "And a recent diagnosis of schizophrenia from your previous psychiatrist. Are you aware of that?"

So they'd made it official. I was a bona fide schizophrenic. Another crazy mountain girl, just like the rest of them.

The doctor flipped a page. "I understand you have a prayer you like to say?"

"Is that a crime? Praying?"

She pursed her lips. "You know, Althea, schizophrenia is no laughing matter."

"I wasn't making a joke."

No response. "But the illness can be managed so that you can live a full, productive life, maybe even at home, surrounded by your loved ones."

I sighed.

"Are you willing to do what it takes to get better? To listen and learn? Will you trust the process and the doctors here?"

My skin broke out in gooseflesh. "I'll do whatever it takes," I said.

Before dinner, we dispersed for free time. The teenager from the hallway stopped me outside my room.

"You almost died?" she asked.

I pushed open my door. "So they say."

"Who did you see when . . . you know . . ." Her eyes were two desperate shadows. "Jesus? Or a light or something?"

I thought back to the filthy room, the beam of the flashlight, the broken windows. My brother and the pyramid of pills rising out of his hand.

"I didn't see anyone," I said after a couple of seconds. "Sorry."

✦

Dinner was in a dingy cafeteria on the first floor. The patients filed past pans of glistening patties of meat, gray vegetables, and wedges of something I guessed was pie. I took my place in line, keeping an eye on an orderly—a young guy, skinny, with braces, who was pushing a garbage can on wheels around the perimeter of the room.

I took my tray to a table, started pushing the food around in the gravy or sauce or whatever it was, and watched the orderly. He slouched around the room, dumping trays and picking wadded napkins up off the floor. When his can was full, he started toward the back of the cafeteria.

I jumped up and, checking to make sure nobody was watching, followed.

In the kitchen, one guy stood at the sink, going at a stack of pots with a sprayer, his back to me. I scanned the rest of the room, the jumble of freezers, ovens, and shelves stacked with huge cans of vegetables. There was no one else here. I could hear the orderly in the back of the room, jostling the cans. I slipped past the sink, past the shelves of bowls and pots and enormous steel utensils, and turned the corner just as he'd pushed the door open and kicked down the metal doorstop. Between us there was a cluster of cans, all full, ready to be bagged and dumped. The orderly reappeared, and I ducked back behind a massive steel refrigerator.

"Dude, give me a hand!" he yelled into the kitchen.

"What?" came from the guy at the sink.

"Come back here and help me!"

There was no answer and the orderly heaved a sigh, then fought through the cans back into the kitchen.

I scooted out from behind the refrigerator and darted out the door. Crossed the paved area and ran to the administration building.

About fifteen minutes later, as I was leaving, two burly orderlies met me at the door.

"No need to manhandle me," I said to the huge guy who'd hooked my right arm. "I just got lost."

He chuckled. "Whatever you say. But rules are rules. No patients allowed in admin."

"Did Denise call you?" When I'd casually slipped past the woman's deserted desk and down the hall into Beth's office, I'd assumed she was in the bathroom. Excavating her teeth, probably. Disgusting Denise.

"The food-services guys," he said.

"Everybody's doing paint-a-pot in the community room," the other guy said.

"Paint-a-pot." I nodded gravely. "Well, thank God you came when you did. I would've hated to miss that."

Even though we were headed back to the land of gray, I was feeling pretty buoyant. Sure, I sucked at being an escape artist. Sure, the meds were dulling me, but I was confident of one thing: sooner or later, Beth would pull her keyboard out from its hidden desk tray and find, taped to the top of it, the hastily scrawled note I'd left her.

Chapter Thirty-One

Thursday, September 27, 2012
Tuscaloosa, Alabama

Three days until my thirtieth birthday, and no word from Beth. Not a peep. Not only that, but I hadn't been able to get within spitting distance of the admin building. They'd taken away my outdoor privileges and added a couple more pills to my daily cocktail.

At any time, Wynn could pick up the phone and have me shipped off to the other side of the country. Or pop in and strangle me in my sleep himself. I knew this, which should've made me a wreck. But it didn't. I wasn't afraid.

He must've thought I knew something. Information that would be useful to him.

He needed me.

Or maybe I was overestimating my value to Wynn. Maybe it was just the pills blunting the edges. Even though I knew they were leaving their cloudy film over every inch of my nervous system, I found myself looking forward to the morning and evening concoction doled out to me. Nothing could beat it—that smooth, downward glide from dinnertime to lights out.

Nights were another story. That was when the dreams came. Nightmares starring Trix and Collie, Wynn and Walter. Terror and violence. Blood everywhere. Usually around three o'clock in the morning, I'd jerk back to consciousness and lie in my bed, drenched in sweat, trying to slow my racing pulse. Fear surrounded me, filled up the corners of my room, wafted between my sheets.

Maybe that was the real reason I wasn't scared of Wynn. Maybe I actually wished he would sneak into my room one night and put me out of my misery.

Then, finally, I was told I had a visitor. When I saw her, standing in a block of sunlight by the sagging sofa in the community room, my heart slammed in my chest.

"You look tired, Althea." Molly Robb held her arms out to me. "But really so much better."

I didn't move. She was wrapped in a beige trench, the belt cinched tightly around her tiny waist. I wondered if she had a gun hidden inside the folds. A cloth soaked in chloroform. Nylon zip ties.

"You're fuller somehow"—her hands went to her cheeks and she patted them, like an overgrown toddler—"in the face."

"It's the meds. They bloat you. And thanks so much for mentioning it."

I stormed out and down the hall. I could hear her scurrying, mouse-like, just a couple of yards behind me. I rounded the corner and slammed the door to my room, but she pushed it open and swanned into the room. I backed against the far wall.

"Get out," I said. There was a telltale tremor in my voice, and I knew she heard it.

She smiled—a slow, cruel twist of her carefully lined lips. "I've already signed you out. Just for a couple of hours, and then I'll bring you back. I'm taking you to see your father."

"Dad wants to see me?"

"It's so near the end," she went on. "Wynn decided to let you see him one last time before he passed."

I didn't move. "He's . . . It's really the end? Really?"

She pursed her lips. "I'm so sorry, hon."

I still didn't move.

"I know it's difficult to face this, but you have to be strong. This is your father we're talking about. You don't want to let him slip away without having settled your differences and said your good-byes."

I pressed my fingers to my temples.

I couldn't think. My brain was so filled with fog.

"Why didn't Wynn come?" I asked her.

"He's busy. And we're a team. We're all three a team, right?"

She held out her hand, and, God help me, I took it. I let her lead me down the hall and through the ward to the nurses' station. Then, escorted by an orderly, through the series of steel-cage doors and down the stairs to the lobby. She pulled me by the wrist, kicking open the double doors of the building with her bow-tipped flats. When we hit the parking lot, I finally pulled against her, squinting in the light.

It was one of those September days where the sky was so blue and the leaves so crisply outlined against it, it made your eyes water. But the sun didn't blind me to the black SUV idling in the far corner of the lot. It wasn't Molly Robb's car. My nerves twanged, and I tasted something weird and metallic in my mouth. Fear.

I turned to her. "The staff told Wynn I ran, didn't they?"

She didn't answer.

"So now that Wynn knows locking me in this hellhole and drugging me like a fucking circus elephant isn't going to intimidate me, he's got to do more."

She forced a smile. "You're confused, Althea. No one's out to get you."

"Who's in the SUV, Molly Robb?" I asked.

I saw it then, the flash of hatred in her eyes. The naked disgust. It wasn't just Wynn who wanted me out of the way. I'd messed up her plans for a glorious career as a politician's wife, and now she wanted me gone too. To my sister-in-law, I was nothing but a problem to be solved.

"Is my brother going to kill me?" I said. "You're going to kill me now?"

She clawed at my arm, but I twisted away from her.

"Because I ruined your plans?" I screamed.

She caught my upper arm and clamped down. She leaned into my ear. "Shut up." She shoved me hard, and I stumbled forward.

"Where are you taking me?" She didn't answer, just kept pushing me toward the SUV.

I didn't know if that ominous vehicle was whisking me off to another hospital or back home to see my father or to some isolated spot in the woods outside of town where one of Wynn's cronies was going to shoot me in the back of the head and leave me for the crows. All I knew was there was no chance, not one chance in hell, that I was going without a fight.

I wrenched away from Molly Robb, dropped to my knees on the asphalt, and started screaming like I had really and truly lost my mind. She turned back to me, her eyes bulging, her hands making helpless flapping motions. I inhaled and screamed again, louder this time, and I saw a back window of the SUV lower.

"Help me!" I screamed into the air, praying those damn orderlies would finally show up when I needed them. I dropped to the pavement, flailing, scratching at the asphalt. And then I heard footsteps pounding from somewhere in the lot.

"What's going on?" It was a woman's voice. A familiar one.

"She's . . . I had permission to take her off campus but she's . . ." Molly Robb's voice came out choked.

"Althea?"

I stopped screaming and tilted my face up. Beth loomed over me, her nimbus of curls blotting out the sun. She planted her hands on her hips.

"You can't take this patient out today," she said.

"I have written permission from her brother. She's going to see her dying father."

"Well, not today. She has a medical appointment."

I scrambled to my feet.

Molly Robb snorted. "She'll be back later this evening. Reschedule it."

Beth waved over an orderly who'd just exited the building. He broke into a jog. She turned back and sniffed at Molly Robb. "I'm sorry. We can't reschedule. The OB-GYN is only here once a month, and it's a legal thing. The state gets very particular when we're dealing with a pregnant patient."

I almost laughed at the gobsmacked look that came over Molly Robb. She glanced back at the SUV, then at me, then at Beth, her jaw working.

"She's . . . pregnant?" she asked.

"And has a duodenal ulcer. She's in no shape to be leaving. In fact, she really should be lying down." Beth laid a hand on my shoulder. "My supervisor would have my head if he knew you were trying to take her off campus."

"Her brother—" But then she shut her mouth. I shot Beth a grateful look, and next thing I knew, my trench-coated sister-in-law was heading toward the SUV. In seconds, the black vehicle peeled out of the lot, its tires trailing twin puffs of white dust.

Beth sent the orderly away and hustled me back into the cool lobby. She sat me on the scratchy plaid sofa and took my hand. She searched my face.

"Are you okay?"

"Yes," I said. "I'm fine. I just . . . I don't know what I would've done if you hadn't shown up when you did."

"Where was she taking you?"

"I don't know." I looked in her eyes. "Away."

A couple of nurses walked past, and she released my hand. When they'd passed, she leaned closer and spoke in a low voice. "I'm sorry it took me so long to get back to you. I had to think."

"You did fine. You showed up just in time. And with a great story, by the way. Although maybe a touch over the top, with an ulcer and a pregnancy."

She didn't smile.

"Beth?"

"After you left the note, I got your file. The thing about the ulcer's true."

As if on cue, I felt a wave of nausea roll through me.

"Go on," I said.

She ducked her head. "They did a blood test at DCH Regional, that first night."

"Okay."

"You are pregnant."

I put out my hands on my knees, locked my elbows, and stared down at the sofa's dirt-colored polyester fabric. A million different thoughts flung themselves around the inside of my head, colliding, zinging past each other.

Pregnant.

With Jay's baby.

A life had started inside me, just weeks ago. It was now a part of me. A part I'd already put in jeopardy when I swallowed those pills. A part that was about to be swept up in a battle I didn't know how to fight.

Beth's eyes softened. "Althea. I'm so sorry I had to tell you like this. I'm sorry I told her."

I felt like I'd been gut-punched. "I don't care about that. I just . . .
Oh God. I've been taking all those meds."

"Whatever they're giving you is safe. The pregnancy, the ulcer—it's
all on your chart."

"On my chart? You mean, everybody knows but me? Why didn't
they say anything?"

She shook her head.

"It was Wynn," I said. "It had to be. He must've told them not to
talk. He doesn't want me to know."

"Althea, why wouldn't he?" Her eyes had shuttered now, and she
had stiffened in her seat. I felt a jolt of fear. She didn't believe me.

"I don't know. I don't know. Because it would make me run,
maybe?" I felt a wildness swirling up inside me. A funnel cloud of
panic. I wanted to break out of this crazy place and run as fast and far
as I could until I lost myself. I gripped the sofa beneath me, holding
my body down. I couldn't lose it now, I couldn't afford to. I needed
Beth's help. "It's like I said in the note. Wynn made me take the pills.
He wanted it to look like I was trying to kill myself, and he wanted
me locked up here. But I didn't try to kill myself. And I'm not schizophrenic. I'm not. You've got to believe me."

Desperation rose inside me, and the nausea on top of it. I wished
I would just get sick right here, right now, all over the stained carpet. I
wanted to purge everything—the meds, the fear. The past.

"I do," she said and laid her hand on mine. "Althea, I do believe
you. The minute I saw your name in our intake file, I thought it
was odd that your brother had put you here. Pritchard is a state
hospital. The end of the line for people who don't have insurance or
who can't pay for private care. Or who don't have any family who
can take them in."

I blinked at her, aware of the sensation that something was crack-
ing inside me—the sludge of meds coating my nervous system that had

hardened to a brittle shield. Someone was finally listening. I told myself to sit still. Not to rush anything. I swallowed, feeling my face warm.

"And then I got your note."

I squeezed her hand.

"But, Althea, if your brother forced you to take the pills, if he really hurt you, we should call the police."

I was sweating now. I could feel a trickle roll down between my breasts. "No. I don't want the police involved, not yet. I can't risk it."

"Risk what? You're not making any sense. The police can stop your brother. Put him away for what he's done to you."

"No. It's not that simple. I don't have time. My father's the only one who knows what happened to my mother. Right now, in the state he's in, he can't tell me anything. So I've got to find somebody else. Somebody who knew her family. I have to go back to where it all started, and I've got to do it in three days."

"Then call the police. Turn your brother in, and go do what you have to do."

I gritted my teeth. "I'm telling you, it won't work. They know him. They're on his side. Everybody trusts Wynn like they trusted my father. I'm just the schizophrenic, junkie little sister who's trying to smear the family name."

"You can hire a lawyer. Take him to court."

Now wasn't the time to talk about my approaching thirtieth birthday or red ravens and gold dust and the honeysuckle girl. Maybe all that stuff was real, maybe there was more to my impending doom than just a megalomaniacal brother.

But it didn't matter right now. And it didn't change the fact that he was hell-bent on locking me up and maybe even killing me to keep the truth about our family quiet. If I wanted to be free, I had to find the truth before he got to me.

"I can't explain everything right now." I lowered my voice. "But trust me. There's something in my family's history, something terrible that Wynn is determined to keep quiet. He's probably going to be furious when he finds out his wife botched the job today. Next time, and there will be a next time, he'll come for me himself. And there won't be anything I can do to stop him."

A doctor, my doctor, swept in through the front door and stopped at the front desk. She spoke to the receptionist, then rested an elbow on the counter. Her gaze wandered over to us. I lifted a hand in greeting, and Beth straightened beside me. She smoothed her blouse.

"I appreciate you sharing this with me," she said in a loud voice. "And I'll see what I can do." Then she rose and disappeared through the front doors.

Chapter Thirty-Two

October 1937
Sybil Valley, Alabama

Howell marched the whole way home from the revival in silence, his hand on Jinn's back. Walter and Collie fell into a somber line behind their parents.

The foursome followed the gravel road that led from the church past the feed store and the general store and the firehouse. When they passed the turnoff for the schoolhouse, Jinn held her breath. Her blood beat so hard, she could hear it in her head. She kept walking, through town and up the fern-choked path to their cabin.

On the front porch, Howell collapsed into one of the rocking chairs. He stared off into the darkness, a hank of blond hair falling into his eyes.

Jinn shooed Walter and Collie inside. "Bed."

They obeyed. Or at least, she thought they had, until a few minutes later when Walter reappeared, holding her daddy's .22 rifle in front of his chest like a grim child soldier.

The boy looked at his father. "It ain't right for somebody like him to come up here, all up on his high horse, telling us how we ought to do things. We ought not allow him to shame us like that."

Howell bolted up.

"Get back inside, Walter," Jinn said quickly, before Howell tore into the boy. "And put that gun in the cabinet."

Walter acted like he hadn't heard a thing. His eyes were fixed on his father's face. After a few long moments, Howell spoke.

"Go on, boy." His voice sounded thin and tired.

Walter turned and disappeared inside the house, and Howell settled back in his rocker. Jinn rested one hand on the doorjamb.

"Why's he got Daddy's gun?" she finally asked.

"Vernon gave it to him. He thought it was time. The boy's grown now."

There was no arguing with that. But, all the same, Jinn felt that somehow time had sped up, a river current after the spring melt. Everything was happening faster than it should. She wondered if Tom and Willie were still at the schoolhouse. Waiting and hoping she was going to come. She wondered if there was still a chance for her and Tom.

But she shouldn't think about that.

God had done a miracle and made Howell right.

She took off her sweater and dropped it on the other rocking chair. Rested one hand on her chest. The night was soft, a velvety fall mountain night, the warmest she'd ever felt. The breeze was like a caress across her neck.

"What did you say to him?" Jinn asked. "To Brother Jarrod?"

He sighed. "I said I had been a weak man. A bad husband." His voice had an unsteady quality to it, which gave her a peculiar sense that there was something just ahead of them, something large and terrible, out in the distance, waiting to engulf them. "I told him I knocked you around."

"Well," Jinn said.

He was quiet for a moment or two longer. "I didn't tell him all of it. I didn't tell him the worst part." He peered into the darkness, like there was something to see in it. "I haven't been strong with you, Jinn, not in the way a husband should. I've let you run wild, and I haven't done nothing to stop it."

Jinn felt a sensation like the porch was tilting under her. She gripped the doorjamb.

"Your daddy warned me. He went through this with your mama, so he knows. But I didn't listen." She was quiet. "You're planning to take that money and run off with Tom Stocker, aren't you?"

She flushed hot, then went dead cold. "Who said that?"

"It don't matter, Jinn. Your daddy don't like how this kind of talk reflects on the family." He spoke in a low voice. "The thing is, I can't have it. I got to do my duty as a man and a husband."

He stood. They were face to face, but he seemed to tower over her.

"I told Brother Jarrod and God that I vowed to be a better husband, and that's what I aim to do. I'm going to do what's right for this family, Jinn. So you'll be off to Pritchard in the morning."

❧

Right before bed, when Howell went out back to wash up, Jinn slipped out the front door. She flew across the yard, clattered down into the cellar, and took the last bottle of honeysuckle wine. She didn't want to leave it behind for Howell to smash.

It had been some time since the altar call. An hour, at least. But maybe Tom was still at the school. She hugged the bottle to her chest and ran, her breath ragged in her ears, all the way back down to town. When she veered into the schoolyard, she saw it was deserted. Tom and Willie had already gone.

She stood frozen in the dark.

Now she'd have to run back up Old Cemetery, right past the path to her cabin, to get to Tom's house. By that time, though, Howell would be waiting for her at the head of the path, her case packed for Pritchard.

But what else could she do?

She walked around the side of the school, and what she saw nearly made her faint. There was a woman, dressed in white, languidly leaning against the metal railing of the steps. She was smoking.

"Lord," Jinn gasped.

"Hey there," the woman said. "What are you doing out here this time a night?"

Jinn took a step forward, into the light of the moon. It was Dove Jarrod, the preacher's wife. Now that she was closer, Jinn could see Dove was no more than a teenager. Seventeen or eighteen, at the most.

"I'm . . . just out for a walk," Jinn said.

"Me too." Dove smiled and took a deep drag of her cigarette. "How's your husband feeling?"

"Oh. Good, I guess."

"The Holy Spirit will flat wear you out with all that convicting of sin." She released a plume of smoke from her red lips. "What's his big secret? He got a chippie in Chattanooga? Or is he a pansy? You know, at the Ballyhoo in Chicago the men dance with each other in French silk peignoirs."

Jinn didn't know what to say about pansies or chippies or peignoirs, nor was she exactly clear on what any of those things were. She had to get going. Tom's house was a ways away. Howell might've even gone up there already to look for her.

"What you got there?" Dove asked, nodding at the bottle of wine.

Jinn looked down. She had forgotten about it.

"Let's see that."

Jinn handed over the bottle.

Dove studied the label. "Honeysuckle, hm. You're Jinn, I take it?"

Jinn nodded. "Jinn Wooten."

Dove smiled at her. "Dove Jarrod. Let's drink it." She unscrewed the cap and tipped the bottle into her mouth. "Oh, that's good, Mrs. Wooten. You've got a talent. You really make it with honeysuckle?"

"Yes." She cleared her throat. "Well, excuse me, but I got to get going."

"Where you off to?"

Jinn toed the dirt.

"I get it." Dove smiled. "Don't want to talk about it. Makes me awful curious, though. Awful curious. Your husband know where you are?"

Jinn didn't answer.

"Hm. I'm going to say . . . no, he doesn't."

Jinn realized her hands were trembling. She clasped them behind her back.

Dove smiled. "There's trouble between you two, isn't there?" She took another sip and narrowed her eyes at Jinn, like she was studying on something. "Don't be embarrassed about it. I could see that earlier, in the meeting. I could see it just by looking at you two. Just taking a shot, but I'm going to say . . . you've had it up to here with his catting around, and tonight, you've finally decided to run off. Is it with another man? Is that why you came here, to meet the other man?"

Jinn blinked in shock. "How'd you know?"

Dove widened her eyes. "I've been doing this a long time."

"How?"

"Witness of the Holy Spirit." Dove tapped the ash off her cigarette. "None of my business, but if I was you, I wouldn't go after that man. Not tonight." She sucked on her cigarette again and blew out a cloud of smoke. "He's not here, which means either he's changed his mind or something went wrong. Either way, it's no good."

Jinn felt her face grow warm. The Holy Spirit certainly didn't seem to mind telling folks' secrets. She wondered if He had told her about Pritchard too. Her face burned now, thinking about it.

"If it was me," Dove continued, "and I'm saying this in the strictest hypothetical sense, because I've never done anything like this, I'd let the dust settle a bit first before you gave it another try."

"I can't go home," Jinn said.

"Well, running off in the night all by yourself isn't the way to go about it. And standing here in the schoolyard with a bottle of wine makes you look guilty as hell."

Jinn blinked at the word *hell*.

Dove pushed off the railing. "As it happens, I myself am going out to do an errand. If you'd like to come along, I wouldn't mind it, not atall."

Jinn looked up the road, then back at Dove. She was right. Tom would wait for her, she knew it. He loved her. She'd let things settle with Howell, then they'd make another plan.

"How about it?" Dove said. "If anybody tries to say you were running off, I'll vouch for you. Say you came with me to do the work of the Lord."

"Where are we going?"

"Good question." She closed her eyes. Inhaled. "I'm thinking . . . up the mountain. That way." She pointed behind the school.

Jinn realized her heart had slowed and the trembling had stopped.

"What's the errand?" she asked. She found she was genuinely curious now.

But Dove just shrugged. "That's the fun of it. I never rightly know 'til I get there."

They walked—through the schoolyard and up the mountain path. Up into the thick woods, past the place where Tom had showed her the dead calf. Eventually, they stepped out of the woods and onto the open slope of the mountainside. Jagged stumps dotted muddy slides where the lumber companies had swept through, sawing down trees and skidding the logs down to the stream.

"Who lives in that house?" Dove pointed to the next hill over, where the moon shone on a tiny cabin ringed by more stumps.

"The Tippetts," Jinn said.

"They have a girl?" Dove's silk dress glowed against the mountainside. She looked like a ghost up there on the ridge, the trees her haunted backdrop.

"The youngest," Jinn said. "Vonnie."

The Tippetts' house was a pathetic place, a shanty made with odds and ends of boards that had mostly rotted through and looked wet all the time. Dove skipped right up the sagging front steps and knocked on the door. It swung open, revealing Mr. Tippett, a gaunt man, yellow from many years of drinking moonshine and clinging for dear life to the damp mountain.

"Good evening, sir." Dove's bright voice rang out in the night. "I've come to see your daughter."

At the foot of the steps, Jinn cringed. Everybody knew the Tippetts were involved in bad business, that one of the pale sons had once threatened a forest ranger with a hatchet. She was pretty sure Dove would set Mr. Tippett on edge, but he was just staring at her blankly.

"I'm Charles Jarrod's wife," she said. "We missed you at the meeting tonight."

Jinn's heart smashed against her ribs. Would Mr. Tippett have heard anything about Howell sending her to Pritchard? Would he know her husband was out looking for her now?

"Well . . ." Mr. Tippett shifted a fraction and peered down at Dove, taking in the dress, the lipstick, the hair.

"You know Charles Jarrod, the evangelist?"

"I heard a him."

"I know you'd a been there tonight with the rest of them if it hadn't been for your girl. She's a handful, right? Stubborn? Lazy?"

Jinn thought she detected a hint of twang in Dove's voice. Maybe this was her way of buttering folks up, taking on their way of talking.

"Somebody say something to that fact?" Mr. Tippett's eyes fell on Jinn. She shrunk down a little, wishing the shadows would swallow her.

"Oh, no," Dove said. "I got the message direct." She pointed up, and Mr. Tippett followed her finger, stared up at the soggy, overhanging roof. "If you'll let me in, I can give her the Word of the Lord and straighten her right up."

"She won't listen to you," Mr. Tippett said. "She's hard."

Jinn felt a tendril of fear snake through her. She wondered if she could just turn and run, let the darkness of the mountain swallow her. But before she could consider it further, Dove motioned to her to follow.

Dove had suggested Mr. Tippett stay on the porch, and, meek as a lamb, he obeyed. The girl, no more than fourteen, was in the back bedroom curled into a crescent on a narrow iron bed. In her hands she held a handkerchief, knotted and wet from perspiration. She looked up at Dove when the women entered the room, her face puckered in a focused way Jinn instantly recognized.

"Jinn?" she said between clenched teeth.

"Hey, Vonnie."

"I'm Jinn's friend," Dove said and sat on the bed beside Vonnie, being careful not to jostle her. "Have you passed it yet?"

"No. How'd you—?"

"How long has it been?"

"I been bleeding for seven days." The girl looked quickly at Jinn, then back to Dove, in confusion. "I told my pap it was regular female trouble. Did he send for you?"

"No. He doesn't know anything about the baby, and you have my word he won't," Dove said. "Can I put my hands on you?" Dove asked, and the girl nodded. "Jinn, come here," Dove said. Jinn kneeled beside the bed, right at the girl's head. "Put your hand on her." Jinn rested her fingertips on the girl's thin arm. "No," Dove said. "Her stomach." Jinn slid her fingers down until she could feel Vonnie's flat stomach. The girl winced.

Vonnie gazed into Dove's eyes. "I didn't want no baby." She flicked a look at Jinn. "But I changed my mind. I don't think it matters how it got here, do you?"

Jinn shook her head.

"I think it'd be nice to have a little girl."

"Well, God willing, it's gonna take, and you're gonna have yourself one," Dove said. "I'll do my best. But I ain't the one in charge."

Her hand rested right next to Jinn's on Vonnie's stomach, which was trembling slightly and hot as an oven. In fact, there seemed to be waves of heat radiating from where Dove sat on the bed. She began to speak in low tones, words Jinn couldn't make out, and Jinn felt herself sway as the walls of the cabin fell away and light pierced her skin and bones. She felt herself floating in space, buoyed by the music of Dove's words and the heat and the light.

Then she felt a rush of heat jolt through her and tingle down her arms and legs. Her scalp prickled and goose bumps raised on her arms. She opened her eyes. Vonnie's face was relaxed now, and she'd unfurled, stretching into the quilt. The handkerchief lay beside her. Jinn recognized the fine embroidery and the initials stitched with a fine, gold thread. *VA.* Vernon Alford.

She swallowed, then turned away to find Dove. The other woman's eyes had gone glassy.

"Did it work?" Jinn whispered.

Dove slid off the bed and smoothed her hair. "I'd say yes."

Jinn scrambled up. "But, what if she—"

"We've done our part." She leaned to Vonnie and whispered into her ear. Then she turned back to Jinn. "Time to scat."

"What did you say to her?"

"I told her not to say the daddy's name. Not for nothing."

For the second time that night, Dove took Jinn's hand, but this time, Jinn gripped it just as tightly in return. Other than little Collie, no one had held her hand in such a long time, and it just about filled her to overflowing. Made her want to shout out loud.

Mr. Tippett stood when they came out on the porch, but Dove didn't even say good night. The two of them breezed right past him and tripped, hand in hand, down the front steps and onto the muddy, stump-spotted slope below.

Chapter Thirty-Three

Friday, September 28, 2012
Tuscaloosa, Alabama

The next morning, a giant, mustachioed orderly stuck his head in my room.

"Visitor in the community room," he said.

I stopped in the doorway when I saw Jay. He was standing with his back to me, wearing khakis and a crisp blue button-down. His hair was wet, his hands in his pockets.

A couple of patients played that infuriating Hungry Hippo game on the other side of the room, banging on the levers like a bunch of toddlers. The sound clacked through the room, giving me a headache. Jay's attention was fastened on one of the pissers in the corner under the TV, an elderly lady named Melva, who'd done her business, then leaned over the armrest of her wheelchair to observe the yellow lake pooling under her chair.

I stared at the back of his head, mesmerized by the swoops of honey-colored hair, grooved by the teeth of a comb. It was a marvel of sculptural perfection.

Will the baby have his hair?
Will we ever make love again?
Is he still working with Wynn?

"Visiting hours end at eight," the nurse said behind me, and Jay turned. His eyes lit up—brown, warm—and I resisted the urge to run straight into his arms. Bury my face in his chest, breathe the scent of him in. Confess I loved him and wanted to be with him forever.

"Hey," I said.

His face was open, his eyes gentle as always. I could see his pulse throbbing in his neck. I wanted to press my lips against the spot. Or punch him, really hard.

"Hey," he said.

"Hey."

Forget the pleasantries, I thought. *Just rip off the bandage.*

"Your car's gone," I said. "They impounded it."

"What is it with you and my car?" He flashed a smile, but I didn't return it. "Don't worry about it. I got my mom's."

"Okay. Well, sorry, anyway. Again."

He ran a nervous hand through his hair.

"I didn't think you would see me," he said. "But the woman who called—Beth—she promised me you would."

"What else did she say?"

"Just that I should come as soon as I could."

I tried to focus on breathing. Staying upright. I had work to do.

"We should sit," he said.

"I'll stand."

He was looking at the purple-yellow bruise that stretched all the way to my chin.

"What happened?"

"Why don't you tell me?"

He frowned. "I don't know what you mean."

"Wynn did it."

His eyes widened.

"What? He didn't tell you? He doesn't tell his stooges every move he's making?"

He reddened. "Just tell me what happened."

"I was on my way to see Terri and Traci Wooten. Apparently, Rowe was following me and handed me over to Wynn. Who took me to Old Pritchard, up to one of the rooms. He forced me to take a bottle of pills."

"I'll kill him," he said between clenched teeth. "I'll kill both of them."

"I appreciate the sentiment, but they wouldn't have found me if it hadn't been for you. So, you know, fuck you."

He was staring at me with that guilty-as-hell look on his face. A duplicate of the one I'd seen as I'd driven away from him and Wynn and the restaurant.

"I didn't tell them where you were," he said. "Not Wynn. And not Rowe, I swear. I didn't even know where you were."

"Not even with the car's remote access thing?"

"No."

"But you set me up at the restaurant in Birmingham."

"Yes . . ."

"You told Wynn I was going to be there."

"Wynn said he wanted to help you, and I believed him. I was an idiot. I didn't know what he was planning, and I knew I'd made a mistake the minute I saw your face. So I left it alone. I left you alone. Wynn and Rowe tracked you on their own."

I felt words, sentences, and paragraphs multiplying so fast I thought they might geyser up my throat and out of my mouth before I could stop them. But I couldn't let that happen; I had to be careful. Smart.

"Tell me something," I said.

"Anything."

I cleared my throat. "Why did you come find me that night in the clearing . . . at my father's party?"

He flushed again, and I felt a stab of fear in my chest.

"He said you could use a friend."

"Who said?"

"Wynn." His face had gone from pink to deep red. "He asked me to hang out with you. Keep your mind off your dad's health . . . and all the other stuff you'd been through in the past year."

"In exchange for what?"

He was quiet.

"What, Jay?"

"A job. Later, after he got elected."

"Fuck you."

"I told him no, Althea." He looked down at his clasped hands. "I told him I didn't need anything to spend time with you. I wanted to do it."

I barely suppressed an eye roll.

His flush had faded, and he was looking at me with an intensity that unsettled me. "You have to believe me, Althea. It was good, being with you, really good. It made me happy. Made me want to sort out my shit. But it was selfish, in a way. I see that now, and I'm sorry."

"You knew what he was planning. You knew he wanted to lock me up when you got him to meet you at the restaurant."

"I know, I know. But he kept calling me, Althea, the whole time we were together, swearing he wanted to help you. He said he wanted to look after you. I didn't buy it, not completely, but I thought I could get him to back off. I was going to make him a deal at the restaurant. Offer him a campaign contribution and maybe convince him to let me take you away somewhere. I didn't know who I was dealing with. I didn't see the truth—that he wanted to hurt you, really hurt you. That you were the sane one, and he was the crazy one."

"And you couldn't share this plan with me?"

"If I had told you what I was going to do, that Wynn had asked me to hang out with you and that I was going to bargain with him, you'd have been gone in a shot."

"Maybe not."

Jay gave me a look that said he knew I was lying.

"Why couldn't you have just told me the truth?" I said.

He swallowed. "At the party he told me I was the only person who could get through to you. That I was somebody from your past who had never hurt you. I didn't want to mess that up. I was worried about you. He said you were sick."

"I *am* sick. The drugs, the drinking, what happened to my mother . . . Everything made me crazy. I've been seeing things for years, did you know that? Gold on my hands. Red birds . . ." My voice trailed off.

His brow furrowed.

"It's this thing . . . ," I said. "This thing I can't quite shake. I wanted to believe it was the drugs, but it still happens sometimes. I see crazy shit."

"Stress can do weird things."

"Make you see the exact same crazy shit, over and over again, for twenty-five years?"

He was quiet for a really long time.

"I'm pregnant," I finally said into the silence. His mouth dropped open. I spoke again, in a louder voice. "I'm going to have a baby."

It was the first time I had said it out loud.

I was going to be a mother. The mother of his child.

I waited, steeling myself for the disappointment, the moment when he backed away. I kept my face neutral. It wouldn't surprise me if, over-whelmed with the bomb I'd just dropped, Jay got up and walked right out of the building.

"I'm sorry, I'm . . ." He passed his hand over his mouth. "You're . . ."

"What?" I rested both hands on my stomach, as if I could shield the baby from what Jay was going to say.

"It's a surprise," he said. "That's all. I guess . . . I guess, congratulations to you."

"Okay, thanks," I said slowly. "Congratulations to you too."

His eyes widened, then he thumbed at his nose a few times, sniffed, and looked up at the ceiling.

"Jay?"

He didn't answer me.

"Jay, say something."

His eyes dropped down and locked on mine. He looked scared, entirely freaked out, in fact, and my heart quickened.

"Are you sure?" he asked.

I nodded. "Absolutely. Without a doubt. The baby is yours."

He nodded. Sniffed some more. "Okay," he said. "Okay."

"So," I said.

"Yeah," he said.

I heaved a sigh. Closed my eyes.

"How are you feeling . . . about all of it?" he said.

"I don't know what I am, exactly. Wynn gave me pills," I said. "A lot of them."

"Don't think about that right now," he said. "It's going to be fine."

I thought suddenly what a good father he'd be. Steady. Reassuring. If I let him back into my life. Forgave him for working with Wynn.

I had two days until my birthday. Two days. Was I willing to face my thirtieth birthday alone? Without Jay? I thought of waking up, smothered in a cloud of schizophrenia. Out of my mind, maybe even to the point of being suicidal. Or being tracked down by the honeysuckle girl, right here at Pritchard, confronted with some horrific reality or evil mountain spell or whatever she had that pushed Trix and Collie over the edge.

I had no idea what to expect, not even this late in the game. And now there was a baby in the mix. I didn't want to go into this alone, but I didn't know if Jay could be trusted. I was clear on one thing, though.

"If something happens to me," I said, "you have to take care of her. Promise me that, okay?"

"Her?"

"Promise me. You'll take care of her, no matter what."

"I promise, Althea," he said. "Nothing will happen to her. Or you. I'm going to look after you too. If you'll let me."

I sighed. "I don't know, Jay. I just don't know."

"Okay. Fair enough."

He picked up my hand and put it over his. Then flipped his up to grasp mine. I felt the warmth of his skin, the pressure of his fingers, and something else: a folded piece of paper pressed between our palms.

"You don't have to believe me," he said. "Or even love me."

I curled my fingers around the paper.

He leaned forward. Whispered in my ear. "You can just use me for my day pass."

<hr />

Forty-five minutes later, we were at the Wootens' house, but, just as I feared, the BMW was gone. And probably the gun as well. We went on to the hotel, where I spoke with the woman at the front desk. Luckily for me, they'd boxed my things and stored them in the back room.

"Some guy came in here. Tried to get us to give him your stuff," she said, after she'd retrieved the items. "Didn't like the look of him. I said you had to give the okay."

I thanked her and took the box to the car. Pulled out the cigar box and opened the lid. Everything was still there. I ran my finger over the barrette. The ivory bird stretched out in flight.

A bird.

Rowe had said the woman my mom met with had the name of a bird.

We made a quick supply run—clean clothes and new phone to replace the one Wynn had taken—and then I found Sybil Valley on the map, and we set off. We drove north to the first in a chain of mountains, the foothills of the Appalachians in Alabama. Brood Mountain was a lush dome, covered in green and, even in the summer, a good ten degrees cooler than the rest of the state. It was close to noon by the time we arrived at a rambling, shingled bed-and-breakfast perched on the edge of the mountain, and after Jay checked us in, I fell instantly asleep on top of the covers of a huge quilt-covered bed. When I awoke, I was alone. In the fireplace, a plucky little fire crackled between fake logs.

I spent the next half hour throwing up in the bathroom. When I finally emerged, showered, teeth brushed, Jay put down the magazine he'd been thumbing through.

"Feel better?" I nodded and sank back onto the bed. He pointed at the bedside table. "I brought you some tea. Peppermint. The lady who owns this place said it was good for morning sickness."

I sipped the tea, then opened the cigar box and pulled out the wine label. I smoothed it on the bed in front of me. "'Tom Stocker, Old Cemetery Road,'" I read. "No idea who he is. Or was."

"Not the honeysuckle girl, obviously," Jay said. "But maybe he knew who she was."

"He's probably long gone by now. If Jinn wrote that, it would've been all the way back in the 1930s."

"The woman who owns this place, she told me the valley's full of Stockers."

I sat up. "She did?"

"Maybe we can find someone up here who knew him. A family member?"

I was quiet.

"Are you up for this?" he asked.

"I only have two more days. I have to be."

He sighed. "Nothing's going to happen to you, Althea."

I didn't answer. I wasn't so sure.

"If you're worried about Wynn, we can still go away. Anywhere, as far away as you want. But there's no bad magic coming, I swear."

I put down the mug. "I appreciate everything you're saying. I do. But I can't give up now. I have to know what this thing is. If I'm mentally unstable, if I'm going to have some kind of psychotic break on my birthday, I'll need you here to help me. To keep the baby safe. If it's something else—something really bad about my family, and Wynn tries to keep me from . . . from publicizing it . . ."

He stared at me, unblinking.

"Then we're going to need each other that much more," I finished.

He slumped back. "Jesus. What the hell are we digging into here?"

"I don't know. But any minute now Wynn's going to figure out I've gotten out of the hospital—he may have already—and he'll be coming after me. I can't stop now. I have to find out what happened to Jinn, and I have to do it fast."

He pointed at the wine label on the quilt before me. "Then this is where we start."

Chapter Thirty-Four

Friday, September 28, 2012
Sybil Valley, Alabama

Old Cemetery Road was exactly that—a half-paved road that mean-dered up the mountain past an old, mossy cemetery. From the car I thought I saw a crumbling headstone bearing the name Wooten. The sight sent a chill through me.

The lady at the bed-and-breakfast had told us the Stocker place was roughly three-quarters of the way up the mountain, an old but immacu-late two-story brick Italianate that crowned a couple hundred acres of the area's best pasture and farmland. According to her, Tom Stocker's father, a shrewd businessman and entrepreneur, had struck gold in Georgia back in the late 1800s, then settled this land in Alabama and instructed his children in the intricacies of the stock market. Evidently they all amassed quite a bit of wealth, including Tom. Most of them moved away to the surrounding cities—Birmingham or Chattanooga—after securing their fortunes, but Tom stayed on the mountain, as did his son, William, now in his late seventies.

Our hostess told us everybody in Sybil Valley knew William Stocker. Elected mayor multiple times throughout the past decade, he'd established the town as a sort of festival Mecca. If tourists weren't coming here for the apple-picking festival, they were enjoying a book fair or wine-tasting event. He'd built a quaint country diner, a music venue, and a small Swiss chalet-style hotel, but these days he mostly just ran his few head of cattle and fished.

Stocker appeared to be eating his dinner on the front porch when we pulled into his gravel drive. He lowered a newspaper, took off his glasses, and watched us climb out of the car. William Stocker might be big money, but he was still mountain folk, and I'd heard they regarded strangers with more than the usual small-town level of suspicion. When I reached the porch steps, I lifted my hand in greeting.

"Mr. Stocker?" I could feel myself trembling so I clasped my hands together. "I'm Althea Bell, from Mobile. This is my friend, Jay Cheramie."

"How do?" He eyed the both of us coolly. "Can I help you?"

"I'm here in town trying to do some research on my great-grandmother. She lived up here a long time ago. I thought you might be able to tell me something about her."

"I just may. What was her last name?"

"Wooten."

"We got a lot of Wootens around here. What was her first name?"

"Jinn. I'm not even sure of her maiden name."

He put down his paper then. "It was Alford," he said. "She was Jinn Alford before she married Howell Wooten." He stood up, skirted the table, and came down the steps. He put his glasses back on his nose and took a closer look at me. "You're her great-granddaughter, you say?"

I nodded, my heart thumping. "Did you know her?"

"I knew her son, Walter." He was still looking at me. "When I was a boy. He was a few years older than me. My father knew Jinn well."

Jackpot.

"I'm trying to find out what happened to her," I said.

"How do you mean?"

"How she died."

He didn't flinch. "I don't know anything about that."

"I've heard she had a bit of a reputation. Maybe your father mentioned something about that?"

"I don't think so. At least, not to me."

"Did you ever hear things from other people? Gossip, maybe?"

"I know the Wootens were good Christian people. They went to the Baptist church, and Howell never spoke against his wife."

"Why would he? Because of this?" I held up the label. He straightened.

"Yes. Jinn made her own wine and sold it. Which was a bit . . . out of the ordinary."

"You mean illegal?"

"Borderline. The state had just made the sale of alcohol legal—four years after the rest of the country—but only under their strict supervision. I'm pretty sure Jinn's wine didn't have the official government stamp of approval. The folks up here have always liked to do things their own way. It's possible she could've brought some trouble on her family." He hesitated a fraction of a second. "There was something else. People said she and her husband had a falling-out over her wine business. That she left him."

"For another man?"

His eyes flickered. "Some said. I never thought it was so."

I flipped the label over, held it up to him. He adjusted his glasses and read the inscription.

"Well, I'll be," he breathed.

"Did Jinn run off with your father, Mr. Stocker?" I said.

I thought I detected his face flushing, but he ducked his head, scratched at his jaw. "No, he was a widower—my mother died soon after I was born—and he never did remarry. We left town for a bit, we went over to Georgia for a while . . . but it was just the two of us, nobody else. And it was after Jinn left. We moved back a couple of years later, and my father died right here on this mountain, back in 1991."

I decided to lay all my cards on the table for William Stocker. "Jinn's daughter, Collie, kept that label with your father's name written on it for many years. I assume because Jinn wanted her to find him. I've been told Jinn had some kind of episode when she turned thirty—a nervous breakdown or some kind of psychotic break—and then disappeared. I've wondered if she might've been sent away. To Pritchard Hospital."

He didn't nod or look surprised. His face was a stone.

I went on. "The same thing happened to Collie."

That glimmer in his eyes again. "I knew Collie."

"Well, she had some kind of breakdown at thirty too and ended up at Pritchard. It happened to Collie's daughter, my mother, as well. At age thirty, oddly enough. Although I can't prove it, I'm pretty sure my father had her locked up. She died like the other two, under question-able circumstances."

He studied me so long I began to think he'd determined I was crazy and he was plotting a strategy to extricate himself from this conversation.

"So you're telling me," he finally said, "that you think the same thing's going to happen to you?"

"You could say I'm concerned, yes."

"I gather you're close to turning thirty . . ."

"In two days."

He nodded once, then averted his gaze and folded his arms over his chest so tightly it seemed like an act of self-preservation. His gaze traveled out to the fields where a couple of cows were lowing about something—then he spoke.

"I do know a few things about Jinn Wooten and my father." The lines along his mouth deepened and his eyes dimmed. "Not that I've ever felt it was right to share any of them. My father was a very private man."

"Please," I said. "I have no desire to ruin anyone's reputation. I just want to know the truth about my great-grandmother."

He scratched his cheek and gazed out over his property. "The last time any of us saw Jinn Wooten was the night of a church revival, for an itinerant preacher. It was the talk of the town. Everyone went to the service that night. But not us. My father was . . . well, he seemed agitated that night."

He clamped his mouth shut, but I wondered if there was more.

"You don't remember anything else?"

"Well. Some folks said she ran off with the preacher."

"Do you think that's what happened?"

He hesitated.

"You can't tell me . . . anything."

He gave me a rueful smile. Then shook his head. "She didn't run off with the preacher."

I pulled out the wine label and handed it to him. "As far as I know, Collie never contacted your father. Do you know why Jinn would've wanted her to?"

"By God." He whipped off his glasses and scrubbed at his eyes. "I can't believe I . . . I'd almost forgotten." He looked at me. "I have something for you. Do you mind waiting?"

He went inside. The big door, gleaming white with an ornate medallion, slammed shut behind him. Jay and I exchanged glances and waited in silence. After a few minutes, he reappeared with a small coin purse made of blue silk, held together with a metal snap of tarnished silver.

He handed it to me. I opened it and pulled out a thick stack of neatly folded vintage bills.

William Stocker cleared his throat. "Before my father died, he told me a little bit about Jinn. About their friendship. I'm fairly certain they were things he'd never told anyone. He was a respectful man, Miss Bell, a good man. Jinn asked him to hold that fifty dollars. For Collie. But she never came back for it."

The breeze made the bills flutter in my fingers. Fifty dollars hidden away for a young daughter. Something about it seemed so sad.

"I suppose it's yours now." He adjusted his glasses. "It was a lot of money back then and worth something now too, vintage bills like that."

"I don't know what to say." I smiled at him. "I mean, thank you."

He nodded. "Jinn Wooten didn't leave her family, and she didn't run off with some preacher." His voice wavered. "I don't know exactly what happened to her that night, but I'll tell you this—she wouldn't have left town. She was in love with my father. And he was in love with her."

"Mr. Stocker—"

But evidently we were done because he nodded at us, then turned and headed up the porch steps, leaving his half-eaten dinner behind him.

Chapter Thirty-Five

William Stocker had said Jinn and her husband, Howell, attended the Baptist church. It wasn't much to go on, and I didn't even know what I could possibly find there, but I decided it was a place to start.

There were three Baptist churches in the valley. (Not to mention two Methodists, one Community Bible, and a broken-down roadside shack with a hand-painted sign that read "Yahweh Holiness Tabernacle.") We chose the oldest-looking one, just up the road from town, a traditional white clapboard with a green roof and spire.

We climbed the worn steps and entered the cool, dim sanctuary. The room smelled of mildew and lemon Pledge. Two banks of glossy wooden pews flanked a center aisle of mauve carpet that ended at a simple white podium emblazoned with a painted gold cross.

From the warren of doors adjacent to the pulpit, a pasty man with Down syndrome emerged and lumbered toward us. He had a thick shingle of greasy hair and a green baseball jacket embroidered with the words "BROTHER BOB."

"Hey there," Jay called out. "Mind if we look around?"

He stopped and inspected us. Scratched his head. "You have your letter here?"

"We're not members, just visitors passing through town," I said. "Just wanted to look around if we could."

Brother Bob nodded. "Brother Larry will be by later."

"Okay," I said. "We'll just look around for now, if that's all right."

Jay's phone buzzed, echoing in the empty room.

"No phone calls in the church," Brother Bob said. "No music or beer either."

Jay handed the phone to me, and I scuttled out to the vestibule. I shut the heavy wooden double doors behind me. They clunked loudly in the hush of the church.

"Hello?"

"Althea, it's Beth Barnes from Pritchard." My breath caught in my throat.

"Is everything okay? You're not in trouble, are you?"

"No, not yet. They don't expect you back until lights-out. It's just . . . someone came by the hospital asking for you, a woman, and I thought I should call."

"Who?"

"She wouldn't give her name. She said she was family."

Could it have been Molly Robb again? *Shit.* But no. Beth had seen Molly Robb when she'd attempted to abduct me the first time. So who was it?

"What did she look like?"

"I wasn't here when she came. One of the interns talked to her."

"Listen, Beth," I said. "You've got to tell her, or anyone else who comes looking for me, you don't know where I am—"

"Althea," she said. "I *don't* know where you are."

"Right," I said. "Look, if anyone else shows up looking for me, tell them I'm . . ." I peeked through the crack in the double doors at Jay, who was gazing intently at some photographs on the wall. Brother Bob was circling behind him. "Tell them you think I went to Paris. With my boyfriend."

"Althea. You should come back. Call the police and tell them what your brother's done. I'll go with you and back you up."

"I know. I know. I will. I just . . ." I bit my lip. "There are some things I have to do first."

"Well, good luck," Beth said and hung up. I pushed through the doors, back into the sanctuary.

The entire length of it was covered in rows and rows of framed photographs. There were dozens of them, some black-and-white, some color, stretching from the balcony to the chair rail, all encased in identical dime-store frames. There were grainy shots of picnics and rummage sales, revivals and singings from past decades. All the way back to the thirties.

"Holy shit," I said, my voice echoing in the silence. Brother Bob glared at me, and I put one apologetic finger over my lips. "Sorry."

I waved Jay over to where I stood. The pictures in front of me were faded from years in the sun. I pointed to a series of three arranged under the pitched roof: the first showed a group of men in undershirts posing in front of a large, white tent, and the second was the same tent at night, filled with people.

I pointed to the third photograph; a close-up portrait. Jay's eyes widened.

Three people—two men, one woman, in front of the same tent. The woman, fine-boned and pale, was a beauty, with delicate features and a shiny, waved bob. Her head was turned to the side, and I could see her hair was pinned back on one side with a uniquely shaped barrette. The photo was grainy, but it could have been a bird with its wings outstretched.

It might've been.

"The barrette?" I said.

Jay hung over my shoulder. "I dunno. Maybe."

I looked at the bottom of the photo. Tiny letters spelled out the inscription: *Br. Daley, Br. and Mrs. Charles Jarrod.*

"Mrs. Charles Jarrod." I spelled the last name out for him.

Jay was already tapping away at his phone.

"Brother Jarrod preached here in 1937," a voice behind us said. Jay and I spun. Brother Bob was pointing to the photo. "He was from California. That's Brother Daley, the pastor back then with him. And his wife. Her name was Dove. Dove Davidson Jarrod."

Dove. A bird name. My heart kicked into overdrive.

"She was outlaw Dell Davidson's half sister. Some people said she made that up, though, nobody knows. They came to Sybil Valley in October 1937 to do a healing revival."

Jay and I exchanged stunned looks.

"You know who all these people are?" I asked Brother Bob.

He waved his arm at the wall. "I've worked here ten years. I've memorized them all," he said proudly.

"Listen to this." Jay read from his phone. "'Charles Jarrod passed away in 1956 of cancer at his home in San Diego, after which . . .'" He paused at this point and pronounced each word deliberately. *"Dove Jarrod returned to the state of Alabama where she currently resides.'"*

"You're kidding me." I grabbed the phone. "It really says that?"

He leaned over, and we read it together. "Is she here?" he said. I looked at the guy in the green jacket. "Does Dove Jarrod live in Sybil Valley?"

"No. But she's come to see Jean before. I seen her in town a time or two. She's real old. Dead now, probably."

My heart sunk, then leapt again. "You said Jean? Jean who?"

"Jean Tippett. She lives down by the creek."

"Finally," I said. I sank down onto a pew and rested my head back, feeling simultaneously lightheaded and nauseated. Here, at last, was someone who might've owned the hair barrette. Dove Jarrod. Maybe she was my honeysuckle girl. Maybe.

Jean Tippett's shingled cottage nestled on a shale slope that led down to a creek, just as Brother Bob had described. When we got out of the car, we could hear the creek running somewhere out back. I wished I could circle past the house and head to the water. Hide in the woods. Maybe I was just afraid of what I'd find inside.

Jay took my hand—I'd noticed he'd been doing this more and more—and together we walked up the dirt lane to the house. The yard was exploding with perennials, all kept in check by a low wall of stones. The door and shutters were painted a deep eggplant, window boxes overrun with a mass of blooms. A fairy-tale cottage.

I knocked on the door. There was no answer, not even a rustling from inside the house. All I could hear was the sound of the bees swarming the black-eyed Susans. I knocked again, a little louder in case Jean had hearing difficulties. Nothing. I turned to Jay.

"She's in there." He nodded at a puddle of water beneath a window box just to the left of the front porch. "She just watered her plants." He scanned the yard. A beat-up Oldsmobile sat on the far side of the house.

"What the hell," I growled in frustration. "Why won't she answer?" I looked into Jay's eyes, feeling the enormous dread I'd been keeping at bay for almost a whole month, creeping toward me.

My confidence was slipping. I was going to face my thirtieth birthday like Trix, Collie, and Jinn had faced theirs—exposed. In a position of weakness. I hadn't found the road map. In fact, the way ahead looked as dangerous and confusing as when I first started.

I took the brass-and-ivory barrette out of the cigar box and laid it in the center of Jean Tippett's green, plastic welcome mat. A last offering. We walked back to the car, and Jay climbed in, rested his head against the seat. I looked over my shoulder, hesitated, then wheeled back.

"What are you doing?" he called after me.

I didn't answer, just leapt up the front steps and began beating on the door with the flat of my palms, slapping at it until I thought it might rattle off its hinges. I'd curled my hands into fists and continued to pound when he got out of the car and ran to me. He touched my shoulder, but I shrugged him off.

"Open up," I shouted. "Let us in, goddamn it, or I'm going to kick down your door!"

"Althea, come on."

I kept banging.

"Stop it!" he said. "Stop!" He touched my arm but I jerked away.

"She's in there," I said, panting. "I've had enough of this bullshit. She knew we were coming. This is a small town. I bet Stocker called her." I dug my fingers into my hair, curled them into fists. "I don't know, Jay. I don't know what I'm trying to do here. This is crazy . . . this whole thing. Maybe I should just forget everything."

"Okay, let's just—"

"I can't go on like this. I've got . . . I have other concerns now."

"And we'll do whatever we have to do. I know what I said before, Althea, but I don't know. I'm starting to think you need to keep going. Find out the truth."

"I don't think I can. I don't."

"I'll help you . . ."

But I'd already backed across Jean's front porch, stumbled down the steps and around the side of the house. I slipped into the woods that bordered Jean's backyard, weaving my way through the trees, unable to stifle the sobs that tore at my throat. I came upon a meadow, and a sharp, sweet smell enfolded me—honeysuckle, moss, cold water. I stopped for a minute, my whole body trembling, the tears still falling. I dashed them away. Started off in a new direction.

I could hear my breath coming fast and the sound of the grass as I thrashed my way across the field. At last, I reached the creek. Broad and shallow, it sparked and tumbled over rocks, dancing its way down the mountain. I collapsed on the mossy bank, eyes squeezed shut and fists clenched.

A few minutes later, the sound of crashing underbrush brought me back to reality.

Jay stood behind me, in the grass, the sunlight behind him making his edges glow. He was so beautiful, feet planted wide and hair tousled. I turned my back to him.

"I can't do this anymore," I said. "I just . . . can't."

"I know you feel that way." He dropped down beside me. "But I don't believe it. You aren't a person who gives up."

I sighed. "Yes, I am. That's exactly who I am." I squinted out over the flashing creek. "I stole pills, Jay. From your mom's bathroom drawer. From the nurse at Val's place. I was keeping them . . . for later. It made me feel better, just knowing they were there."

He was quiet.

"And now . . . with the baby . . . I can't do that stuff anymore. And I don't have anything left that makes me feel safe."

He put his arm around me. I thought of the way he'd bumped my shoulder a few weeks ago in the clearing beside my house. I remembered the way the gesture had practically turned me inside out. It had been exactly thirteen days ago. Thirteen days, but it felt like a century. I had changed so much. Everything had changed.

He nodded at the creek and the waterfall. "Beautiful, don't you think? Magical, even."

I said nothing.

"There's a story here, you know."

I wound a blade of grass around my finger, then split it. "I hate stories. I don't ever want to hear another story as long as I live."

"So you're really going to give up?"

I flicked the grass away. "You don't understand. These stories—they've torn me up. Ripped me to pieces. My mother, my grandmother, they were at everyone's mercy. They couldn't save themselves; they couldn't do anything for themselves. I don't want that. I want to be okay. To be strong. To take care of myself."

"How long have I known you, Althea?"

I shrugged. "I don't know."

"Since we were eight," he said. "We were eight when you walked down to my house and asked if I wanted to go sailing. You were this little wild child, dirty feet, mismatching clothes. You weren't afraid of anything. You shoved me in that Sunfish and sailed us all the way down to the bay like a fucking pirate."

I shook my head, unwilling to trust myself to speak.

"You'll be okay, Althea. You have so much more than those women ever had."

"What?" I looked at him. "What do I have that makes me so different?"

"Their stories, the things they put in that box. You have Trix and Collie and Jinn inside you. It's not true what you said before, that you were bad odds. I think you're excellent odds, Althea. Really excellent odds."

Whether it was true or not, I needed to believe him. I couldn't face my future alone. I was losing my grip. I let my body fall against him, let him put his arms around me, and settled there.

Chapter Thirty-Six

Saturday, September 29, 2012
Sybil Valley, Alabama

The next morning, over coffee and English muffins, I told Jay I wanted to go back to Jean Tippett's. He sat back in his chair.

"Don't say it," I said. "Not one word about pregnancy hormones, okay? I realize I'm all over the map. But what you said by the creek? You were right. We have to talk to her."

But when we pulled up to Jean's house for the second time in twelve hours, my stomach flipped. She was waiting for us on the front porch. She looked to be in her seventies, nearly as wide as she was tall, with deep-brown eyes set in a sun-weathered face. She didn't seem the least bit surprised to see us climbing out of our car; she just waited with folded hands and a placid expression. I wondered who'd called her— Brother Bob or William Stocker or the lady who owned the bed-and-breakfast. *Word must travel as fast as electricity up here in Sybil Valley.*

"I'm Jean," she said when we reached the front gate. "You must be Althea and Jay."

"Yes, ma'am," I said, surprised my voice worked.

She motioned for us to follow her into the house.

As we passed the tiny living room, Jay rested his hand on my back and heat emanated out from it, all over my body. I was glad he was here. Glad he would hear Jean's story with me. In the kitchen, we found a small table covered with a gingham tablecloth and set with mugs.

Jean motioned for us to sit and began to pour coffee.

"I'm glad you came back," she said. "I was hoping you would. William called and gave me all kinds of hell for not answering my door."

I nodded even though I had no idea how Stocker had known we'd come here, or that Jean hadn't answered her door.

"I apologize for that. I was . . ." She pushed the sugar and cream toward us. "I think I was just hoping if I ignored you, the whole situation would just go away."

"The whole situation?"

"Well, Dove, you know. And Jinn. All that."

I felt Jay's hand steady me.

"We don't know much," he said. I was grateful. My throat seemed to have constricted to a pinhole. "We've only been able to find out scraps of information about what happened to the women in Althea's family. And all of it seems to point to Dove Jarrod."

She nodded, then let out a long, quavering sigh. "Yes. You're right. Dove is responsible for many things."

I leaned forward. "Do you know their story? Dove and Jinn's?"

"I do."

"Will you tell me?"

She held my gaze. "I will. But first I have to return this."

She slid the barrette, Dove's barrette, across the table toward me.

"It was a gift from President Roosevelt, you know," she said. "Brother Charles and Dove visited the White House, in '35 or '36, I think. The president was a thoughtful man. I don't guess he had any idea Dove wasn't her real name." She clasped her hands on the table. "It was kind of you to leave it. But it belongs to you. It's come a long way, and you should keep it."

I couldn't tell if my heart was thumping from fear or expectation or a combination of both, but I didn't care anymore. I had come too far to care.

"Please," I said. "Tell me. Tell me everything."

She pushed back her chair, rose, and walked out of the room. When she returned, she was holding a bound scrapbook. She laid it on the table in front of me, and I opened it. Sepia-toned photographs, dozens of them, and newspaper clippings spilled out of the yellowed pages.

"Dove gave this to me," she began in a quiet voice. "She said she couldn't bear to look at it anymore. Couldn't even stand to have it in her house."

I opened the book. Saw the picture of a handsome, barrel-chested man dressed in a white suit and bow tie.

Jean nodded at the picture. "Charles Jarrod was quite famous in his day. One of the original Pentecostals. They traveled around the country, gathering crowds of sinners to listen to them preach. Sounded like a bunch of hollering and carrying on to me, but people liked that kind of thing back then. They enjoyed being fussed at. Made them feel better about all the sin they'd done. He used to call the people 'whiskey-soaked and Sabbath-breaking.' Tell them he was going to drive them right back into the arms of God."

I flipped the pages. The man in the white suit stood on stage after stage, before masses of people. Then there were the shots of people kneeling before him or sprawled out on the ground, his hands on their heads. Children in wheelchairs, women on crutches. Men, in overalls and suits, their faces wet with tears.

"A faith healer," I said.

"People called them evangelists, tent revivalists. But yes, healing was part of his ministry. So was Dove."

I felt a trickle of sweat under my arms. "You knew her?"

Jean smiled, a brief, bright flash that made her look like a young girl. "She came looking for me one day, when I was thirty. The same way she came looking for your grandmother and your mother. She found me and told me her story. My story."

"I'm nearly thirty. Why hasn't she found me?"

Her eyes dimmed again. "Things went wrong with the others. I expect Dove thought she would be putting you in danger if she contacted you." She paused. "What happened to Jinn, to Collie, and then to your mama? It was Dove who set all that business in motion. She didn't mean to, and she was sorry for it—Lord, I can't tell you how sorry—but she was the cause of it all."

I swallowed. My throat felt coated in sandpaper.

"When Dove was younger," she went on. "She had the notion that she could make things right. But we can't always fix the past. She learned that."

I closed the book, pushed it to the side.

"The thirties were a difficult time," Jean said. "People were broken after the war, split on Prohibition, and devastated by the Depression. They were looking for answers to their problems. And who better to provide those answers than God? So, like I said, Charles Jarrod offered them God. They ate it up, every last bit of the show. And it was some show—speaking in tongues, healings. All kinds of miracles. The people up here in the mountains were used to old-time preachers who told them they needed to be baptized with water. Well, Charles Jarrod preached the baptism of the Spirit, you know. The baptism of fire.

"There were people who reported miracles in Jarrod's services. People claimed to see feathers fall from the air, supposedly from angel wings. Or oil dripping from people's skin. A few said they saw gold dust on their hands. They called it the anointing of the Lord."

A chill moved down my spine.

"If you asked me," she said. "I'd have to say there was at least one miracle—one real miracle—that occurred in Sybil Valley."

Chapter Thirty-Seven

October 1937
Sybil Valley, Alabama

After they left the Tippetts', Jinn took Dove to the meadow where the honeysuckle grew. Howell had probably already been here, searching for her. Or maybe he hadn't bothered. Maybe he'd gone directly up to Tom Stocker's house. The not knowing didn't feel so scary now. In fact, there in the meadow, with Dove, Jinn felt her heart lift.

The hollow was wild and tangled and silver in the moonlight. Jinn could hear the rush of the branch just beyond the stand of poplars. It sounded just like the murmurs of a crowd under a tent.

"I had a hunch you had secrets," Dove said.

"I don't," Jinn said, then thought of Tom Stocker and the calf in the woods behind the school. Pritchard. "Well, not really. Everybody knows about this place. I pick so much honeysuckle out here, they say you can smell it on my hands." She offered her palms, and Dove sniffed.

"Well, how about that?" Dove said. Grinned slyly. "You know, I have a secret too." She smoothed her hair. "It's called Clairol Titian Red. Underneath this, it's the color of mouse shit."

Jinn laughed. "That's your secret?"

"Oh, that's just the beginning." She raised one brow. "I got more. I got secrets as big as the Hindenburg. But I don't talk. A girl can't just give out her secrets, willy-nilly."

Jinn marveled at the girl. She didn't seem to be afraid of anything, not gallivanting around in the dark, busting into people's houses, or saying whatever she pleased to whomever she pleased. Talk about setting the world on fire. This girl was Myrna Loy times one hundred.

"Let's go for a swim," Dove said and scampered off to the water's edge. The dark enveloped her, and for an instant, Jinn lost sight of the white dress. She ran to catch up. Just upstream the water cascaded into a waterfall. When Dove saw it, she crowed with glee, peeled off her dress and sat down in her slip, letting the water splash over her shoulders. Jinn watched her from the bank.

"Come on in!" Dove shouted. Jinn skipped across the rocks, and when she reached Dove, the younger woman reached up out of the water and caught her hand. She pulled her onto a scarred altar of a rock, right in the middle of the creek. They settled there, Jinn wringing out the hem of her dress and Dove lazing back on her elbows.

"I wish I had a place like this to hide. You'd never smoke me out of this place. No sir." She glanced at Jinn's half-soaked dress. "Look at us, what a couple of crazy girls we are. What do you think the evangelist would say?"

Jinn shrugged.

Dove jumped up and pulled the straps of her slip over her pale shoulders. It puddled around her feet. "Mrs. Jarrod," she drawled in a deep voice. "I do declare. Your underdrawers are showing."

Off came the bra.

"Mrs. Jarrod! Why your *brassiere*! It's fallen right off your bosoms!"

Jinn giggled as Dove shimmied her underpants down her hips. "Woman! Don't you know the Lord Jesus Christ sees *everything*? What must He be thinking?"

She tossed her clothes toward the far bank. She winked at Jinn. "Why, I don't know, Brother Jarrod . . . That He did a damn fine job on this?" She twitched her pearly bottom.

Jinn had never in her whole life seen another woman naked, let alone one as beautiful as Dove Jarrod. Something inside her surged with rebellion. It made her feel strong. It made her want to howl into the dark, go wild and strip down to nothing herself.

There was a splash, and Jinn turned back. Dove surfaced from the water with a shriek. "Goddamn it! That's colder than Buffalo in January!"

Jinn didn't know exactly what made her do it, but she stood then and peeled off her dress. The slip and underwear too. The night air caressed her skin, the curves of her shoulders, breasts, and belly. Down around her hips and between her thighs. Soft as velvet. She liked it out here—in the dark, beside the water. She liked how free she felt with Dove.

Drawing a deep breath, Jinn jumped in the water, windmilling her arms and squealing at the icy shock.

They swam as the night deepened and settled around them, the stars seeming to drop slowly until they were just above the treetops. Jinn found herself telling Dove about almost everything: the ladies from Chattanooga, the wine. Howell and the money, her mother and father. She even told Dove about Tom Stocker and the poor, dead calf. The only subject she left out was Pritchard. When her throat finally ran dry, they climbed out and collapsed, side by side, on the flat rock beside the waterfall.

"You ever been to Hollywood?" Jinn asked Dove.

"Been there and back."

"Did you have a screen test?"

Dove stretched. "I could have. This one man, a real big-shot producer, he said he wanted to screen test me in his office. But I never went. He wasn't on the up-and-up."

"What do you mean?"

"There wasn't no movie."

"How did you know?"

"Oh, you know," Dove said. "Well, *I* knew, anyhow."

"Because of your gift?"

Dove burst into laughter. "Lord, girl, you're a stitch, aren't you? You planning a trip to Hollywood?"

"Maybe," Jinn said.

"With your Tom?"

And then, in a flash, Jinn knew why she was there in the meadow with Dove Jarrod. The Holy Spirit had led her there. He'd made Howell confess at the tent; He'd gotten him to tell Jinn he was planning to send her to Pritchard. He'd even made Jinn late to meet Tom, so Tom would go home, but it had all been for a reason.

It had all been for Dove.

The Spirit had led her to Dove, a woman with a gift. A woman who wasn't afraid of anything.

"They're going to send me to Pritchard," Jinn said, all at once. "The sanitarium down in Tuscaloosa. They're sending me tomorrow."

Dove's eyes sharpened, and she propped up on one elbow. "Why would they send you there?" Her voice was quiet.

"Because of the wine . . . and Tom."

Dove looked down then, intently studied her fingers as they laced and unlaced through each other. "Pritchard," she said, almost to herself.

Jinn spoke. "Have you been there?"

"Oh, goodness, no." But Jinn thought certainly there was more than that, because she'd suddenly shrunken, her boisterous sound and color melting away in the dark.

She grabbed Dove's hand, held it tight, and Dove flicked a look at her. It was so dark Jinn couldn't read the expression in the woman's eyes. "Won't you please tell Brother Charles what they're planning? Ask him if he wouldn't talk to Howell for me?"

She pulled her hand away. "Charles wouldn't want me to come between a man and his wife. It's not my place. I'm sure you'll be right as rain. They have doctors at those places. Lots of room to roam—"

"How can you say that?" Jinn interrupted. "It's the loony bin." She sat back. "You, of all people. I thought you'd understand."

"There's nothing I can do."

"But you can!" Jinn's voice rose to a screech. "You said you'd vouch for me."

"Jinn, hush." Dove glanced around. "You have to hush."

"I can't go there."

"You will, if that's what they want. But don't be afraid because you'll have the Lord. You can do anything, with His help."

Jinn stared at her. "What?"

"With the anointing of the Lord," Dove said. "You can do any-thing. It's everything. For the healing of the nations. For visions of the past and prophecies of the future."

It sounded like a line from one of Brother Jarrod's advertising bills. Disappointment rose like a suffocating fog in Jinn's chest. A fog that threatened to cut off her breath, choke her to death.

"You're talking about all that with Vonnie Tippett?" she said.

Dove moved toward the edge of the rock and began playing with a spray of water from the fall, fluttering her fingers in and out, in and out. She watched the smooth sheet part like a curtain under her hand.

"Yes. That was the anointing. It's a funny thing. Gives me feelings about people. I see something in my head. Or someone who needs prayer. And, well, you were there. I find them and . . . ring-a-ding-ding." She looked back at Jinn. "It's a gift. A very good thing for a girl to have. A handy thing no matter what situation she finds herself in."

"I don't need a gift," Jinn said. Her heart was really thundering away now. She swallowed, trying to slow it. "I need someone to talk to my husband."

Dove went back to her fluttering.

Jinn moved closer, wrung her hands. "He'd listen to Brother Charles, after what happened at the meeting tonight. You could ask him if he'd go up and pay Howell a visit. Talk to him. Brother Charles listens to you. I know he does. I saw it."

Dove shook her head.

"Dove."

Dove turned her face as stony as the rock they sat on. "I'm sorry, Jinn, I can't. I truly can't. It's not my place to tell your husband how to handle his family. This is the way it is—no one can stop him from sending you to Pritchard if that's what he's bound and determined to do. No one but God himself."

Tears spilled down Jinn's cheeks and into her mouth. She gulped them down, tasted their salty tang. That was the only thing you could do with tears, she thought. Swallow them.

So that was the end of it. Dove would not help her, and Jinn would be sent to Pritchard, away from all she knew and loved.

Jinn dropped her head and began to sob.

"Oh, Jinn," Dove said.

Jinn thought of Collie and Walter, of Howell and her mother. Her little cabin. The white church. The mountain and valley she loved. Then an image of Tom. *Tom.* His broad shoulders and kind eyes. He'd never held her, not the way she wanted. They'd never lain together in a bed. Never . . . She would go to Pritchard, and all she'd known would be lost to her.

She covered her face with her hands, but she couldn't stop the tears. She wanted to, but she couldn't. If Dove didn't help her, all of it was lost to her now.

She felt Dove move to her, take her hands. "I'm awfully sorry, Jinn. You'll never know how sorry I am. You'll just have to be very strong, that's all. Stronger than you've ever been before."

Jinn dug her fingers into Dove's arm. Pulled the woman in close.

"Give it to me," Jinn whispered fiercely, eye to eye with Dove. "I'm begging you."

Dove recoiled. "What—"

"The anointing. The gift."

"Oh, I can't—"

Jinn held fast. "You have to. Please." Her voice had risen again, precariously close to a shriek. "Give it to me. Please!"

And another thing. Her skin was prickling under Dove's touch. Fairly crackling with electricity. That was proof, wasn't it? That the gift was real? That she was feeling the fire Brother Charles talked about?

"I wish I could help you," Dove said. "But, I don't think it's—"

"I'm thirty today," Jinn said. "It's my birthday." She managed a smile. "Don't you see? You can give me a gift right now—right this minute—a birthday gift that'll make everything different from here on out. You can change everything."

Dove's eyes looked hooded and sad. After a long moment, she pulled the barrette out of her hair and clipped it into Jinn's. "There you go. It's for you."

"I won't tell anyone," Jinn squeezed Dove's hands again. And she thought, as her skin touched the other woman's, that she felt the twinge again, the prickling of her skin—a sign something was happening. She looked into Dove's eyes.

Dove looked down at their entwined fingers.

"Please."

Dove sighed. Then, at last, she lifted one hand, laid it gently over Jinn's eyes. Took a breath. "Do you receive the fire, Jinn Wooten?" she said. Her voice was subdued.

Jinn thought of Howell and the hymns, Vonnie and the creek. She thought of the calf strung up between two pines and the pressure of Tom Stocker's fingers on the back of her head when he kissed her. Even after all the begging and pleading, the truth was, she didn't know if the fire was real. She wanted it to be, that much she knew. She needed it to be.

"Jinn?" Dove said.

"Yes," Jinn said. "I receive it."

Jinn thought she felt a zap of something, a bolt of some kind of light surge through her. It didn't come from the sky, like she expected. It bubbled up from somewhere inside her, as if it had been there all along—waiting, biding its time, before exploding and shooting up and out of her body.

Was this the fire? Or was it the thick honeysuckle vines, finally constricting and choking her, driving her mad? She thought of her mother, lying in bed. She thought of the Lurie girl, who'd climbed to the top of the fire tower and, in full view of the town, stripped down to nothing and threatened to jump. This wasn't a breakdown. Whatever this was shook her body and lit her up from the inside. This thing made her feel invincible.

"Jinn?" It was Dove, still beside her.

Jinn reached for her. "Don't leave me." She was crying still, and she felt suddenly heavy, like two huge hands had her by the shoulders, rattling her bones and teeth. But she wasn't afraid anymore. She was ready for whatever lay before her.

She lifted her hands and pressed the tips of her fingers to her mouth. Her lips were open, they felt cold, and she could feel her breath coming out in staccato puffs.

Just then she heard a shout, from somewhere upstream, in the woods.

Howell.

She looked at Dove. Her face looked like an angel, the makeup washed away. She looked like something not of the mountain. Not even of earth.

"They can't hurt me now, can they?" Jinn said.

Dove bit her lip. But she didn't say a word.

Jinn waited for the men to come. She felt the fire roar through her, calming her, making her feel like she'd drunk a whole bottle of honeysuckle wine. Charles Jarrod appeared first. He'd taken off his suit coat and removed his tie, and his hair had sprung loose from its pomade. His white wingtips glowed in the grass.

"Have you seen my wife?" he called across the water to her.

Jinn looked behind her, but Dove had vanished. She turned back to Jarrod and tried to answer him but she couldn't find her voice. Then Howell was there. And Walter, holding the .22 at his side.

"Jinn," Howell called, and she went to him, plunging into the water, fighting the current. She scrabbled her way up the bank and stood before Howell.

"Son of a bitch," he said.

"I lost . . . " she gasped.

"What?" He leaned closer.

"I lost my dress."

He straightened, looked her up and down. "Looks like you've lost your mind." Jinn couldn't look him in the eye; she couldn't have straightened her body, even if she'd wanted to. "Oh, Jinn. I *told* you."

Then Jinn saw someone step out of the trees. She stared at the figure, her breath shallow, heart skittering, like it was some dreaded haunt from a ghost story. She felt a tear slip down her face and her nose start to run. A warm trickle ran down the inside of her thigh.

Vernon Alford was an average-size man, with knobby arms and legs and a soft belly that spilled over his work pants. A good head of white hair waved back from his temples and fell clear to his shoulders. He had a deep voice—everyone said he should've been a preacher—and through the years, he had dressed up as Santa Claus and gone to the post office, where the kids swarmed over him and told him what they wanted for Christmas. Jinn had never sat on his lap. She'd known he wasn't Santa.

Vernon walked to his trembling daughter and hitched up his pants. "What's this?" he asked Howell. He looked at Jinn, who shook her head, mute. He began to unhook his suspenders. "You're gonna speak to me about this. Howell done got me up out of bed in the middle of the night, and, by God, you're gonna speak."

Chapter Thirty-Eight

Saturday, September 29, 2012
Sybil Valley, Alabama

Jean had trailed off, her gaze drifting somewhere beyond us. The coffee had gone cold, and my stomach was rumbling. But I didn't register any of it. I couldn't think. I pressed my hands against my face, just to remind myself I was really sitting in this room.

My mother had been serious, deadly serious, that night in the clearing with me. The honeysuckle girl was a real person, and her name was Dove Jarrod. Jinn had known her. Collie had met with her and so had my mother. And Mom had meant for me to find her as well. To figure out what had really happened to Jinn. And why the secret had been kept from all of us.

"You've got to finish," I pleaded. "You can't stop there."

"I've told all I know." Jean sighed, looking tired and distracted, every bit her age. "I suppose Vernon beat Jinn. Back then, the men got away with that kind of thing, more than folks would like to admit. But what happened after that, what they did with her, I don't know. Dove would never tell me."

My eyes burned with tears. "So, after all this . . . after I learn the honeysuckle girl really existed and, not only that, actually knew my great-grandmother . . . that's it? That's the end of it?"

In answer, she rose, collected our mugs, and lumbered to the sink.

"You're Vonnie Tippett's daughter, aren't you?" I asked. "The one Dove and Jinn prayed for?"

She kept her back to us. "I am."

"How did Dove know your mother was pregnant? Did she really have a gift? Is that the miracle you were talking about?"

She faced me. "I'd sound like a nut if I said I believed that, now wouldn't I? And they'd have to put me in Pritchard."

"Do you believe it?"

Jean shrugged and went to work cleaning the mugs under a spray of water. "On the other hand, Brother Jarrod had a pretty professional outfit going. He had a solid reputation as a prophet and healer to keep up, and I can't imagine he left much of that kind of thing up to chance."

Jay cut in. "Look, Jean, it doesn't matter if Brother Jarrod was lying or telling the truth. It matters if you are."

She seemed unperturbed by his dig. "I've told you everything I know."

"This is a small community," I said. "There had to have been rumors about what happened to Jinn."

"Oh, there were rumors, all right." She stacked the mugs in a dish rack and looked out the window. "Let's see. Jinn's daddy and her husband caught her in a tryst with Tom Stocker. They caught her with Charles Jarrod—they caught her with *Dove Jarrod*—and chased her out of the valley, clear down to Birmingham. Or to Mobile. Some people said Howell put her in Pritchard. Some said, when Vernon and Howell caught her doing whatever she was doing, she was so ashamed and humiliated she ran up the mountain and jumped off the cliff."

"I need the truth, Jean."

She turned. "Then you'll have to talk to Dove because I don't know it."

"And how do you propose I do that?" I shot back. "Seeing as she's dead."

"I never said that."

"You—" I blinked. Gulped. The room spun around me, sunlight and gingham and the smell of stale coffee whirling into a hot, smeary blur. What was she saying?

"Dove's not dead," Jean said and laughed. "She's well into her nineties, granted, but she's very healthy."

"You're kidding me."

"No. I'm not. Dove Jarrod's alive and well."

I stood, my chair scraping the wood floor. "She won't be for long, not if I don't get to her soon. My brother's after her, after her story, just like I am. I'm afraid he'll hurt her if he finds her. You have to tell me where she is. Please. She's in danger."

"She won't want to see you. It's not safe, not for either of you."

"I know. Don't you understand? That's exactly what I'm saying. She may have been safe before, but everything's changed. If my brother figures out she's alive—and I'll bet he has—he'll come for her."

She wiped her hands on the dish towel and hung it neatly over the dishwasher handle. She studied me for a second or two, then seemed to arrive at a conclusion.

"She lives in a little house. Down in Tuscaloosa."

My eyes widened.

"Right across the highway from Pritchard Hospital," she went on. "But she's not going to talk to you."

Jay and I exchanged glances.

"Then you're coming with us," I said.

Back in Tuscaloosa, Jay, Jean, and I sped past the crumbling gates of Old Pritchard, and I sank deeper into the cushioned leather of the seat. But I couldn't help looking back.

The spires stood out against the blue sky, and the brick walls of the place were furred with ancient vines. Honeysuckle, I thought, or, more aptly, poison ivy. The windows that weren't boarded over with plywood gaped like empty eye sockets, lined with mold and cobwebs instead of scar tissue.

I thought of Jean's story, all the things Jinn had told Dove that night at the creek about the honeysuckle wine, the money, and Tom Stocker. Her own mother, neglected and wasting away in that upstairs bedroom. The mutilated calf.

Of course the whole thing could be twenty-four-carat bullshit—a tale concocted by Jean or Dove or even Jinn. Dove hadn't told anyone else the story. That, in itself, bathed the whole thing in a certain unbelievable glow.

It could all be a lie.

But if it was true, I had to admit my great-grandmother had faced a terrifying evil. The men Jinn lived with had been monsters—her son, father, and husband. And all she'd had to defend herself was the flimsy farce of spiritual protection offered by a carnival con woman. A woman who pretended she could bestow the power of God on people.

Jinn must have been desperate. She'd fallen under the spell of Dove's mumbo jumbo, believing she'd received a miraculous gift. The men at the creek—Howell and Walter and Vernon—had witnessed Jinn's breakdown. No doubt they'd wanted to keep it quiet.

"Is that it?" Jay asked Jean, interrupting my thoughts.

I followed his pointed finger to a simple white house in the distance. It was positioned just across the road from the Pritchard soccer field. The house sat in a thicket of cedar trees, and other than the immaculately neat yard bordered on all four sides by a silver-gray board fence, nothing about the place was remarkable. Jay pulled the car onto a slight rise on the side of the road, and we stared at the house.

"That's it?" I asked. "That's Dove's house?"

"What did you expect?" Jean said.

"I don't know—a little enchanted hideaway in a hollowed-out tree?" I let out my breath. "I can't believe it. She'd been right across from the hospital, all along. I'd been a hundred yards away, and I never even knew it."

I studied what I could see of the place. There was no car in the adjacent carport, which made sense. Dove was in her late nineties; she probably no longer drove. I wondered who looked after her, who picked up her groceries and medication. Did anyone come to cook or clean for her? Play cards or watch movies with her?

"I guess she likes her privacy. Except . . ." My eyes swept the place, and all at once, my pulse ratcheted up. "It looks like the gate's open."

The doorbell echoed through the house—the sound of wind chimes—but no one answered.

The minute we stepped over the threshold, I knew something was wrong. All the lights were on, and jazz music was playing from a stereo. Two back windows, one on either side of a neatly swept fireplace, were cracked open to let in the late-September breeze.

Nothing looked out of place. Framed photographs lined the mantel—Dove and her husband Charles, or just Dove alone, in black-and-white and color, through the years. She'd grown more beautiful with time, her red hair turning to silver, then white. I could see the ethereal beauty Jean had described. The girl Jinn had been drawn to.

"Something's not right," Jean said.

I picked up what looked like a recent snapshot—Dove in her garden, floppy straw hat hanging down behind her, head thrown back in laughter. She had on red lipstick, and her hair was smoothed back into an impossibly perfect chignon.

"I took that," Jean said. "Her birthday." She glanced around uneasily.

Jay called to us. In the kitchen, on the table, there was a half-eaten plate of food—wilted salad, brown rice, and a hardened wedge of cheese. An overturned glass of water lay broken in a puddle on the linoleum floor. I felt the panic rise in my throat.

"He has her." I locked eyes with Jay. "Wynn."

"Where?"

"I don't know. He could've taken her anywhere. To one of the rooms at Old Pritchard where he took me. Or farther back on the property, in the woods, near the cemetery." I mopped my face with my hand. "He could've taken her back to Mobile."

"Why would he do that?" Jean asked.

"It's secluded, down by the river. He could take his time getting the story out of her. And then, when he's gotten what he's after . . ." I grabbed Jay's hand. "If he's gone home, I have to go after them. You and Jean search the hospital and the grounds."

Jean listed slightly, then put out a hand to the counter.

"I'm coming with you," Jay said.

"No," I said. "You have to stay with Jean. If Wynn sees her, she'll be in danger too."

"I don't want you going down there alone," he said. "Not in your condition."

"Don't be ridiculous. I'll be fine."

His lips tightened.

"I'll be careful, I swear. If I see Wynn has Dove, I'll call the police. Right away. Look." I pointed to the plate of food on the kitchen table. "Wynn—or one of his guys—surprised her while she was eating lunch. They can't have been gone that long."

He just stood there, shaking his head, eyes flinty.

I turned to Jean. "If I leave now, I'll be in Mobile by five, right behind them. If you don't hear from me by five thirty, call the police. Or the governor. Or whoever will listen to what you have to say. But if he's really taken her there, I have to go now."

"I'll go," Jay said. "You stay here with Jean."

"No. And no way I'm setting foot back on Pritchard property."

"He could kill you, Althea."

"I won't let him." I put my hand on his arm. "Jay, listen to me. You have to let me do this. Face him on my own. It's like you said before, don't you see? It's for all of them. I have to do this for Trix, Collie, and Jinn."

"Listen to her, Jay," Jean said.

"Thank you," I said.

Jay inhaled once, then released the breath. Pulled the car keys out of his pocket and held them out to me.

"Five thirty," he said.

I took the keys. "Five thirty. Call the police, make sure Jean's safe, and then come find me."

Chapter Thirty-Nine

Saturday, September 29, 2012
Mobile, Alabama

I chanted the *Veni, Creator Spiritus* in a loop all the way down to Mobile. At first, tears streamed down my face, but after a while, they dried, and I felt a calmness steal over me. A strength I'd never felt before. I felt my mother near me. My mother and Collie and Jinn.

At last, I spun into the drive of my childhood home, behind a familiar-looking black SUV. I sprang out of the car and ran to the front steps, then pulled up short. There was no sign of life in the front windows, no lights on in the slanting afternoon sun. I could smell the salty air, see the river sparkling just beyond the house. But there was only silence. An eerie silence blanketing the whole place.

I rounded the side of the house, gazed upriver, then down.

Wynn's boat was gone. Which meant he could've taken Dove somewhere. Out to the bay or out toward the gulf. Or the boat could simply be at the marina, getting its yearly service, for that matter. I studied the matted grass for some kind of sign—footprints or a dropped handkerchief or something for me to follow—then felt like laughing and crying at the same time. Like I had any tracking abilities whatsoever. Like Dove was going to know I was coming and was going to leave me clues.

I straightened, my eyes closed, listening to the sounds of the river. The distant putt of boat motors, the wind in the pines above me, a neighbor's leaf blower. An egret squawked overhead, a great, deep-throated call I felt like I hadn't heard in a hundred years, and my eyes snapped open. Should I go inside and search the house? Or just hide? Wait for Wynn to make the move first?

Somewhere, in the distance, a door slammed.

My head swiveled to the woods.

The sound had come from the other end of the property, from the vicinity of a broken-down wharf on the far side of the woods. The old dock was abandoned and concealed by the bramble of the woods, along with an old shed where my mother used to keep her crab traps.

Breaking into a run, I slipped into the thicket of trees. I ran through the clearing and back into the tangle, crunching over pine needles, stumbling. I broke through the opposite side of the woods and skidded to a stop. Wynn was standing just off the dock, on the shore, waiting. He had his hands in the pockets of his seersucker suit, a pink bow tie at his neck. He looked like he'd just come from an Edwardian-era ice-cream social.

I shaded my eyes against the setting sun. "What have you done with her?" I said. "Where's Dove?"

He glowered at me. "You know you can't just waltz out of a place like Pritchard. You're in violation of a court order."

"I'm about to lose my mind in two days," I said mildly. "I'm just here to see if there's anything I can do to stop it."

He sighed, waved his hand. "Where's your boyfriend?"

"I sent him home. I told him this was a family matter."

He cocked his head. "Really?"

"Really. You and I can handle this alone. There's no reason to involve anyone else. Not Jay. Not Dove."

"You know that's not true." He jutted his chin, regarded me coolly. "Dove's essential. She's the one with the secret."

"What have you done with her?" I asked.

He smiled.

I lunged at him. Buried my hands in his slick, black hair and clenched as hard as I could. Then, with all my strength, I pulled. He screamed and clawed at me, but I didn't stop. I just kept pushing and pulling, yanking his head back and forth, my fingers anchored in his hair.

"Stop!" he screamed, and I finally did. He staggered backward among the mud and the reeds, and I saw what I'd done. His hair—his perfect hair—was actually a mass of plugs, running all along his scalp in neat little rows like they'd been planted by a miniature, methodical farmer. I'd pulled them out by the roots. Now many of them had come loose and lay on the shoulders of his suit. His head oozed red and white.

He glared at me and spit. "You little bitch!" He touched his scalp gingerly and examined his fingertips in disgust. He wiped them on his pants. "You know, I am getting really tired of dealing with you. I have been very patient. Endlessly patient. We all have, Althea, while you've done nothing but dragged this family's name through the mud."

All I could do was stare at him and those disgusting, bleeding plugs.

"I'm tired of making excuses for you," he went on. "I'm tired of the constant, never-ending damage control I'm obligated to do because you won't *pull yourself together!*"

He was trembling, and a blue vein throbbed in his forehead under a smear of blood. "I have a career to attend to, do you understand that? I have important—*meaningful*—work to do. I am carrying on Dad's legacy. Does that word have any meaning to you?" He mopped his face and looked out over the river. "All of us—me, Dad, Molly Robb—would've been fine if you had just kept going down the path you were on. I mean, don't get me wrong, it's not an easy thing to watch, someone you love destroying herself. But with you, it was an inevitability."

He turned back to me. "Here's the way it works. I am me. You are you. Molly Robb is Molly Robb. Do you understand? We all have our roles to fulfill. You don't suddenly get to decide you're someone else. Some hero. Some *whistle-blower*"—he spit this word out—"who can screw everything up for everybody else. You need to go back to doing what you do best, Althea. Killing yourself."

Shaking, I watched him amble down the dock. I felt hollow, like my insides had just been scraped out. I couldn't cry. I couldn't make a sound.

He was already at the end of the dock, where he fumbled with the door of the rotted shed and then disappeared inside. Before I could start toward him, the door banged open again and he reappeared, pulling a woman behind him. He pushed her to the end of the wharf, all the way to the edge, then turned her to face me.

I caught my breath, felt my heart thump in my chest.

Dove.

She was tiny, a bird of a woman. Her white hair was smoothed back in a bun, just like in the pictures at her house, and she wore a white caftan, which hung off her delicate bones like a waterfall. Her face was bare, save for a smudge of red lipstick. The way the light of the dipping sun glowed behind her, I thought she might be some kind of character out of a movie. An angel. Or some strange twist of my own imagination.

I dug in my pocket for my phone and, with shaking fingers, tapped out a call to 9-1-1.

"Put down the phone, Althea," Wynn shouted to me.

I froze, lowered it. I could hear the faint sound of buzzing.

"Come down here," he called. "Come talk to Dove."

I moved toward them, down the wharf, stopping just a couple of yards short. Wynn had a vise grip on Dove's arm, and he was breathing hard, blood smeared down his temples.

"My God," I whispered. "You're real."

She smiled, dimples cleaving both cheeks, and I could see the network of veins beneath her translucent skin. As I studied her, she searched my face too, each of us cataloging the other's features. She reached out a hand, like she meant to brush my cheek with her fingertips, but we were too far apart and she lowered it again.

I felt my skin tingle where she would have touched me.

"Hang it up, Althea," Wynn said. He nodded down at my phone. I realized there was a voice, tinny and faraway, coming from it. "Hang it up now. And throw it in the water." He twisted Dove's arm, and her smile turned into a wince. I hit the button.

"If you want to hear her story," he snapped. "If you want her alive, you'll throw it in the water now."

I did.

"What are you going to do, Wynn?"

Behind us, the sun was sinking into the bay, way down at the mouth of the river. The river was high, detritus from recent storms swirling past the slimy, sunken piers. Water sloshed up in the gaps left by rotted boards, turning the whole surface of the dock into a slippery, treacherous square.

It was getting darker by the minute, and we were hidden from everyone, beyond the curve of the tangled bank. Soon to be cloaked in total darkness. No one would see what happened here.

"I like drowning," Wynn said. "It's an efficient way to go. And it happens frequently enough, accidentally—to elderly ladies on medication, in their bathtubs. To addicts with suicidal tendencies." He regarded me coolly. "I should probably take care of you first. She can't run."

"Wynn," I said, as calmly as I could. "Let's go back up to the house. Let Dove tell us her story."

He barked out a laugh. "No. No, I don't think so. I don't think I give a shit about her story anymore, Althea. All I want to do is finish up with you two here and find someplace to get myself a good, stiff drink. Or three."

Dove looked out over the river. She didn't seem scared. She didn't seem worried in the least. I took one tentative step closer to them.

"You can't commit murder to keep our family secrets buried," I said. I took another step. "Politicians get away with all kinds of stuff. Affairs, drug addiction, tax evasion. Just call a press conference, tell them everything, and it'll blow over in a month."

"Don't be so naive, Althea," he growled. "Our uncle was Klan. So I already have that one, massive, humiliating strike against me. I may win governor, but can you imagine what it's going to take for a man with a murdering white supremacist in his bloodline to get into the White House?"

"Killing Dove is not going to fix that."

He sent me a scornful look. "Didn't you learn anything from all your detective work? It wasn't just Walter who stirred shit up. There are other stories—other questionable events that our family has been involved in—and I will have to account for every single one of them in a presidential campaign. It's not right. It's not fair. Because, God knows, I didn't do anything. But that's the way it works these days. The media doesn't let anything go. All it takes is one news report, one Internet article, and you're finished."

"Wynn—"

"So I'm taking care of it now. I'm burying everything *now.*"

"People died, Wynn."

He sighed. "Oh, who's to say what really happened? It was so long ago. Regardless, it's our family, Althea. Our business. Walter understood that. And Dad."

He shook his head and turned back to Dove.

My gut twisted. So our father had done something horrible, too.

I moved toward them but his free arm shot out, warning me from coming any closer. As he did, both rotted boards underneath his feet cracked and split. With one jerk and flail of his body, he fell into the gap, his entire lower half disappearing into the river below.

I cried out, and Wynn clawed at the surrounding planks. He dug his fingers into the cracks and blinked down at the swirling, black water.

"Jesus," he gasped. "My leg. I think it's broken."

I dropped to my knees and reached out to him, now wedged between a narrow two-foot gap.

"Jesus, it really hurts," he said, sputtering. "I think the bone tore through."

I studied him for a split second. He was my brother. He needed me.

"Give me your hand," I said.

He didn't, though, just tilted his head back, an offering to the sky, now sprayed with stars. He started to laugh, a manic, high-pitched cackle that rose up into the darkness. I sat back on my heels and watched him for a couple of moments.

"This is fucked up," he said, after winding down. "So fucked up."

I looked over my shoulder. "Dove? Are you okay?"

She nodded, and I turned back to Wynn. His face was a mess of blood and water, and it shone a pale, greenish hue in the moonlight. He looked bad. Weak. I wondered how bad his leg was.

"Give me your hands," I said. "I'm going to pull you out."

"You can't. I'm too heavy. I'll swim around," Wynn said.

I eyed him. "What about your leg?"

"I'll be fine. I'll go under the dock and swim to the bank." He gave me a look I couldn't quite read, at least not in the dark. "I'm sorry, Althea," he said. "Okay? I'm really sorry. For everything."

I didn't know how to answer.

"Althea. I said I was sorry."

And then, his body seemed to rise out of the water slightly, almost imperceptibly. He looked down at the choppy water in confusion. Then it happened again—he bobbed up, then back down again, as if buoyed by something beneath him.

"What—" he said, then stopped.

Behind him, pushing the water into the shape of a long, deadly arrow, I saw the brown, pebbled back of an alligator. I wanted to yell out, to warn him, but I couldn't make the sounds connect to one another. I couldn't push them out of my throat.

But Wynn could. From between the broken boards, he let out the most piercing, high-pitched shriek I'd ever heard. And he began to move too—thrashing back and forth wildly, flailing his arms in the air in an effort to grab hold of something, anything. He managed to snag a piece of the dock, dig his fingers into the soft wood.

He groaned and tried to heave himself up. But he was weak, and he couldn't manage to lift himself more than an inch or two out of the water. His head dropped to the wharf, and he scratched at it fiercely, panting like he'd just run a marathon.

Before I was able to reach him, he was screaming again, kicking and bucking in the churn. I extended my arm. He caught me, and we held fast. I hooked one hand under his armpit, pulling him in a bit, bracing myself with the other hand. His eyes flashed a wild, metallic sheen. Something primal I'd never seen before.

"I've got you," I said.

He pressed his face against mine and made a strange sound in my ear. A low, whining hum. I locked my arm around his torso, tried to dig the toes of my shoes into the crack between the boards.

"Hold on," I said. I felt one of his arms tighten around my back. "I'm going to get you out."

"Jesus, Althea," he gasped. "My leg . . . It got my leg . . ."

"I know. It's okay. I've got you." I growled through clenched teeth and pulled with all I had, straining to get his sodden body over the boards. I threw my weight back again and again until the muscles in my back cramped.

When I looked into the block of darkness behind Wynn, there was nothing, just the gentle undulations of the river. Then, in an instant, twin crests rippled up and zoomed through the ink-black water toward us. A half a second later, Wynn screamed. It was a horrible, shrill, unearthly sound, and it rang in my ear. I might've screamed too; I don't know. He jerked, one hard, violent shudder. I held him but he lurched sideways, out of my grasp. I watched in horror as his face contorted in agony. His body shuddered once more, and was swallowed beneath the surface of the river. I know I screamed then.

I backed away from the narrow opening, the water still lapping the edge.

"Althea." It was Dove, behind me. I turned. "Go. Go to the house. Call the police."

I nodded and ran down the wharf and into the woods, blinded by tears, my ears filled with the sound of my sobs. They came out in a low, keening hum, exactly the same as the last sounds I'd heard from my brother.

Chapter Forty

Sunday, September 30, 2012
Mobile, Alabama

Sometime in the early morning hours, the nurse called my name. My river-soaked clothes had mostly dried, and I was curled up in the vinyl hospital lounge chair beside my father's bed. Her voice jolted me out of my ragged, nightmare-filled sleep, back to consciousness and the antiseptic smell of the hospital room. I opened my eyes. They burned with grit.

"Sorry to wake you," she said. "The police are here. They want to talk to you." Her face was carefully arranged in a neutral expression.

I craned my neck and looked past her into the dim hall. I could see the outline of Jay's shoulder and hear the rumble of his voice. He'd caught them already, was probably telling them they could talk to me later. I glanced at my father. He looked the same as he had last night. White. Deathly still. Breathing on his own, but just barely.

"I'll be out in a minute. I need to use the bathroom."

"Of course. Oh, and happy birthday." She nodded toward Jay. "He said you're thirty today."

"Yeah," I said. "Thanks."

She beamed a cheerful smile. "That's a big one."

When the door shut, I unfolded from the chair. My muscles and joints screamed in protest; my tongue felt huge and furry. Forget thirty, I felt sixty.

After I'd gotten back to the house, after the police and Jay had shown up, my father had had a rare moment of lucidity. In halting phrases that looped forward and backward in time, he'd told me his story.

The Haldol had wrecked Mom, left her physically shaky and mentally diminished. She chanted her Latin prayer all day, every day. He was afraid for her safety and ours. And then, when Mom had met up with the woman from the mountain, she'd snapped.

That night, she threatened to tell the family secrets she claimed to have learned. She promised to ruin her uncle Walter and her husband—even her young son's future career—if they didn't come clean. Panicked, Elder whisked her off to Pritchard. He convinced a young paramedic, Woodrow Smart, to sign a phony death certificate and told everyone my mother died of an aneurysm. Soon after, Smart died from an accidental fall. My father hadn't had anything to do with it.

In the next days, Dad and Walter had argued about the best course of action. Dad had wanted to keep my mother at Pritchard; he felt she was safe there. Walter disagreed. And one night, he took matters into his own hands. He drove to Tuscaloosa and walked into my mother's room in the hospital, where he fed his niece an entire bottle of Haldol.

After I finished up in the bathroom, I returned to Dad's bedside. His face glowed an eerie white under the fluorescent hospital lamp. I tried not to focus on his frail form, just on the features of his face. The ones that felt familiar to me. The lines of his nose. The creases on his forehead.

"So today's the day," I said. "My thirtieth birthday."

I lifted my hand, let it hover over his head, then lowered it, until the pads of my fingers rested on his forehead. He felt warm, and my fingertips tingled ever so slightly—a frisson of electricity between my skin and his. I touched him along his temple, over his fragile skin, and down his jaw. Leaned closer and cupped his face between both my hands.

His eyelids fluttered, then opened.

His mouth stretched in what looked like a smile. "Thea."

Thea. I hadn't heard that name in so long. Not since I was very little, before my mother died.

"I'm here."

"How's my girl?" He touched a strand of my hair.

"I'm good."

"I want to say . . ." He swallowed. "Walter didn't tell me what he was gonna do . . . to your mother."

"Dad, it's okay. You don't—"

"No." He fumbled for my hands. "No. I knew. I knew who Walter was. I knew, and I didn't stop him." He coughed out a sob. "I didn't stop him."

I gathered my father into my arms, shushing him, stroking his face. After a while, he quieted, and I drew back.

"Thea," he said once more.

"I'm here. But listen. I have something to tell you now." My hand drifted down to my stomach. "You're going to be a grandfather."

Chapter Forty-One

October 2012
Mobile, Alabama

I buried my father six days after my birthday. Six days I sat by his bedside, watching him sink deeper into himself until there was almost nothing left. Maybe it was a sense of daughterly duty—he didn't have anyone left but me—but the fact was, I loved him. As much as I wanted to, I couldn't deny it.

Maybe I was just grateful he'd used his last few moments of lucidity to tell me the truth. Maybe it wasn't love I felt but relief that the whole thing would be over soon. In his own messed-up way, I think my father believed he was protecting Wynn and me. I think he loved us. But I don't know. I really don't. How could anyone call that love?

After Dad's service, Jay suggested I stay with him. He was worried about my mental health, I think, and the baby—but I was grateful, whatever the reason. I packed up a couple of things and headed down the road, happy to be away from that house, so steeped in memory and sadness.

He also mentioned that Dove had called him. I let it simmer for the time being. I needed a little more time before I heard another story. Even if it was the final one.

Some fisherman found Wynn downriver, his pink bow tie still knotted in place and both legs bitten off just above the knee. An accident, the police concluded, and Molly Robb didn't contradict them. She ended up in the spotlight after all, my power-hungry sister-in-law, not exactly the way she'd always dreamed, but as the bereaved widow of a fallen politico. She seemed pretty happy with her new role. She collected Wynn's life insurance and moved back to Birmingham to live with her family. I heard soon after that she'd started dating a state senator.

❧

One crisp Sunday morning, Jay and I drove back to Tuscaloosa to see Dove. When she saw us at her front door, she broke into an enormous smile.

"Are you ready?" she asked me.

I looked back at Pritchard—the field and woods and spires of the old building on the other side of the highway—and turned back to her. "Yes."

Dove served us soup, but I couldn't eat. The only thing I felt capable of doing there in Dove's tiny, cozy living room was holding Jay's hand as I waited for her to tell us the rest of the story I'd been waiting a lifetime to hear. Jinn's story.

"Where do I begin?" Dove finally asked me.

"Jinn's father had come to the creek," I said. "He'd found her there. Naked."

"Yes." Dove smoothed the napkin on her lap. "That's right."

And that was where she started.

Chapter Forty-Two

October 1937
Sybil Valley, Alabama

Vernon Alford studied his daughter, who was kneeling in the moonlit mud. Charles Jarrod, Howell, and young Walter flanked the white-haired man. The boy held his rifle and watched his naked mother with his opaque eyes.

"We were doing the work of the Lord."

Vernon chuckled. "Were you, now?"

"She prayed for me," Jinn gasped out. "The evangelist's wife."

"Well. All right, then."

"She prays for folks. For ladies."

"What kinda praying is that?" Vernon Alford folded his arms. He turned and cocked an eyebrow at Charles Jarrod. "In the middle of the night, in a creek? Without a stitch of clothes?"

Jinn didn't speak.

"Did that woman take off your dress?"

"No, sir. I did. We wanted to . . . We went swimming."

Vernon took one step closer and peered down at Jinn. "What's a matter with you?" He looked back at Howell. Vernon stretched the suspenders between his hands. Jinn tensed. "Why you shaking all over like that?" he said.

She didn't answer. He raised the suspenders and hit her once across the shoulders. She bit her lip to keep from crying out.

He jerked a thumb at Howell. "Get on back home."

Jinn dropped to all fours and listened for Howell's footsteps, waited for him to move across the meadow, through the trees, and back home. Howell would take Walter and go home to Collie. Her children would be safe if her father sent her to Pritchard. Because he would most definitely do that now. Now that she'd been touched.

That's what she was, she thought, touched. Touched with insanity. Touched with the fire of God. Funny how the two felt one and the same. Maybe they were.

When she looked up, she saw that Howell and Walter were still standing behind her father. She couldn't see their faces, but their bodies seemed to sway with the tree branches in the honeysuckle-scented wind. Charles Jarrod had vanished. He must've gone to search for Dove. She noticed Vernon held Walter's rifle now.

He cleared his phlegmy lungs. "Tomorrow you'll go on to Pritchard, you hear? I shoulda sent your mother there, years ago, but I wasn't enough of a man. But Howell . . . Howell's different. He's a fine, strong man."

She sat back and stretched out her hands to her father, but she could only reach the barrel of the rifle. She grabbed it with both hands and, using it to steady herself, pulled herself upright. The gun began to vibrate in her grip, and the vibration traveled down the barrel into the stock and into Vernon's arms. He looked down with horrified fascination. The shaking traveled from his arms to his chest, down the trunk of his body. He leapt back like he'd been snake-bit, tearing the gun from Jinn's hands.

She dropped forward again. Her brain filled and buzzed with words. Whole sentences, paragraphs even, sharp dark letters on a white sheet of paper. She could read them, just as if she was holding them in front of her, like a telegram. Was this how it happened for Dove? Words like on a telegram? Or was her mind playing tricks on her? She saw something clearly now—a *V* and an *A* embroidered in the corner of a handkerchief.

She lifted her head, her hair swaying. "I saw the Tippett girl tonight," she heard herself say. "Vonnie Tippett."

She could hear her father's breath come out of his mouth in a whoosh, like he'd been gut-punched. The gun slid down to his side.

"What do I care about that?" he said.

"I believe she'll be having her baby in three or four months."

"So?"

"She saved it. She saved your baby." Jinn looked up at Vernon from the ground. She waited, but he didn't answer. "Does Mama know?"

She felt the air around them still as he took aim at her. She looked at the grass and mud between her fingers. There was a small flower pressed into the dirt—a honeysuckle blossom, yellow-gold and crushed. She moved her hand to cover it and rolled it against her palm, back and forth, shivering and trembling. The scent of the flower rose to her nostrils, a comfort.

"I don't know what you're talking so crazy about."

She closed her eyes. She could feel the brightness, the electricity humming inside her, and instantly, she knew that she could rise up out of her body if she wanted to. She could float up to the sky in her mind. Rise up and become a part of whatever was beyond it, heaven or the Milky Way. That was the beauty of being touched.

Only.

Only she would have to leave Tom behind. Dear, kind Tom with his soft eyes and bright smile. And their eternally unfinished conversation. But what did it matter? She was leaving him anyway, wasn't she? She was going to Pritchard.

"Jinny!" Vernon Alford's voice sounded shrill, nothing like a man's. More like a wounded deer. Or a calf. His voice was nothing but the bleat of an animal.

"Jinny," he said again. "You better keep your damn crazy mouth shut."

She didn't want to go to Pritchard, even though Dove had said the gift would keep her safe there. If she went, she would never be able to make wine or go to California with Tom or see her children grow up. She'd gotten it all wrong, telling her father about Vonnie right off the bat. She should've been braver, gone on to Pritchard, waited for Tom to come or the gift to see her through.

Now it was too late.

Vernon moved to his daughter. Touched the barrette Dove had given her. It slid right out of her wet hair, coming away easily in his hand. He turned it over, squinting at the design. He turned, tossed it back to young Walter. "Get rid a that."

He faced her again. "Well? You ain't got nothing to say?"

She didn't. She only had thoughts of Collie and Tom and the home they could have made if she hadn't been so afraid. She had thoughts of standing under Tom's stair, kissing his mouth, feeling his body under her touch. She had thoughts, too, of the mountain. Of the sky and the stars and whatever might lay beyond.

But her father was waiting, and she should say something. He didn't like to be defied.

"Shy don't set the world on fire," was what she said. Because those words were the only ones that made sense to her now. Because they seemed just right for all that had happened in her life.

When she heard the crack of Walter's .22 and tasted the gunpowder and blood in her mouth, she knew that at last, she had truly spoken her mind.

Chapter Forty-Three

October 2012
Tuscaloosa, Alabama

"They all knew," I said. "Howell. Walter. And your husband. They all saw Vernon Alford shoot his daughter."

She nodded.

"You saw it too," I said.

"I did."

"Good God, Dove!" I struggled to keep my voice level. "Why didn't you tell anyone?"

She looked at the fire. It had smoldered down to embers, spilling over the hearth and filling the room with a thin haze of graying smoke. "Charles said mountain people didn't like outsiders interfering with their business. He said they might kill us too if we didn't stay out of it. We packed up our things and left Sybil Valley that night. We never spoke about Jinn, or what happened, again."

"Okay. So then, if you wanted nothing to do with all that business, why did you come back to Alabama? Why did you move across the street from Pritchard? And where do Collie and Trix fit in to all this?"

She folded and refolded her hands. "I don't expect you to understand. But there's always been something about this place. Something that won't let me go." Her gaze flicked from me to the window, the one that looked out onto the hospital. "It's difficult to explain."

"What are you talking about?"

"What question do you want me to answer first?" she said.

I shifted on the sofa. "According to Jean, you were a wild child—this rebel who snuck around behind her husband's back, barging your way into peoples' houses, laying hands on total strangers. So why were you afraid to go to the police? You could've told the truth, Dove, gotten justice for Jinn. But you ran away."

"I wanted to tell," Dove said. She stared down at her hands. "Every day after that, for twenty-five years, I wanted to tell. I did, finally. Not the police. It was Collie. I found Collie."

"When she was thirty," I said.

"You know, after Jinn disappeared, Howell moved Walter and Collie down to Birmingham. She went to college for a while, studied art. Paid for it herself. She never went back to live with Howell, though. She always thought maybe he'd had something to do with her mother's disappearance." Dove put a hand on her chest. "When I told her the truth about what those men had done to her mother, she cried and cried."

"But why didn't you tell her earlier? Why wait until thirty?"

Dove shook her head. "All I can say is, I've always thought thirty was a special age for women. When they come into their own, get on solid ground."

"But she wasn't on solid ground. She was already involved in some activities that her family was unhappy about. Walter was KKK, and not about to let his little sister tarnish the Wooten family name. After she met with you, she went to see him. She told him everything—the giant, horrifying family secret that Vernon Alford shot and killed his daughter, then hid the body. I don't know if she threatened to make the story public, if she threatened his life. But whatever happened, for Walter, it was the last straw. He had to shut her down. He put Collie in Pritchard, then later, he went back and killed her. *Murdered* her."

"I know," Dove said. "I think I saw him bury her."

A shock wave traveled through me. I leapt up. "What are you talking about? How could you have seen that?"

Dove stood. She was trembling too, and she clasped her hands in front of her. "There are many of them buried there. Just across the street, at Pritchard. They used to do it in secret, at night . . . the ones they didn't want anyone to know about. They ones they killed."

"My God," Jay said.

"After I met with Collie, I went back to Birmingham," Dove said. "Just to make sure she was okay. But she was gone. I heard she'd been sent to Pritchard, so I came back here and I waited. One day, when the patients were out, I thought I saw her walking the grounds. She looked bad. Pale and sick. I was concerned for her, worried that I shouldn't have told her. She wasn't strong enough."

I thought of the records I'd read. The horrible things they'd done to my grandmother.

"One night I couldn't sleep. I made myself a cup of tea and walked out onto the porch. Just to look at the stars, to get some fresh air. At least that was what I told myself. Maybe I knew what was about to happen." Her eyes shone, filmed over with memories. "I saw two men, digging a grave. Burying a body. I went to Pritchard a couple of days later. I gave them a false name, asked to see Collie Crane. They told me she'd died. I asked to see her grave but they couldn't find it in her records. They said the information hadn't been updated yet."

I felt faint. Disoriented with horror and confusion. "Who were the men?"

"One was police, I believe. He looked to be in uniform. And I could see his squad car nearby. The other one . . ." She faltered.

"Dove."

Her eyes met mine. "The other one was Walter Wooten."

"You saw him?"

She was quiet.

"If you didn't see him, how did you know it was him?"

"I *knew*. The way I've always known things. In here." She clutched at her chest. "I was scared, but I stuck to the trees along the side of the field. I got closer just as they were throwing the dirt in. When he was done, the one man picked up a rifle with an engraved stock plate. A rifle I'd seen before."

I shook my head. I couldn't tell if anything she was saying was true. Somehow, magically, she'd known the figure burying a body was Walter? Then she'd gotten close enough—in the dark, no less—to see engraving on the side of a rifle?

And yet . . .

When Trix had gone up to Walter's house, taken the gun and threatened to tell what he'd done, Walter had killed her. Would he have done that if she hadn't been on to something?

I turned my attention back to Dove. "So, if you knew it was Walter, why didn't you turn him in?"

She shook her head. "I told you, Althea. The other man was a police officer. And that wasn't the first time I'd seen the police at Pritchard. They came other nights, too. They helped bury the bodies."

"The police?"

"Yes. The police." She gave me a rueful look. "Althea. This is Alabama. No matter what people want to believe, in this state, the past is still very much alive."

"If that's true, why would you do it?" I asked. "Why in the world would you get involved again and pull Trix into it?"

"I couldn't forget the things I'd seen. I couldn't sleep. It weighed on me."

"So you had to unburden your conscience and, as a result, my mother ended up in the same hellhole as Collie?"

"Yes," she said. "God forgive me, yes." She shook her head. She was trembling, her eyes watering, but I didn't feel sorry for anything I'd said. She'd nearly destroyed my family, robbed me of my mother and grandmother. I had no sympathy for her.

"I saw what happened then," she said quietly. "And it was terrible. So terrible."

I blinked in disbelief. What did she mean, she *saw*? What was she saying?

She looked from Jay to me, like she'd read my mind. "I know where your mother is."

In the deepening dusk, we crossed the road in front of Dove's house. Stepped onto Pritchard's soccer field.

Or what used to be the soccer field. It was a construction site now. The goals had been removed, the area excavated and marked with wooden stakes, pink plastic markers, and two-by- fours. The squat administrative building glowed behind the field, and the U-shaped residential hall behind that. In the distance, stalwart sentinel over the whole scene, stood Old Pritchard.

A cement mixer rumbled at the far end of the field. It was pouring gray sludge into the staked area. Watching just beyond the mixer were three men—a hospital security guard, a beefy man in a red fleece, and Gene Northcut. My mouth went dry.

I turned to Jay. "This is the memorial Wynn was talking about. He and Gene Northcut were going to put it right on top of the bodies. To hide them."

"You really think your mother is here?" he said in disbelief. "And Collie and Jinn?"

"I don't know," I said. "Dove?"

Dove lifted her hand, pointed a knobby finger at a spot just to the left of the mixer.

"There." Her voice was steady.

She turned ninety degrees to the left. Pointed at another area of bare ground on the far side of the excavated site, beneath a cluster of dark pines that thrust toward the pink-swept sky. "There."

She nodded at our feet. "And here."

Before I even knew what I was doing, I was down on my knees, clawing at the earth like some kind of demented dog.

"Althea!" I heard, and then Jay hauled me up by the shoulders.

"They're watching." He brushed the hair out of my face, then turned and looked behind him. I followed his gaze. The three men beside the cement mixer were standing shoulder to shoulder, staring.

"I don't care. They can't do this." I tore out of Jay's grasp and stumbled across the field, waving my arms at them like a maniac. "Stop!" I shouted. "Stop!" The man operating the mixer stuck his head out the window and stared. "Stop pouring!" I screamed over the roar of the equipment. My eyes flicked to Mr. Northcut's deer-antler cane. The handle of it looked as sharp as an ice pick. Then I caught sight of his face. His features had hardened.

"You can't pour here," I called out to the group again. "You have to stop."

The three men conferred among themselves, then Red Fleece walked to the truck and spoke to the driver. The stream of cement stopped, and the truck idled. The four of us walked over to the men. I saw, out of the corner of my eye, the security guard's hand drop to his gun holster.

I laser-focused on Northcut. I could see he was trying to place me, his brain clicking through the internal files. "You have to stop working here right away," I said.

"Well, hey there," he said. "I know you." He looked at Red Fleece. "I know her."

"You do?" Red Fleece crossed his arms over his chest, feigning boredom.

Northcut smiled. It was an unpleasant smile. An oily one. "You're Wynn Bell's sister."

"That's right." I tucked my dirt-clotted hands behind me. "Althea."

"Althea. Of course. This is my nephew, Bennett."

I ignored the introduction.

"Now what were you saying?" Northcut asked.

"This area can't be disturbed. There are—" I glanced at Dove. "This field is a cemetery."

"No, it's not," Red Fleece said. Then he laughed.

"It is," I said.

"You're mistaken," he said. "It absolutely is *not*."

"I have proof that more than one body is buried in this field," I said. The security guard unsnapped the strap on his walkie and went a couple of yards away from us. Beyond him, I saw the door to the administrative building open. Beth stuck her head out, scanned our little group, then walked briskly to the security guard.

"Proof?" Red Fleece turned to Northcut. "You have got to be kidding me."

"Miss Bell—" Northcut said.

"It's common knowledge where Pritchard's cemeteries are located," Red Fleece said over him. "At the rear of the old property and in the woods."

Northcut's smile stretched further, revealing a set of too-white teeth. "Bennett, a moment, if you don't mind." He addressed me. "This area of Pritchard has been promised to the Alabama Historical Association, Miss Bell. To build a memorial for the hospital. Your brother"—his nostrils flared—"God rest his soul—arranged it all. One of his last acts on this earth."

Red Fleece clapped his hands together. "So you should all just head on home."

I didn't move. I could feel Dove and Jay behind me, the strength of their presence.

"Tell me something," I asked Northcut. "Why are you out here at dusk, pouring cement over this field? Why not wait until morning to start the job?"

Red Fleece and Northcut stared at me. Neither said a word.

"Why are you in such a hurry?" I asked. "What are you hiding?"

Silence.

"What are you afraid people will find in this field if you don't cover it with an entire layer of *concrete*?" I was breathless now, my voice high and loud. I pointed at the old man. "I know," I said. "I know what's going on."

The security guard broke in. "I've called the sheriff. And the president of the hospital."

"Good," I said. "Perfect. I'll wait until they get here."

"You folks are going to need to clear off the property," he said.

"We're staying right here until they plow up this whole fucking field."

They shook their heads and chuckled.

The mixer operator swung down from his seat and shambled toward us. "Where are you saying someone's buried?" he asked me.

I looked at Dove. She pointed to just past him.

She spoke out clearly. "Several of them are buried there."

The field fell silent. I heard a door bang open from somewhere— the administrative building, most likely.

"Several of them?" The mixer operator pushed up the brim of his hat and peered at Dove.

"I saw the men do it. Bury them, at night. I live over there, so I could see it all."

Red Fleece, the security guard, and the mixer operator gaped at her. Only Northcut didn't. He glanced furtively at the brick building behind him. The parking lot.

"What men?" the security guard asked. "When?"

She shrugged. "Different men. Different years."

"Come again?"

Dove's face had taken on a vacant look, and I could see she'd left us. She'd left the field, the purple night, and the construction site. She'd gone somewhere far away.

"Back in the 1920s there was a passageway." Her voice had gone soft. "That led out from the east wing."

I shivered. Here it was: the promise of a door about to be unlocked and opened.

"An underground tunnel connected the main building and another set of barracks behind it. They put the dangerous patients out there, and some of the nurses and orderlies used the tunnel to travel back and forth between the buildings. They didn't like to use it, unless it was storming. They thought it was haunted. Halfway down the passageway, there was a small chute, with a trapdoor that opened to the outside. They used to shovel in coal that way, long ago, to be delivered to the furnaces in both buildings. If you knew how, you could wriggle up the chute and get out of the trapdoor."

She began to drift toward the magnolia. Its leaves shone in the rising moon. I looked at Jay, and Red Fleece and Northcut exchanged glances. We followed her all the way to the tree. She stopped and looked up at it.

"They chained the trapdoor, but it was nothing but a piece of rotted wood. They didn't feed us much back then, and I was a small thing. I could push the door up and slip through the crack with no problem. No one ever saw me."

She turned to me. Her face had broken open, and her eyes were on fire. Her hands pressed against her heart.

"I was born here," she said. "At Prichard. Ruth Lurie was my name. My mother was Anna. They said she threw herself off a fire tower on top of Brood Mountain because she was pregnant with her brother's child.

Her family put her in Pritchard, and the doctors kept her chained to a bed. Because she was a runner."

I felt tears rising in my eyes.

"When I got to be about six or seven, I used to sneak out at night. I'd go down to the tunnel, slip out the coal door, walk in the moonlight. That's when I first saw them—the men burying the patients. They were the severely disabled ones they'd raped and beaten. The violent ones, the failed medical experiments. The ones who'd frozen to death because they'd hosed them down and left them too long in the cold.

"They brought them in from the outside too. Bodies. White and black. I saw policemen, more than once, unload them. Wrapped in quilts and blankets.

"The day my mother turned thirty, I woke up early; it was still dark. During the night, while I was asleep, she'd knocked out the glass from the transom above the door. Used one of the restraints they left behind to hang herself. They buried her in this field." Her voice cracked. "I left her there and snuck down to the tunnel. I slipped out the trapdoor and ran. Across the field. Through the woods. I ran all night. I was twelve."

Twelve. A child, all alone in a world of terror and confusion.

I wanted to tell Dove to stop talking, to tell her she didn't have to reveal any more, not in front of these people. This was her story and hers alone, and no one had any right to know it. But my throat was burning, and the words wouldn't form.

Dove gazed out into the night. "I kept running, all the way to California. I knew if they found me they'd put me back. I never wanted to go back. I couldn't go back to the place where my mother . . ."

She faltered, and Jay moved to us. I could feel the warmth of his body near mine.

"Several years later, Charles wanted to come out this way. I was scared. I didn't want to come, but I also felt like there was something waiting for me here, back in Alabama."

Dove smiled at me. Squeezed my hand.

"Your great-grandmother, Jinn. I met her at the revival. She said they were going to send her to Pritchard. I couldn't bear it for her. I just couldn't bear it . . ."

She stopped.

"You saw what her father did to her," I said. "And you knew where they would bury her, didn't you? You knew where they buried women like her."

Her gaze didn't waver. "I had a good idea. Yes."

"She's here," I breathed. "Jinn's buried here."

Dove looked behind her, at the spots she'd indicated. "And Trix too, I'm fairly certain." She turned to us. Her face looked so much older now, shadowed by lines and folds. "I moved back here after my husband passed. I knew Jinn had to be here. I knew I had to tell Collie. It was my responsibility. I was terrified of being here, but I felt like I had to watch over the place, to see who else disappeared."

Her hand gripped mine tighter.

"I thought if I told them," Dove said, "told Collie and Trix, they could make it right, and I could leave this place forever—finally be rid of it. But I was wrong, and they paid for my cowardice. I wasn't going to see the same thing done to you. I was not going to betray you the way I'd betrayed your mother and your grandmother."

I nodded, unable to speak.

"Forgive me, Althea. Please forgive me."

I went to her and gathered her into my arms. I held her and we were both crying, then Jay joined us. The three of us stood there, locked together.

"You people heard the guard," Northcut barked. "You need to clear on out of here."

Dove, Jay, and I separated.

I turned to Northcut. "You knew Walter Wooten. My uncle. Didn't you?"

He said nothing.

"Tell me something, Mr. Northcut, did you ever see Walter Wooten discharge a .22-caliber rifle in the perpetration of a crime?" I stepped closer to him. He was trembling now. With fear or anger or both. "A murder, maybe? You ever help Walter Wooten kill anyone, Mr. Northcut? Bury them in the middle of the night, in this very field?"

His eyes hardened. "I never did nothing. It was your family that did all that. All your kind—they were trash. Nothing but trash."

"A few were," I said. "But not all of them. Not all of them."

He started to reply, his eyes blazing with disgust, when we heard the piercing wail of a siren in the distance. His mouth clapped shut and his hand wobbled on the head of his cane as he turned to search for his nephew. That's when I realized we'd done it. Dove and I had stopped them.

It was over.

Jay's hand found mine, and I laced my fingers through his. I wrapped my other arm around Dove's waist, and together the three of us walked in the direction of the flashing red and blue lights.

Epilogue

I am my mother's daughter.
The honeysuckle girl is real.
The gold dust and the red raven were reminders
That she had a gift for me.

❧

When the state got the proper clearances to excavate the site, we were there—Jay, Beth, Dove, and I, huddled together against the late-November wind. We watched as they unearthed the first skull.

"Sweet Jesus," the workman said, and we all bent over the freshly excavated hole. After using a backhoe for the initial digging, the crew had been using picks and shovels and brushes to carefully turn up the ground. He was standing at the deepest point, at least six feet down, a shovel in his hand. He looked up at us.

"There's a lot of bones down here." He shook his head. "It's like I just hit a whole cemetery."

He had. They identified dozens of remains—Jinn's and Collie's among them. Both had bullets in their skulls, fired from a .22 rifle. They found my mother too, on the opposite side of the field, closer to the road. There was no bullet with her bones, but I knew what Walter had done to her just the same.

They found others. Missing men from Birmingham, including Lindy's brother Dante. Lost men, women, and children who'd become too difficult for their families or society to handle. Pritchard, supposed refuge for the tormented, had become their tomb.

I found Walter's rifle at Dad's house, hidden in the back of a closet. Wynn must've found it in Jay's car after all. I wondered why he hadn't just taken it down to the dock and thrown it in the river, where the mud would have held it forever. He must've wanted to keep it—a gruesome memento of our twisted legacy. I didn't want it, though. I didn't want to ever see it again. I drove up to Tuscaloosa and handed it over to the officer who was working the Pritchard case.

After the excavation, Dove sold her house and planned to move back to California, where she'd lived with her husband Charles Jarrod so long ago. The thought of her going out there alone tore at me, and I begged her to move in with Jay and me. She refused.

She'd only been out there a month when I got the call that she'd died peacefully, in her sleep.

❧

Ruth Trix Cheramie was born in the middle of June. She was perfect and beautiful, with a full head of fiery-red hair and the sweetest upturned eyes I'd ever seen.

I hold her at night, whenever I can get Jay to relinquish her. I sing to her and tell her stories about her grandmother and all the women who went before her. I tell her about gold dust and red ravens and special gifts that some women have. Gifts of touching and knowing. Healing. I tell her the stories like I believe them. I don't know, maybe I do.

One day, when she's older, I'll show my daughter a trick I learned once, as a little girl in a magical clearing ringed with magnolia. I'll show her how to draw out the stamen from between the petals of a honeysuckle bloom and taste the tiny drop of sweetness that comes from the flower.

Acknowledgments

There are many people to whom I owe a huge debt of gratitude.

My spectacular agent, Amy Cloughley, a deep well of patience, good humor, and editing prowess, who championed this book from start to finish.

My incredible editor, Kelli Martin, and the Lake Union team: Danielle Marshall, Shannon O'Neill, Meredith Jacobson, Gabriella Dumpit, Christy Caldwell, Tyler Stoops, and all the others. Thank you all for making this book shine.

Chris Negron, my first, most dedicated and tireless beta reader. Hats off for slogging through a million different versions of this book and always, with gentleness and tact, pressing me to make it better. The Atlanta Writers Club, and the extraordinary Atlanta Writers Conference and Roswell Critique Group, the latter two organized and run with infectious wit by George Weinstein. Team Erratica: Chris Negron, Becky Albertalli, and Manda Pullen. Chips and salsa on the outdoor patio with y'all make good news even more special and bad news easier to bear.

My early readers: Rick Carpenter, Katy Shelton, Kevin Whitehead, Ashley Taylor, Gloria Schulz, Amanda Silva, Karen Hardy, Shelby James, Laura Watson, Randy Watson, and Shannon Holden. Thank you for the input, suggestions, and edits.

My junior-high English teacher, Sandi Flowers, the first person who ever said that something I wrote was good . . . and then read it out loud to the whole class. You made me believe I could be a writer.

Anne and Henry Drake, who instilled in me their own fierce love for books and story. Henry Drake, Kathleen Drake, Katy Shelton, John Shelton, Danner Drake, and Jennifer Drake, each encouraging, each inspirational, each gifted historians, humanitarians, businesspeople, writers, and craftsmen in their own rights. Nancy and Richard Carpenter, Karen and Jim Brim, Lee, Ashley, Brandon, Amy, and Daniel Taylor. Thanks to all of you for cheering me along the way.

Rick—words cannot express how much I appreciate you every day. Noah, Alex, and Everett—the only thing more fun than writing this book is being your mom.

About the Author

Photo © 2015 Christina DeVictor

Emily Carpenter, a former actor, producer, screenwriter, and behind-the-scenes soap opera assistant, graduated with a bachelor of arts degree from Auburn University. Born and raised in Birmingham, Alabama, she now lives in Georgia with her family. *Burying the Honeysuckle Girls* is her first novel. Visit Emily online at www.emilycarpenterauthor.com.